Ambition's Woman

Ambition's Woman

Jeanne Jones

M. EVANS AND COMPANY, INC.

NEW YORK

Library of Congress Cataloging in Publication Data

Jones, Jeanne.
  Ambition's woman.

  I. Title.
PS3560.0492A8 813'.54   81-9721

ISBN 0-87131-359-6   AACR2

M. Evans and Company, Inc.
216 East 49 Street
New York, New York 10017

Design by Diane Gedymin

Manufactured in the United States of America

9 8 7 6 5 4 3 2 1

To Ted, for all the right reasons

Each honest calling, each walk of life, has its own elite, its own aristocracy based on excellence of performance.

James Bryant Conant

Part One

Chapter One

AT 1:05 IN THE AFTERNOON of a late March day in 1980, Mike D'Amato hovered nervously behind the ornate nineteenth century mahogany music stand that served as a reservations desk in the foyer of his lavish new restaurant on Wilshire Boulevard. His mood veered back and forth between anticipation and anxiety. The brass-bound revolving door began to turn and he stiffened slightly. But it was only a second-echelon agent from William Morris with some starlet in tow. D'Amato gave an almost imperceptible nod to Joseph, his maître d', who moved forward to greet them. D'Amato himself was waiting for someone far more important to appear.

Al Cartoccio, open for only three months, had been conceived as a magnet for people with expensive tastes and extensive influence, for those whose power imbued them with glamour, and those whose beauty had brought them power. Not that Mike D'Amato had any aversion to serving the merely rich either. But for a restaurant on the scale of his new venture to be launched successfully, you needed to attract the real heavyweights. You wanted to see Nancy Reagan, escaping from the rigors of the primary trail by having a gossipy lunch with Jerry Zipkin. If an aide to Governor Brown made a reservation for four you hoped that the governor himself might show up—while praying that if Linda Ronstadt was along she wouldn't try to turn the premises into a roller rink, the way she had the Brown Derby. The only trouble with politicians in a presidential election year was that you had to set aside a table for their Secret Service agents, who always chose the cheapest dishes on the menu. Frank Sinatra's bodyguards, on the other hand, always ate as well as Ol' Blue Eyes himself.

And when such people patronized your restaurant, the anonymous rich were sure to follow. They might be too obscure even to qualify for an American Express "Do you know who I am?" commercial, but so long as they had a wallet full of plastic money, Mike D'Amato was happy to serve them. He'd seat them up front so they could watch the celebrities parade by to their secluded tables at the back. In Los Angeles, the truly famous always demanded a table in the rear; in New York they would insist upon being seated up front. It was one of the few mysteries of the restaurant business that D'Amato had never quite fathomed.

But while movie stars and sports heroes and men who wanted to be President attracted those who took pleasure in merely being in the same room with the famous, there were a few people who were even more important to the restaurant's success, who could help you or hurt you in more complicated ways. Not the restaurant critics. Mike D'Amato wasn't afraid of that secretive lot, with their assumed names and the wigs and bizarre hats with which they tried to disguise their identity. D'Amato ran a taut ship, and he had a superb chef in the kitchen, imported—or, more accurately, stolen—from Ranieri's in Rome. The critics didn't faze him. In fact, during his twenty-five years in the business he'd come to appreciate their efforts at anonymity. Because it was when you knew who you were dealing with that things were most likely to go wrong, when the waiters would turn unaccountably butterfingered, or the chef, trying to overreach himself, would produce an inexplicable disaster. The problem didn't arise as much with the usual run of celebrities, who were for the most part surprisingly forgiving. It was when a Julia Child or a James Beard or an Andrea Harrington walked into a restaurant that the staff was likely to get the jitters. It was always the stars of your own profession, D'Amato believed, who were the most intimidating.

Mike D'Amato's eyes flickered once again toward the entrance. Sid Fogel, the producer of Andrea Harrington's nationally syndicated television show, "Gourmet Adventures," had already been seated. Her ladyship, as people called her behind her back, was bound to arrive momentarily. Even she wouldn't dare to keep Sid Fogel waiting more than ten minutes. D'Amato turned the pages of the reservations book, not really seeing the names. On the occasions she had dined at his previous restaurant, La Fenice, in Beverly Hills, Andrea Harrington had always been very charming, but this was her first visit to his new establishment, and that was something to worry about. She could do him a great deal of good. She sometimes mentioned restaurants favorably on her program, and if she was truly impressed she might even tape a segment in a restaurant she particularly liked. But she was also dangerous. The clientele of her catering firm was comprised of exactly the kind of Hollywood high rollers D'Amato wanted for customers, and he knew that a casually disparaging word from her in the right places could do him a great deal of damage.

His palms were sweating and he was about to reach for his handkerchief when the door began to revolve once more. And then she was standing there, fifteen feet way across the deep purple carpet.

Like any first-class maître d' or experienced restaurant owner, Mike D'Amato had learned to make instant and yet surprisingly subtle appraisals of people. You could tell a great deal about a person by the way he or she entered a restaurant. It wasn't just a matter of the style or quality of the clothes they wore, although he had a sharp eye for sartorial detail. It was the way people stood, the expressions on their faces, how their eyes moved. He could spot at once the man who would inevitably complain about something before the meal was over; he knew which woman would talk too loudly before she had even opened her mouth. He could tell who would be knowledgeable and decisive about ordering and who would be hesitant and need advice. People who were unsure of themselves were in one sense all alike; you didn't have to worry about them much because they were afraid of revealing their

11

ignorance. But there were many different kinds of self-assurance. There was the brash impatient self-assurance of a man like Sid Fogel. There was the understated blue-blooded self-assurance of people who had always had money and had never had to fight for what they wanted. Then there were the survivors, the ones who had been through it all and were still on top in spite of everything. You often saw that quality in actresses over fifty who were still stars, women who had been declared legends by Blackglama furs and had the coats in their closets to prove it.

But there was something special about the self-assurance radiated by Lady Andrea Harrington. She was an American in spite of her title, which she had gained through marriage, though in Mike D'Amato's opinion she might as well have been born to it, for she had the ability to be graceful and authoritative at the same time. It was surprising to find that combination in a woman who was only in her early thirties. There were plenty of authoritative young women around these days—they marched into Mike D'Amato's restaurant every day—but there was often something stiff-shouldered about them, as though they were working too hard at it.

As D'Amato moved toward her now, Andrea Harrington inclined her head slightly and smiled, her honey-blond hair catching the light as she did so. As always, she appeared tanned, but so lightly and smoothly that she might have acquired her coloring by basking in moonlight instead of under the sun. Her eyes, as she looked into his, were an intense sea blue, not the blue of the Mediterranean, but of colder, more northern waters. They were eyes that measured you even when the rest of the face was smiling.

"Lady Andrea, how delightful to see you," Mike D'Amato said, his voice taking on a slight croon as he bowed and kissed her hand. "Congratulations on your award tonight. It's an honor to have you here on such a special day."

This one doesn't miss a trick, Andrea Harrington thought. She found Mike D'Amato's manner too unctuous by half, but

12

it amused rather than annoyed her. And he did know how to run a restaurant. There were a lot of talented kids around who could do exciting, innovative things in the kitchen, but it took an old hand who had come up through the ranks like Mike D'Amato to make a place run with the quiet purr of a Rolls-Royce.

Andrea almost giggled at her own comparison, for her new Rolls, butter colored with caramel seats, had been delivered the day before. It was almost an exact replica of the one her late husband, Sir George Harrington, had had waiting for her when they returned from their honeymoon in Venice. But then it had been lost, irretrievably sacrificed like everything else. She had promised herself she would have another one someday and now she did. But giggles were not an expected element of her public repertoire, and she contained herself, saying to Mike D'Amato, "I've heard very good things about your new effort here, Mike. I hope you're going to coddle me shamelessly today."

"It will be our pleasure, Lady Andrea. Would you like to meet the chef? His English isn't much, but he's very charming."

"Perhaps after lunch, Mike. Is Mr. Fogel here yet?"

"Yes, he arrived a few minutes ago. I'll take you to your table."

He led the way across the foyer and down the three steps into the spacious, high-ceilinged dining room. Andrea liked the room at once. It was as clever a mixture of the old and the new as she had encountered in some time, with a round antique bar at its center, where a lavish assortment of hors d'oeuvres was displayed. Purple tablecloths echoed the color of the carpet, and the pale beige walls were hung at intervals with old mirrors in a variety of wood frames, giving a reflective glitter to the room but placed high enough so that you wouldn't have to stare at yourself while eating. The pressed-tin ceiling had been lacquered dark brown and pleasantly diffused

13

the light from the brass wall sconces. Chrome and leather chairs added an enlivening contemporary touch.

As she moved through the room, conversations faltered momentarily and then rippled forward on a slightly different note as diners recognized her. It was one of those subtle tributes to her success that Andrea had grown used to in the past two years.

At a table just to one side, Baxter Robinson, the gossip columnist of the *Los Angeles Times*, was sitting with a beachboy type whose face Andrea vaguely recognized from some series or television movie. Mike D'Amato would no doubt be making every effort to persuade Baxter to report on Andrea's presence in the restaurant in his column the next day. That would be less difficult than he probably suspected. Andrea and Baxter had a little-known but mutually beneficial agreement. She often supplied him with the choice tidbits of gossip about upcoming social events gleaned from the many important clients of her catering firm, and he in turn saw to it that she was regularly and flatteringly mentioned in his column. She hesitated momentarily. It wouldn't be a good idea to have people realize quite how chummy she and Baxter were—they might begin to figure out how he got some of his juicier items. He had once told her that she was one of his two best sources. The other was a telephone operator at the Beverly Hills Hotel whom he paid to eavesdrop on the guests' calls.

Baxter was waving at her now, and she didn't want to appear to snub him either. "I'm just going to say a word to Mr. Robinson," she told Mike D'Amato, who beamed and replied, "Of course, Lady Andrea."

Baxter had the good sense to greet her formally rather than as Andrea, darling. "You must be thrilled about tonight," he said.

"It's always nice to be appreciated. Will you be there?"

"I wouldn't miss it. Let me introduce you to Rod Trager," he said, gesturing to the beachboy with a hint of proprietary glee.

14

Rod smiled and looked as though he were going to shake hands but thought better of it. The boy had teeth to burn. Andrea wondered idly if Baxter had actually made it with him. Rod seemed very macho, but that didn't mean anything anymore, as Andrea herself had discovered more than once. Of course it didn't really matter whether he were straight or gay—beachboys didn't care where they stuck it so long as it furthered their career, which was just as well for the Baxter Robinsons of the world. Baxter had fuzzy white hair and a small red nose. Andrea privately referred to him as Baxter Rabbit.

"I gather you're having lunch with Sid," Baxter said. "Planning next season are you?"

Andrea supposed this was an innocent inquiry, but considering what she was about to spring on Sid, it made her vaguely nervous.

"Yes, getting a head start. It's nice to see you, Baxter." She nodded at Rod Trager. It didn't seem possible he could actually sit down in pants that tight, she thought. Either he had robbed his sock drawer or Baxter had himself a real find.

When she reached their table, Sid was looking impatient. "How's Baxter Rabbit?" he asked, standing to greet her.

"Twitching with anticipation as always."

"I'll never understand how that kind of faggot can get to be so powerful."

"By being ruthless, of course. Just like you."

Sid grunted and kissed her lightly on both cheeks. This continental greeting always amused Andrea, since she had realized it was reserved for women with whom Sid had previously had affairs. Women he was currently having affairs with he kissed on the mouth. For the rest, it was one cheek. Andrea wasn't sure if he was fully aware of making these distinctions, or whether it was merely an unconscious reflex. It was probably deliberate. Sid seldom did anything that hadn't been planned in advance.

Andrea seated herself in the chair Mike D'Amato had

15

reappeared to pull out for her, and slipped out of her beige suede cape. She had heard that the color scheme of Al Cartoccio was purple and brown, and so had chosen to wear a Mary McFadden dress of lavender silk. It not only went with the setting, but she knew she looked particularly smashing in it. When you were about to ask for a couple of hundred thousand dollars, it seemed wise to look as irresistible as possible. Besides, it never hurt to remind ex-lovers of what they were missing.

Mike D'Amato hovered. "Would you like a cocktail, Lady Andrea?"

"A glass of champagne, please, Mike." Andrea almost invariably drank champagne. Sid had sometimes accused her of doing so for effect, but she genuinely preferred it to anything else. She had been a very young woman when she had first promised herself that someday she would be able to afford to drink it whenever she pleased.

"Make mine a martini on the rocks. With an olive," Sid requested curtly, not bothering to look at Mike D'Amato.

Andrea winced inwardly. Damn him, Sid would never learn. He *looked* like a gentleman, his dark curly hair always perfectly cut, worn just long enough to show its luxuriance without becoming unruly, his lean, six-foot frame elegantly attired in Armani suits. And he could be extremely charming, especially to women. But in some ways he was a boor. He was not a man who bothered with the more subtle social niceties. To him a restaurant owner was little different from a busboy —they were both there to wait on him and he would treat them with equal disinterest.

She gave Mike D'Amato a compensatory smile, but though he inclined his head graciously, she could tell he was annoyed.

Sid was sitting back in his chair studying her. She returned his gaze unwaveringly, the blue of her eyes even further intensified by the touch of iridescent ultramarine on the lids. She knew he must be curious as to why she had arranged this luncheon, but she didn't want to hurry things. Let him wonder for a while.

16

"I was watching your entrance," Sid said. "You get better at it all the time."

"I wasn't especially aware of making an entrance," said Andrea, with absolute untruth.

"You're a lying bitch, my dear. You've learned how to put on the star act, and you know it. I like that. When I first met you, you were poised, sure of yourself. And beautiful, of course. But you didn't have that extra dimension you do now. Now you're commanding."

Andrea laughed, unable to suppress her delight. It wasn't the word *star* that delighted her. It was the word *commanding*. Sid couldn't possibly know what that word meant to her, the terrible sound of it repeating in her ears, for it was a story she never told anyone if she could help it. But she had never forgotten the words coming at her out of the eighth row of the Colonial Theatre in Boston as she stood on the stage trembling, on the edge of hysteria.

"You've got to be more commanding, Andrea. I can't tell you how to do it. You've got to find it in yourself. But you've got to be commanding in this scene or the scene won't work. And if this scene doesn't work, the play won't work, and we're going to be dead on arrival when we open in New York. Now come on. Dig down and find it."

But all she'd been able to find was terror and the knowledge that she'd been right all along, that she wasn't good enough, her success had been a fluke, and it was all going to fall apart because the one thing she couldn't find it in herself to be was commanding.

But she knew now, she'd learned how, and Sid's words were sweeter than he knew. But she wasn't going to let him know that. Their drinks arrived, and as they clinked glasses Andrea said, "Tell me, Sid, why is it that when you give me a compliment you always start out with an insult?"

"What insult?"

"Lying bitch."

"That's not an insult, Andy, that's a simple statement of fact."

17

"You mean the way you're a manipulative bastard?"

"Exactly."

They smiled at each other with the kind of wry complicity that only people who've laughed and fought and made love together can share. Their affair had been over for a year and a half now, and although things had been rocky for a while, they had come out of it good friends. Andrea was happy about that but not really surprised. They were both strong, independent people, each enjoying personal success.

Andrea had noticed that among television and movie people, sexual liaisons often evolved successfully into friendship when the two partners were of equal standing. It was only when one person was famous and the other a nobody that a dreadful fracas like one of those palimony suits erupted. If you were a celebrity yourself, a broken affair or even a broken marriage meant the loss of a particular partner but not the collapse of your very identity. But if your status was merely a matter of reflected glory you had nothing to fall back on. To lose a lover could be shattering, but it was even worse to be reduced once again to a nobody. Andrea knew. It had happened to her. There were a lot of things it was easier to take in stride when you were a somebody. Some of her friends, and most of her enemies, she was well aware, would have said that she had simply become harder over the years. But there was more to it than that. She had become certain of her own worth—certain enough to put a very high price on it.

But before Andrea named that still escalating price to Sid, she wanted something to eat. Something special, something sumptuous. Tonight she would make amends. The food at the awards dinner wouldn't be worth eating anyway.

Mike D'Amato brought the menus, their covers a handsome, dark, shiny purple, as burnished as the skin of an eggplant. He discussed the possibilities with her while Sid perused the listings in silence.

"A little seafood salad to begin with, Lady Andrea? It's very fresh, slightly piccante. I think you would enjoy it."

18

"That sounds lovely," said Andrea, "but I think I'd prefer some pasta. Only a half portion, but something very special."

"I know just the thing. It's not on the menu, but Luigi made some beautiful tortellini this morning, stuffed with a forcemeat of sweetbreads. Very delicate, they need only a little butter and cream."

"Perfect," Andrea said, calculating to herself the economics of such a dish. As a forcemeat for tortellini, a few pounds of sweetbreads could be made to go a long way. It might be an idea worth stealing. "And of course I must have something in parchment. What do you suggest?"

"The fresh crab, without question. It was flown in from Alaska overnight. The cartoccio seals in the juices, so that it is very tender, very sweet. You can't eat better crab."

"Wonderful. And a small salad of arugula, with lemon juice only."

"Certainly, Lady Andrea."

Sid Fogel ordered oysters on the half shell and a veal chop *alla pizzaiola*. Tasty, no doubt, but highly unimaginative, in Andrea's opinion.

"You should have had something in parchment," she said mischievously.

"Andy, you know I hate to have you tell me what to eat."

"Just trying to be helpful."

"Like hell. Just trying to put me down, is more like it. As if it weren't annoying enough to have to sit here and listen to you la-dee-dahing it with that smarmy ass-kisser. You really are a bit much, you know."

"It works," said Andrea.

"Image-wise? I suppose it does."

Andrea didn't exactly overlook her image, it was true. But there were more hardheaded reasons for currying favor with chefs and restaurant owners, and for trying unusual items on menus. She needed fresh ideas constantly, both for her television show and for her catering firm. Like fashion designs, recipes were marvelously easy to plagiarize. Just as you could alter the cut of a dress minutely and produce a garment that was different enough to avoid being sued but that still could pass for a creation of the latest Coty Award winner, so you could change a single ingredient in a recipe, substituting leeks for shallots or tarragon for chervil, and claim the result as your own. Every chef, every author of cookbooks, did it all the time. On the other hand, if you wanted the precise recipe and were willing to give credit, you had to flatter the chef into telling you his secrets. Andrea was certainly not above either flattery or plagiarism in the pursuit of her career. You couldn't be if you wanted to survive.

"It's not just the image, Sid. When I first started out in this business I thought of myself as better than the people who hired me. But I realized damn fast that that wasn't the way they looked at it. The possibility of hiring some titled bitch to do her cooking for her gives the average stockbroker's wife an orgasm on the spot. So the Lady Andrea Harrington bit is important, I grant you. But it's also a kind of armor, and believe me you need all the protection you can get. Did you know that one of the cardinal rules among restaurant owners is never to go into the kitchen to fire a chef?"

"Why not?" asked Sid, with genuine curiosity.

"Because that's where the knives are."

Sid put his head back and laughed. He was especially attractive when he laughed, Andrea had always felt. It took the steel out of his gray eyes. "I guess I'd better watch my step," Sid said. "Is that why you always carry your own set of knives when we tape on location?"

"Not really. There are other ways to intimidate people." Andrea took a sip of champagne. "Actually, in the food world the invisible knives are almost as dangerous as the real ones. Everyone carries those around with them, which is why you need armor. And part of mine is what you call la-dee-dahing. As I say, it works."

Sid could not really quarrel with Andrea on that point. He supposed that most people Andrea dealt with recognized that there was a mailed fist beneath the velvet glove. Curiously, though, it was quite another side of her that came across most strongly on television.

Like Julia Child before her, she had an uncanny ability to convey to other people her own pleasure in food. But while the hearty Mrs. Child's great triumph was to make gourmet cooking seem accessible to ordinary people, it was Andrea's special talent to make cooking seem an extension of her own sensuality. When Julia dropped a roast potato on the floor and then replaced it on the serving platter, reminding her viewers that they were usually alone in the kitchen, or when she disguised a crack in a rolled omelet with a little extra sauce, she reassured people that they too could make a mistake and get away with it. She had taken the intimidation out of gourmet cooking.

What Andrea did was to subtly suggest the connection between food and sex—or at least romance. She paid far more attention to making a dish look beautiful than Julia did, and focused as much attention on table decorations and food presentation as she did on the cooking itself. Andrea emphasized style, creating an atmosphere of glamorous sensual allure. And she did it in a way that managed to suggest, however subliminally, that eating was not only a sensual act in itself, but a prelude to other pleasures of the flesh.

Andrea, sensing that Sid was momentarily relaxed and mellow, decided that it was time to get down to business. "I've been going over the new contract, Sid. And I have to tell you that I'm not satisfied. You've upped the budget for individual shows, and I appreciate that. But I also want a larger share of the profits." Andrea leaned forward, her large blue eyes fixed on his. "I'm sure you realize that I'm being underpaid."

Sid chuckled. It was not a genuine laugh but simply the stock response of a man accustomed to turning down demands for money. "No, Andy, I'm sorry but I don't realize that. I

21

suspected that you might *think* you were underpaid, but you're not."

Andrea had not really expected him to say anything else. "Then you're not paying attention to your books, Sid."

"There's nothing I pay any closer attention to. Your first season was a loss. It picked up a lot at the end, I grant you. We attracted a number of new advertisers and were able to charge a higher premium per minute. But the year as a whole was still in the red. This past year's profits just barely made up for the first year's losses."

"Considerably more than barely, Sid. I know what the figures are."

Sid's face went suddenly hard, his long jaw muscles pulled taut. "In other words there's somebody in my office I ought to fire."

Andrea shrugged. "I don't think you should bother. I'd just find another sympathetic friend."

Sid paused for a moment and then changed tactics. "The answer is still no. But I'll make you a promise for next year."

"This year, Sid. Or there won't be a next year. There won't even be a this year. I won't sign the contract as it stands."

"Such gratitude, Andrea." Sid only called her Andrea when he was annoyed, although that was what she usually preferred to be called.

"What were you making with your catering firm when I met you? Fifty, sixty thousand for yourself? By your own admission it didn't give you much pleasure curing the frigidity of stockbrokers' wives. Now you really can feel better than they are. Right? By putting you on television I made you into a national celebrity. I quadrupled your income. Now you've got not only your New York firm but a branch out here. Thanks to me. The reason that Beverly Hills crowd took to you so fast is that you're a celebrity yourself. There are dozens of catering firms, Andy. The reason yours is on top is that I put you on television. You ought to be thanking me, not holding me up."

22

"Sid." She gave his name two syllables. "You under-estimate me. You gave me the chance to become famous sooner than it might have happened otherwise. But it would have happened. And even though you gave me the opportunity, I was the one who made it work. It was my idea to change the format and get us out of the studio. If we hadn't done that there wouldn't be a show anymore. It would have died the first year. You know that as well as I do. So we owe each other. All I want is my share of what was made together. That's all."

"I think you want more than your share, Andrea."

Despite the intensity of their feelings, they had not raised their voices above a conversational level, and Andrea felt no embarrassment at the sudden appearance of a waiter bringing them their first course. "That looks lovely," she said. "Thank you."

She did not immediately reply to Sid's accusation. Instead she speared one of the small perfect rounds of pasta that had been placed before her—navels of Venus, they were sometimes called in Italy. She tasted. The pasta was perfectly done, with a slight *al dente* resistance but none of the toughness found in inferior tortellini. The sweetbread filling was smooth and subtle but avoided blandness. She detected a hint of truffle, and a mere suggestion of brandy. Quite marvelous.

She speared another tortellini and held it out to Sid as though they were still lovers. He looked as though he might refuse, but then leaned forward and took it off her fork into his mouth.

More than her share, Sid had accused. She didn't believe that was true. Always, as far back as she could remember, she had wanted more than she had. But that was not the same thing as more than she deserved. Growing up in Cleveland, ordinary Andrea Nilsson then, everyone had seemed to have more than she did. No, of course there had been others with much less. But she had always been far more conscious of those with more. Her father, a second-generation Swedish-

23

American, had taught English at Brixton Academy, a private girls' school, where his salary was only a little more than twice a year's tuition for a boarding student. As a faculty child, Andrea had gone to Brixton for free, but the contrast between the lives of the other girls and her own had made her even more determined to someday get all the things they had and she didn't. They had more new clothes in their closets than she had old ones. They flew to the Bahamas or Hawaii for Christmas and to Europe in the summer. They were girls who had horses and their own cars, girls whose families' summer cottages had fourteen rooms. Andrea had been popular at school—she had never let them realize how jealous she was. More than her share? She didn't think so. It wasn't what was fair in life, it was what was attainable.

"Let me put it this way, Sid," Andrea said. "I know what I deserve and I won't settle for less. What you did for me or I did for you in the past is beside the point. The show's going to be picked up by markets in another thirty cities this coming season. Your advertising revenues are going to double. And I want my share of that."

Studying his remaining oyster as though he suspected it of being spoiled, Sid did not reply for a moment. Then he looked up. "I suppose you think you're terribly clever, springing this on me today. Did you figure I couldn't be ungentle-manly enough to spoil your big evening? The thing is, Andy, I'm not all that impressed with awards. And you're not exactly getting an Emmy. The Independent Broadcasters Association is important, but it's not in the same league as the majors."

"You know damn well I've outdrawn network programs in several cities," Andrea snapped.

"Sure, that's why you're getting an award."

"I believe the citation reads, 'To Lady Andrea Harrington for her innovative contributions to television programming,' etcetera, etcetera."

"Oh, for Christ's sake, Andy. You don't really buy that stuff, do you? Those station owners don't give a shit about innovative programming. All that interests them is that you knocked Sheriff Lobo on his ass in the ratings a couple of times. Which doesn't take much, I might add. It's all about money, honey."

"You really think the award should have gone to you, don't you, Sid."

"No. We've been through this before. It was your ideas that saved the show, as you were so quick to make clear to Baxter Rabbit and all your other columnist friends. If there's going to be an award, you deserve it. But don't go thinking it has anything to do with quality. The bottom line is that you've turned out to be commercial and they didn't expect it. So they give you a pat on the back."

"Sid, darling, I think you just made a mistake. If I am so bloody commercial, then surely I deserve more money. Right?"

Sid suddenly laughed. "I keep forgetting how damned tough and smart you are. Okay, Andy, let's not fight about it. I'll give you an extra three thousand a show."

"I was thinking of seven."

"You are a greedy bitch, aren't you?"

"A little while ago it was lying bitch."

"Both if you like."

Andrea reached across the table and covered Sid's hand with her own. "We shouldn't be fighting, Sid. We have too much in common. We've shared too much."

"That becomes clearer by the minute," he replied, withdrawing his hand. "And you can forget the seductive overtures."

"Sid, what I've asked for is what I deserve. At the very least. And you can certainly afford to give it to me."

"It has nothing to do with what I can afford. You still owe me for what I've done for you, God damn it. You should be happy to get two thousand."

"It's not enough."

"That's all there is, kid. That's it."

"Then I won't sign."

25

Sid flung down his fork. "Oh, come off it, Andy. What kind of a fool do you take me for? You love the power that show gives you. Nothing would make you give it up. Don't make idle threats. It doesn't pay."

"It's not an idle threat, Sid. I have the catering firm to fall back on. And eventually I'd find another producer for the show. You know that. It might take a while, but I'd be back on television. Don't forget that I own the rights to the title."

"How could I forget? I realized that was a mistake the minute I agreed to it. I should know better than to make contractual agreements in mid-fuck."

Andrea merely smiled.

Sid looked away from her. He was usually the one who did the pushing around. He was only thirty-six and had five shows on television, including Andrea's. The others were game shows of the kind that critics invariably referred to as sleaze or junk. But with his very first show, "Honeymoon Roulette," he had discovered that by aiming for the lowest common denominator in public taste the highest possible profits could be realized. He'd produced "Gourmet Adventures with Lady Andrea Harrington" partly to prove that he could turn out a class show if he wanted to. It had given him a hard, sweet pleasure when the critics raved about it. Somewhat to his surprise, it had turned out to be financially successful, too. Not like his other shows, at least not yet, but the prospects were very good. He could give Andrea what she wanted, but it would mean taking it out of his own pocket, and he genuinely felt that she still owed him. The books weren't balanced yet in his mind, even though they were on paper. She owed him more than she was willing to admit. That, more than anything, was what made him angry. Besides, he was convinced she would back down. There was no way she was going to give up the status she'd achieved.

"Okay," he said. "So there won't be a show this coming season. Have it your way. Maybe you can find another pro-

26

ducer to seduce into backing you. But you know, my dear, you're not really *that* good in bed. And you're not as important as you think you are."

Andrea felt a sudden chill. She nearly shivered.

Sid devoured his last oyster and pushed back his chair. "Give me a call if you change your mind. But don't wait too long, Andy. We have to start gearing up soon, you know."

He stood.

"Sorry not to stay for the chop. But, as you say, I probably should have had something in parchment."

And he strode away toward the door.

Andrea was stunned.

Sid had walked out on her before, it was true, but that had been when their affair was coming to an end, in the course of an intensely emotional and personal argument. It never would have occurred to her that he would walk out in the middle of a business conversation. Especially in a public place, the bastard.

Mike D'Amato materialized at her side. "Should I hold your main courses, Lady Andrea?"

"I beg your pardon?"

"Your main courses." He gestured toward Sid's empty chair.

"Oh. No. No, Mike. Mr. Fogel won't be returning."

"I hope there was nothing wrong with his oysters?"

Andrea nearly laughed in his face. How typical. She had just been told to go to hell, but Mike D'Amato was concerned only that she might give him a bad report card. "No, of course not. Mr. Fogel's beeper rang, which means there must be some absolute disaster on the set," Andrea lied with what she hoped was some plausibility.

"Shall I bring your crab, then?"

Her appetite was gone. But it would hardly do for her to leave, too. "Yes, please, Mike. I'm looking forward to it."

Why had Sid reacted so strongly? She knew he could afford to let her have the money she wanted. Unless there was

27

some secret financial problem she didn't know about. Or was it that he was still more emotionally involved with her than she had thought? He'd acted like a jealous lover.

You're not *that* good in bed.

That wasn't what a *friend* said to you when he was angry, not even a friend who was a former lover. Her head began to ache. She would have liked to put her face between her hands and massage her temples. But she couldn't, not here.

She had a sudden feeling of apprehension, and glanced around to see if Baxter Robinson were still in the restaurant. It would be very unpleasant to have him report in his column that Sid had walked out on her in the middle of lunch. That would have to be stopped.

But his table was empty and had been entirely reset. He must have left before Sid had. Still, she'd have to face him tonight at the awards dinner. She had a strong premonition that Sid would not be there, and Baxter, along with everyone else, would want to know why. Unless they already knew. All it would take would be for Sid to tell one or two people, and the whole town would know. There was no place in the world that gossip traveled faster. And there she'd be, all decked out in one of the most smashing outfits she had ever owned but feeling absolutely naked, with everyone snickering behind their napkin. It was the kind of drama they loved in LA, triumph contradicted by disaster.

Sid had been right, of course. She had attacked him today exactly because she had thought he'd be unable to refuse her on this particular day. Ungentlemanly enough, he'd said. She'd forgotten that Sid, for all his external gloss, was not a gentleman and never would be. He was a street fighter. And now he'd turned her ploy against her. Unless she called him and begged forgiveness, he wouldn't show up tonight. Unless she accepted his terms, he'd let it be known that he'd had it. Greedy bitch, he'd say to anyone who would listen.

Mike D'Amato set a plate down in front of her. She hadn't

heard him coming and almost jumped. And he stood there waiting for her approval.

Carefully she opened the pale brown parchment envelope. The sweet briny odor of crab wafted upward with the escaping steam. Bathed in butter, the large white and pink chunks of shellfish were surrounded by glistening snow peas and tiny whole mushrooms, each of which had been lovingly fluted. In the center there was a perfect black diamond of a truffle. That was for her, she knew, a special addition to the dish. And she would not be charged an extra twenty dollars for it, either.

"It's absolutely beautiful, Mike," Andrea said, and prayed that he would go away. And then she added, "Perhaps we can tape a segment here next year. Would you be amenable to that?"

Mike D'Amato turned pale and then beet red. "I, I," he said, stuttering, "can't imagine anything more exciting."

She smiled at him. At least she hoped it came across as a smile rather than a grimace. "Wonderful. We'll get back to you on that."

"Thank you, Lady Andrea. Thank you very much." And he backed away, bowing and then scraping, literally, against the table behind him.

She could not possibly eat more than a bite or two. She could get away with that, of course—she was famous for merely tasting dishes. Her slender waist attested to her restraint, and Mike D'Amato would not be offended. He probably wouldn't even notice, with the prospect of having his restaurant featured on her show dancing before his eyes. He wouldn't know until tomorrow that there might not be a show.

Andrea's house just to the north of Beverly Hills had originally been built by Stephan Goltshak, one of Hollywood's top set decorators in the fifties and sixties. With only nine rooms it was not large by the overblown standards of movie people, but it was marked by the taste and the flair for the

29

dramatic that had won him two Academy Awards. The two L-shaped wings of the house opened off a central glass-roofed foyer with a small reflecting pool, a room filled with the scent of the gardenias and begonias that bloomed in tiers along the walls. Glass doors on the far side of the foyer opened onto a cypress-lined walk that led down to the swimming pool, and to the separate studio beyond it which Andrea had converted into an office and small test kitchen.

Andrea loved the house. It was a haven to which she gratefully returned from her many cross-country trips. But today, after her disastrous luncheon with Sid, she did not feel the usual sense of imminent relaxation as she turned into the steep, winding driveway.

The red Volkswagen Rabbit belonging to Gabriella Crowley, Andrea's chief West Coast assistant, was parked in front of the house. Andrea brought her Rolls to a sharp stop beside it, churning the white gravel, and then hurried through the house and down the path between the cypresses to the studio.

As she entered the office at the front of the studio, Gabriella looked up from her desk. Her dark eyes registered immediate concern. "Something's wrong," she said.

Andrea flopped down into the big Dansk swivel chair behind her own desk. "I wish for once you weren't right, Gabriella, but as always you're dead on target."

"Sid's being difficult?"

"Sid's being impossible. He walked out on me in the middle of lunch, the bastard. Not to mention threatening to cancel the show."

Gabriella sighed and brought one hand to her head in a very Latin expression of dismay. From her father, a San Diego lawyer and later a district judge, Gabriella had inherited a cool, shrewd mind, but from her mother, a Mexican film actress who had come to Hollywood in the thirties and appeared in small parts in several westerns before marrying Richard Crowley, Gabriella had acquired certain gestures that were charmingly at odds with her otherwise very controlled personality.

Andrea looked across at her expectantly. "Aren't you going to say, 'I told you so?' "

"I didn't really."

"No, you just asked, with your usual discreetness, if Sid could really be expected to cough up that much. I wish you'd told me I was being a damn fool."

"But that's not what I thought, Andrea. After all, you do have a way of persuading people to do what you want. It was just that I thought maybe you should have had Mr. Danforth feel things out first. He called a couple of minutes ago, by the way."

Bucky Danforth was Andrea's lawyer and accountant; he could not quite have been called her manager—she was her own manager, which she suddenly was beginning to feel might be a mistake—but Bucky was one of the few people she allowed to tell her off. Which no doubt was what he was about to do. "He's probably heard from Sid," Andrea said. "I wouldn't be surprised if the whole goddamn town knew by now."

"No." Gabriella shook her head. "Surely not. I can't believe Sid would let the show die just over money. It's the one prestige show he has and that's important to him. Everyone would accuse him of being a tasteless money-grubber all over again, just when he was beginning to rise above that reputation."

"Oh, I don't think he really wants to lose the show, either. But by putting out the rumor that he's canceling it, he could put all the blame on me."

"But Andrea, what he really wants is for you to back down a little. And spreading rumors all over town would just make it more difficult for you to do that. He knows your pride."

Andrea made a kind of growl in her throat. "My pride! God knows I've had to swallow it often enough. But not this time."

Gabriella simply spread her hands. It was a gesture that said, "Don't ask me if you're not going to listen." Which was fair enough, Andrea had to admit.

"I suppose I'd better call Bucky Danforth."

Gabriella nodded. "Do you want me to stay for a while? I don't really have to be at the kitchens until four."

"You'd better go. If everything isn't perfect for Mrs. Berriman's soiree she'll start screaming again. I thought she was going to take my head off when she found out I couldn't *personally* supervise tonight. 'But this was agreed upon months ago, Lady Andrea,'" Andrea said in perfect imitation of Mrs. Berriman's nasal whine.

"Oh, you needn't worry about that. I talked to her this afternoon, and after some reflection she's come around to the view that having the party the same night that you're getting the award is a coup, even if you can't be there *personally*."

Andrea and Gabriella looked at each other for a moment and burst out laughing. Both women knew perfectly well that everything would go just as smoothly with Gabriella in charge. But Andrea was the star, and Gabriella was the understudy, and people like Mrs. Berriman always turned in their tickets if the star couldn't appear. As Andrea herself knew from long-ago and painful experience, there were times when the understudy was better than the star. But you couldn't tell that to the likes of Mrs. Berriman. If you weren't a star, in her mind, then you didn't exist.

"Were you able to round up enough Iranian caviar?" Andrea asked. Only Mrs. Berriman, with her disdain for everything that had not received the ultimate in accolades, would have insisted upon Iranian caviar while the hostages were still being held. Andrea sincerely doubted that the woman, who was famous for her consumption of martinis, would be able to taste the difference if you gave her catfish roe, but she would be certain to look at the labels on the cans, and she wanted them to be Iranian, regardless of what was going on in the world.

"Yes. Luigi, in Santa Monica, dug some up for us, God knows from where. I doubt that it's first quality, although the can he opened for me was all right. I hope we don't find sludge in the rest of them. He gave a great show of letting me pick the test can myself, but you know Luigi. I always feel as though I'm in the middle of a reverse shell game when I'm dealing with him. He wills you to pick the right one. Not that it matters. Mrs. Berriman only cares what the—"

"Label says," Andrea finished for her, but this time she did not join in Gabriella's laughter.

"Well, I'll go along then," Gabriella said. "Try to enjoy tonight, my dear. It will all work out."

"I don't know. But thank you."

Andrea sat for a moment after Gabriella had left, trying to steel herself for what she suspected would be an unpleasant conversation. But then again, maybe Bucky didn't know about Sid.

She dialed.

The receptionist told her that Mr. Danforth was on another line but that he'd given instructions to be interrupted if Lady Andrea called. Andrea's heart skipped a beat. Bucky didn't usually interrupt calls.

"Andrea." The voice was measured, low.

"Yes. You called, Bucky?"

"I gather you've gotten yourself into a major pickle."

"Sid called you?"

"The man himself."

"And suggested that you marinate me in pepper sauce and cook me over a slow fire?"

"Something like that. Why didn't you tell me you were making demands on that scale. I could have told you he wouldn't buy."

"Because I knew he wouldn't in fact buy from you. I thought I could get away with it if I played it right."

"That's reasonable, I suppose. Up to a point. So what went wrong?"

"I don't know. I guess I'm not the seductress I thought."

"Apparently not, my dear. I hope you're better at eating crow."

"I'll be damned if I will," Andrea almost shouted.

33

"Now you listen to me, for once. I think the man is serious about canceling the show."

"He can't be. It means too much to him. Gabriella said—"

"Gabriella is a hell of a smart lady. And so are you. But there's something else involved here. I think you've somehow got Sid's macho up. He thinks he's been played for a sucker. It doesn't have anything to do with the money as such. It has to do with feelings."

"What do you mean feelings?"

"Well, is there any chance he might still be in love with you?"

"Oh, for God's sake. I'm not sure he ever was. I don't think Sid falls in love with women, he just falls in love with the idea of having certain women for a certain length of time."

"Maybe there's more to him than that, Andrea."

"I just don't believe that's the problem. He did seem strangely emotional today, but I can't imagine—" Andrea faltered.

"Or can you?"

"Well, it certainly isn't going to *help* any even if I could imagine it. What am I supposed to do? Spring out of his closet in the middle of the night in a Frederick's negligee? It's absurd."

"You misunderstand me, my dear. I'm not talking about sex. I'm talking about the fact that he may think you're trying to get money out of him on the basis of what he once felt for you, and maybe still feels for you in some way. He feels used, it's my guess, and he doesn't like it."

Andrea was silent for a moment. There was something in what Bucky was saying, she had to admit it, at least in regard to the way she had come on to Sid today, but she didn't really believe he was that sensitive.

"So what am I supposed to do, Bucky?"

"I don't know exactly. You'll have to use your intuition. But I do know you're going to have to back down at least in part."

34

"I won't do that."

"Look, Andrea, think of it this way. You can sacrifice a little of your pride and ask for a bit less, or you can sacrifice your new Rolls. I told you to wait on that until the contract had been signed. If you lose the show you can't afford to keep up the payments on a Rolls, and that's all there is to it. You're going to be seriously strapped. As you're well aware, you still have investors to pay off on the catering firm. Including me. Lose the show and it's going to be strictly no frills for at least another year."

"You certainly know how to hit home, Bucky." Andrea's first Rolls had been a present, but in the end she had lost it. To buy one for herself was a reward for what she had accomplished on her own. It was a symbol to her of her ability to survive all calamities. She couldn't lose this one too. She couldn't bear the thought of it.

"Well, I can't think about it now. I've got to pull myself together for tonight. I have a feeling Sid won't show up, and people will be asking questions. So if you'll excuse me, Bucky, I'm going to go practice putting on my best front. I'll talk to you again in a couple of days."

"Okay, my dear. And Andrea, try to have some fun tonight. You deserve it. You deserve what you're asking from Sid. But he's a stubborn man. You ought to know that better than anyone. You'll get what you want in the long run. But I don't think you can have it right now. And if you don't compromise now, you may be throwing away that long run. But enough said. Take care."

"Yes. Thank you, Bucky," she said automatically, thinking immediately that she didn't have much to thank him for.

Andrea sat for a few moments looking around her office. Hardly anyone but she and Gabriella ever came here, yet she had furnished and decorated it as though it were for public display. The desks were teak, the chairs covered in leather, the small sofa upholstered in suede. Even the filing cabinets were the most expensive available, the walls painted to match their glossy green. It could all have been done simply, efficiently, and even attractively for a third the price, but Andrea was not comfortable unless she was surrounded by the best. She wanted and needed that glow that came from knowing that it couldn't have been done better. It wasn't for show, for others; it was for herself.

And now it was in jeopardy.

She left the office and began to walk slowly back up to the main house. As she reached the pool, screened from view on three sides by cypresses, she was startled by the sound of Rick Trumbull's voice. He had been due to fly in from Nevada, where he was playing his first starring role in a contemporary western, to accompany her to the award ceremonies tonight, but she hadn't expected him before six. Ordinarily she would have been happy and excited that he was early, but today it simply seemed one more complication.

Rick was stretched out on the yellow cushions of a chaise longue talking with Jim, Andrea's houseman. Jim was a Vietnamese refugee, but he was so determined to leave behind his and his wife's memories of that beleaguered country, and to become assimilated into his adopted one, that he had insisted upon being called by an American name. Jim was the closest equivalent he could devise; his wife called herself Em. He had apparently just brought Rick a drink, and they were engaged in a curious conversation that was in fact a kind of language lesson for Jim.

"Camera," said Rick. "Movie camera." He made a circle of his hands and peered through them. Jim nodded. "On a boom."

"Fire?" asked Jim in alarm.

"No. God, how do I explain this? A boom is a machine to carry the camera. High in the air." He gestured desperately.

Jim saw Andrea first, and bowed, looking slightly embarrassed, although she did not in the least mind such attempts to improve his English. He was a highly intelligent man, who had been in the importing business before the destruction of

36

his country. The gratitude that he and Em showed her for giving them the opportunity to be mere servants, when they had once had servants of their own, sometimes made Andrea feel almost guilty. But she understood. Her own world, after all, had twice collapsed around her in the past.

"May I bring you something, Lady Andrea?" Jim asked.

"No, not at the moment. Thank you, Jim."

He bowed again and left them.

Rick had gotten up from the chaise, and now he came to her and embraced her. He was wearing only a bikini—unlike most of the young men of southern California who insisted upon wearing surfing shorts, Rick was vain enough to prefer the tan line left by the briefest of suits—and Andrea could feel the strong warmth of his body. She held him for a long moment.

"Hello, love," he said. "A dust storm kicked up so I was able to get away early." He held both her hands and looked her up and down. "You look fabulous."

"Well, I don't feel fabulous."

"What's the matter?"

"Sid Fogel has made it clear that he'd rather cancel the show than give me the money I want."

"Christ. Was he nasty about it?"

"He was very unpleasant."

"The bastard."

"My word exactly."

"That's terrible, baby." Rick embraced her again. He was one of those men for whom sex was the answer to all problems, for whom comforting a woman was immediately arousing, and Andrea could feel him beginning to get an erection as he pressed tightly against her.

She broke away from him, gently.

"Shall we go inside?" he asked, smiling.

"Not right now, Rick. I'm very upset. I'm sorry."

"I know you're upset. I understand. I thought we could take your mind off it."

Andrea looked at him. He was an extraordinarily handsome young man, with blue eyes and almost black hair; his jaw had just enough ruggedness to it to keep him from being too pretty, too soft looking. There were those who thought he could become a major star. Andrea wasn't sure about that. He hadn't shown much depth as an actor so far, but he radiated manliness and sincerity, and that had been enough to make a lot of other actors into stars.

Half of Hollywood would have liked to get Rick Trumbull into bed, and there were those who were jealous enough to wonder aloud what he was doing with a woman six years older than himself. Andrea was not much amused by such talk; at thirty-three she was older than Rick, yes, but she hardly considered herself an "older woman" in the usual sense. Yet there was something slightly mysterious about their relationship. Andrea was used to having men fall in love with her, but most of them had been complicated, sophisticated men. Rick was neither. Perhaps that was one of the things she found attractive about him—she always knew exactly what he was thinking and there was no need to play any games. But at this moment, she wished that Rick were a little more complex, that he had a more subtle understanding of the world. He'd been on location for ten days, and had come home to find her troubled, and she knew he would not really be able to comprehend why she felt that making love with him wouldn't help. He simply had never learned that there were some things you couldn't overcome that way.

He stood there in the sun, a beautiful, broad-shouldered, long-legged celebration of the flesh, looking extremely puzzled.

"I was looking forward to seeing you so much," she said. She touched him on the shoulder. "You know that. But the last thing in the world I feel like right now is sex."

"Jesus, you really are upset. I wish I could wring Sid Fogel's neck for you."

"It isn't just Sid. I'm angry with him, but I'm also angry with myself. Sid is stubborn, but so am I. Gabriella and Bucky

Danforth think I should back down. But I'm not sure I can bring myself to do that. I keep thinking that there must be some way to bring Sid around. But then I get a kind of sinking feeling. I look at this house, these trees, this pool, and I know they could all be gone from my life, just like that. It happens all the time out here."

Rick shrugged his strong tanned shoulders. "Well, I've never really had anything much to lose up to now. But I guess I understand a little of what you're feeling. You know Bob Brandon? He's playing one of the heavies in my movie. Well, two years ago he got his big break, just the way this should be mine. But the movie was never released. It's just sitting there in cans someplace. And he'd thought everything was about to happen for him, bought a house in Laurel Canyon, the whole thing, and then he couldn't pay for it. Nobody's seen the movie, so producers and directors think maybe it's his fault it was never released, that he couldn't hack it. So he's back to playing secondary parts, and he wonders if he'll ever get another chance. It makes you think. What if my movie was never released?"

Andrea took his hand, and their fingers intertwined. She gave him a quick kiss. "We have to leave in a couple of hours. I guess I'd better go try to start to pull myself together."

"Okay. I think I'll swim a few laps. I'll be up in a little while."

She squeezed his hand once more and left him there in the sun.

At awards ceremonies over the years, whether she was there herself or merely watching on television, Andrea had always been astonished at the getups that famous women had allowed themselves to be persuaded to wear. You knew that they had spent many thousands of dollars in order to make an impression, yet most of them ended up looking like high-class hookers. There were always a few who looked elegant, whose taste and class upstaged all the rest—Merle Oberon, even in her last years, Lee Remick, Kim Novak, who designed her own clothes and knew precisely how to show herself off to best advantage. But the rest of them, even when they enlisted the services of the world's most famous designers, usually looked like refugees from a Ringling Brothers grand parade. There were too many sequins and too many feathers, ruffles, and flounces, which made the woman look like a lampshade; skirts were too tight or slit to the naval. They were costumes, not evening gowns. And they did the most bizarre things with their hair, creating constructions to rival the Leaning Tower of Pisa, ratting it to look like tumbleweed, or separating it into snake-like strands that would have been the envy of Medusa herself.

Andrea knew that in the midst of such eccentric gaudiness, a little understatement could be like a fresh breeze from the sea on an August night. Three years ago, Hayes Caldwell, in the months when he had been trying to persuade her to marry him and spend the rest of her life shuttling around the world with him, had brought her a length of silk from Bangkok. She had not wanted to marry him, rich and charming as he was; she had wanted to have her own life, to make her own success, and the silk had seemed at the time one more in a series of reminders that he could give her anything she wanted. Hayes was still giving her presents from time to time, in fact. They were still reminders, perhaps. It was difficult to know.

The silk had been stored away in a cedar chest, buried but not forgotten. She had taken it out recently, unwrapped it, and spread it across her canopied mahogany bed and left it there for a day, glancing at it when she went in and out of the room. It was of the colors of peacock feathers, but those colors were so true and the design so subtle that the cloth looked as though it were almost of nature's own creation.

She had taken the silk to a young designer named Susan Scott who was not yet very well known but whom Andrea was convinced soon would be. Susan had grown up in Hong Kong, where her father had been a representative for IBM, and Andrea had discovered that she had a particular flair when

40

working with silk. The resulting gown was a triumph of free-floating fragility with a trailing scarf like a butterfly's wings. It was eye-stopping yet simple, and its colors seemed to shift subtly as she moved.

As she arrived at the Beverly Hilton for the awards ceremony that night, a tuxedoed Rick at her side, she could tell by the way the television cameramen with minicams on their shoulders converged on them, suddenly deserting a starlet with overexposed breasts and a hairdo that must have required at least two cans of lacquer, that she had contrived exactly the effect she wanted. The moment Andrea had put on her gown, in fact, and looked at herself in the mirror, she had begun to regain her control. She was determined that no one who hadn't heard she'd had a traumatic afternoon would ever guess it, and that those who might have heard any rumors would judge from her composure that the rumors must be false.

As she and Rick made their way to their table, Andrea distinctly heard the young second wife of a local television executive say, "I'd kill for that dress," and a companion reply, "Not to mention the man." Andrea smiled to herself. No woman could ask for two more satisfying expressions of envy.

This was not the kind of event to draw out the Gregory Pecks and Frank Sinatras; it was not to be telecast live, though a half-hour program would be put together which independent stations across the country could use at their convenience. But many of the major stars of syndicated television could be spotted around the room—Dinah Shore, looking as fresh as ever, Mike Douglas, Monty Hall, and Peter Marshall, the personalities who provided the real backbone of television programming, day in and day out through the years. In the back of her mind, Andrea looked forward to the day when she would have a network show, when she would be nominated for an Emmy and not merely be receiving a special award from the independent stations. But she did not look down on those who had made it in the world of syndication. It was a different league, but in its own way it was just as tough. And it was full of survivors, people whose shows had been canceled by the networks at one time or another but who had proved that there was a lasting affection for them among viewers across the country, who had gone out and produced their own shows when the networks yanked them off the air. They were people who knew how to pick themselves up by their bootstraps. And tonight of all nights it made Andrea feel happy to be among that kind of survivor.

Andrea and Rick had been seated at a table for eight, along with an English producer and director and their wives. Andrea had not seen their British-made mini-series that had appeared on the independent stations the previous fall, but she explained that she seldom had the time to see even her own show except at special screenings. It turned out that Andrea and the producer had mutual acquaintances in London, which helped take her mind off the fact that there were two empty chairs at their table that should have been occupied by Sid Fogel and his current lady friend, a young soap opera actress.

She had doubted that Sid would put in an appearance, and as the waiters began to serve the first course, an avocado stuffed with shrimp, she knew for certain that he would not arrive. Sid was never late, especially not to functions of this sort.

"I wonder who our missing companions are," the producer remarked later, as he cut into his veal chop. That would make the second veal chop Sid had missed out on today, Andrea reflected with a sudden feeling of anxiety. But she managed to reply, very coolly, "Oh, that's my producer. I can't imagine what's happened to him."

Rick glanced at her and suppressed a grin. He still did not seem to fully comprehend how seriously disturbed she was, Andrea thought. The fact of Sid's absence simply underlined the situation. But Rick and Sid did not get along well, and she supposed Rick was actually rather pleased Sid wasn't there. What was ominous to her was probably a relief to him.

It was going to be a long evening. Andrea's special award was not to be presented until near the end. At least she knew it was actually going to be given to her. As the lights were partially lowered and the ceremonies began, Andrea's mind drifted back to the 1966 Tony Awards, when she had sat nervously in the audience for more than two hours not knowing what was going to happen. She had been just barely twenty, and yet found herself competing with Lee Remick and Rosemary Harris for Best Actress in a Play. In one way she had wanted to win, but in another she had been afraid. It had all happened too fast. She had been a different person then. She had not wanted the responsibility of winning. She had not as yet even gotten used to the responsibility that was hers when the curtain went up each night. The previous year she had been only a college girl, a drama major who had got lucky.

She had been a nobody who had become suddenly and unexpectedly famous, and she had had to do as much acting offstage as she did on, because she had not really found out who she was. That would take years.

Andrea sat at her table, applauding dutifully as an endless series of presenters and award winners came and went. She tried to look attentive, in case one of the wandering minicams should suddenly zoom in on her, but her mind was full of memories. She did not usually think a great deal about the past, but in the half darkness of the ballroom, knowing what to expect as the evening wore on, she found it difficult to concentrate on the present.

But then at last it was her turn. They began by showing a number of clips from the show. The clips had been cleverly chosen to show the progress through a six-course dinner, though each course was being served in a different restaurant or home, as she talked with Julia Child in Cambridge, Joseph Baum at Windows on the World, and Danny Kaye in Hollywood. It was a mixture of actual food preparation and interviews with celebrities of the food and entertainment worlds that had made her show a success—her idea, not Sid's, she reminded herself—and the editor of the brief tribute had caught the show's ambience very well. She was happy with it.

"It gives me great pleasure to present this special award to a very lovely and talented woman, Lady Andrea Harrington."

The applause began, genuinely enthusiastic, and Andrea rose from her table and began to walk toward the stage.

Part Two

Chapter Two

AT 7:15 P.M. ON THE THIRD MONDAY in September 1965, the opening night curtain was scheduled to rise on a new comedy called *Playing by Ear* at the Morosco Theatre on Forty-fifth Street. Andrea could still hardly believe it was happening. The playwright, David Summers, was a young assistant professor of drama at Northwestern, where a production of the play had been mounted with a cast of students from the School of Drama the previous March. Like Arthur Kopit's *Oh Dad, Poor Dad* at Harvard a few years earlier, the play had been such a success that a string of Broadway producers had flown out to see it. Now, after a tryout on the summer circuit, it was about to open on Broadway, and alone among the members of the original Northwestern cast, Andrea was recreating her role.

Walking along Forty-fifth Street on the way to the theater during the two weeks of previews, past the Imperial Theatre where *Fiddler on the Roof* would be celebrating the beginning of its second year the night after Andrea opened, with *The Odd Couple* playing right across the street, it seemed like a miracle to her that she could possibly be entering the stage door of the Morosco to give a performance before a Broadway audience on the same street where Zero Mostel and Walter Matthau were packing them in every night.

Not that *Playing by Ear* was exactly packing them in. The preview houses were only about two-thirds full, and the audience was not there to see her, or even the play, since David Summers was as unknown a quantity as a playwright as she was an actress. They were coming to see Barry Lawrence; with two big hits in a row to his credit, theatergoers seemed to feel that any play he appeared in was likely to be worth seeing. Even so the advance sale was small and it would all depend on the critics. Barry himself was confident they did have a hit, but his reason for it scared her to death.

Saturday night after the last preview, he took her to dinner at Sardi's and in introducing her to Vincent Sardi, he said, "You're going to have to make room on your walls for a new caricature, Vinny. Come Monday night this young lady is going to be a star."

After they were seated, Andrea said, "I wish you wouldn't build me up so much. It gives me the heebie-jeebies."

"It's your play, Andrea. Audiences are falling in love with you already, and once the critics have told them how good you are you'll be getting more applause than I do. It's beginning to happen already. All they need is to be reassured that you're as wonderful as they think you are. Starting Tuesday morning your phone is going to be ringing off the wall with people wanting interviews. Midwestern college girl becomes overnight star—they're going to love it."

It was true that audiences had been responding very enthusiastically to her, but Barry's words made it seem as though the success or failure of the play ultimately rested on her shoulders even more than on his. It wasn't something she wanted to hear. It was too terrifying a thought.

But it was a thought she could not get out of her head all day Sunday. She wished there had been a performance, or at least a rehearsal, that day to take her mind off the opening, but Jack Hoffman, in his directorial wisdom, had said that rest would do more good than any further work. To get out of the apartment and distract herself she went to see the movie *Darling* late Sunday afternoon. She was fascinated by it; as the story of a young woman who became an overnight celebrity, though, it increased her nervousness. If Barry was right, if Jack was right, if all the people who'd put so much faith in her were right, the same kind of thing could happen to Andrea. And it all depended on what she did opening night.

Monday afternoon, before she left her apartment, Andrea threw up the little lunch she had eaten. She felt weak and light-headed when she arrived at the theater. It seemed entirely possible that she would start retching again right out on stage. Her hands were trembling so that it took two tries to get her makeup on straight. But once it was on she began to feel a little calmer. In her head she went over the new lines that had been inserted in the first scene on Thursday and the revamped blocking in the second act.

The fifteen-minute call came and then Barry knocked on her dressing room door.

"Nervous?" he asked.

"Petrified."

"Good. So am I."

"I don't believe you."

"Then how come I'm already on my third pack of cigarettes today? Listen, young lady, anybody who doesn't get nervous on opening night doesn't belong out there. It gets the adrenaline going."

"I don't need any more adrenaline. How often do people drop dead on stage?"

"Not often enough, sweetheart," said Barry with a laugh. "There are times when you wish you could, but tonight's not going to be one of them. We've got our first full house, and it's packed with people who wish us well, and they're going to laugh in all the right places, great big laughs. And after the first five minutes we're going to be having the time of our lives. You'll see."

The assistant stage manager poked his head in at the door. "Five minutes," he said.

Barry gave her a hug. "Let's go get 'em," he said.

She stood in a kind of trance waiting for her entrance. The stage manager gave a hand signal and the curtain rose. There was applause for the set, and even more applause a few moments later when Barry made his entrance. He was, after all, a star, and the audience wanted to say hello. There would be no applause for her, of course. Nobody knew her. It was up to her to make them her friends so that the next time they would want to say hello. Even her parents weren't there. They'd wanted to be but she had persuaded them to wait until the following week.

Her entrance required split-second timing. She had to burst through the door, come to a dead stop, retreat backwards out the door, close it, wait, knock and come in again. Including Barry's two lines, there were five laughs that could be had, provided everything went just right.

She turned the knob and rushed into the room with three walls. She came to a stop. Beyond the absent fourth wall a thousand people laughed.

At the end there were eight curtain calls. She had the first solo call, and there were bravos and people stood, almost everybody seemed to be standing and she felt the most extraordinary exhilaration she had ever experienced. And then it was Barry's turn and the applause stayed steady but it did not rise above what she had gotten. On the eighth call, Barry took her hand and led her out onto the stage with him. They bowed once and then he let go of her hand and stepped back. She bowed again, and she felt Barry leaving the stage. She could not see or hear him but she could feel him withdrawing. He was leaving her there alone. It was in his contract that he was to have the last bow, but he was giving it to her, and as the curtain came down for the final time she felt tears start to her eyes.

Offstage he was standing smiling at her, and then as they hugged the tears began to stream down her cheeks. "You shouldn't have done that," Andrea said.

"Oh, yes, I should have, sweetheart. It's going to be like that from now on. I'm not dumb, you know. I told you this was your show, and it is. I had a hundred friends out there tonight, and several hundred more fans, and even so you got as much of an ovation as I did. Starting tomorrow, you'll get a bigger one. And if I can't have the biggest ovation, at least

I can get points for magnanimously giving you the spotlight. They'll like me for doing that, they'll say I'm a prince. Earl Wilson will mention it in his column, and that will be good for my image, and good for you and good for the show. I'm not doing it just for you. It's a way of holding my own."

"You are a prince, Barry."

"Ummm," said Barry, making a yes and no gesture with his hands. "Let's put it this way. You could have found yourself playing opposite someone who was dumb, and he would have hated you for being so good. I'll take that much credit. You could have done worse."

Andrea was still crying. "Thank you so much. So much for everything."

"Sure. But it's time to stop crying and get yourself cleaned up before they start invading your dressing room. Besides, we have a party to go to. And there are those reviews to wait for. You better save some tears. I don't think you'll need any sad tears, but with those bastards you never know. The night isn't over yet."

The party was held at the East Sixties townhouse of one of the producers, Karen Bolling, who had amassed a multi-million dollar fortune in the course of running through three husbands. The first had been a playboy Argentinian with vast land holdings and a habit of discarding wives as casually as he changed hotels. Karen, it was said, had been perfectly well aware that she wouldn't last long and could not have cared less so long as the payoff was large enough. A second husband, with more oil wells than neckties, of which he owned an endless collection, had been killed when his private plane crashed following engine failure. Despite her huge inheritance, Karen had not neglected to sue the manufacturer for an additional million dollars in damages.

Her friends claimed that she had actually been distraught over the death of her third husband, a mere banker, who succumbed to a ruptured appendix. Her enemies suggested she had fed him a diet of grape seeds to bring on the attack.

At any rate, she had sworn she would never marry again. Certainly there was no need to do so, since she had enough money to back at least two Broadway flops a year without even noticing the dent in her bank account. In her first two years of dabbling in the theater she had in fact lost an estimated million and half, but apparently had developed better, or at least more commercial, judgment since. Much to the dismay of those who disliked her, her last five shows had been hits.

Barry Lawrence had explained to Andrea that the size and location of opening night parties was a major public relations consideration. If the show was a big musical and you were pretty sure you had a hit, you took over the St. Regis Roof or Tavern on the Green and threw a party for three hundred. If you thought it might be a flop you invited an extra two hundred in the hopes that celebrity glitter would overwhelm the bad notices. Actually, that sometimes worked, helped along by the fact that the public's taste was, thankfully, far less exclusive than the critics', especially when it came to musicals. If you were producing a straight play with a small cast, the upstairs room at Sardi's was a favored location. It wasn't all that expensive, and the walls were covered with pictures of Broadway legends who had had their own share of flops, giving everyone the reassuring sense that next time around it might turn out more happily.

A party held at a producer's house or apartment could mean one of two things. Either everyone knew that disaster was at hand, and preferred to conduct the funeral ceremonies as privately as possible, or nobody was quite sure what the critics would say but at least had a good deal of hope. The difference between those two possibilities could be immediately detected by the quality of the catered buffet, Barry believed. And if that were the case, Karen Bolling had a good deal of hope.

The fourteen-foot table in the high-ceilinged dining room with its gold-damask-covered walls was laden with the most expensive of delicacies. An enormous silver tureen was piled high with what Andrea thought must be several pounds of caviar. "Ah," said Barry, ignoring the toast points and digging in with a spoon. "Beluga. Karen is keeping the faith."

To Andrea the buffet was awesome. She had grown up in the midst of good food; her mother had run a tiny restaurant in Cleveland that served lunch and tea, and Andrea had sometimes helped her lay out the platters of artfully decorated open-face Swedish sandwiches that were the restaurant's main attraction. When her mother gave a party at home it was always a smorgasbord, with several varieties of herring, shrimp, salads, cold meats, Swedish meatballs, and potato casseroles, all very attractively presented. But Andrea had never seen anything like this display, not even at the homes of the rich girls with whom she had gone to school. On a three-foot platter shaped like a fish, gossamer slices of smoked salmon overlapped like the shining scales of some sea creature imagined by Botticelli. What Andrea took to be chicken breasts in aspic she later discovered to be pheasant. On a more mundane level there was potato salad, but it had been intricately studded with uniformlly cut pieces of red and green pepper so that it looked like a miniature Persian carpet. There was a pyramid constructed from medallions of foie gras and, in the center of the table, a decoration that looked like a vase of flowers, except that the petals were formed of shrimp and bay scallops, each with its own toothpick. And those were only the cold dishes.

She wished suddenly that she had had her parents come east for the opening after all, instead of the following weekend. Her mother would have loved this; it was so beautiful and so lavish. The terrible thing was that Andrea didn't think she could eat any of it, or any more than a very little. She ought to be ravenous, there was nothing in her stomach, but she was still too excited and nervous to eat.

It had taken her forever to make her way into the dining room. The assembled guests had applauded when she entered the party, and everyone wanted to talk with her, congratulate her, ask her how she felt. Fortunately, Barry and his wife, Maddy, had rescued her. "I'm sure this young lady needs some sustenance," Maddy had said, taking her by the hand and leading her away from an elderly gentleman who claimed to have attended every Broadway opening night for the past forty years. But now that she was faced with all this glorious food, she couldn't bear the thought of eating it. To be polite, she took tiny helpings of a few dishes; maybe she'd be able to nibble at them later.

The dining room was becoming very crowded, and Andrea made her way back into the living room, taking a glass of champagne from the silver tray proffered by a waiter as she passed. Karen Bolling swept up to her and led her to a big wing chair which Andrea gratefully sank into.

"You were absolutely wonderful tonight, my dear," Karen said. Karen was at least fifty, but she had had her face lifted during the summer, and she looked no more than thirty-five. "You've been splendid all along, of course, but tonight you had an extra shine."

"Thank you, but I think what was lighting me up was simply pure terror."

"Oh, you performers always say that. If anyone should be terrified, it's me. After all, I had three hundred and fifty thousand dollars riding on the evening."

Karen was famous for being nothing if not direct, and Andrea laughed. "You have a point."

"Well, you're going to have a long run, child, I can feel it. And a long career. I was a bit dubious when Jack insisted that he keep you from the production at Northwestern. After all, you hadn't had much experience, but Jack directed two other shows for me and I trust him. He was adamant about you, and he was right."

"I hope the critics agree."

"Oh, don't worry about them. I had my spies planted in seats all around them, and it's going to be fine. They give themselves away you know, when they don't like a play. They all have their little quirks, writing all the time in their nasty little notebooks hardly ever looking at the stage, or getting all fidgety, or even falling asleep. That's a very bad sign. But there was none of that tonight. I'm not in the least worried."

Andrea had originally been a little intimidated by Karen Bolling. She was so unbelievably rich, and obviously a very tough lady, but the toughness was sheathed in a certain degree of humor. She had been very nice to Andrea, finding her an apartment on West End Avenue that Andrea could move into the moment she arrived in New York from their brief summer tour. That hadn't been too difficult for Karen, of course, since she had inherited the building from her third husband. But Andrea was grateful nevertheless; she doubted that she could have dealt with apartment hunting along with all the other pressures. During the two-week rehearsal period before the summer tour she had stayed with Jack Hoffman and his wife, Lucy, in their duplex garden apartment on Charles Street in the Village. She had been nervous about that, afraid that if Jack had had any second thoughts about casting her it could become a very awkward situation. But she had begun to realize that it was another way Jack had devised to show his confidence in her and to make her relax. She had never been alone in New York before, and staying in a hotel would have been lonely and perhaps a little frightening. Jack had understood that. They had all been so understanding and so nice.

Well, almost everyone, she thought, as she saw Maria Davino approaching with some young man. Maria was twenty-seven, she had had a great deal of experience, and Andrea had known the moment they met that Maria was something less than thrilled to be understudying a twenty-year-old nobody from the boondocks. Maria had never had a Broadway lead, but she had worked continuously for years in summer stock, in Off-Broadway, and in smaller parts in two Broadway shows. Andrea was naive in some ways about New York theater, but

55

she wasn't too green to understand that someone who had been in the business for ten years was not going to be happy to play second fiddle to a girl who appeared out of nowhere. She'd decided that the only way to handle the situation was to play to Maria's ego by asking advice even when she already knew the answer. Up to a point, it had worked. Maria had been extremely cool at the beginning, and Andrea knew that she was praying Andrea's inexperience would trip her up, making it possible for Maria herself to inherit the part. Occasionally, Andrea had seen her watching from the wings when Andrea was onstage, studying her with a kind of mixed admiration and fury. But after the first few performances on the summer tour, Maria seemed to accept the inevitable, and had become almost a friend.

Maria's family had originally come from Northern Italy and she was almost as blond as Andrea, with high cheekbones and very blue eyes. She was very dressed up tonight, more so than Andrea really, wearing a floor-length dress of black satin with a very low-cut bodice. It looked a little incongruous next to the young man she was with, who was dressed in beige corduroys and a brown tweed sports coat that obviously had seen better days.

"Mrs. Bolling," Maria said, "I don't think you've met Terry McKenna."

"Karen, dear, Karen. Are you in the theater, young man?"

Before Terry McKenna could get out a word, Maria was answering for him. It was just like her, Andrea thought. "Terry's directed a lot of showcases and two plays at La Mama. And next month he's doing the new Orton play at the Theatre de Lys."

"The big step from Off-Off to Off," said Terry with a laugh.

"I'll be sure to see it," Karen said. "Now let me find one of those disappearing waiters and send him around with some more champagne."

"And this of course is Andrea Nilsson," Maria said, with a slightly fixed smile.

"I wanted to tell you how absolutely wonderful I thought you were," Terry said, and Maria's smile became more fixed than ever.

"Thank you very much." Andrea found Terry very attractive. He had a slightly gangly, unkempt air about him that contrasted with the keen intelligence of his eyes. And she liked his extremely curly light brown hair; it was the kind of hair that made her want to run her fingers through it. She wondered idly if Maria had gotten her hooks into Terry; she'd never mentioned him and was supposedly living alone, but there was definitely something proprietary about the way she treated him.

"Even Maria thinks you're pretty good," Terry added with a mischievous expression.

Maria looked as though she might punch him, but forced a laugh.

"Maria's been a tremendous help," Andrea said quickly, and reached up to take her hand. "It's quite a transition from a college auditorium to the Morosco Theatre. She made it a lot easier."

"I went to Northwestern, too, you know," Terry said.

"Small world," Andrea exclaimed, and tried not to wince. That was a phrase she was trying to stop saying; it sounded increasingly gauche to her ears, since she had discovered that Broadway theater was one of tightest and smallest worlds imaginable. "Did you have any courses with David Summers?"

"Oh, yes. I really should go congratulate our esteemed playwright before he gets too loaded to recognize me."

Andrea laughed. "Yes, I think he's even more nervous now than I was before the performance. He was very calm then, came around and wished everybody well. But he seems to be getting more hysterical by the minute."

"I don't blame him," Terry said. "He has to know what a terrific production of his play it is, so if anybody is going to be put through the buzz saw by the critics it'll be him. You can't fault the performances or the direction. But I think he'll come out all right. It's not art, but it's great fun, and that's what audiences prefer anyway, even if the critics don't."

As the evening wore on, Andrea began to wish that everyone would stop talking about the critics so much. It was beginning to make her nervous all over again. But it seemed to be an obsessional refrain. One man, Andrea never found out who, claimed that he had been standing at the urinal next to Howard Taubman of the *Times* at intermission, and that he had suddenly chuckled. This piece of arcane information was considered highly significant by some, since Howard Taubman was not regarded as having much of a sense of humor. The story was passed around the party from group to group like an oracular pronouncement carried down from Mount Olympus. Andrea heard it twice, fifteen minutes apart, and the second time it had been wishfully or wickedly embellished to suggest that the poor man had laughed so suddenly that he'd dribbled on his shoe.

In the book-lined sitting room on the third floor of Karen Bolling's townhouse, the large console television set was flanked by smaller sets that had been moved in from Karen's bedroom and the guestroom, so that all three major New York stations could be tuned in simultaneously. Local news programs had been reviewing theater for a dozen years, since they had first stepped into the gap left by the 1953 newspaper strike to review *Kismet*, but none of the television critics had anything like the kind of power the critics of the daily newspapers did. A one- or two-minute review simply didn't have the kind of impact that a full-scale printed opinion did, but they could provide an early indication of which way the wind was blowing while everyone waited for the first editions of the papers to appear.

By eleven o'clock most of those who had direct connections with the show were crowded into the sitting room, looking over one another's shoulders at one of the three television sets, even though the reviews weren't likely to be aired until fifteen or twenty minutes into the news. Simply to hear the announcement that a new Broadway play would be reviewed created a special kind of anticipatory tension in the room, though. Everyone began to talk a little faster and a little more loudly. Sudden giggles and self-conscious laughs punctuated the din, as bad jokes and reminiscences of other such nights were shared.

"This is the worst part of it," Barry said to Andrea. "The waiting. It's even worse than to be panned when they actually open their mouth and start spouting."

"I can't imagine you being panned."

"Oh, my dear. How about, 'Barry Lawrence is, as usual, very charming'—sounds good so far, right—'in a part that calls for far more steel.' They love to start you off thinking you're going to get off unscathed, and then stick it to you after the comma."

"You're scaring me to death." Andrea was in fact beginning to feel a little queasy again, and she set down her champagne glass on the table beside her. "I never thought I could get enough champagne," she added, "but I think all those little bubbles are turning into one great big one in my stomach."

"That's why I always drink Scotch. Harder on the liver but easier on the intestines."

Suddenly, on Channel 4, appropriately following an Alka Seltzer commercial, Edward Newton's grave presence filled the screen. The room was immediately silent.

"Every Broadway season needs a romantic comedy or two for reasons of commerce if not art," Newton began in his deep voice. "And in *Playing by Ear* we have one that seems sufficiently diverting to become a hit. Its romance is not too sticky and its comedy is actually funny a good deal of the time. Another in the long line of plays descended from Shaw's *Pygmalion*, *Playing by Ear* once again brings us a confrontation between a free spirit and a know-it-all, with the plot revolving around the question of who will change whom the most. As in *A Thousand Clowns* a few seasons ago, the free spirit is an older man and the know-it-all is a young woman. As the former, Barry Lawrence is a charming as ever, but—"

"Uh oh, here we go," Barry muttered under his breath.

"—he plays the part with a kind of bravura zaniness that adds zest to his customary expertise. Broadway newcomer Andrea Nilsson is more than a match for him. In a tricky role, she manages to make the heroine's stubborn righteousness both funny and curiously endearing, and she is even touching when her certainty finally begins to unravel. Jack Hoffman has directed with the pace and ingenuity we have come to expect of him. *Playing by Ear* is great fun."

A cheer went up and Andrea and Barry hugged each other. Andrea felt a great surge of relief, a release of tension that surprised her—she hadn't fully realized how much anxiety she had been carrying around with her for the past few months. One good review did not make a hit, she knew, but at least somebody had said that she was good. Better than good. Funny and endearing and touching. That couldn't be taken away from her no matter what the rest of them said.

But everything was quiet again. Both CBS and ABC were covering the opening simultaneously. Andrea tried to listen to both at once, catching a phrase here and a phrase there: "lightweight but perfectly tailored"; "delightfully sure of herself"; "the evening zips along"; "both lovely and funny"; and, best of all, "Broadway has a new star."

People had been telling Andrea for weeks that the play could make her a star, but she hadn't been able to connect those words with herself. Until coming to New York for rehearsals before the summer tour, she had seen only two Broadway plays in her life, when her parents had brought her to New York on brief vacation trips—*My Fair Lady* when she was twelve and *The Miracle Worker* when she was fifteen. Julie Andrews was a star, and so was Anne Bancroft, and she had wanted to be like them, to have her picture in magazines, to have people applaud her. She had wanted that since she was a child. But it had never occurred to her that it could happen so soon and so quickly. She had expected to finish college and then come to New York and work at whatever jobs she could find to support herself while she gradually made a reputation as an actress. She'd been prepared for it to be hard, and full of disappointment, before she finally made a name for herself. To have had it happen when she was still so young, out of nowhere, made it all seem a little unreal. To hear a critic proclaim her a star was terribly exciting, and she felt an almost physical sense of joy. But although she had spent years daydreaming about what it would be like to be a star, what she would feel, how she would behave, she did not at this moment feel what she had thought she would. She had expected to feel a sense of power, but instead what she felt was a kind of awe at the strange workings of fate.

The television sets were turned off and everyone went back downstairs to the living room, where the assistant stage manager had just arrived with stacks of early editions of the *New York Times* and the *Daily News*. Howard Taubman had indeed enjoyed himself, although in the way of *Times* critics he made it clear that the play was not perhaps entirely worth the attention of serious theatergoers. But the performances were, he went on, praising both Barry and Andrea lavishly. John Chapman, writing for the less snooty *Daily News*, was as enthusiastic about the play as he was the production.

"Ladies and gentlemen," Jack Hoffman announced. "We have a hit."

Terry McKenna came up to Andrea with a glass in each hand. "I think you deserve some more champagne," he said.

"Thank you, Terry," she said, accepting the glass.

"How does it feel?"

Andrea laughed. "I don't think I'll really know until tomorrow. I'm in a kind of a daze."

"That's reasonable."

"It must be strange for Maria," Andrea said, and immediately wished she hadn't. She was getting a little high.

Terry shrugged. "Being an understudy is better than not

working, believe me. But I was surprised when she agreed to do it. I've known Maria for a long time and she doesn't exactly have the tiniest of egos."

"Oh, I thought you were, well—" Andrea stammered to a stop.

"Lovers? No, just old friends. Maria's a lesbian, you know."

"What? No, I didn't." Andrea felt very naive.

"Well, now that you know we're not attached, could I ask you to have dinner with me after the show some night?"

Andrea hesitated momentarialy, she wasn't quite sure why. Terry was very attractive. Perhaps that was just it. She felt a slight spark between them, and she wasn't at all sure she wanted to feel any sparks just yet. She needed time to absorb all that was happening to her. But she didn't want to say no, either. "All right. That would be nice."

"What about Saturday night?"

"Well, the show's dark on Sunday. I think I'm just going to want to go home and sleep for about twenty hours. Could we make it early next week instead?"

"Sure. Say Monday?"

"Fine."

"I'll be waiting for you backstage," said Terry McKenna.

It took Terry McKenna three weeks of patient courtship to get Andrea into bed. He was not used to courting women. If a woman he was attracted to didn't respond to him sexually after two or three encounters—and they usually did—he almost always moved on to other possibilities. There were too many attractive young women in New York to waste time on fruitless quests. Being a director didn't hurt. He was beginning to be well known in Off-Off Broadway circles, and he gave the impression of being a comer, someone who was likely to make it big eventually, someone worth knowing in the business. There were thousands of actresses out of work in New York, and every time he directed a showcase production, or a play at La Mama, a couple of dozen new faces always showed up at auditions.

In the theater world, even more than in most, it was whom you knew that was important. Most jobs came because you'd worked with a director or stage manager or another actor before, or because a friend recommended you for a part. It was possible sometimes to get a part without having any connections, but it was harder and depended a lot more on luck. Terry McKenna knew the rules, and he knew his own growing power, and he used it. Not that he would cast an actress just because she slept with him, or refuse to cast her because she didn't—a director didn't help himself any professionally if his cast wasn't as good as he could make it. But Terry had found that the good actress and the good lay coincided often enough so that he couldn't be bothered with chasing after difficult cases.

Andrea was different, though. For one thing he wanted her badly. The moment she had walked out on the stage of the Morosco Theatre opening night he had wanted her. It wasn't exactly love at first sight; Terry didn't really think in those terms. But he felt a stronger attraction to her than he had to anyone in a long time, and it had become more intense when he met her at Karen Bolling's party. She seemed older than her years in some ways, a woman, not a girl, yet there was still a vulnerability to her, the special promise of a flower that had not fully opened.

He was also willing to be patient because whatever happened it wouldn't hurt to be seen with her. She was suddenly a star, an overnight sensation. In the ten days following the opening, her photograph had appeared in the *Times*, the *Post*, *Newsweek*, and *Look*. She was being recognized on the street and in restaurants and shops. When he was with her he knew that people were wondering who *he* was, and envying him. That was a good feeling. He was certain she was attracted to him too, but needed time to sort out her feelings. She was obviously going through a lot, with her life changing so dramatically, and he understood that she needed to get used to being so suddenly important.

When he took her out after the theater during those first weeks, he avoided going to theater-district restaurants like Sardi's or Downey's where she was sure to be recognized. He even shied away from Joe Allen, the poor actor's Sardi's, where he was likely to run into people he knew himself. They went instead to small neighborhood restaurants in the Village or on the West Side, places where Andrea could get out of the limelight and relax. She talked much more than he did. He loved to listen to her slightly husky voice, with the sexy little catch to it, as she told him with a kind of awed excitement about the famous people who kept coming backstage to meet her and congratulate her. Sometimes she talked about her parents, about Brixton where her father taught and she'd gone to school, about her mother's small Swedish restaurant in Cleveland.

"It was so strange when they came to see the play," she said. "Backstage afterwards they seemed so shy, almost scared in a way. I've been telling them I wanted to be an actress since I was ten or eleven, of course, and they've seen me in school plays for years, and they came up to Northwestern and saw me in this part, but I don't think they were quite ready for all this." She laughed. "I'm not sure I'm quite ready myself."

And Terry reached out across the table and covered her hand with his. She was quiet for a long moment and looked at him steadily and smiled at him. She did not shy away from him physically. When they walked along the street she took his arm, and their knees would touch when they sat together, and she kissed him goodnight when he took her back to her apartment, a few blocks from his own small place on West Eighty-second Street. She kissed him on the mouth, but they were quick sweet kisses, affectionate but also reserved. He didn't suggest she come back to his place, or that he come up to hers. He waited for her to make that move; he was sure it would be a mistake to push her.

She surprised him when it finally happened. It was a rainy Saturday night in the second week of October. There was a gusting wind and a temperature that felt more like November. Terry had decided they should have dinner close by, but when Andrea had finally freed herself of backstage visitors she announced to him that they were going back to her apartment to eat.

"It was such a miserable day," Andrea said, "that I thought it would be nicer to just have a quiet dinner at home instead of running around the city."

"That sounds terrific. You're sure you feel like cooking, though? You must be tired."

"Actually I feel very up. We had wonderful audiences, even at the matinee. I was afraid they might be kind of grumpy after sloshing to the theater in the rain, but they were falling in the aisles laughing. And besides, the meal is pretty much ready."

Andrea had reserved a taxi, which was waiting right outside the Morosco, and they were at her apartment in just over ten minutes.

"Things are a little sparse, still," Andrea said, "but I'm gradually getting things together."

To Terry, whose apartment was furnished largely with repainted cast-offs he'd picked up on the streets of Manhattan, Andrea's place seemed more luxurious than sparse. There was a big butter-yellow sofa, two white wicker easy chairs with Marimekko cushions, a glass-topped coffee table, and a huge white flokkati rug on the polished hardwood floor. There were as yet few pictures, but the walls were freshly white and the room had a bright, sunny feeling to it that instantly obliterated the memory of the rain outside.

They went into the kitchen and Andrea poured herself a glass of white wine while Terry mixed himself a Scotch and soda. From the refrigerator she took out a foil-covered cookie pan, an oval Le Creuset baking dish, and a thick sirloin.

"It looks like a feast."

"Let's hope," Andrea said, uncovering the cookie pan.

"These are for hors d'oeuvres, a little crab on toast, and they just have to go under the broiler for a couple of minutes."

"What's that?" Terry asked, pointing to the oval dish.

"It's called Jansson's Temptation. My father's favorite dish in the world. It's just potatoes and onions and anchovies and heavy cream, but they all meld together in a way that's . . ."

"Very tempting."

Andrea laughed. "Exactly."

Terry had discovered over the past few years that when it came to cooking, actresses fell into one of two categories. Either they were wonderful cooks, or they could barely boil an egg, and most of the younger ones seemed to fall into the latter category. He wasn't sure if that was because they were rebelling against housewifery in general, or because they spent so much time grabbing meals on the run and eating in restaurants on the road that they just never got the chance to learn what to do in the kitchen. He wasn't surprised that Andrea liked to cook—after all, her mother ran a restaurant, even if it was a very small one—but he was surprised to discover that watching her work in the kitchen turned him on sexually to the point that he was getting an erection. Maybe it was just that this was the first time they'd been alone together in her apartment, and his expectations were aroused. But there seemed to be something more to it than that. There was something about the way she moved around the kitchen, so absorbed and so graceful, that made him want to put his arms around her and pull her to him.

Terry couldn't decide whether to turn away discreetly or stay where he was leaning against the woodblock counter and hope that Andrea would notice what was happening to him.

She pulled open the broiler and took out the cookie sheet. The tops of the canapés had turned light brown and were bubbling slightly. He could smell butter and sherry and some herb, dill maybe, and by the time Andrea had transferred the rounds to a small platter he was in control of himself again.

He hadn't realized how hungry he was. He consumed two

thirds of the crab rounds and the larger portion of the sirloin, which Andrea liked as rare as he did, and he simply couldn't stop eating the Jansson's Temptation. "Your father is a wise man," he told Andrea. "That's one of the best things I ever tasted. You're a wonderful cook."

She smiled at him, giving a small toss of her blond hair. "It's just things I learned from my mother. I should have asked you if you liked anchovies, so many people don't, but they're what makes Jansson's Temptation different."

"People who don't like anchovies are making a big mistake. Now why don't you let me do the dishes?"

Terry hated doing dishes. His own sink was always piled high with several day's worth. But he thought it was a good idea to offer, and the meal had certainly been worth a few minutes at hard labor.

"There's a dishwasher. We just have to rinse."

Terry scrubbed the plates off and Andrea stacked them in the machine. As she turned the dial to start the cycle, he impulsively embraced her from behind, putting his hands around her waist, and snuggling his head down between her neck and her shoulder. She smelled slightly of stage makeup still, a sweet rich odor he loved.

Andrea turned around in his arms and kissed him, her lips moist and soft, her tongue delicately teasing his own. He held her tightly against him, his hands moving down her tapering back. She rotated her hips slightly, rubbing against him, pressing into his hardness.

Then she drew her face back from his and said, "I think we'd better go into the bedroom."

He'd never wanted to hear those words so much.

It had been important to Andrea that she be the one to initiate their affair. She had wanted to be absolutely sure of her feelings, certain of her sexual responsiveness to Terry. She had needed to test him, to reassure herself that he felt something strong for her as a person and was not simply attracted to her physically. From her past experience, she had come to the conclusion that there were too many men in the world whose feelings toward women were governed almost exclusively by their genitals. Her first sexual experience had occurred during the summer between high school and college, when she had been invited for a long weekend to the Lake Erie summer house of Cynthia Borden, one of the wealthiest of her many rich classmates at Brixton Academy. She had been rather surprised, since she and Cynthia, while not enemies, were not exactly close friends either. Andrea had quickly discovered that she had been invited because Cynthia's older brother Rob had insisted upon it. He was in his second year at Princeton, and was very handsome, in a homogenized, preppy way. She had had a slight crush on him for years, which he had been smart enough to realize. Together with a lot of smooth talk about having her come east to Princeton in the fall, he had played on her attraction to him and her delight at spending a weekend at the huge lakefront house with its swimming pool and tennis courts and sailboats, and somehow made it seem as though it would be a privilege to sleep with him and unforgivably rude not to. Besides, she was attracted to him and it was time, she told herself, to be initiated into the world of sex—half of her classmates had preceded her already.

For Andrea it had not been a pleasant experience, painful and messy, in fact, though it didn't seem to faze Rob in the least. She learned later that he specialized in virgins, and had known she was one, thanks to his dear sister Cynthia. Andrea had hated herself afterwards, even before she began to realize that there would never be any invitation to Princeton. She had felt used and, most of all, stupid. She had let herself be dazzled by the trappings that surrounded Rob and his family, as though by sleeping with him she could somehow make that world more nearly hers.

And then there had been Scott Durkin. He was thirty, an assistant professor at Northwestern, who taught a course in chamber theater Andrea had taken the spring of her sophomore year. He had a breezy charm that went with his slightly crooked grin and the curious streak of white in his thick, dark hair. Scott had played the flattery game—told her she was the best actress at Northwestern in years, and no one since Paula Prentiss had had such a talent for comedy and she was prettier by a long shot than Paula—and Andrea had been completely swept away. She knew she was good, but Scott's praise gave her new confidence in herself, a sense of being truly special. He made her feel special in bed, too; he had perfected the manly art of seeming to be utterly absorbed in the body of the moment, as though there had never been any other before or would ever be one again. Friends warned Andrea that there had in fact been many bodies before, that Scott ran through undergraduate girls like so many boxes of Kleenex. She didn't doubt that, but she was convinced she was different, special— Scott had convinced her of that with practiced ease. Their affair had lasted all through that spring, and then he had gone to Europe for the summer, saying a dozen times that he wished he could afford to take her with him.

In the fall, of course, he found another protégée, this one with a profound understanding of the rhythms of Shakespearean verse.

There had been no one else during the next year. Andrea had thrown herself into her work, and had had the luck to be cast in *Playing by Ear.* When Scott Durkin had come backstage after the first performance at Northwestern and said, "You see, I told you how good you were," she had looked at him coolly and replied, "Yes, that's probably the only truthful thing you ever told me."

He had merely laughed, but she had felt good about it for days afterward. She still did.

She took Terry by the hand and led him into her bedroom. She turned on a single lamp on the dresser, a lamp with a rose-colored shade that gave the room a soft, warm glow. Even though she had taken the initiative, she felt a sudden shyness.

Terry, as though he understood that, came around the bed to where she was standing.

He leaned toward her, and kissed her, touching her only with his lips, gently, softly. Then he stood back from her and pulled his green turtleneck up over his head. And then he waited, while she removed her blouse. Each of them in turn removed one piece of clothing after another, taking their time, each watching the other uncover one area of flesh after the other.

They moved together, still standing, pressing against each other. It was strange and marvelous, Andrea thought, how different one man's skin was from another man's, how subtle and yet absolutely individual were the variations in the texture of the flesh. Terry was very smooth, his chest almost entirely hairless except for an aureole of soft brown hairs around his nipples. And there was a funny, unexpected tuft of hair at the base of his spine which she felt as she ran her hands down his back and over his buttocks.

Against her abdomen she could feel his hardness pulsing with that strange, insistent strength that always seemed almost separate from the rest of a man's body.

Then he picked her up and gently laid her on the bed, covering her body with his own.

Chapter Three

TERRY McKENNA KEPT HIS OWN apartment on West Eighty-second Street. It wasn't really discussed between them, but Andrea was perfectly happy with the arrangement, and she suspected it was what Terry wanted. He spent the night at her place most of the time, but, again by unspoken agreement, they almost always were apart on Wednesdays, when Andrea had two shows and came home exhausted. Saturdays were different. There were two shows then, too, but the week was over for her, and they could sleep as late as they wanted on Sunday.

Andrea didn't want another relationship in which she felt anxious whenever she was apart from the man. She had allowed herself to become too dependent on Scott Durkin, had defined herself in his terms and thus felt incomplete when she was not with him. Sometimes now when she and Terry spent a day or so apart she wished that he was there, but she did not feel any less her own person. She believed that a certain degree of separation was good for them both. Besides, she and Terry each had friends the other didn't much appreciate. On Terry's side there was Maria Davino, for one. She and Andrea got along fine backstage, and Maria only occasionally made comments that seemed to contain a little more acid than was absolutely necessary. When she said, "I never thought there would be a woman who could domesticate Terry," Andrea was not quite sure whether it was a compliment or some kind of warning, but she just smiled and ignored it. Still, she thought it was better if Maria and Terry occasionally saw each other without her being around; there was always a slight tension when the three of them were together. And Terry had another friend whom Andrea actively loathed, a loud-mouthed jazz drummer named Phil Griglak who smoked a dozen joints a day and couldn't get out a sentence that didn't contain half a dozen expletives. Terry seemed to find him funny, but Andrea thought he was both a boor and a bore. When she finally said as much, Terry stared at her coldly for a moment and then said, "That's too bad. I'll tell you what, let's make a deal. You keep Bruce Halliwell out of my hair and I'll keep Phil out of yours."

Andrea had grown up just down the street from Bruce. He'd been a smart, graceful little boy—too graceful, the other boys had felt—but he'd always managed to hold his own because he knew how to make people laugh. As he'd grown up his sense of humor had become more cutting. He could put a person in his place faster than anyone Andrea had known. After graduating from high school, he'd headed straight for New York. Andrea had received a couple of letters and cards from him, but then they'd lost touch. But he was one of those friends you could always pick up with as though you'd never been apart, and she'd been thrilled when a note from him was brought to her backstage during intermission at a Wednesday matinee in the second week after the opening. She'd left word with the stage doorman to bring him to her dressing room after the performance, and they'd sat there for an hour catching up on each other's lives.

"I saw your name in an ad for the play," Bruce told her, "but it never occurred to me that it was actually you. In fact, I thought, oh, oh, some actress has the same name as Andrea. She'll be furious. Then I saw your picture in the paper and I practically fell down the subway steps."

"You don't sound as though you had much faith in my talents," Andrea said, teasing.

"Oh, I always expected you to make it *someday*, love, but you have rather jumped the gun, you know."

"And how about you, what are you doing?"

"Well, let's see. You knew I got a job with a florist when I first got here. That went on for about eight months. It was a very ritzy outfit and we often did arrangements for parties catered by Max Barron. After he'd seen a few of my more elaborate efforts he decided I ought to come work for him doing the same kind of thing with food centerpieces. Besides, he was mad for my body. So I was with him for a year. But the man was dreadfully possessive and I'm far too young and gorgeous to be chained to any one person's bed, so I went over to his biggest rival, Richard Corliss, and that's where I am now."

The name Richard Corliss struck a bell with Andrea. "Didn't Richard Corliss cater the opening night party for the play, at Karen Bolling's house? There was this gorgeous centerpiece of shrimp and scallops that looked like a vase of flowers."

"Thank you, my dear. That was my work. But I didn't know it was the opening night party for your play. If I'd known I would have insisted on overseeing the party myself, just to surprise you. What a shame. That would have been a delectable moment."

It was comments of this sort that put Terry off when he met Bruce. Bruce was too effete for Terry, just as Phil Griglak was too crude for Andrea. Even so, it annoyed her a little that Terry didn't like Bruce. She could understand why some heterosexual men might be put off by Bruce's manner and attitudes, but she wouldn't have expected that from someone who worked in the theater; it was a world in which even the straightest of men occasionally indulged in a certain degree of campiness and backbiting. Terry never did.

She began to discover, though, that there was a hard-driving, surprisingly tough side to him. She went to watch a run-through of the Joe Orton play he began directing soon after the beginning of their affair, and was astonished at the intensity and single-mindedness with which he worked. When she had first asked him if she could come sit in, he had seemed reluctant.

"I don't much like having outsiders at rehearsals, Andrea. It's distracting."

"I'll sit way in the back and I won't say a word."

He looked at her silently for a moment, and then said, "Well, it might be a tonic for the cast, in fact. You don't mind if I introduce you to them?"

"I don't want to play the visiting star, Terry. I'd just like to watch you work. I'm curious."

"But you are a star, honey. You'd better get used to it. If I don't introduce you they'll all be wondering what you're doing there, instead of concentrating. And, believe me, they need to do some concentrating."

Andrea had begun to realize that Terry saw his relationship with her as an asset to his own career. That was perfectly natural, of course, but it bothered her slightly. If you weren't well known yourself, but were close to someone who was, it was inevitable that your status would improve in other people's eyes. Terry was talented and ambitious, and if the fact that they had become lovers helped him in getting ahead, that was fine. She wanted him to become as successful in his own way as she was.

That would make it easier, in fact. Because she had suddenly come to understand the common complaint of the rich and famous that it was hard to be absolutely certain if you were loved for yourself or for your money or renown. She had always thought there was something a little silly about that kind of doubt. If you were rich enough or famous enough, what difference would it make? Why should it be so important to know exactly why you were loved? She'd doubted that anybody could really know what it was about them that attracted other people, anyway, even if you were just an ordinary person. She knew Terry loved her, she had no doubt about it, but she did find herself wondering if he would have fallen in love with her if she had been just another out-of-work actress when he met her. It was not something she thought about a lot but it crossed her mind occasionally, and it was unsettling when it did.

"Well, maybe it's better if I don't come," she said.

"No, it's okay. I'd like to have you see me work, too. I'll just tell the cast you're coming the day before, and then we won't have to get into a big routine when you're actually there."

So she had gone and watched, and Terry had seemed like a different person. There were, Andrea knew, basically two kinds of good directors. There were those who believed that the real secret of direction lay in good casting of the parts, followed by carefully worked out blocking of the stage action. Within that framework, such directors were inclined to trust the intuition of their actors. They liked to be surprised, liked to give the actor room to experiment. When they were pleasantly surprised they said so, and when they saw something going awry they gently nudged the actor in another direction. Jack Hoffman had been like that, lounging in a seat with his feet up, a relaxed, friendly presence.

But Terry was clearly the other kind of director, one of those who had a very definite idea of how a play should sound and look, almost line by line. He was on his feet almost constantly, roaming the theater with the intensity of a caged animal. When something went wrong on stage he interrupted curtly, speaking in a cool, unemotional voice that was nevertheless intimidating. It was a side of him that Andrea had never seen before. She was startled at first, feeling a kind of disorientation. But as the rehearsal went on she became more and more impressed. The actors clearly respected him, and he was getting the results he wanted.

"Stop. Carole. You're telegraphing. You mustn't move an inch until Lewis says 'money.' "

They did it again.

"Once more," said Terry, "and keep going."

When they broke for ten minutes after the first act, Terry came and sat with her. "So, what do you think?"

"I think it will be a big success. You are a toughie, aren't you?"

Terry smiled, looking pleased. "Surprised?"

"A little at first. But not when I think about it. It's good, Terry."

"It's all right. The cast is trying very hard. This kind of thing needs the stop-on-a-dime technique of British actors. And that's not putting American actors down. The British are completely at sea when they try for passionate American naturalism. But it's a hard kind of play to transplant to this side of the Atlantic. If it gets good reviews it ought to run about five months. Black comedy makes American audiences nervous. They want comedy that's squishy at the center, like a chocolate cream."

"Like *Playing by Ear?*"

"Sure. And don't get me wrong. I would have loved to direct that, squishy or not. Success is success is success. Besides, I would have met you several months earlier."

He squeezed her hand and then got up to call the rehearsal back to order.

Terry turned out to be right about the extent of the play's success. It got good reviews and ran just under six months. His own career got the expected boost, and he was offered three other Off-Broadway assignments. They conflicted with one another in terms of scheduling, however, and he chose to do the most challenging of the three, a revival of Ibsen's *Peer Gynt*. Terry was a strong believer in taking on challenges, in stretching yourself, and he began to push Andrea to start thinking about the future of her own career.

She had a one-year contract, but the play was clearly going to run long beyond that time. Karen Bolling wanted her to sign for a second year, or at least another six months. Barry Lawrence had made it clear that he would be departing, and she didn't want to lose both her stars at once. But Terry thought Andrea ought to move on to something else.

"It's a great mistake to stick with the same part too long, Andrea. Say you sign for another year. Then they'll want you to do the national tour, and people will start wondering if you really can do anything else. That's what happened to Larry Kert. He went on with *West Side Story* for years because he was comfortable with it. It was safe. But you have to take chances or people start thinking you're afraid to stretch yourself, and you get so identified with one part that nobody thinks of you for anything else."

"Yes, Terry, I understand that. But the scripts I'm getting offered are just pale carbon copies of *Playing by Ear*. Why should I give up a terrific part for one that's the same thing but not as good? That's not stretching myself, for God's sake."

"That's not what I'm asking you to do. I think you should do the Claude Eakins play."

"I've told you before, Terry, I don't see myself in that part. I don't think I'm ready for that kind of heavy drama. I don't think I can do it."

"Of course you can do it. Stop underrating yourself."

"I've never done anything like that, Terry, where I have to come on like a tower of strength."

"So you're just going to do romantic comedies for the rest of your life?" There was disgust in Terry's voice.

Andrea threw up her hands. "God damn it, Terry, you know that's not what I'm talking about. There are several parts in Chekov I'd love to play. I'd like to do Nora in *A Doll's House*. There are things in Shakespeare I'd like to try, but that girl in Claude Eakins' play is like some goddamned Antigone or Saint Joan. I'm not ready for it."

"Then go play some Chekov, up at Lincoln Center, or for the Circle in the Square, wherever, somebody's always doing some Chekov. Of course you won't get paid the kind of money you're making now. That's part of the problem, isn't it? You want that two thousand dollars a week."

"Why not?" Andrea was beginning to get angry. "You act as though there were something wrong with money. Well, let me tell you, there isn't. Money isn't everything, but it counts for a hell of a lot, Terry. The whole time I was growing up I was surrounded by people who had things I couldn't have,

77

and now I can have some of them, and I'm going to get more of them."

"Things. It's a disease, Andrea, money's a disease. Sure I'd like to have a few millions to throw around like Karen Bolling. But I wouldn't have a townhouse, and a place in the Hamptons, and a villa in Nice. I'd spend that money producing shows that ought to be seen, even if they lost money, even if the tourists from Kansas and the matrons from Scarsdale didn't want to see them. I'd use my money for creative purposes, not just to buy things."

"Yes, yes, I know, Terry, you're so fucking pure."

Andrea took a deep breath and collapsed back against the cushions of the yellow sofa. A soft April breeze floated in through the open window, cooling her face. They'd never had an argument like this before. They had disagreed, yes, but they had never spoken harsh, unforgivable words, never tried to wound each other. She didn't really understand why it had happened. Why was Terry pressuring her now? She didn't have to make a decision for two and a half months—she'd promised Karen she'd tell her whether or not she was staying with the show by mid-July, when Andrea began her month's vacation.

The rights to the Claude Eakins play were held by Richard Barstow, who had produced the Orton play. Maybe, it occurred to Andrea, Terry thought he might be chosen to direct if she agreed to do the part. Maybe that was why he was so anxious to persuade her that it was right for her. But she didn't dare ask him that now, while they were both angry. It would come out like an accusation, and she didn't want to make things worse.

She looked up at Terry, who sat gazing at her in glum silence. Reaching out to put her hand on his thigh, she said, "I don't want to think about all this anymore right now, Terry. Peace?"

He nodded. "I'm sorry. I guess I was being pushy."

"I'm sorry, too. I love you, you know."

"I love you." He reached over and pulled her to him and

held her silently for a moment. Then he took her face between his hands, his long fingers moving gently against her temples, and kissed her.

The following day Andrea met Bruce Halliwell at Bergdorf Goodman's at one o'clock. She'd asked him to help her shop for a dress to wear to the Tony Awards. Terry didn't know that. She'd just said they were having lunch. But she trusted Bruce's judgment in matters of style; she knew what she wanted, but it helped to have an objective eye confirming your own choices. She hadn't really expected to be nominated for a Tony, and she certainly didn't expect to win. In her own opinion the award belonged to Rosemary Harris in *A Lion in Winter*, although Lee Remick was also a possibility for her performance in *Wait Until Dark*. But on the off chance that she might win, Andrea wanted to look absolutely smashing.

In the past eight months she had bought a lot of clothes, including a suit and two sports jackets for Terry. He'd protested he didn't need clothes, but she had insisted. The truth was that she didn't like arriving at parties at The Dakota or having dinner at Orsini's with a man who looked like a thrift shop on wheels. She'd never quite put it that way, but he had acquiesced. "I guess if I'm going to keep company with such a beautiful woman, I ought to dress the part," he'd said. She didn't think he really minded as much as he claimed, since she'd caught him admiring himself in front of the mirror more than once.

For herself she'd bought a closetful of clothes, dresses and blouses of silk, soft wool jersey skirts, cashmere sweaters and several suede jackets, a half-length silver-fox coat, and almost two dozen pairs of shoes. Her Tony nomination gave her an excuse to be truly extravagant. She wanted something heart-stoppingly gorgeous, and she didn't care what it cost, an evening gown that people would think was a Balmain or a Dior even if it wasn't an original.

She spent almost an hour picking out half a dozen gowns she wanted to try on, and then paraded each of them before

Bruce as he sat on a gilt chair playing his part with elegant aplomb.

"That is a beautiful gown, of course," he would say. "But it doesn't really do you justice."

And later, "Ah, now that is almost perfect, it suits your coloring so well. I'd seriously consider it."

Once or twice both of them were almost consumed with laughter, it was all so reminiscent of an afternoon in Cleveland when they were ten and each of them had taken turns modeling dresses from Bruce's mother's closet while she was out playing bridge.

Andrea had quite purposely saved the gown she really liked best for last. It was of a purple as delicate as the first crocus of spring, a gown that was cut with a youthful but elegant flair. Some of the other gowns Andrea had felt looked a little too mature on her, slightly pretentious. This one was a gown for a woman, not a girl, but it did not give the impression that she was dressing beyond her age.

"That's it," Bruce said. "I know you could go on with this all afternoon, but I'm getting hungry, and you couldn't possibly find anything more lovely."

They walked two blocks up Fifty-seventh Street to have a late lunch at the Russian Tea Room. Between bites of her blini with caviar, Andrea told Bruce about her discussion with Terry, although she called it a debate rather than an argument. "I understand what he's talking about, but I really am afraid of the part in the Eakins play. But of course it would be good for me if I could carry it off."

"Is it a good play?" Bruce asked.

"Yes, I think it's very good."

"Commercial?"

"Who knows? It could be. I think there's an audience for it. It's set in Sweden, which I suppose is one reason why they want me. The heroine is a seventeen-year-old who idolizes her father, and then it begins to come out that he collaborated with the Nazis. It's called *Past History*."

"Lord, it does sound grim."

"No, it's not so much grim as it is very emotionally charged. It's very moving. I think it will make people cry. A lot. But I don't know if I can make people cry. The girl is strong in ways I'm not and weak in ways I'm not. In a way I'm fascinated by it, but I'm scared of it, too. And there's always the question whether it would run. I'd hate to give up *Playing by Ear* for it, and go through all the pressure of trying to bring it off, and then have it close in three weeks."

"Or three days," said Bruce brightly.

"You're a big help."

Bruce grinned wickedly and speared another piece of his chicken Kiev. "I do my best. The thing is, my love, you're always going to be faced with this problem. People pushing you to do something you're not sure about. Obviously, it's important not to let yourself be talked into doing something that's dead wrong for you. But Terry does have a point when he says you have to keep moving. That's even true in the catering business, which is as cutthroat a world as the theater any day. Right now simply everyone is demanding Beef Wellington. But before too long people will start getting tired of it, and the smart caterer will steer his clients toward something new. And you just have to hope that what you suggest will become all the rage itself."

"Yes. Another hit. I suppose I'm asking for too much. I want my next part to be as perfect for me as this one. And I know you don't get all that many parts in a lifetime that are perfect for you. The trouble is, I don't feel entirely secure yet as an actress. I had a lot of good training at Northwestern, but I haven't really had all that much *experience*. It's not that I was typecast in *Playing by Ear*. Susan isn't me, but I can understand everything she's supposed to feel. I know how to communicate what she's feeling. But there are a lot of other feelings I'm not sure I'd be very good at communicating. The Eakins play is full of them. I'm not sure I even begin to understand the kind of burning moral certainty that it calls for."

"Oh, my dear, which of us does? Abject moral confusion is so much more human. And generally quite thrilling to experience, I find."

Andrea laughed. "Yes, that I could play."

"Well, if you win the Tony, you'll be able to name your own game. Just give Tennessee a call and say you want him to write you a play about abject moral confusion. He probably has half a dozen in his files."

"I'm not going to win the Tony. I'm not sure I even want to. It would just make people expect even more of me."

"Nonsense. Of course you want to win."

"Well, it would make my decision easier. I'd feel honor bound to stay on for at least another six months. I really feel that anyway. Karen and Jack took a big chance on me, and I owe them a lot."

"There's your excuse, then."

"Yes, I know. But it is an excuse. It's making a decision by default."

"Andrea, my love, you're contradicting yourself. If you're going to think less of yourself for making a decision by default, then you undoubtedly have it in you to play burning moral certainty. If we all avoided making decisions by default, we'd be much superior beings. Of course, that would make life vastly less entertaining, but never mind."

Andrea laughed again. "Thank you, Bruce, you always make me feel much better about things."

"Yes, well, it's a knack I have, isn't it? You understand, of course, that I seldom take my own advice. But if I can lighten the hearts of my friends I suppose it can't be said that I'm all bad, can it?"

"Oh, I don't know," said Andrea demurely, and they laughed together.

Andrea did not win the Tony Award. She did not even get to wear her new evening gown. Helen Menken, who had been chairman of the Tony Awards board for many years had died in March, and it had been decided to present the awards at an afternoon ceremony at the Rainbow Room, without any public attendance or entertainment. There was talk that the following year the Tony Awards would be presented as a live, nationally broadcast television program for the first time, but on this April afternoon the atmosphere was businesslike rather than festive, an occasion touched by sadness. The winners accepted their awards with quiet dignity. No one raced joyfully to the podium; there was little sense of the exultation of winning.

That made it easier, so far as Andrea was concerned. She was not as tense as she had expected to be. Her mood was reflective as she sat waiting for the Best Actress award to be announced. Rosemary Harris was at the table in front of her, serenely lovely. A few tables away, Lee Remick's red-gold hair shone in the afternoon light streaming through the huge windows of the Art Deco room, high above the city. It was enough for Andrea simply to have been nominated in the company of such accomplished and beautiful women.

A little over a year before, when she had first begun rehearsals for *Playing by Ear* at Northwestern, Andrea would not have even imagined, could not have hoped, to find herself here in the same room with so many of the theater's most accomplished performers. It had been a great year for Broadway, and the Rainbow Room that afternoon was host to more glittering names than Andrea could count. Hal Holbrook and Nicol Williamson, Jack Cassidy and Richard Kiley, Barbara Harris and Julie Harris and Angela Lansbury and Gwen Verdon. It had been the year of *Mark Twain Tonight!* and *Inadmissible Evidence*, of *Cactus Flower* and *Marat/Sade*, of *Man of La Mancha* and *Mame*, and *Sweet Charity* and *On a Clear Day You Can See Forever*. To be a part of it brought Andrea close to tears, but she fought them back because if she were to cry people would think that it was out of disappointment and not out of the sheer wonder of being present.

She felt a kind of relief when Rosemary Harris's name was

announced as Best Actress. In a strange way, it would have made Andrea feel uncomfortable to have won when she was herself convinced that the award belonged to Rosemary. She applauded with genuine pleasure and turned to smile at Terry beside her, whom she suspected was a little overawed by the occasion himself.

Afterwards they went to Karen Bolling's for a small, quiet party. *Playing by Ear* had been nominated in four categories but had not won in any of them. Karen was philosophical about it. "Romantic comedies almost never win Tonys," she said. "The musicals always win for sets and costumes, and that's reasonable, since they've spent an extra five hundred thousand on them. And they always give the Best Play award to something serious. Or pretentious, as the case may be. There's nothing to be done about that. But I wish that once in a while they'd recognize that to act a romantic comedy is just as difficult as to rant and rave and scream in some serious play, but they just won't. That, I think, is unfair."

Terry gave Andrea a significant look across the dinner table, as though to say I told you so.

Almost before she knew what she was doing, Andrea said, "Well, Karen, I want very much to win a Tony someday, so I guess I'll have to learn to rant and rave, but in the meantime I think this is a good moment to tell you I've decided to do *Playing by Ear* for another six months."

"Thank you, my dear Andrea! Thank you, thank you, thank you. A toast to you, and to loyalty. And let's add good sense."

Terry looked as though he had been slapped. His lips moved and he seemed about to blurt out some angry response. But he controlled himself and lifted his glass along with the others.

"Thank you," said Andrea. "After that I'm going to do the Eakins play, if they're willing to wait for me. I think that may be biting off more than I can chew, but everybody else seems to think I can do it. So why not?"

"Of course you can do it," said Terry, whose face was suddenly alight with happiness.

"I'm sure you'll be wonderful," Karen said.

But Barry Lawrence, sitting to Andrea's right, merely smiled at her and said, "You've got guts, kid." Barry had been turning down parts he thought were too serious for him for years; Andrea knew that. She wasn't sure, though, that while he might say she had guts he wasn't really thinking she was making the very mistake he had so carefully avoided for so long.

They were willing to wait for her. She had hoped they might not be, that Richard Barstow would want to get the play on in the fall, or that Claude Eakins himself would protest. But it was only the second Broadway play for Claude, and it was difficult enough to get a serious play produced without complaining about delays or the casting. Barstow was convinced they needed an actress whom the theatergoing public had fallen in love with, someone they associated with a pleasurable evening in the theater instead of with Art with a capital A. She was bait, and she knew it.

The question of who would direct was still open. Barstow had wanted Alan Schneider, who had directed *Who's Afraid of Virginia Woolf?* and *Tiny Alice* so brilliantly, but Albee had a new play for the coming season and there was a scheduling conflict since Barstow had agreed to wait until Andrea was free from *Playing by Ear*. Andrea was sure Terry secretly hoped he might get the nod, although he never brought the subject up. She decided to raise it herself during her vacation, which they spent lying in the sun at Truro on Cape Cod.

They had gone to the Coast Guard beach at Orleans that day, making their way down the steeply inclined dunes to the white sands below. The breakers at Orleans were always high and usually rough, so that few people actually swam there. They just drove up and stood on the cliff overlooking the sea and then drove away again. Terry and Andrea had the beach almost to themselves. Andrea merely got her feet wet, but Terry bodysurfed exuberantly in the breakers, his lean frame cutting through the center of the incessantly rolling waves. Then they stretched out on a blanket in the hot sun, their bodies gleaming with oil, their arms and legs touching occasionally as they turned under the blue sky.

"Has Richard ever said anything to you about the possibility of your directing *Past History*?" Andrea asked, pouring them each a cup of iced tea from a thermos.

Terry looked surprised. "Not in so many words. When he first gave the script to you he asked me to read it and tell him what I thought of it."

"You never told me that."

"Well, I wanted you to do the play. And I didn't want to have you think that I wanted you to do it just because there was a chance I might get offered the director's job." Terry smiled at her disarmingly. "Would you rub some more oil on my back?"

"Sure." She poured a small amount of oil between his shoulder blades and moved her hands slowly up and down his back, feeling the warm, strong flesh.

"I wasn't sure you'd even want to have me direct. My approach is very different from Jack Hoffman's."

"I know."

"And it could be hard on us, on the two of us, on how we feel about each other. Some people who are lovers can work together easily, but with others it just doesn't work. What do you think?"

Andrea shrugged. "I really don't know. I do think I'm going to need all the help I can get with the part, and since you seem to feel so strongly it's right for me, and know me so well, maybe you could help me find my way through it better. But it would be awful if I didn't live up to your expectations."

"I might not live up to yours. Ever think of that?"

"Not really." Andrea looked out at the breaking waves, watching them crash on the sand. Terry was ready for a

Broadway production, and *Past History* would be a good play for him. He had a talent for bringing out the subtext of a scene, orchestrating pauses and stage movements in a way that sharpened and clarified the feelings and ideas that lay below the surface of the text. It was a play that needed that kind of insight.

"Did you ever talk the play over with Richard, give him your ideas about it?"

"Yes. I told him he needed a very daring, very modern set, with half a dozen levels that flowed into one another. I don't think it will work with realistic sets sliding in and out all the time, unless you spent the kind of money you would on a musical."

"What did he say to that?"

"He asked me who should design it. I said Boris Aronson, and he said he agreed with me. I don't know whether Richard can get him, though. He's supposed to be designing that new musical based on *I Am a Camera*. What's it called?"

"*Cabaret*, I think."

"That's right. Anyway, there's a lot of money to be raised before next February. It all depends on the money. Of course, your name helps a lot with that."

Andrea shook her head, her still damp hair clinging to the back of her neck. "That seems so strange. I love it, but it seems very strange to me."

Terry rolled over and sat up, looking into her eyes. He took both her hands in his. "It's not strange. Why do you think it's so strange? You keep talking as though it's all a fluke. And then other times you behave so much like a star it scares me a little. The way you spend money, for instance. I don't really understand sometimes."

"It's very simple, Terry. It really is. I love the idea that people would actually invest thousands and thousands of dollars in a play because I'm going to be in it. I love the applause and the interviews and the famous people who treat me as one of their own. And the money. But I love it so much it frightens me. I'm so afraid it will all just disappear."

"You're not going to let that happen, baby. You know you're not. And I'm not going to let it happen to you."

Afterwards, Andrea was never quite sure whether she had talked Richard Barstow into hiring Terry or whether it had really been his intention all along, provided she agreed with the idea. From Andrea's point of view the best thing about it was that she would be able to work privately with Terry on the part for several months before they actually went into rehearsal. But they weren't able to do much until November. Barry Lawrence left *Playing by Ear* when his contract was up, and Andrea had to spend a considerable amount of time rehearsing with her new co-star. Her name was above the title now, and her salary had been increased to $3,000 a week. The extra thousand dollars went straight into her savings account —she wanted to have a nest egg in case *Past History* did not turn out to be a hit.

Terry was occupied with directing *'Tis Pity She's a Whore* for Circle in the Square, and for most of October they saw less of each other than they had grown used to. He was rehearsing by day and she was performing at night, so that although Terry came over for a late supper and spent the night several times a week, Andrea sometimes found herself feeling rather lonely during the day. She knew she ought to be spending the time learning her lines for *Past History*, but she kept putting it off. Even though she had signed a contract, there was some part of her that still was trying to hold *Past History* at arm's length. She spent most of her daytime hours shopping or going to old movies at the Thalia or the Little Carnegie. In the darkness of those tiny theaters, watching old Bogart movies or the early films of Ingmar Bergman, she would find herself suddenly anxious, thinking, "I must start doing some work."

'Tis Pity She's a Whore, despite its overblown Jacobean plot, turned out to be a great success for Terry and an even

greater one for Maria Davino, whom he had cast in the central role of the incestuous Annabella. Once it had opened, Terry began working with Andrea almost every day on *Past History*. She began to gain confidence during those hour-long sessions in her living room, and the lines began to take on emotional meaning for her. But there were still scenes, especially as the play worked toward its climax, where she felt at sea. Terry was patient and complimentary, and she knew that she was reading the lines well enough, but she had the sense that that was all she was doing, just making them sensible. They were still not coming across with the force of true conviction. The part was very long, as well, and even when a scene went smoothly, she wondered about her ability to put all the scenes together in the kind of mounting crescendo she knew was necessary.

She gave her final performance in *Playing by Ear* on February 18 and went into full rehearsals for *Past History* on the twentieth. By the third week, when they began running the complete play every day, she knew she was in trouble. The early scenes were fine, or at least passable, but she seemed to weaken as the play went on, just when she should have been gathering strength. In the final scene she was supposed to achieve a kind of intense coldness toward her father, a burning coldness, as it were, like dry ice, as Terry put it. And every time, as she waited to make her entrance she felt a dreadful weakness, an anxiety that made her stomach churn and her hands tremble. Even in *Playing by Ear* she had always been nervous, night after night, before the curtain went up. There was nothing strange about that; almost every actor she knew felt some degree of nervousness before a performance. But once the curtain went up everything had been all right in *Playing by Ear*. Now she found herself getting the jitters worse and worse as the play went along.

Richard Barstow came to a run-through and left without speaking to the cast. Andrea had caught a glimpse of his face, however, and it was grim.

She went home every night in a state of total exhaustion.

She started buying frozen foods that just had to be heated up; she had no interest in cooking and had to force herself to eat. Terry seemed withdrawn and frustrated, at times even angry. He never raised his voice to her during rehearsals, but he was like a stranger, his tone formal and cold. For the last five days of rehearsals before leaving for Boston, where they were to play two weeks at the Colonial Theatre, she and Terry did not make love. She was too tired anyway, but more than that, it was as though a fuse had blown. There was suddenly no electricity between them.

The night before the final run-through, she asked Terry to come back after the rehearsal and have dinner with her. He hadn't been able to do that for several nights. There had been production details that had to be worked out, conferences with the lighting designer and the stage manager, meetings with Richard Barstow at which she was sure her own failings were discussed.

They sat across the table from each other in virtual silence, Andrea merely picking at her chicken potpie. "What are we going to do, Terry?"

"What do you mean?"

"I'm not bringing it off, that's what I mean. We both know it."

"You will. Wait and see. Once we get an audience you'll begin to make it work. You'll be able to feel their presence. It'll give you strength."

"You hope."

"Yes, I hope. But I believe that, Andrea. That's what out-of-town tryouts are for. I don't care if you don't finally get it for another two or three weeks. We have two weeks in Boston and two in Philadelphia. By the time we open in New York, you'll have it. And that's all that really counts."

"I don't believe it, Terry. It's too much for me. I don't believe I can do it."

"Listen, Andrea, some of the most famous actors and actresses in the world have said that about parts they were doing, and then they finally made the breakthrough. They finally did do it. There's a famous story about Julie Harris when she was playing Saint Joan in *The Lark*. They were in Boston, too, and after a matinee, she came offstage and sat sobbing in her dressing room, saying just what you're saying. That she couldn't do it. That it was too much for her, too exhausting. But she pulled herself together and she did do it, and a lot of people I know say it was one of the most mesmerizing performances they ever saw anyone give, and she won a Tony for it in the end. I only wish I'd been around to see her do it. So don't think that what you're going through is something special, some hell that's reserved for you alone. It's happened to a lot of people, a lot of the very best people. In fact you could say that it's only untalented people who never feel that they're inadequate. They don't know any better. The fact that you know it's not right means you can find the way to make it right. We've just got to keep going until it happens."

Andrea felt the tension drain away, as though she'd been carrying something too heavy and had finally put it down. "Thank you," she whispered, and began to weep. "Thank you."

Terry got up and came around the table to her and knelt down and held her in his arms.

"Terry," she said, trying to stop crying.

"Yes. I'm here."

"Will you spend the night? I mean, I just want to have you hold me. I just don't want to be alone."

"Sure. Sure I will."

It was better the next day. She felt stronger, she felt as though she were beginning to get there. Several other cast members complimented her after the run-through, and she began to believe that Terry might be right, that she could eventually find her way to the heart of the role. She even felt a certain amount of pleasurable excitement when they flew

91

to Boston the following noon. Ensconced in her suite at the Ritz-Carlton two hours later she felt a new surge of well-being. She stood at the window looking down on the Public Garden where people were strolling in the surprisingly warm mid-March sunshine. The change of scene was good for her, she realized. Her suite was beautiful and the hotel staff had fussed over her as though she were someone truly important. Somewhere in the last three weeks of rehearsal, she had lost the sense of being important, of being a star. Her sense of herself as someone special had been so totally identified with *Playing by Ear* that the rehearsal period had been like a kind of vacuum; she had forgotten that she was more than just an actress struggling with a role, that there were people who envied her, and people who would turn to stare at her in the street, people who wished that they could know her or be her.

The set was being installed that afternoon and evening, the lights adjusted, the costumes distributed to the proper dressing rooms. Terry had to be there, but she was free until morning. She knew that she ought to simply rest, but she was feeling alive again for the first time in weeks and she wanted to do something. She had never been to Boston before, but Max Jacobi, who was co-starring as her father, had played the city many times, and during their rehearsal breaks he had been telling her about its pleasures. It was one of his favorite cities, one of what he termed the three European cities of America, along with San Francisco and New Orleans. One of the things he had told her she must do while they were there was to see the Isabella Stewart Gardner Museum, and from what he had said about it, it seemed the perfect place to while away a quiet afternoon by herself.

It was only a short taxi ride down Huntington Avenue and across The Fenway to the museum, a curious other-worldly structure that Mrs. Gardner had had built to resemble a Venetian palace and stuffed full of the art treasures she had collected throughout Europe. From the moment she entered and got her first glimpse of the beautiful interior garden in the three-story balconied atrium, Andrea was enchanted. It was not just the extraordinary treasures, including one of the world's few surviving Vermeers, that impressed her, but the fact that to wander through its rooms felt like entering into someone else's life. Just as Max had told her, there was the vase of fresh nasturtiums in front of Sargent's famous portrait of Mrs. Gardner, precisely as she had stipulated in her will. She looked out from the painted surface with a regal bearing and an eye so commanding that Andrea felt the portrait might even be capable of making verbal objection should the nasturtiums ever be missing or wilted. How extraordinary, Andrea thought, for a woman to have had such a clear vision of herself and such certainty and power as to be able to ensure that the home she had built for herself would remain exactly the same decades after her death.

During the next few days she kept thinking how glad she was that she had gone there that afternoon. In some strange way Mrs. Gardner's example gave her a new insight into the role she was playing, into the certainty of self that the part required. It was a secret reserve she tried to draw upon during the harrowing days that followed.

On Monday they rehearsed from ten in the morning until almost midnight. It was their first time on the set and the company had voted to dispense with union rules about the length of rehearsals. Andrea knew that some of those with smaller parts would have liked to get out of the theater and go home to their hotels, and that they had voted to suspend the Equity rules to help her, because they knew she needed the time. She thanked them for it sincerely, yet she could not help but think that it would have been unnecessary had she truly mastered her part beforehand. But by the time she returned to the Ritz that night she was too tired even to think about it. She simply tore off her clothes and fell into bed.

Tuesday at noon they ran through the play without stopping, spent a half hour listening to Terry's notes, and went back to their hotels to rest. They opened that night at 8:00

to an almost full house. When the curtain came down at 10:20, Andrea was so tired that she couldn't even gauge the strength of the applause. It had sounded like waves breaking on the shore a half mile away in the middle of the night.

She did not wait up for the reviews. Sleep was the only thing she cared about in the world. When she read them in the morning they were not bad, but not really good, either, at least not for her. The play itself and Max Jacobi were treated with serious respect, but while no one really slammed her, Eliot Norton suggested that she had not "fully realized the potential power of the role," and Elinor Hughes, whom Andrea had been told was a notorious sweetheart, noted that "Andrea Nilsson is here attempting to make the perilous leap from light comedy to serious drama; she is almost across the chasm and I fully expect she will reach the other side when she learns to take a slightly more daring jump." Those words did not depress her; in fact, she thought they were exactly right. But whether she could finally make the jump she still did not know.

There was no time to dwell on it that day, though. She had a matinee and an evening performance to do. She didn't know how she got through them—she went out onstage and said her lines and simply hoped that something out of pure instinct was coming across. It was nothing but guts that she was working on, and she had no idea what effect she was having. On Thursday she slept until three in the afternoon. She had hardly had a single private moment with Terry since they'd arrived in Boston. There was no way of telling what he thought, and she wasn't sure she wanted to hear. But then after the performance Thursday night he came into her dressing room and asked her if she would mind working with him privately for an hour the next afternoon.

"Okay. I'm so tired I'm not sure what I'm doing. But I'll do whatever you think we have to."

She was sitting in front of the mirror, her face smeared

94

with cold cream. Perhaps it was just as well; she hated to think what she looked like under that layer of salve.

"You're almost there, baby. I just want to work on the final scene. I think maybe we can break through it. Okay?"

"Yes. Yes. That's fine."

"Are you all right?"

"What's all right? Tell me, I don't know anymore."

"What you're doing on stage is beginning to be just right. Remember that." He leaned down and kissed her hair. "I love you. Remember that, too."

"I love you," she said. But she didn't feel anything as she said it, just as she didn't feel anything on stage. The words were right, the inflection was right, but she didn't feel a thing.

Then it was sometime in the middle of Friday afternoon. She'd forgotten to put on her watch. They'd been through the long speech in the final scene three times. And Terry still wanted more.

"You've got to be more commanding, Andrea. I can't tell you how to do it. I've given you the blocking to bring it out. I've told you the pauses. You know what's needed. But I can't do it for you. You've got to find it for yourself, in yourself. You have to be commanding in this scene or it won't work. And if this scene doesn't work, the play won't work, and we're going to be dead on arrival in New York. Now come on, dig down and find it."

But she couldn't. She began to sob instead. Maybe she was just too exhausted. Maybe that was it. But she didn't think so. She thought she would never be able to find what Terry wanted. It wasn't there. It was like digging a well where there was no water. You could shovel down and down and down, making a great pile of dirt and sand to one side, but all you had was a pile of sand.

She stood on the stage of the Colonial Theatre in the harsh brightness of the work lights and wept. The auditorium itself was almost completely dark. Terry was standing only a few rows back but she couldn't see him. He was just a silhouette against the blackness beyond.

"All right," he said. "Let's call it quits. You need some rest. I wouldn't be surprised if it wasn't finally there tonight. Just get some rest."

The Ritz was just a few hundred yards across the Common and the Public Garden, but they took a taxi. As they went through the revolving brass door of the Ritz, Andrea saw Maria Davino's face through the glass, like an apparition, passing through in the opposite direction. But she was not an apparition. She continued around and came back into the lobby.

"Andrea!"

"Hello, Maria."

Maria gave her a big hug, holding her in her arms for a long moment. Then she turned away and kissed Terry demurely on both cheeks.

"What brings you to Boston?" Andrea asked, already sure of the truth.

"I came up to see the play, of course. I'm looking forward so much."

Andrea tried to pull herself together. "Well, we'll see you backstage afterwards then. I'd suggest we have a drink, but what I desperately need right now is a nap."

"Of course. I'll see you tonight," Maria said, and hugged Andrea again.

As they were going up in the elevator, Andrea asked Terry, "What is she doing here?"

Terry glanced at the elevator operator, who with practiced tact was doing his best to pretend to be deaf. "She came up to see the show. Just as she said. She's a friend, Andrea. My friend and your friend."

"And knows damn well she can do this part better than I can. She's had a whole lot more experience at being burning cold."

"That's really not called for, Andrea. You already have an understudy. Let's not add paranoia into the mix."

"Oh, no, let's not do that. Excuse me, but this is my floor."

"Get some rest, please."

"I'll try," Andrea said as the door closed between them.

No one who was in the Colonial Theatre in Boston on that March night in 1967 ever forgot the performance of Andrea Nilsson. Not the twelve hundred members of the audience, not the stage crew, and particularly not the actors. Years later, in his autobiography, Max Jacobi would say that it was at once the most wonderful and the most terrifying evening he had ever spent on stage. "Every actor," he wrote, "has moments when they go beyond themselves. Sometimes it is the pressure of an opening night, or the reaction to some personal problem that seems insoluble. Or it may be something that another actor on the stage does, something so naked and liberating that you forget who you are and simply respond to what is being given to you."

Andrea's own memory of that night was hazy. But she could not forget that as she stood on the stage in the final scene she found herself expressing a rage she did not even know existed within her. Her body as she stood there was almost rigid. But the sounds coming out of her throat were something unimaginable. They terrified her. They belonged to someone else—she hoped she could not make them on her own. And in her terror at what was happening to her, as she stood stock-still on that stage, the tears poured down her cheeks even as her voice cried out in tones of icy retribution.

When the curtain came down, the audience was for several moments absolutely silent. And then, almost as one, they stood and began to cheer.

There could have been many more curtain calls, but as soon as the final programmed bow was over, Andrea stumbled offstage and immediately fell to her knees, sobbing uncontrollably. Max Jacobi knelt down beside her and rubbed her back and murmured over and over again, "It's all right, Andrea. It's all right."

And then Terry was there, holding her and saying. "What are you crying about? You were magnificent. Unbelievable. I didn't think you could do it. I really didn't. Andrea? Andrea! You were wonderful. It's all there now. It's all there."

Andrea heard herself saying, "Yes, yes, yes, I know. I know." And she was sobbing again. "I never want to feel that way again. I don't want to feel those things. I can't deal with it. I can't—I can't do it. I can't be like that. I can't. I can't do it."

Her face was in her hands, her body shaking with anguish. "I can't do that. I can't go through this night after night after night after night. I can't. I can't."

"Come on," Terry was saying. "Come on. Of course you can. You just found it too suddenly, that's all. Tomorrow you'll be able to do the same thing and you'll be in absolute control of yourself. But you'll know what to do, how to do it. You'll be able to make it happen every time. But *you* won't feel this way. The audience will. You'll feel it, but not like this. It will be all right. I promise you."

"No. No. No! It won't be all right. I can't." She was aware of the people standing around her in a broken ring. Cast members and stagehands and others, too, she didn't know who they were. She could see faces, she knew who the faces belonged to, she knew their names. There was David. He was the stage manager. He was a nice guy. I know his face and his voice. I know who he is. And he's looking at me so strangely. And Max. Max is crying too. Max. Max. Please don't cry. Please.

There was Terry's voice, she knew it was Terry, very softly in her ear. "Remember. Remember what I told you, the story about Julie Harris. She went through something like this. Something like it. And she won the fucking Tony, baby. That's what she did. And you will, too. That's what you should be thinking about, baby. You're going to win the fucking Tony."

Andrea heard herself again, her voice. But it was as it had been onstage. It wasn't her. It was some voice coming out of her mouth from some place she didn't know. And the voice was screaming, screaming now, "I'm not Julie Harris. I'm not Julie Harris. I can't. I can't, I can't, I can't do it. I can't.

"I can't!"

Chapter Four

IN HER BARE FEET, wearing a filmy peach-colored negligee, Andrea moved slowly down the long upstairs corridor of Oakridge Manor. Twice she stopped momentarily and listened. At the third door on the right she paused and put her hand on the knob, but then hesitated again as though afraid to turn it.

Suddenly, from behind her, a stern voice asked, "What do you think you're doing?"

Andrea jumped in fright and wheeled around to face the nurse standing in the dim light farther down the corridor.

"Nothing," Andrea said, "nothing." Her voice was steady, but she could not prevent herself from shivering.

"Cut," called out John Sanders, the young English film director. "You can print that."

Sanders, a tall thin man with glasses and unruly hair came over to Andrea. "Loved the shiver," he said.

"Thank you, John, but that wasn't acting. It's incipient pneumonia."

"Here you are, Miss Nilsson." Betty, the wardrobe assistant, put a pair of slippers at Andrea's feet and helped her into a heavy wool housecoat.

"If it's this cold in May, I hate to think what it must be like in this house in December," Andrea said.

"Shh," warned Sanders. "That's the owner standing over there. Making sure we aren't desecrating his house unduly, I gather. Anyway, love, you mustn't criticize the English climate or the temperature of English houses. It adds to the impression that all Americans are spoiled rotten. Besides, no one would dream of wearing a lacy thing like you've got on in one of these drafty old manor houses, at any time of year."

"Then why am I wearing one?" Andrea asked in mock exasperation.

"You wouldn't look sexy in flannel up to your earlobes, dear. Not even you. Now, don't forget the shiver when we do the close-up. And keep that marvelous trapped expression, it's perfect."

That wouldn't be difficult either, Andrea reflected. The character actress playing the nurse looked very much like the officious tyrant who had attended her when Terry and Richard Barstow had hustled her off to Massachusetts General after her collapse backstage at the Colonial Theatre. She hadn't wanted to go to the hospital, but her sobbing protestations had just given Terry more reason to insist. They'd kept her there for three days—it had seemed like weeks—and she had quickly come to look on the nurses more as jailers than anything else. That had been more than two years ago, but Andrea had not forgotten the mingled rage and fear she had felt at the time. It was easy to draw on it now.

"Look, love," John Sanders was saying, "it's going to take a while to set up your reaction shot. Sir George wants to meet you. Maybe he'll even give you a glass of sherry."

"Sir George?"

"Sir George Harrington, love. Oakridge Manor is his house. Country house, of course. It's been in his family for absolute generations."

"How nice for him," Andrea said with some flippancy.

Actually, despite her complaints about the cold, Andrea had fallen in love with Oakridge Manor on first sight, as it appeared suddenly on a slight rise at the end of the winding drive up through the oak woods. Like many eighteenth century English manor houses, its exterior was of plain locally quarried stone, impressive but not in any way elaborate. That plain facade, however, gave way to an Italianate interior of beautifully proportioned neoclassical rooms decorated with elegant moldings, squares and rectangles of varying sizes that divided the walls of the rooms into subtly changing patterns.

Almost all the windows were recessed; there were cushioned window seats everywhere. One of Andrea's childhood friends had had window seats in her bedroom, and Andrea had always envied them. Many of the lovely rooms in Sir George's house were in turmoil now, of course, with electrical cables running across the floor in all directions and lights and cameras hulking in corners, strange steel and aluminum invaders. Andrea wished she had encountered the manor under less hectic circumstances, but even in the midst of the chaos of filming it seemed to retain its dignity.

Because she loved his house, Andrea decided that it would be pleasant to meet Sir George, even though she wasn't really in the mood for chitchat. "I'm not presentable," she said to John Sanders, indicating her robe.

"My dear, he's already seen you in your negligee while we were shooting. Besides, he's an English bachelor of the old school. It really won't matter."

"You mean he's gay?"

"Oh, I wouldn't say that exactly. Classic English indeterminate is more like it. No doubt he'll marry one day. He's the last of his line, and these people hate to see a baronetcy come to an end. It isn't done, if one can help it."

John Sanders took her down the hall and introduced them. Sir George took her hand and bowed slightly. He was a tall, handsome man, with a long face and a strong Anglo-Saxon jaw. His hair was graying slightly, and he had deep-set intelligent eyes. Andrea guessed that he must be in his late forties, but despite his slightly rumpled tweed suit there was something quite dashing about him.

"It will be at least half an hour," John Sanders said, and left them together while he prepared the next shot.

"Why don't we go downstairs, Miss Nilsson? I have a fire going in the library. I'm afraid you must be rather chilled."

"Well," Andrea replied lightly, "John said I shouldn't admit it or you'd think I was just one more spoiled American. So I'll blame it on the costume designer. They never do take working conditions into account."

102

Sir George laughed, quite genuinely, it seemed, and put a hand under her elbow as they descended the stairs. After ushering Andrea into the library, he excused himself to get tea. "Since I'm only down from London for the day, I didn't bring the servants with me and I don't want to put Mr. Sanders' people to any bother. So if you'll just sit by the fire for a few moments, I'll get it myself."

Warming herself in a big wing chair, Andrea looked around the room. One wall was lined with books, almost all of them leather bound. The gold leaf of the titles on their spines reflected the light of the fire and the meager intermittent rays of May sunshine from the high windows hung with red velvet drapes. The cushions of the window seats were of red and gold brocade, and there was a table between them on which an array of lacquered Oriental boxes was displayed. And there were portraits hung here and there, their gilt frames in the styles of successive eras, some simple, others ornate. It was a room with a feeling of continuity, Andrea decided; it was as though it had absorbed bits and pieces of the personalities of the people who had lived in the house over the generations. It was a very human room, with a warmth to it that came from something far more intangible than the quietly crackling fire. Andrea began to relax. She felt curiously at home.

Sir George returned, carrying a silver tray set with an exquisite porcelain tea service decorated with miniature roses. The cup was so delicate Andrea was almost afraid to pick it up. "How beautiful," she exclaimed.

"Yes, they are rather nice. My great-great-grandfather brought them back from China, in 1829 I think it was. That's his portrait over the fire. One of the family's more successful merchants. The Victorians were quite mad about Oriental objects, of course, and he made a considerable fortune in the China trade."

Sir George said this as though the accumulation of that fortune were utterly unconnected with his own life or station; it was presented as mere historical fact. When she was growing up in Cleveland, Andrea had gone to school with girls whose families represented both old and new money. There was a difference between them, she had soon realized. The families with old money behaved as though money were unimportant, though they spent it very carefully. The families with new money spent it freely but seemed obsessed with it. Andrea had often wondered if it were possible to become newly rich and still live as though one had always been so. It suddenly occurred to her now that, despite its aura of old money, Oakridge Manor might well have been built with what had then been new money.

"Who built Oakridge Manor originally?" she asked, and immediately regretted it. She sounded like a tourist.

But Sir George seemed pleased with her interest. "That was Samuel Harrington," he said, offering her a plate of Scotch shortbread. "Quite a brilliant man in his way, a botanist, a bit of an inventor, essayist. But he dabbled too much, instead of sticking to one thing, and he's not much remembered. Fortunately, he married well, and his wife let him spend her money as he pleased. He built this house in 1739. It's a very sensible house, especially for that period, only twenty-one rooms. But he got a fine architect, John Wood the Elder. The truly grandiose houses of that time have almost all passed into public hands. No one can afford the upkeep or the inheritance taxes. I'm very lucky that Samuel Harrington built well but modestly."

Andrea did not really think twenty-one rooms was all that modest, but she supposed it depended on your perspective. Not that Sir George seemed to be trying to impress her. He did not talk down. She liked him very much, in fact. He had a calm urbanity that made her feel comfortable and safe. So many of the younger men Andrea knew, whether American or English, were so brashly ambitious, always on the make in every conceivable way. Sir George was refreshingly mellow. Perhaps it was just that he was older, but she suspected that his having led a life of titled privilege probably had something to do with it as well. It was strange that he hadn't married. He was such a husbandly kind of man.

"I'm surprised you'd let a film crew invade your house this way," she said. "It seems like a violation of it somehow."

"Well, I'm an old friend of one of the producers. And I'd seen the adaptations of Huxley and E. M. Forster young John Sanders directed for the BBC. They were very impressive. When I found out he'd be directing, I knew the house would be beautifully photographed. It seemed quite an amusing idea."

"Yes, John is very good. He gives you time to get things exactly right. Of course, that's one of the luxuries of working on a feature film. I've done three movies for American television in the past year and a half, and the schedule is killing."

"Is this your first trip to England?"

"Yes, it is. I wish I had a chance to see more of it, it's so lovely out here in the country. But I'm planning to spend a couple of weeks in London when my scenes are completed. So at least I'll have a chance to explore the city some."

There was a knock at the door. "Come in," said Sir George.

It was the second assistant director, a beefy young man with the remnants of a cockney accent. "You're wanted on the set, Miss Nilsson. Ten minutes, please."

"Thank you, Bobby."

He nodded and closed the door behind him.

"Well, back to work. Thank you so much for the tea. I wish I could sit here for the rest of the afternoon."

"It's been my pleasure, I assure you. You won't be filming on Sunday, will you?"

"No, the unions see to that, thank God."

"Would you have lunch with me, then? There are a number of quite excellent restaurants in the area. And we could drive about some afterwards."

Andrea, somewhat surprised, hesitated. She was supposed to spend Sunday with Kevin Willoughby, the young English actor playing opposite her. He wanted to show her Stonehenge, he said, although she knew perfectly well that what he really wanted was to sleep with her. Sir George's invitation would be an excuse to keep Kevin in his place.

"I think that would be marvelous," Andrea said. "What time should I be ready?"

"Say about twelve thirty. You're staying at the Boar's Head in the village, I gather."

"Yes, that's right. I'll look forward to Sunday, then."

Sir George smiled and took her hand once more.

Andrea often ate dinner in her room at the Boar's Head Inn, but that evening she agreed to join Kevin Willoughby in the dining room, hoping it would take the sting out of her announcement that she wouldn't be going to Stonehenge with him on Sunday. The dining room was almost full, as usual. Not only were a number of the cast and crew staying at the inn, but it had a reputation for serving quite decent food, and drew a considerable number of diners from the surrounding area. Andrea did not entirely understand the inn's popularity. True, the smoked salmon and oysters on the half shell were excellent, and the kitchen did justice to roast beef, Dover sole, and duck, but anything that aspired to French cuisine was ruined by heavy, floury sauces. And the vegetables were appalling, especially the ubiquitous brussels sprouts that were invariably gray, watery, and mushy at the center. John Sanders explained that it was a national failing; the English liked their brussels sprouts gray and that was all there was to it.

Still, the dining room itself was attractive, with its beamed ceiling and heavy wood tables, and dominated by a huge fireplace festooned with antique cooking utensils. Eating in her room was quiet and restful at the end of the long days of shooting, and it meant she didn't have to dress again after soaking in a hot tub, but sometimes it was nice to have some company. John Sanders, who was always funny and interesting, was her preferred dinner companion, but when she was in the mood she also found Kevin Willoughby's attentions pleasantly amusing in their way.

He was quite a beautiful young man, with dark eyes, dark curly hair, and smooth, deep-toned skin. He looked more Italian than English, in fact. When she told him so he had announced that he was descended from a Roman legionnaire, which was perfectly possible, she supposed, although she suspected it was more likely that he had gypsy blood. Certainly he had a kind of gypsy male arrogance, seeming to take it for granted that any woman he wanted would simply fall into his arms. Andrea derived a certain wicked pleasure from resisting his charms, but she also liked him, and she did not want to make him angry.

She had intended to break the news to him about Sunday late in the meal, but he brought the matter up himself when they were still on their first course. The day had turned even colder, it was raining steadily, and Andrea had ordered turtle soup. It was undoubtedly canned, but it had been dressed up with a good dollop of sherry and was soothingly hot.

"I hope this rain doesn't go on for too long," Kevin said. "At this time of year it can last for a week. If it does, maybe we should go to Blenheim Palace instead of to Stonehenge."

"Oh, I wanted to speak to you about Sunday, Kevin. I'm afraid I'm going to have to back out on that. I'm sorry."

Kevin looked as crestfallen as any child denied a trip to the fair. "Damn it all. I thought we were on."

"Well, I'm afraid I'm being utterly selfish, but Sir George Harrington asked me to spend the day with him, and I couldn't resist."

"Really. Well, it can't be the old man's sex appeal, so I suppose it's his title that impresses you. You Americans are all alike. You ought to realize that decrepit baronets are as common as sixpence over here."

"I'd hardly call him decrepit, Kevin. In fact I find him quite attractive. And it's not just his title, although it will be fun to talk about when I'm back in New York, I admit. It's just that there's something fascinating about a family and a title that go back hundreds of years, that are older than America is."

"That's complete rot, Andrea. My family goes back to the bloody Crusades. It's just that most of them spent their lives cleaning up slops after the nobility, and tilling their fields, and getting killed in their wars. I can't understand why a supposedly democratic country like America should go all squishy about all those titled leeches who've been draining this country dry for centuries."

Andrea was surprised. Kevin was sounding like someone out of a John Osborne play. Maybe he was just playing at being the angry young man, but she didn't think so. He had seemed so self-absorbed that it had never occurred to her that he might have any social grievances. "Well, you're right, of course, Kevin. I mean, it does seem odd that Americans should be so romantic about the English nobility. I suppose it's exactly because we don't have much of that, just our presidents and Rockefellers, and there aren't many of them. But you must have some romantic feelings about it, too. Why else would you take me to Blenheim Castle?"

"Palace."

"Sorry. Palace."

Kevin stared down at his half-finished onion soup as though he were trying to compose himself. He looked up, his dark eyes gentler now. "I'm sorry. I really do understand. I suddenly got the chance to go to a royal benefit a couple of years ago, you know, one of those film openings where the Queen shows up and gives movie starlets a chance to curtsey to her, and I stayed away from my grandmother's eightieth birthday party in order to go. So even I'm affected by the mystique sometimes."

"Was your grandmother upset?"

"Hardly. She was much more excited about my meeting the Queen than she was about her party." Kevin smiled at her. "I'll tell you what. I won't complain any more if you'll promise to spend as much time with me as possible in London after we finish shooting."

Andrea looked across the table at Kevin's handsome, sensual face. She had to admit to herself that she did find him more interesting as the days passed. There was something about him that made her want to touch him. She felt that more than with any man since she had finally drifted apart from Terry six months before. The idea of having an affair with Kevin was not something she dismissed, but she really hadn't decided. Sex for the sake of sex, without a bond that transcended mere physicality, had always bothered her, perhaps more than it should have. It seemed like making love in the dark; if you couldn't see someone's eyes, the expressions on his face, then, it seemed to her, it might as well be anyone, and she did not want just anyone.

Sometimes she thought it would have been better if she had broken off with Terry sharply, cleanly, long before. She had intended to. She had felt she never wanted to see him again during the first few weeks after her collapse backstage in Boston. She had been full of fury then, angry with herself for having let herself be talked into doing a part she knew was wrong for her, and even angrier with Terry. She convinced herself that the only reason Terry had encouraged her, goaded her into doing the part, was that that was the only way he would have a chance to direct. In the hospital she had said as much, throwing the yellow roses he had brought her across the room.

"That's not true, Andrea. I believed you could do it. I admit that during rehearsals I began to think I was wrong. But then last night you proved you could do it."

"Once. I did it right once. I can't do that every night. I just don't have the strength."

"Andrea—"

"Please go away, Terry. I don't want to see you. I don't want to talk about it. The only thing I want is to get out of here. I'm going to leave this afternoon, I don't care what you say."

"You can't just leave. The doctor has to sign a release."

"What am I, a prisoner?"

"Look, Andrea, if you are insisting on leaving the show, it's a good idea for you to stay here a few days. We've already put out a statement saying you have a severe viral infection, and that we don't know when you'll be able to return to the show. Now that's to help you. It gives you a cover, so everyone won't be saying you were fired or just not up to the part or whatever."

"They'll say that anyway. I suppose Maria is going to take over? I suppose that was all planned."

"That's what Richard wants, yes."

"Really. How wonderful for her. I suppose she's superb."

"I don't know, Andrea. She's not going on until Monday night."

"Monday! You mean she's learning the part in two days? I'll bet she's had the script for weeks."

Terry looked pained, caught. "Yes, she's had it for a while, but I didn't know it. I swear I didn't know it. It was Richard's doing. I honestly thought she'd just come up to see the show on her own."

"Like shit."

Terry tried to take her hand but she pulled it away. "I don't blame you for being angry," he said. "I don't like it either. But I'm telling you the truth. I love you, Andrea. I wouldn't do that to you."

"Get out, Terry. Get out of here. Get out!" And she had started on a crying jag that made her realize she wasn't at all ready to leave the hospital. She refused to see Terry over the next two days, though, and when she was released Tuesday morning she had flown immediately to Cleveland, home to her parents.

During the next few weeks her parents had seemed as bewildered by her sullen withdrawal as they had been by her

110

sudden success on Broadway a year and a half earlier. She hardly went out. She didn't want to see people, to have to answer their questions or endure their sympathetic avoidance of the subject of her career. Terry kept calling, almost every day, but she refused to come to the phone and would not answer it if she was alone in the house. She was sleeping twelve hours a day, and when awake, she felt only half alive. And, strangely, she did not feel at home. The house she had grown up in had been a happy, busy place. Despite the fact that there had never been enough money to do or have all the things she wanted, the things her parents had wanted for her, too, it had been a house full of dreams and plans for the future, her future. But it was no longer a place to dream. The future could only consist in doing. It was not a place she could hide, or even feel comfortable. She knew she had to leave, go back to New York. She told herself so every day, but still she did not leave.

Maria Davino wrote her a letter. Andrea did not open it for several hours. She considered tearing it up unread. But she was curious. Maria had not done anything to her, she had done it to herself. Maria hadn't betrayed her; Terry had.

The letter was short.

> Dear Andrea,
> There is a misunderstanding that has to be cleared up.
> I'm probably the last person you want to hear from,
> but I have to tell you that whatever you may feel about
> me, you are wrong to blame Terry. He truly did not
> know that I had a script. Richard Barstow swore me to
> secrecy, and if things had turned out differently, only
> Richard and I would ever have known about it. Terry is
> desperately unhappy about all this. He loves you. Please,
> for your sake and for his, talk to him.
> Come back to us all.
> Maria
> P.S. You were magnificent, you know, that Friday.

111

Two days later, Andrea flew back to New York. During the long taxi ride in from Kennedy she had felt an initial apprehension that had slowly changed to exhilaration as the taxi approached Manhattan. The cab entered the narrow tube of the Midtown Tunnel and exited into the sudden light of an April afternoon in New York. The deceptively fragile-looking trees on East Thirty-third Street were beginning to leaf out. It was just after five, and the streets surged with people, people struggling onto buses, streaming into supermarkets, cramming into bars. Or just hurrying home.

The rush-hour traffic was heavy, and it took more than half an hour to get to her apartment building. The doorman greeted her with what seemed to be genuine pleasure and carried her bags to the elevator. And then she was turning the key in her door. The lights were on and she drew back.

"Who's there?"

"It's all right. It's me."

She could not see him from where she stood in the vestibule. But she began to cry, happily. And then he was there, holding her in his arms. "I had to be here," he said. "I just had to. Your mother called and told me you were coming."

She couldn't speak. She just held on to him.

Yet it had never been quite the same. Their gradual drawing apart had been more sad than painful, but it had left her feeling drained, reluctant to commit herself to another relationship. There had been other young men, though none quite as handsome as Kevin Willoughby, who had tempted her in the last several months, but she had always held back. She wasn't sure quite what she was looking for in a man, but she could tell when it was not there. It wasn't there with Kevin, although his sudden blast at nobility had aroused her curiosity and made her feel there was perhaps more to him than she had imagined. She wasn't averse to spending some time with him when she was in London, but she didn't want to raise his hopes too high, either.

"Well, of course I'll see you in London, Kevin. But I have a lot of plans already. An old friend of mine, Bruce Halliwell, is going to be there on vacation, and I'll be seeing a good deal of him. But I'm sure I'll be free for lunch or dinner at some point."

Kevin looked annoyed, and Andrea thought for a moment that he was going to say something rude, but after a moment he replied. "I suppose I'd best consider myself lucky to have some of your time, then. Is your friend an American, too?"

"Bruce? Yes, we virtually grew up together." Andrea supposed she ought to tell Kevin Bruce was gay, but decided not to. Let him wonder what their relationship was.

Kevin was studying her in a slightly unsettling way. "You're a person with a plan for life, aren't you?" he said unexpectedly.

"What do you mean, a plan?"

"Well, I think we're different kinds of people. There are people who know what they want in life, who have a particular destination in mind, and they don't like to be sidetracked. And then there are people, like me, for example, who take life more as it comes, and try to have as good a time as possible along the way. I think you're the first kind."

Once again, Andrea was somewhat surprised. "I did have a very specific plan once, I admit. But it didn't work out quite the way I had wanted. I do know what I want for myself, but I'm not sure right at the moment that I have a very concrete plan about how to get it."

"What *do* you want?"

Andrea laughed, trying to put it lightly, "Oh, just to be very rich and very famous."

"A Liz Taylor?"

"I wouldn't mind. I could do without Richard Burton, though."

"Couldn't we all. Well, I hope you get what you want, Andrea. But you really ought to relax and have a little fun sometimes, too, you know."

"I'll keep that in mind," Andrea said.

*　*　*

The Sunday of Andrea's planned excursion with Sir George brought with it a change in the weather and the first real intimations of summer. The temperature was in the upper seventies, the sky a bright Wedgwood blue with only a few high puffy clouds. After a long rainy spring, the meadows and woodlands were so lushly and brilliantly green that they looked painted. Clumps of white and yellow wildflowers bloomed effervescently along the roadside, and pink or scarlet rambling roses opened their buds along low stone walls. In the course of the afternoon they made a wide circle through the secluded valleys and hamlets of Gloucestershire, Sir George's black and silver Bentley purring smoothly over the winding country roads and through the narrow streets of Stow-on-the-Wold, Chipping Campden, and Upper and Lower Slaughter. Each of these Cotswold villages had a character of its own, but they all had about them a sense of harmony and peace. Perhaps, Andrea thought, it was the constant use of the same local honey-colored stone that had been used in building Oakridge Manor. She felt as though she were traveling back into the past, into the tranquillity of a lost age. As they were leaving Stow-on-the-Wold she looked back at it, half expecting it to have suddenly disappeared like the enchanted village in *Brigadoon*. When she told Sir George of her feeling, he smiled and said, "Yes, one does have that sense about these places. I'm glad that you feel it. It's a part of the essence of rural England, I think."

They had luncheon at another old manor house near Tewkesbury, the ancient town on the Avon, a house that had been converted into a country inn and restaurant by James Curry, one of England's leading food writers and restaurateurs. Curry was an acquaintance of Sir George's and had reserved a table for them in a small, quiet side dining room. Their view was over a lawn that sloped gently down to a large pond where swans floated regally in the dappled light near the reedy shore.

114

The round table for two by the floor-length window was draped in pale yellow linen and set with napkins as green as English grass, cut-glass goblets, and antique silver.

"What a lovely place." Andrea had expected Sir George to take her somewhere rather special, but the Swansleigh Inn was even more elegant and beautiful than she could have hoped.

"Yes, isn't it? James spent nearly two years restoring the house and collecting the silverware and china. It's all antique. The glassware is new, but it's a Waterford pattern that goes back more than a century."

Andrea had been to more than one restaurant in New York that was expensively and elegantly adorned where the food had been disappointing, but here the exquisitely calligraphed menu gave promise of a meal equal to the surroundings. "This is going to be difficult," she said. "There are so many interesting possibilities."

"Yes, it's a very unusual and imaginative listing, more so than most London restaurants. James has never confined himself to any particular cuisine, so you'll often find dishes that originated in France and Italy and Scandinavia and even the Far East on a single day's menu. But somehow everything works well with everything else. I think it's rather a feat."

"Well, you're going to have to help me. I'll never make up my mind on my own. What do you especially recommend?" Andrea asked this more as a matter of politeness than anything else. In general, she loathed having a man tell her what to order, but it seemed appropriate to defer to Sir George's judgment on this occasion.

"Well, let me see. Among the first courses, I happen to be particulary fond of the fried mussels with béarnaise sauce. And there's a quite wonderful dish of pureed mushrooms and a round of foie gras on a toasted slice of brioche. Yes, here it is. *Croûte Landaise*. And if you want something simple, I'd suggest the smoked eel, which is as good here as you'll get anywhere."

Andrea laughed. "I don't think this is getting any easier. What about main courses? Maybe I should work backwards."

Sir George appeared to be enjoying himself. "That is even more difficult," he said, smiling. "However, the goose with garlic sauce is extraordinary if you like garlic. A great deal of garlic, I should add. And the medallions of veal wrapped in cheese crepes are very special. Or the pigeon in red wine." And Sir George laughed, too. "Frankly, I can't think of anything I wouldn't recommend."

Andrea had grown up eating mussels, not fresh ones, since they were almost never available in the Midwest, but canned ones imported from Denmark. The texture of fresh mussels, she had discovered in New York, was quite different, and since she had never had them fried, she decided on that as a first course. Again because it was new to her, she settled on the pigeon as a main course.

Sir George ordered the *Croûte Landaise,* saying that he wanted her to have a taste of it, and the goose. He insisted that they have a half bottle of white wine with the first course and a full bottle of claret to follow. "In America you'd call it a Bordeaux," Sir George explained. "I can attest to the wines, since they were imported by my own firm."

"You're a wine importer?" Andrea was surprised.

"Oh, yes, it's been a family business for over a hundred years. I have very good people running it for me, so I don't spend anything like full time on it. But I do have a large say in the choice of vineyards we deal with. The white is something quite special, a 1961 Châteauneuf-du-Pape. White Châteauneuf-du-Pape is almost unavailable in America, I believe. Only a small quantity is produced and it's very much in demand in France and Britain. We don't let it escape across the Atlantic. And the claret is a Margaux from Château-Laurent, 1957. I think you'll like it. It's robust enough to stand up to the goose and the pigeon."

Andrea was woefully ignorant about wine, and the few people she had known who considered themselves expert—

116

Richard Barstow had been one—had always seemed to her rather pretentious about the whole matter, behaving as though they were ordained priests of some elite cult. But Sir George, perhaps because he really did know what he was talking about, was pleasantly matter-of-fact. She didn't have the feeling, as she had with other men, that he was trying to prove his superiority; he was simply casually discussing something he happened to know a great deal about.

"But enough about wine," Sir George said. "I'd like to hear more about you. John Sanders tells me that you starred in New York in *Playing by Ear*. I hadn't realized that. I saw the play only last month in London. I must say it seems a shame you couldn't have done it here."

"Well, as you probably know, the American and British actors' unions are both very difficult when it comes to importing a star from abroad. You have to prove that the star is virtually irreplaceable, and I wasn't in that category. But to tell the truth, after doing it for a year and a half on Broadway, I'm not sure I would have wanted to recreate it in London anyway." This was only partially the truth; Andrea was not at all sure that she would ever act on the stage again. The trauma of *Past History* had left her with a lingering wariness about performing for live audiences, night after night. With a film, you could always do another take, and that made her feel far more secure.

"I've heard that many actors with stage experience find making films rather boring," Sir George said. "Do you find that to be true?"

"Sometimes. I prefer acting in films, though." Andrea hesitated for a moment, and then began to tell Sir George about her experience with *Past History*. It was an episode in her life that she almost never discussed with anyone, and she wasn't quite sure why she felt the urge to confide in Sir George. It was not just that she was sure he would be sympathetic and nonjudgmental. John Sanders would have been too, more than likely, but she wouldn't have even considered telling him,

117

perhaps simply because he was a director. In a sense it was almost like unburdening oneself to a fellow traveler on a ship or a long plane trip, someone you might or might not ever see again. But as she talked she began to realize that there was more to it than that. She wanted Sir George to know more about her; she wanted to reach out to him, to make contact with him on some more personal level. And although she couldn't have said why, she had the feeling that that was what he wanted of her, even expected of her.

She didn't go into great detail in telling her story, and touched only lightly on her relationship with Terry, but she found a certain release in talking about what had happened. It was as though she were finally putting it behind her in a more complete way than she ever had before.

"I suppose the strangest part of it," she said, "was that it should have been so frightening to finally find the character that night. It was like opening up a part of myself that I had never known was there. I just couldn't handle it."

"I can understand that," Sir George replied softly, almost regretfully. "I was in the R.A.F. during the Second War, and there was a moment when we had first begun to retaliate against the Germans when I realized that I was taking a kind of obscene pleasure in dropping bombs on them, that I was enjoying killing. It shook me very badly. It wasn't something I wanted to discover in myself, either."

As they looked at each other in silence for a moment across the exquisitely set yellow table, Andrea felt a sudden bond between them. Almost simultaneously, they picked up their crystal wine glasses and delicately touched one to the other.

Their luncheon was superb. Andrea's mussels, crisp on the outside, were almost meltingly tender within, without the slightest hint of sand, and the tarragon tang of the béarnaise sauce complemented them perfectly. Her pigeon surprised her. She would not have imagined that such a small bird could be so sweet and succulent. It was presented on a delicately fried croustade, surrounded by tiny onions and small mushroom caps, the sauce a perfectly balanced blend of winey tartness and the sweetness of thyme and bayleaf. The taste she had of Sir George's goose was equally delicious, the flesh of the bird moist and not at all greasy, the garlic sauce pungent but free of any sharpness or bitterness. They considered having a cold lemon soufflé for dessert, but decided they were too full, and Sir George suggested that instead they stop for tea later in the afternoon at a small hotel noted for its pastry.

After lunch they drove south to the inland seaport of Gloucester, and spent an hour exploring the cathedral. "It's one of my favorites among the British cathedrals," Sir George explained. "Most people prefer Salisbury because it was built in such a short period of time and its architecture is so consistent. But it's exactly because Gloucester Cathedral took so long to build—from the eleventh century to the fifteenth—that makes it so fascinating. You can see a kind of capsule history of English architecture in its various sections." Looking upward at the high Norman vaulting of the central nave, Andrea felt a sense of awe she had not expected. She had never been especially religious; raised a Lutheran, she had found little sense of mystery or spirituality in the modest and quiet tenets of her church. But the very idea of generation after generation laboring through four hundred years to complete such a massive cathedral in this quiet corner of England was in itself strangely uplifting. And yet she suddenly wondered if she would have felt quite the same way if she had been standing there with Kevin Willoughby instead of with Sir George. Kevin, for all his talk about his family going back to the Crusades, had a very modern temperament; he seemed to have little connection with the past. But Sir George somehow belonged to that past and seemed at one with it.

As he showed her the tomb of Edward II, murdered in 1327 with a hot poker by henchmen of his wife, Queen Isabella, Andrea suddenly shivered. "Are you cold?" he asked, and put his arm around her shoulder. "Let's go walk in the cloisters. It will be warmer there."

Strolling through the cloisters, their exquisite fan tracery

119

so intricate it might have been carved from ivory instead of stone, Andrea suddenly linked her arm through Sir George's. "This is so beautiful," she said. "I feel in another world."

"You are," he said, smiling down at her. "Tourists come here by the thousands, but the congregation is terribly small. On some Sundays there are fewer worshipers than clergy and members of the choir. It's that way all over England. I'm not a religious man myself, but it sometimes seems very sad. These cathedrals were built with great sacrifice by living people, who knew they would never see them finished, because they believed in something. Now they're really nothing but museums. It seems to me that few of us really believe in anything but ourselves anymore. And many of us can't even manage that."

Andrea paused for a moment and reached out to touch the stone of the nearest arch. The late-afternoon sun had warmed the stone, but she could feel the coldness beneath it. She touched it first with her fingertips and then laid her palm flat against it.

Behind her, Sir George asked quietly, "What do you feel?"

Andrea felt many things, things too complicated to say easily. Her hand still against the stone, she looked over her shoulder and smiled at him. "History," she said with a slight laugh.

Sir George looked startled, and she turned toward him. "What is it?"

He hesitated. He shook his head slightly. "Just one of those very strange moments. Someone else, a young woman about your own age, gave me the same answer a long time ago." His voice was very gentle, reflective.

"Here?" Andrea asked.

"No, not here." He smiled. "Come, let's go have tea."

She took his arm again, and as they made their way out of the cathedral into the late-afternoon sunlight, Andrea thought, I could make this man fall in love with me. If I wanted to.

Part Three

Chapter Five

SIR GEORGE'S LARGE WHITE HOUSE in Eaton Square in London was run with great efficiency—and a good deal of intramural squabbling—by Mrs. Evelyn, a plump, white-haired woman in her sixties, and Jeremy Butts, who had been born into a family of small shopkeepers in Cheapside, but who had long since mastered the haughty disdain of the traditional English butler and gentleman's private manservant. Mrs. Evelyn had known Sir George since he was a boy when, still in her teens, she had first gone to work for his recently widowed mother in this same house more than forty years earlier. Since Jeremy had been in Sir George's employ for a mere fifteen years, Mrs. Evelyn quite naturally felt that it was her household. But because Jeremy had a far greater knowledge of Sir George's intimate affairs, the question of their relative status had eventually been contested to the point of a friendly yet still combative draw.

When Sir George had announced to them that a Miss Andrea Nilsson, an American film actress, was to be his house guest for two weeks, both Mrs. Evelyn and Jeremy had begun their separate speculations on this development. Houseguests at Eaton Square were not rare, although Sir George more commonly entertained during long weekends at Oakridge Manor. In earlier years, those who did stay at Eaton Square were usually young men, from France or Italy or Scandinavia, whom it was understood that Sir George was putting up while they found London lodgings of their own. But more recently there had been two women who had been guests at Eaton Square. One, a French countess in her early thirties, to whom Mrs. Evelyn had taken an immediate dislike despite the fact that she was properly of Sir George's own class. She was officious and cold, and Mrs. Evelyn had been delighted when she had departed in a fury after an argument with Sir George, which Jeremy had overheard but refused to discuss with Mrs. Evelyn. The other had been a very pretty Swedish girl, vivacious but also a bit silly. Her giggles and informality had seemed out of place in the elegant house.

It was Mrs. Evelyn's certainty—to which Jeremy also somewhat reluctantly subscribed—that Sir George had given some consideration to marrying each of these women, and that their stays at Eaton Square had been in some way a kind of test. The prospect of Sir George's taking a wife was one that both Mrs. Evelyn and Jeremy looked on with a mixture of approval and apprehension. Sir George had been an only child, and if he did not himself father a son, his ancient line would come to an end and his title would pass into oblivion. That was too common an occurrence these days, and Sir George's servants, both of whom cherished the England that once had been, hoped that he would indeed marry. But as they had distinctly proprietary feelings about Sir George and his house, they were greatly concerned as to the character of any future mistress of the household. The fact that Sir George's upcoming house-guest was an American was not taken as a good sign. Winston Churchill's mother had been an American, of course. But she had been of another and more genteel age. And then there had been the dreadful Mrs. Simpson who had seduced their King right off his throne. It might be 1969, but to Mrs. Evelyn and Jeremy, an American did not seem an appropriate vessel for the continuation of Sir George's line. Nationality aside, however, the fact that the young woman was a film actress was what most deeply disturbed Mrs. Evelyn.

Jeremy pointed out that Princess Grace of Monaco had been not only an American but a film actress. "She's a great lady, as regal as any true princess," he insisted. "And a good deal more so than some I could name."

Mrs. Evelyn did not rise to this reference to Princess Margaret, for whom Jeremy regularly expressed contempt but

124

for whom Mrs. Evelyn felt rather sorry. "Princess Grace was always too good for the films," she said. "And at least she was as famous as any woman on earth. Whoever heard of this Andrea what's-her-name. I still don't understand why Sir George allowed them to make a film at Oakridge Manor in the first place. Why, any shopgirl will be able to say she's been there, as it were."

Jeremy, who knew that Sir George had been paid 20,000 pounds for the use of the manor, could have explained this seemingly wayward action of their master's, but did not. The curious state of Sir George's finances were even less Mrs. Evelyn's business than they were Jeremy's.

Andrea's actual arrival, however, mitigated some of their qualms. She drew up in a limousine, and even though Jeremy quite correctly judged that it had been rented by the film company, it was at least a sign that she was a person of some status. Upon being introduced to Jeremy she had smiled and nodded, but had extended her hand to Mrs. Evelyn, whom Sir George identified as his housekeeper of twenty-five years' standing. This subtle distinction in etiquette had greatly pleased Mrs. Evelyn, and even been approved of by Jeremy. Despite being an American and a film actress, Miss Nilsson appeared to have some understanding of what it was to be a lady.

At dinner that night, Jeremy noted that she dealt with the first course of stuffed artichokes with practiced expertise, as she did with the fingerbowl that followed. She commented approvingly on the rare pinkness of the rack of lamb—a continental degree of doneness that Sir George, in contrast to most Englishmen, insisted upon—and seemed delighted and even rather touched by the dessert, a cold lemon soufflé that apparently carried some special meaning for her and for Sir George.

"Her table manners are impeccable," Jeremy reported to Mrs. Evelyn, "and she seems to know about food. She asked me to congratulate you, in fact."

Mrs. Evelyn, who had had to put aside many of her own

prejudices over the years in order to cater to Sir George's rather French tastes in cuisine, beamed at this compliment, and when she carried Andrea's breakfast tray upstairs the following morning, she saw to it that it bore a fresh rosebud from the garden.

"What a lovely rose," Andrea said, picking up the crystal bud vase and sniffing the fragrance. The half-opened flower was silvery pink, shading at the center to a true rose pink, each of its half-opened petals veined with a deeper tone. "Do you know what it's called?"

"They call it the Empress Josephine, Ma'am," Mrs. Evelyn replied. "It's a very old kind, but the master could tell you more about that. He's a great fancier of roses and knows the stories about all of them."

After Mrs. Evelyn had left her, Andrea sat by the window overlooking the garden, where other roses bloomed, and nibbled at her breakfast. There were hot muffins and three kinds of jam, gooseberry, raspberry, and a grapefruit marmalade, all delicious, but she seldom had much appetite for breakfast and ate sparingly. Watching the birds swooping down on the ornate wrought-iron feeder at the back of the garden, Andrea reflected on her good fortune. To be staying here in Sir George's home was proving far pleasanter than a stay in even the most luxurious hotel. When at the end of their Sunday together Sir George had offered his hospitality, she had made a show of reticence, saying that she didn't want to be a nuisance to him. But just as she'd expected, he had insisted there would be no difficulty, indeed it would be his pleasure, and she had accepted. Sir George had told her to feel free to come and go as she pleased, but that he hoped she would join him for a few special occasions he would like to plan for them. The first of those special occasions was to be this evening, a performance by the Royal Ballet of Sir Frederick Ashton's new production of *The Sleeping Beauty*, with Margot Fonteyn as Princess Aurora and Rudolf Nureyev as the Prince.

She had not intended to bring an evening gown to England

with her, but Bruce Halliwell had told her she was crazy. "You never know who you may meet or what you may be doing, love. Be prepared." He had been right, of course, and she had packed the pale purple gown she and Bruce had picked out at Bergdorf's for the Tony Awards. She had worn it only twice, and its simple, elegant cut remained perfectly in style. But she had forgotten to pack the matching shoes, so her first object today was to shop for a new pair. She had considered asking Sir George where to go, but decided that he probably wouldn't know—even married men seldom seemed to know where their wives bought shoes, only that they cost too much. Fortunately, expecting to be on her own in London, she had brought along Kate Simon's new guide to the city, which listed a variety of possibilities. She set out at mid-morning and managed to consume three hours trying on one glorious pair after another at Kurt Geiger, Les Jumelles, and Anello & Davide, deciding to skip lunch altogether since Sir George had said they would have high tea at five and dinner after the performance. She bought three pairs of shoes and a pair of boots in the course of her excursion, none of them sensible but all of them beautiful, including a pair of silver kid shoes for that evening.

"I'm afraid I got completely carried away," she told Sir George at tea. "In part I guess it was the salesmen. They all behaved like the prince searching for Cinderella. You don't get that kind of devout attention in New York, even in the very best stores."

Sir George chuckled. "Yes, I think it's probably true that one gets the most attentive and polite service in London shops of any city in the world. I don't know how much longer that will last, but it's a happy remnant of the past."

Andrea was also getting carried away eating. She was absolutely ravenous, and although she knew that "high" tea indicated a virtual meal, she had not been prepared for quite such an extensive spread. There were both watercress and cucumber sandwiches, hot oyster fritters, stuffed eggs with

127

caviar, brandy snaps filled with whipped cream, and a marmalade cake.

"We're going to be joining Myra and Charles Brockton in their box this evening," Sir George said, helping himself to another oyster fritter. "I think you'll find them very engaging, especially Myra. She's had quite an extraordinary life. She was an opera singer in Vienna before the war, and was beginning to make quite a name for herself. But she was Jewish and even though she was married to a Gentile, a stage designer I believe he was, she had the sense to get out. He stayed behind and they were divorced after the war. Then she married a distant cousin of the Queen, who got himself killed climbing the Himalayas. After that there was an Italian conductor. That didn't last long either. Myra's explanation is that he found lady harpists totally irresistible. At any rate, she and Charles have been married a dozen years now. I should tell you that he was knighted a year ago, so you should probably call him Sir Charles. These newly elevated sorts take it all very seriously. But Myra will probably ask you to call her just that almost at once. She's had the title of Lady twice now and could not care less."

"She sounds quite marvelous," said Andrea, thinking immediately of Karen Bolling and her series of husbands. She hadn't realized they were joining anyone, and it made her slightly nervous. Especially someone titled. Sir George had told her to call him simply George, but she was finding it hard to do, and had been avoiding the issue by not calling him anything. "What was Sir Charles knighted for?" she asked, hoping that he wasn't some former cabinet minister or admiral; she knew virtually nothing about British politics.

"He's in the recording industry. Myra says he was knighted for recognizing that rock-and-roll was one of Britain's few exportable commodities, which isn't far from the mark. The Beatles and the Rolling Stones have done more for our balance of payments than most of our other industries combined."

"The Beatles and the ballet. It sounds as though he has wide-ranging tastes."

"Actually, he loathes popular music, and as for the ballet, he'll probably go to sleep. But Myra's on the Board of Governors of Covent Garden, so they have a box. It's fortunate they do, in fact, or we simply wouldn't be going tonight. Everyone wants to see the new *Sleeping Beauty*, especially when Margot and Rudy are dancing. No one expects Margot to go on dancing the prima ballerina roles much longer. Aurora is the only one she still does in fact. So there's not a ticket to be had."

Although every ballet fan in New York took the liberty of calling Fonteyn and Nureyev by their first names even if they'd never gotten any closer to them than the last row of the Third Ring, Andrea suspected that Sir George might actually know them, perhaps even quite well. She certainly wasn't going to be gauche enough to ask, though. In fact, she was beginning to think that the best way to deal with the evening to come would be to murmur, "How lovely," at appropriate moments and otherwise keep quiet unless she was spoken to.

With a half hour to change, Andrea was ready at 6:15. As she began to descend the staircase, Sir George was standing at the bottom with his back to her, talking to Jeremy. "You won't need to return to Covent Garden for us, Jeremy. The Brocktons will be taking us in their car after the performance and Lady Myra has insisted that we allow Jacob to drive us home after dinner."

"Very good, Sir." Jeremy, with an almost imperceptible motion of his head indicated to Sir George that Andrea was on the stairs above them. Sir George turned and looked up at her.

"How very beautiful you look, my dear," he said, his voice warm with pleasure, coming forward to take her hand as she reached the last step.

"Thank you, George," she said quietly, experiencing a sudden surge of confidence. She was beginning to feel entirely comfortable with him, to have that sense that she had known him far longer and far better than she actually had. He himself was dressed in white tie and tails, which he wore not only with elegance but with the casualness that only those who have spent their lives in evening clothes can muster. Andrea had met very few American men who did not give the impression of having been trussed up like a Thanksgiving turkey when forced to wear formal dress.

A half hour later Jeremy pulled into the line of limousines and taxis drawn up before the Royal Opera House. Andrea had ridden in limousines on a number of occasions over the past few years, but they had always been rented, or provided by producers. Even Karen Bolling had usually taken taxis. To ride in a private car driven by a personal chauffeur was a new experience, one that brought Andrea a secret interior smile. How nice it would have been, she thought, if instead of taking taxis back and forth across London today while shopping for shoes, she had had Jeremy waiting to sweep her off from one shop to another.

They had arrived before Sir Charles and Lady Myra, and Andrea had a chance to sit for a few minutes in their Grand Tier box and look out over the opera house at the audience as it gradually filled the great red, gold, and cream-colored hall. She had never liked the Metropolitan Opera House at Lincoln Center in New York. It had seemed garish instead of ornate, an uneasy compromise between the old and the new. Here there was a glow, a sense of rightness, a true grandeur shining forth from the cherubs that decorated the front of each box, the gilt of the proscenium arch and the massive red curtain emblazoned with the royal coat of arms. It was a hall made for kings and queens, not merely for mayors and governors and the occasional bored president. Andrea, she thought, you are a dreadful snob, and then she smiled happily at the notion.

The Brocktons arrived five minutes before curtain time. Lady Myra proved to be a woman of appropriately operatic build and expansiveness. But she carried her weight with a grace and authority that Andrea saw at once would make other women seem diminished rather than slender. Sir Charles, portly and white haired, appeared to be perfectly happy to let his wife take command. She insisted that Andrea sit with her at the front of the box. "George is tall enough to see over you and I'm big enough to hide Charles from any snooping opera glasses if he decides to take a nap," she explained.

Andrea was enthralled by the performance, by the soaring fairy-tale sets, the magical transformation of the stage through a mere fog machine and lighting into a vast blue lake through which the Prince sailed toward his destiny, by the filigreed opulence of the costumes. Nureyev, at the height of his career, was breathtaking in the power of his leaps, but Andrea was almost more impressed by the loving and self-effacing way that he partnered Margot Fonteyn, presenting her to the audience as though she were the rarest and most beautiful princess who had ever existed, a nymph discovered in a dream.

"This has been the loveliest evening I've spent in a very long time," Andrea told Sir George later, as they were being driven home following the champagne supper at the Brocktons' Mayfair townhouse. It was nearly one in the morning, and the London streets were far more deserted than New York's thoroughfares would have been at that hour. She knew that London was an early-closing city, although that did not seem to be the case for the wealthy; she was surprised at the number of chauffeur-driven cars making their way through the quiet streets.

"I'm very glad you enjoyed yourself," Sir George said in a matter-of-fact tone that made Andrea realize that such evenings were probably quite routine to him. It was a routine she could happily embrace, the kind of life she had always wanted for herself.

"You were quite right about Myra," she said. "She really is very amusing and extremely nice. She said that she would ring me up in a day or so to see if we could arrange a lunch."

Sir George chuckled.

"What did I say?" Andrea asked, slightly puzzled.

"Ring me up. Instead of telephone. You're picking up British usage very quickly."

Andrea laughed herself. "You know, I wasn't even aware

of it. It must sound awfully phony coming from an American."

"Not at all, my dear. It's charming. I'm glad you and Myra hit it off so well, although I'm not surprised. She's a very good person to know in London. She has a great deal of influence with many very important people, but at the same time she doesn't take herself too seriously. She could be a good friend for you to have."

Andrea didn't know quite what to make of these remarks. They didn't seem like the kind of thing you would say to a foreign visitor who was planning to be in England for only another two weeks, less really. She cast a sidelong glance at Sir George, and her heart began to race just slightly. But there was nothing she quite dared to say.

The Brocktons' Rolls-Royce turned a corner. "Well, we're just about home," said Sir George.

Bruce Halliwell had arrived from New York that same night, and by pre-arrangement, she called him the next morning at his hotel near Sloane Square, a comfortable but not at all elegant hostelry that he patronized for the simple reason that the management had a policy of simply not noticing when you brought some young man back to your room at peculiar hours. Bruce knew London quite well; he had been introduced to it initially by the florist he had worked for when he first arrived in New York, and had made several subsequent trips on his own. He was a devotee of King's Road, which he referred to as the Christopher Street of London. Andrea was not particularly interested in the flower children of King's Road, but she was curious about its renowned off-beat boutiques, and agreed to meet Bruce for lunch at Alexander's, with the promise of a full tour of the shops to follow.

Going down the steep stairs from King's Road and entering Alexander's cellar premises was to pass from a daylight world into a nighttime ambience of candlelit tables and after-dark allure. The waiter who brought their menus was a slender, smoky-eyed young man. His sensual Mediterranean manner gave the impression that he himself could probably be ordered up for dessert. In fact, as she looked around the alcoved dining room with its horizontal dividing beams, it occurred to Andrea that she had never seen so many gorgeous waiters in one restaurant.

"Do you come here for the food or the waiters?" she asked Bruce.

"Well," he said, laughing, "the food is very pleasant, but rumor does have it that the waiters are truly delicious. It's regarded as a must stop for faggots on tour. But women always seem to enjoy themselves here, too. The boys are reputed to be extremely unprejudiced."

"Are you ever not on the prowl, Bruce?"

"Never. But right at the moment I'm far more interested in this duke or whatever he is you seem to have snared for yourself."

"He's a baronet. The last of a very old line. And I certainly wouldn't say I'd snared him."

"What would you say, then?"

"He's simply a very kind man who took a liking to me, and offered to put me up while I was in London.'

"Oh, come on, Andrea, that sounds terribly dreary. How many times had you seen him before he extended this invitation?"

"Twice."

"I call that snaring, although it may be that he's the one doing it. Even I don't move much faster than that. Is he divorced?"

"No, apparently he's never married."

"And how old is he?"

"Late forties, I'd guess."

"Old enough to be your father."

"Yes." Andrea was slightly annoyed at Bruce's tone. "From a couple of things he's said, I get the impression I remind him of some young woman he knew once, a long time ago."

"Oh, God, a lost love."

"I think I'll begin with the gazpacho," Andrea said coolly.

"I'm sorry. I'm being awfully flip, aren't I?"

"Yes, Bruce."

"All right. Let's be serious then. Is he interested in you sexually?"

"Not in the usual sense. I mean he hasn't made even the slightest kind of pass, but he does seem attracted to me. He takes my arm a lot."

Bruce rolled his eyes. "Well, the English are so weird about sex, the upper classes anyway. I suppose that might almost pass for assault. I'm afraid you'll have to take the initiative yourself, my dear."

"Sexually? I'm not sure I'm interested in him sexually. I feel very comfortable with him. I guess I'm getting quite fond of him. And he's certainly a handsome man. But I don't think he's the kind of man you have a fling with, even if I wanted that."

"No, of course, you want to marry him."

"Really, Bruce." Andrea put her menu down with a slap. "Aren't you getting a little ahead of things?"

"I'm only trying to help out, Andrea. I think you'd make a lovely addition to the London social register. And God knows these English noble families need a little fresh blood. Their chromosomes are just about shot. And don't tell me you wouldn't like to have a house in London and an estate in the country and get driven around by a chauffeur. Not to mention having people calling you Lady Andrea. I know you. You've wanted a mansion and hot and cold running servants and all that since you were eight and had a jealous fit when Susie Williams got a pony for her birthday."

"I did not have a jealous fit."

"You most certainly did. I remember *everything*, you know. You said, 'I hate her,' four times in succession, each one louder than the last."

Andrea had to laugh. "God but you have an encyclopedic memory for people's worst moments. I grant you I hated her, but it wasn't because of the pony. It was because she was an absolute bitch by the time she was three."

"Nevertheless you've always wanted to be wildly rich, and now you've got your chance. And with a title thrown in. How can you resist?"

"Bruce, this is absurd. He hasn't the slightest thought of marrying me. People keep saying he's bound to marry eventually, just to get an heir. But I'm sure there are lots of young English women who'd fill the bill much better than I would."

"You say he hasn't the slightest thought of marrying *you*. You didn't say you don't have the slightest thought of marrying him."

Andrea tried to look severe, but couldn't help smiling. She had never been able to fool Bruce. "It makes a nice fantasy," she said.

"Fantasies are for fulfilling, my dear."

"Some are. But not this one. You know, it has occurred to me that I could make the man fall in love with me. But I'm not sure it's possible for me to fall in love with him."

"Is that important? It doesn't always help, does it?"

Andrea sighed. "No, it doesn't. I think in most cases one person gives more love than he or she gets back. And maybe it's more tranquil to be the one who's loved, to know that *you* don't have to worry. But I'm not sure I want to give up the excitement of fully loving someone just to be taken care of."

"Let me put it this way, then, Andrea. If he asked you to marry him, would you?"

Andrea knew the answer to Bruce's question, but she hesitated to be completely honest even with him. It would be taking a step toward something she wasn't fully ready to admit even to herself. Besides, it could be that she was reading more into Sir George's attentions than she ought to be. She didn't want to make a fool of herself.

"Come on, answer the question."

"I'd be tempted," she said quietly, taking a half step, leaving herself a loophole.

"And so you should be. I'll tell you what, Andrea. We're

going to change our plans for the afternoon. You can wander along King's Road anytime by yourself, and you'd probably have more fun trying on things endlessly without me."

"You mean you'd have more fun."

"That, too. We're going to Harrods instead. There are some things I want to have shipped back to New York, and in the process I'll give you a taste of what it could be like to be Lady Andrea Harrington."

"All right. I know Harrods is supposed to be the most glamorous department store in the world, and I was going to look for some clothes there eventually, so why not? But what are you going to buy?"

"Not clothes, love. We're going to the Valhalla food halls."

"Valhalla?"

"And not misnamed. If you're into food, they are heaven on earth. For a caterer like myself it is a positively orgasmic experience. There's nothing like it in the United States. You could take Bloomingdale's gourmet shop and quadruple it in size, and add Macy's butcher shop expanded the same way, and throw in a trip up and down Ninth Avenue in the Forties and Fifties for fruits and vegetables and fish, and include the three best pastry shops in New York and put them all under one roof and you still wouldn't equal the food halls of Harrods. You'll see. And if you were Lady Andrea, you'd have a charge account."

"You're trying to manipulate me, Bruce."

"Just helping you to see the light. That's all."

In 1848 a certain Mr. Harrod opened a small grocer's shop, lit by paraffin lamps, on the Brompton Road in what was then a poor section of London. Within fifty years it had grown to be the largest store in the world, extending for an eighth of a mile along Brompton Road, by then one of the main arteries of newly fashionable Kensington. The six-story building, occupying an island site bordered by the Brompton Road, Basil

Street, Hans Crescent, and Hans Road, its walls faced with terracotta and topped by a huge dome, had achieved the dimensions of a secular cathedral. It had become a palace of commerce.

Andrea knew that it was enormous and world famous, but still she was not prepared for its grandeur, for the top-hatted, green-coated doorman who rushed to open the door of the taxi as it pulled up, for the bowing of the pin-striped clerks who looked as though they were dressed for the opera, for the sheer scope of the vast food halls. There were endless aisles of delicacies in shining glass jars, hand-painted tins, and crockery pots, ranging in size from a single ounce to a full gallon, containing pale green artichoke hearts and white asparagus, olives the size of robins' eggs stuffed with almonds and onions and pimientos and anchovies, layered like glistening jewels. There were jams and jellies and marmalades from a dozen countries, their colors a shining rainbow of hues, and hundreds of varieties of teas, biscuits, and cookies in tins that were in themselves works of art. Fresh fruits and vegetables were displayed as though they were treasures from Tiffany's— oranges from Spain, avocados from Israel, dates from Egypt, and pomegranates from Madagascar. There were pearly white endive from Belgium, black radishes from Germany, bunches of carrots no bigger than a finger and tied like a nosegay, everything as bright and clean as though it had been washed in the morning dew.

Live lobsters lazed in one tank, trout darted in another. There were rows and rows of fish laid out on chopped ice— whole fish, their scales bright red or satiny white, black as caviar, or iridescent with greens and blues; dozens of kinds of fish cut into perfect fillets or plump glistening steaks; mounds of mussels, clams, and oysters; scallops still in the shell, their bright orange coral attached; a half dozen grades of shrimp, tiny tentacled squid, and huge wings of skate. Smoked fish and salt-cured fish, whole sides of salmon waiting to be sliced paper thin or carried off in their entirety for some lavish buffet—there was simply no end to it.

"I didn't even know scallops had coral," Andrea said. "I've never seen them in their shells."

"They don't in American waters. That's the reason Coquilles St. Jacques are always a little better in Europe; they chop up the coral and add it to the sauce." Bruce smiled. "Mystery revealed."

Across the wide aisle in the meat department pheasants and quail still in plumage were hanging from stainless steel hooks. In the refrigerated cases were racks of lamb and tiny rosy chops, crowns of pork filled with stuffing, the upraised ends of the bones decorated with paper frills. There were suckling pigs, roasts of beef large enough to feed thirty, and two-inch filets mignons trimmed to scarlet perfection. There were boned and tied veal roasts and scallopine as pale and thin as parchment. Lamb kidneys that gleamed like mahogany were laid out next to lacy honeycomb tripe. And there were nearly two dozen kinds of sausages, from the English banger to the Polish kielbasa.

"You're quite right, Bruce. This place is fit for the gods." She giggled suddenly, realizing that she was whispering. "I wouldn't have believed it if I hadn't seen it. I'm still not sure I believe it."

"And to think you could shop here every day."

"Enough of that. Please, Bruce. I told you, fantasies are nice, but let's not get carried away."

"Very well, be like that. You always were stubborn."

Later that afternoon, after Bruce had finished buying more than a thousand dollars worth of preserved delicacies that were difficult to come by in New York, the Harrods doorman had ushered her into a large black cab as though it were some golden coach. As she rode back to Eaton Square, Andrea found that she could not get those fantasies out of her mind. At the same time she was convinced it was all nonsense.

"It's ridiculous," she muttered aloud.

"What's that, Miss?" the cabby asked, half turning his head.

"Sorry, driver. It's nothing. I was just talking to myself."

"That's quite all right, Miss. In this world, we have to just say things right out sometimes. I do it myself when I haven't got a fare."

Over the next few days, Andrea whirled around London at the kind of pace maintained by the tourist making a once-in-a-lifetime trip. One day it was the National Gallery, another the Tate. There were hours spent shopping, at Liberty's for presents to take back to New York, at Jaeger for a suit for herself, a soft heather blue, at Wallis for a silk blouse from Paris to go with it. She sandwiched in a quick lunch with Kevin at the Salisbury, the very Victorian pub on Shaftesbury Avenue in the heart of the theater district, all red plush and shining brass and dark wood and mirrors, followed by a quick tour of Carnaby Street, whose shops full of raucous hippy clothes Kevin seemed to think amusing but which she found merely tacky. He was not too happy with this on-the-fly encounter, and she agreed to let him take her to Hampton Court two days later when Sir George would be away on an overnight business trip to Paris.

Sir George seemed vaguely bemused by all her rushing about. "The sheer energy of Americans astonishes me," he commented with a smile. "But then I suppose one could also say that we British have become chronically lazy."

"Oh, I like the slower pace here. It's just that I want to see as much as I can."

"Perhaps you should plan a longer stay."

In one sense Andrea had hoped to hear him say that, but his tone had been merely conversational. It could simply be a matter of politeness on his part, and she didn't want to take him up on the idea too quickly. "I wish I could," she replied, trying to suggest that there was some important reason for returning to New York, although in fact she had no specific plans. She was up for two or three roles, but she hadn't signed any contracts yet.

They were having dinner at Eaton Square that evening, since Sir George had to catch an early plane to Paris the next morning. The night before they'd gone to see Alan Ayckbourn's comedy *How the Other Half Loves*, starring Robert Morley, and as much as Andrea had enjoyed it, she was rather glad to have a quiet and early evening in the tender care of Jeremy and Mrs. Evelyn. She had been overdoing things a bit, there was no question about it.

"What kind of marathon day have you planned for yourself while I'm in Paris?" Sir George asked.

He was teasing her, Andrea realized. He hadn't really done that before, and she blushed slightly. "Well, Kevin Willoughby has insisted on driving me out to Hampton Court."

"Oh, yes." Sir George busied himself with an asparagus spear, holding it poised just above the plate with the sterling silver tongs she herself was having such fun using for the first time. It reminded her of the first time she had ever used escargot tongs at Karen Bolling's, grasping the tongs in the left hand and using the tiny silver fork to try to extract the reluctant snail. She had felt dreadfully inept then, but the asparagus was giving her no problems.

"An extremely handsome young man," Sir George continued after a pause, and lifted the asparagus to his mouth.

"Yes," Andrea said. "It would be nicer, though, if he weren't quite so aware of it himself," she added quickly.

"Do you find him interesting otherwise?" Sir George asked, without looking up.

"He's not as shallow as I first thought, but the reason I'm going tomorrow is that I broke an engagement with him to spend that Sunday with you in the Cotswolds. He was rather hurt, I think, so I'm trying to make it up to him."

Sir George looked across at her. "I hadn't realized. I'm very flattered."

"I know this may sound strange," Andrea said, "since

140

Kevin is a year older than I am, but he's really kind of a child."

"That doesn't sound strange at all," Sir George said quietly. "But I am glad you feel that way."

Andrea didn't know what to reply to that remark and so kept silent. Two years ago she would have felt uncomfortable with silence and would have blurted out something regardless. But she was instinctively certain that Sir George respected silence and that to have spoken just then would have been out of place. She sensed that there was more to what he had said than was apparent on the surface, but that he didn't really expect or want her to make too much of it, at least not yet.

The following afternoon, Andrea and Kevin spent more than two hours touring the imposing red brick palace where Henry VIII had lived out much of his tempestuous life, acquiring and discarding wives with despotic abandon. Then, after wandering for a while in the gardens, which in contrast to Henry's life were rigidly ordered in the French style, Kevin insisted that they conclude their excursion by venturing into the famous boxwood maze near the front gates. Andrea was tired from walking, and not at all attracted by the possibility of spending another half hour trying to find their way out of complex green pathways, but Kevin insisted. "You can't really say you've been to Hampton Court until you've gone through the maze," he said, taking her firmly by the arm.

Within five minutes, he had disappeared. One moment he had been at her side. The next he was gone, swallowed up by the high hedges. Andrea was distinctly annoyed.

"Kevin," she called out. "Kevin. Kevin!"

There was no answer. Obviously, he had slipped away deliberately, just like a mischievous child. "Kevin, this isn't funny. Where the hell are you? Kevin! God damn you!"

She kept moving forward, turning this way and that. Reaching a dead end, she heard children's voices squealing with delight on the other side of the impenetrable foliage.

Their pleasure only irritated her further, and she turned back muttering under her breath. "God damn son of a bitch."

Moments later she was suddenly grabbed from behind. She let out a shriek of surprise, which was quickly stifled as Kevin spun her around and kissed her passionately, his tongue pressing deep into her mouth.

She pushed him away violently, kicking him in the shins.

"What's your bloody problem?" Kevin asked, his eyes flashing darkly.

"It seems to be you," she said furiously.

"Well, I hope to God you're not saving yourself for that old closet queen in Eaton Square. I doubt if he can even get it up."

Andrea drew her hand back and slapped him across the face as hard as she could.

Kevin put a hand to his face, stunned. But it was Andrea who suddenly began to cry. She'd never hit anyone in her life before, and her anger turned abruptly to shock. "I'm sorry, Kevin. I'm sorry."

For a moment she thought he might hit her back, but he just stood staring at her. He took a deep breath and said, "I'm sorry, too. Christ, we are a pair. Let's just forget this, shall we? It won't happen again."

"What?"

"I've got the message, Andrea. We're just going to be friends. Is that all right? Can we be friends?"

"I suppose," Andrea said, but she looked away from him as she spoke.

"All right. We're going to get out of here now. I—I apologize."

"Yes. All right. Let's just get out of here."

"Okay. I know the way. Come on, just follow me."

Kevin turned and began to walk back the way she had come.

Lying in bed that night at Eaton Square, Andrea's mind kept returning fitfully to the maze at Hampton Court. Kevin had clearly taken her slap as a sexual rebuke. Perhaps it had been in part, but the more she thought about it, the more she understood that her primary reaction had to do with his insulting remark about Sir George. It surprised her to realize that she felt so strongly protective. But it was even more unsettling that in some secret emotional recess of her being she had come to link herself with Sir George; it was not just that she was insulted for him but that she herself felt personally injured.

It was after one in the morning and she had been lying awake for nearly an hour. Eating alone in the big house that night she had a strong sense of how empty it seemed without George, despite the solicitude of Jeremy and Mrs. Evelyn. She had missed him, far more than she would have expected. She turned again in her bed, but her body was taut and pulsing and she could not find comfort. Throwing back the lace embroidered sheet, she got up and went to the windows. She drew back the curtains part way. It was a cloudy night and the sky was milky, reflecting the lights of London back down upon the city. She had given up smoking more than a year ago, but she had a sudden craving for a cigarette. Perhaps what she really needed was a cup of hot milk, her mother's old remedy for insomnia.

Only Mrs. Evelyn slept at the house, Jeremy had a flat of his own. But Mrs. Evelyn's rooms were above the kitchen, reached by a back stairway, and Andrea didn't want to wake her or have her think there was a prowler. Still, she had been told to consider the house her own and she decided to make her way downstairs.

She had some trouble finding the light switches, especially in the dining room, and when she did the sudden illumination from the crystal chandelier above the shining mahogany table made her blink. She paused for a moment surveying the room, the Queen Anne chairs upholstered in gold brocade to match the window drapes, the great silver platter, punch bowl, and samovar displayed on the eighteenth century sideboard, the priceless Rose Medallion bowl occupying its own ebony stand in one corner. When she and George had eaten at home, he had always seated himself at the head of the table with Andrea to his right. For a moment she imagined herself sitting at the opposite end of the long table, presiding with him over a dinner party, their guests seated on either side, Jeremy serving quail, or trout with béarnaise sauce, or—

Lady Andrea Harrington. It was a role she could play. She wouldn't have thought so only a few weeks ago, but she knew now that she could. It would be the best role she had ever had. But was it a role she could sustain over the years, that she would be happy playing for a run without end? The very fact that she thought of it as a role gave her pause. She had no doubt that she could carry off the public aspects of being Lady Andrea Harrington, but she would also be a wife, the wife of a man she still knew very little about beyond his charm and kindness, a man who had not married even though he was the last of his line, a man whose chief and perhaps only reason for marrying after all this time would be to ensure an heir.

As she passed on into the butler's pantry, its long rows of glass-fronted cabinets holding half a dozen neatly ordered sets of glistening antique china, she speculated on just why Sir George had never married. Was it simply the trauma of a lost love, as Bruce had suggested? Or was he impotent, or sterile, or perhaps homosexual? A masculine appearance, which he certainly had, meant little, as she had learned over the years, in terms of sexual preference. Kevin's taunts nagged at her. She could imagine herself being held close by George, sleeping beside him, but it was in some curious way difficult to imagine being sexually excited by him. It was hard to think of him naked, in fact, stripped of his Savile Row tweeds and his shirts from Gieves. A man like Kevin Willoughby was difficult not to think of in terms of sex, of smooth-muscled nakedness. A man like Sir George, for all his handsomeness, seemed defined instead by his clothes.

144

Andrea took milk from the refrigerator and found a sauce-pan to heat it in. There was china—plain white servants' china, it occurred to her—in a cupboard, and she took down a cup and saucer, poured out her steaming milk, and sat down at the heavy oak table at one side of the large kitchen. Suddenly she heard footsteps on the floor above. Mrs. Evelyn's voice called out sternly, "Who's down there?"

"It's just me, Mrs. Evelyn. Andrea Nilsson."

Mrs. Evelyn came downstairs, and as she entered the kitchen Andrea began to apologize. "I'm sorry I woke you up. I couldn't sleep and I thought some hot milk might help."

"That's all right, Miss. You gave me a bit of a start is all. I wasn't asleep myself, I got so engrossed in one of those lovely chillers by Mrs. Christie. It's an old one but I'd forgotten how it comes out. Perhaps I'll have a spot of tea myself if you wouldn't mind the company."

"That would be very nice."

"The house always seems so empty when the master is away," said Mrs. Evelyn, busying herself with the teapot.

"Yes, I felt that myself. Do you know what time Sir George will be returning tomorrow? I thought I might do a little sightseeing, but I'd like to be here when he gets home."

"A bit before four o'clock, Jeremy says. The master likes to get home before tea."

"You're very fond of him, aren't you?"

"He's a lovely man. Of course, I've known him since he was just a sprite. It may sound a bit presumptuous but I think of him almost like a nephew or some such. You'd never know it now, he's such a dignified gentleman, but he was quite a bundle of mischief as a boy." There was a slight pause and then with her back to Andrea as she poured boiling water into her teacup, Mrs. Evelyn added, "A big house like this needs a child running about to bring it to life."

Andrea had no idea how to reply to this statement. It seemed as though it might be an invitation to discuss Sir George's unmarried state, but she was afraid of saying the wrong thing. She had never given much thought to having children herself. Her ambitions had always taken other directions, and even conflicted with the idea of children. Even with Terry she had never really thought about it. Yet Mrs. Evelyn's words suddenly opened up in her mind a flashing vision of a future in which there would be a child, her child, running through the rooms of this house in Eaton Square, tearing into the kitchen to pester Mrs. Evelyn for cookies.

It was not so much that she wanted such a child—what she wanted was the kind of life that the house itself implied. But the very fact that she could, all at once, imagine the existence of a child of hers as a part of such a life brought her confused feelings into a new focus. She knew, suddenly and completely, that she wanted to marry George Harrington.

For ten minutes more, Andrea sat with Mrs. Evelyn, chatting about her past few days in London. She then went back upstairs to bed and fell asleep almost at once.

When George Harrington returned from Paris the following afternoon, he found Andrea waiting for him in the drawing room. As he came through the door she walked toward him, wearing a white pleated linen skirt and a green silk blouse, her blond hair loose about her shoulders, looking as fresh and bright as a daffodil. "Welcome home," she said, coming right up to him, smiling, and he took her hands in his and leaned forward to kiss her cheek. But she surprised him by kissing him on the mouth, lightly and quickly.

"I'm so happy to see you," he said. "I thought you'd probably be out and about the city."

"I did go out for a while, but Mrs. Evelyn told me you'd be back in time for tea and I thought it would be nice to be here."

"I couldn't be more delighted."

He had in fact considered asking Andrea if she wanted to accompany him to Paris, but that had seemed a little forward, suggestive of an intimacy she might find offensive.

But in the end it had proved a good thing that he had gone alone, for it had brought home to him how much pleasure he took in her company. She had occupied his thoughts so completely that he had not even gone to any of his usual haunts on the Left Bank to seek out a young man's company for the night. To find her waiting for him on his return suggested to him that she had missed him too, perhaps. Sir George was not good at reading the emotions of women, they had always left him somewhat baffled, but he had sensed something new and more complex in her attitude toward him as she had walked across the drawing room to greet him.

"I brought you a little something from Paris," he said, taking a small box from his pocket.

It was a gold pin, a spray of lily of the valley carved in the Art Nouveau style, each blossom delineated by a tiny pearl.

"Oh, how beautiful," Andrea said. "You shouldn't have, you know."

"Nonsense. I saw it in a shop window and it immediately made me think of you. One always regrets it if one resists such impulses."

She smiled at him, her blue eyes bright and shining. "I'm glad you didn't resist. It's lovely."

Jeremy brought in the tea tray, and as though in response to some change in the atmosphere set the tray down in front of Andrea rather than Sir George for the first time since she had been staying at Eaton Square.

"Shall I pour?" Andrea asked.

"Please." Sir George watched her as she did so. She had beautiful hands, he thought, long and slender, very feminine but strong too in their way.

He appreciated beauty in women. His sexual preference for young men was truly that—a preference, and not a matter of fearing or disliking women. There was a story he had wanted to tell Andrea, but had not been able to bring himself to. Now, suddenly, he felt that he could.

"There's something I want to tell you, Andrea. When I

147

first saw you, filming that scene in the upper hallway at Oakridge Manor, I was really quite startled. You reminded me so
much of a young woman I was engaged to marry during the
war. Her name was Maggie. She was the daughter of a very
distinguished clergyman here in London. But I lost her in a
very terrible way. It was in 1944, she was just twenty-one then.
I was on leave. I'd been wounded slightly, nothing too serious.
I was on my way to her home in Chelsea, walking, and there
was an air raid warning. Buzz bombs, you know. I was only
about three blocks from her house. I went into one of the
shelters. You could hear the bombs droning overhead. But the
worst moment was always when they stopped making any
noise, because it meant they were going to fall. There was
one right above us, and then it was silent, and we heard the
explosion, very close by. I ran out, I ran to Maggie's house,
and it was gone, and the houses on either side. Just rubble.
And then, underneath a fallen door I saw her arm. I pulled at
her, and the arm—the arm just came away, half of it."

Andrea put her hands to her face. "Oh, my God," she said.
"How awful. How awful." There were tears in her eyes, as
she looked at him.

"It was a very long time ago," he said, his voice almost
steady. "But I wanted to tell you."

He could have said more, but did not. He could have told
her that for years after that he had found it difficult to respond
to any woman on a deep emotional level. It had not been until
he entered his forties that he had begun to consider marriage
once again, not only because he wanted an heir, but because
of a sense that there was something missing from his life. He
led a busy life, but in many ways a less than full one. Both
the house at Eaton Square and Oakridge Manor seemed to
him sometimes unoccupied, houses not homes, full of the past
but at present empty. Yet the women he had become interested in over the past few years had never seemed quite right.
Some of them had been a little silly, girls not women. Others
had seemed cold and managerial. He had not felt truly com-

148

fortable with any of them, and it had begun to seem that it might be impossible for him to find such comfort with any woman.

When he had first seen Andrea he had been not only startled but curious. The American women he had met over the years had always seemed a bit intimidating, so sure of themselves, calculating even. But while Andrea was clearly very sure of herself in some ways, he sensed in her a kind of yearning, even a degree of frustration that he found attractive; in some odd way it seemed to match his own sense of unfulfillment. As they had driven around the Cotswolds that first Sunday together, he had found himself taking pleasure in her own delight. When she had looked back at Stow-on-the-Wold and told him that she half expected it to have disappeared, he had been curiously moved, her reaction was so congruent with his own feelings. It had been at that moment that he had first considered asking her to stay at Eaton Square while she was in London. When she had touched the stone archway in the cloisters of Gloucester Cathedral, he had been certain that he wanted to know her better.

Now, as she silently handed him a fresh cup of tea, he was swept up by the feeling that she belonged here in this room in this house. It was as though it had been waiting for her—and he also suspected that she might have been searching for it.

"My dear," he said, taking her hand in his. "I wish that I had asked you to come to Paris with me. I missed you, to tell you the truth."

She squeezed his hand. "And I missed you. Much more than I expected."

"Tell me. Must you really go back to America next week?"

"I should. I don't want to."

"It would make me very happy to have you stay longer."

She appeared to hesitate. "They want me for a part, but it wouldn't be for a month or so."

"Ah, yes, there is your career."

149

She was silent for a long moment. "Perhaps I shouldn't say this, George. But when I'm with you my career doesn't seem very important."

"Then there is really no reason to hurry back to New York, is there?"

She looked straight at him with her very blue eyes. "No, there really isn't."

"Then you must stay here. Mustn't you?"

Andrea looked away for a moment and then back at him. She shook her head slightly, as though she did not know how to answer. At last she smiled and said, "I think perhaps so," she said.

Andrea was surprised by the warmth and firmness of his body. She couldn't have said why, but she had expected his skin to be cool. Some old myth about "blue blood," she supposed. They had been almost shy with each other in their first moments of nakedness, pressing tentatively one against the other. Perhaps, Andrea thought, it was because this was in some way a test, for both of them she suspected, not a test of their feelings but of the instinctive responses of the flesh, the secret urgings of the blood, the tingling anticipations of the nerve endings, the feel of skin upon skin.

He smelled subtly of sandalwood, clean and masculine; his large hands moved over her body with surprising delicacy, he kissed her eyelids, her neck. She could feel the largeness of his genitals against her thigh, and then he began to enter her, very slowly and gently, but at the same time with a certain sureness.

Andrea moved to meet him, her arms clasping him to her. It was going to be all right.

"My dear," said Myra Brockton, leaning confidentially across their table in the paneled dining room of the Connaught Hotel, "this is such truly splendid news that I think we must begin with a champagne cocktail. In fact, I've already ordered them."

Andrea laughed. "I think that's a wonderful idea."

"I do think it's a shame though that you and George have decided against a big wedding. I adore big weddings, so long as they're not my own."

"Well, I'm really quite happy for it to be small and private. George said that if we invited more than a dozen people, we'd have to include at least two hundred. I'd rather meet people a little more gradually. George hasn't said so, but I have a feeling that the idea of his marrying an American, and a very young American at that, is going to take some getting used to for some of the people he knows."

"Oh, I wouldn't worry unduly about that, my dear. I went through it all when I married my second husband. A refugee Jewess and former opera singer marrying a cousin of the Queen! They were scandalized, even though he was a very *distant* cousin indeed. You will encounter a good deal of thinly veiled disdain, I'm sure, especially from the women. They'll say things like, 'I suppose you must find life very *different* here than in America,' with the voice going up half an octave on the word *different*. That kind of remark. The thing to do is always to agree with them and then add something or other about how extremely *nice* everyone has been. The English aristocracy is utterly unequipped to deal with being told they're nice, and they'll soon enough let you alone."

Andrea would have giggled aloud, but the waiter, who gave the impression of being a gentleman of vast and serious importance, arrived at that moment with their champagne cocktails.

"You make me feel much better," Andrea said, lifting her glass.

"A toast to your happiness, my dear. We foreigners must stick together." Myra sipped. "How delicious," she said. "As you probably know, George has wanted to marry for some time, and we've all been hoping for it, but I must say some of the prospects did give us pause. There was a French countess who could have chilled our champagne with one glance. Perfectly dreadful woman. Charles and I are so happy it's you, and I assure you that everyone else will be too, once they've gotten to know you."

"Thank you, Myra. If I may return the compliment, I think that one of the nicest things about marrying George is that I'll be able to see a lot of you. I mean that."

"The feeling is mutual, my dear. Half the people I know pretend not to hear me most of the time. I'm very amusing, if I do say so myself, and it's very nice indeed to hear a little appreciative laughter on occasion. And since we're going to be very good friends, I must ask you a terribly indiscreet question."

"Of course," Andrea said, feeling only mild apprehension.

"Well then, are you in love with George?" Myra leaned toward her once again, her ruby necklace swinging forward against the white tablecloth.

If the question had been asked by anyone else, Andrea would have been shocked. She also would have lied. But she felt certain that it was very important to tell Myra the truth, that it would mean the beginning of a true friendship, an alliance, if she was honest. She thought she was probably going to need that alliance, one day, one year, sometime.

"No, Myra, I can't say that I am. I'm very fond of him, very. I know I can be the wife he wants, in all respects. I don't know quite how to put it, but, well, I think I can cherish him without being in love with him. I think that's possible."

Myra leaned back in her chair, beaming. "Without question, my dear. Your honesty itself is proof. I myself have been married four times, as you may know. I married my first husband for love, my second for money and position, my third out of passion, and Charles for the sake of comfortable companionship. There are many kinds of marriages, and I wouldn't say for a moment that those based on love or passion are necessarily the best. Although I *would* venture that sexual passion is almost bound to lead to disaster. A sexually passionate man is almost invariably a sexually promiscuous man. That's an unhappy fact but in my experience a fact nonetheless. I think you will be just what George needs, and I hope that he will make you as happy as I know you can make him. You're a remarkable young woman, Andrea. I seldom say that to anyone and almost never to a woman." Myra began to laugh, a deep, affectionate chortle. "Especially a young one. So consider yourself blessed," she said, and raised her hands momentarily in a mock benediction.

"And now," she said, "what are we going to eat?"

Chapter Six

GEORGE HARRINGTON HAD NOT BEEN so pleased with his life in many years. In the six months since their marriage, Andrea had added new dimensions to his existence in even more ways than he had expected. For many years he had hidden from himself, he now realized, the knowledge of how truly lonely he had been. The sense of emptiness that had hung over the house in Eaton Square for so long, like cobwebs in the corners, had been swept away. It had become a home again, something it had not fully been since his mother's death more than fifteen years earlier.

Aside from redecorating the master bedroom in fresh pastel colors more in keeping with the small Renoir over the fireplace, she had changed the house little. He had told her that she might do as she pleased with it, but she seemed genuinely to cherish the accumulated treasures of successive generations that filled its rooms. She often asked him if he knew the history of various objects or furnishings, and he was surprised at how much he remembered of what his mother had told him over the years. In recounting to Andrea how the Rose Medallion bowl had been brought back directly from China in the hold of one of the last of the clipper ships, or that the ornate mirror in the hallway had been purchased by his great-grandmother on a trip to Venice in the 1840's, he found himself taking considerable pleasure in renewing his acquaintance with his own family history.

But if Andrea had not changed the house physically, she had greatly altered its spirit. When he had been on his own, George had entertained only occasionally and then on a rather small scale. As a bachelor he was not really expected to return the favor of every invitation, and he had spent more evenings out than at home. That had all changed now. They gave a dinner party or an after-theater supper at least twice a week, parties that Andrea arranged with a firm and surprisingly sophisticated hand. George had always left such matters as the choice of table settings and china, the arrangement of flowers, and the preparation of meals entirely to Jeremy and Mrs. Evelyn. Sometimes he suggested a certain dish but the details of the menu had always been Mrs. Evelyn's province, and he had been afraid at first that she and Jeremy might resent Andrea's intrusion into their domain. But Andrea had clearly handled the situation with great tact. Although she had from the first taken a hand in all aspects of the planning of their parties, she had been careful to ask both Mrs. Evelyn and Jeremy for suggestions and advice, and she had obviously won their respect since Mrs. Evelyn had commented only a few weeks after the marriage how nice it was to have a mistress of the house again.

When George had decided to marry Andrea, he had realized that it might be difficult for her at first in terms of gaining full acceptance among the self-appointed doyennes of London society. Some were titled and some were not, but almost all of them took their social standing with more seriousness than George himself really approved of. Indeed, he sometimes found rather comical the inflated importance that many of his acquaintances and even some of his friends accorded to matters of breeding and style. Breeding came first with some, style with others. And if one had enough of either, one could get away with being merely well-off rather than truly rich. If you were old enough, and your lineage sufficiently ancient, you could even get away with virtual impoverishment, especially if your financial downfall had come about because the tides of history, revolution or the leveling effects of industrialism, had swept your power away. That is, reminiscences of past glory could sustain one.

But there was great suspicion of the newly rich, and of

Americans. George knew that Myra Brockton could be of great help to Andrea in dispelling certain prejudices; Myra had been through it all and would be able to guide Andrea around some of the thorniest thickets. If Myra liked you and counted you as a friend, many others would follow. But in the end Andrea would have to do it for herself, and though certain she could do it eventually, George had been astonished at how very speedily she had mastered the arcane rules of the game.

She had done it because she surpassed people's expectations. Although she herself had said to George on several occasions that she still had a great deal to learn, she had natural gifts of style and taste on which to draw while she was learning. There had never been any difficulty in charming the men—she was young and lovely and amusing. But those same qualities could easily have antagonized many of the women. That they did not, George felt, was due to Andrea's instinctive understanding of what was appropriate. The clothes she bought for herself were lovely but they were never flamboyant, and they were chosen to mask rather than to show off her youth. There were no plunging necklines, no slit skirts, but instead a chaste elegance of line and fabric. She managed to appear confident without being brash, to be subtly deferential without seeming either naive or calculating. On several occasions, George overheard her asking various women advice even though, he was aware, she already knew the answers. She was acting, he saw that, but he doubted if anybody else did, except Myra. She seemed to understand instinctively both the demands and the limits of her role, and she played it with great finesse. He was proud of her, and amused by her performance at one and the same time.

But it was her dinner parties that really made the difference. In the early autumn she had begun taking cooking lessons from both the famous Madame Wu, whose small, elegant restaurant in Hampstead, serving dinner only and offering a limited, select menu rather than the endless pages of virtually indistinguishable dishes served by most Chinese restaurants in the city had become the rage of London; and from the authoritarian Jacques Renard, who had been known to throw women out of his classes if they proved to be what he referred to as "dilettantes," by gossiping instead of paying full attention to the achievement of the proper consistency of their *quenelles de brochet*. Whatever Andrea may have gained from these classes in the way of culinary expertise, she clearly needed no lessons in the matter of the presentation of a meal. The china she selected from the long row of cabinets in the butler's pantry, the flowers on the table, even the place cards were orchestrated to complement or echo the colors of the food that was being served. As they sat down to dinner, guests were surprised and charmed to find at each place a handwritten menu—Andrea had found an elderly Austrian with a tiny shop in Notting Hill Gate who did exquisite calligraphy. To find a printed menu at one's place at a large function was one thing; a hand-lettered listing on fine Italian paper in a private home was delightfully unusual.

The same elegance of presentation followed throughout the meal. Each course, for instance, was arranged with delicate artfulness on each person's plate. The usual method of serving in upper-class English homes was to have the butler pass the food on large platters, with each guest helping himself. It took Andrea some coaxing to persuade Mrs. Evelyn and Jeremy that a more stylish effect could be created by serving most dishes in the kitchen, arranging the food in the carefully balanced patterns Andrea had devised and tutored them in. But as the guests exclaimed over how beautiful everything looked, Jeremy and Mrs. Evelyn were soon convinced of the point of doing things Andrea's way, and even began to make suggestions themselves.

Some guests assumed that Andrea had picked up a number of her ideas from the new wave of French cooking then taking hold in France, led by such chefs as Paul Bocuse, Michel Guérard, and the Troisgros brothers. But in fact she knew little of their work, and nouvelle cuisine hadn't yet had any real effect even on the French restaurants of London. Her approach was partly instinctive and partly a legacy from her mother, whose smorgasbord platters had always been small works of art. "If the food is so pretty that people want to just look at it for a minute before eating, they will enjoy the eating more" had always been her motto.

George Harrington's friends were impressed. Instead of the brash young fortune seeker they had feared, they discovered a woman of surprising sophistication and accomplishment. George knew that Andrea had been fully accepted when he overheard old Sir Wilfred Ainsley mention her one afternoon at the Oxford and Cambridge Club. Ensconced in his favorite red leather chair in the paneled library, sipping port instead of tea, Sir Wilfred intoned in the half-shout of the unadmitted deaf, "My wife tells me young George Harrington has found himself quite a splendid wife at last. From America too, the more surprising."

He was addressing his nephew Robert, whom George had been at Oxford with, living just across the hall from him at Magdalen, and who had been to dinner at Eaton Square only the previous week. He had seen George come into the library and George half expected to hear him give Sir Wilfred the warning cough that was so often necessary to prevent the old man from shouting on in what could be embarrassing circumstances. But Robert simply replied, "Yes, she is extremely charming. And a superb hostess I might add."

"Ah, you've been to dinner, then? Lucky fellow, from what I understand."

Andrea laughed delightedly when George repeated this exchange, but she was even more pleased when an item in the society column of the *Times* had noted that an invitation to dinner at Sir George and Lady Harrington's had become particularly coveted that winter season. George tended to the old-school belief that managing to stay out of the newspapers was more of an accomplishment than getting into them, but he was glad for her even so. Americans, after all, looked at the matter of publicity from an entirely different angle. And it was the *Times,* not the *Evening Standard.* Besides, the glow on her face when she came rushing into his study with the paper gave him great pleasure.

"A coveted invitation!" Andrea repeated exultantly after reading the paragraph aloud to him.

"And so it should be," he said smiling.

She leaned over to hug him as he sat at his desk. "I'm so happy, George."

He kissed her cheek. "And I'm very happy for you, my dear," he said.

Soon, though, he thought after she had left him, it would be necessary for them to talk about children again. They had made a pact when they married. Andrea had been very honest with him—she was on the pill, and she wanted to continue taking it for a while. She wanted children, but first she needed time to establish herself as his wife, as Lady Andrea Harrington, time to get to know his friends and to make friends of her own, time to adjust to what was after all a whole new world. And he had agreed; it was a perfectly sensible request. But now she had achieved the standing she wanted, perhaps sooner than she had expected. A child must be next.

He looked out the window at the barren garden, the rose bushes mere pruned twigs, the rhododendron leaves curled inward against the January cold. He would give her another few months before discussing it, until spring, until the first of the roses bloomed. Then it would be time.

At the wheel of the pale yellow Rolls-Royce George had given her as a wedding present, Andrea drove northwest out of London on M-1 heading for Oakridge Manor. She had to make a conscious effort to stay within the speed limit. M-1 was heavily patrolled, as well it should have been, since it was the most dangerous highway in Britain, and one of the most heavily traveled. This was no time for an accident, and yet she could not wait to see George, she knew how thrilled he would be.

It was a late-October day, and drizzly. Ahead of her there seemed to be a break in the weather; she could see the sun shining obliquely through the clouds. She hoped it would clear by the time she reached the manor. The news she had was meant for sunshine. Although a rainbow would be all right, too, she thought, and smiled to herself.

George had been in France for three days. They were to spend the weekend at the manor, and ordinarily Andrea would have been there waiting for him. But Dr. Spann could not give her definite confirmation until late morning, and she had sent Jeremy and Mrs. Evelyn ahead in the Bentley to pick George up at the airport and drive him to Oakridge Manor. When he had called from Paris the night before, she had had a half dozen excuses prepared to explain why she was coming up later in the day, but it hadn't really been necessary to use them since he had a business appointment at the manor in the early afternoon anyway.

Andrea hadn't even told George that she had gone to Dr. Spann; she had wanted to be sure she was right. It had been late April when she had gone off the pill, and although George had not said so directly, she thought that he had somewhat naively expected her to become pregnant almost at once. She'd told him that when a woman had been on the pill for a number of years, it often took two or three months for the body to return to normal fertility cycles. But it had been more than five months now, and she knew that he was impatient, however much he tried to hide it. In a cabinet in his study there was a collection of antique toy soldiers, exquisitely realistic miniatures. She had never seen him touch them until one afternoon this past September when she had found him rearranging them. He had actually blushed, and she had not really believed him when he told her that he was merely wondering how much they were worth these days. She was certain he was thinking of the possible son who might one day play with them as he had long ago.

Because she realized how much he cared, she hadn't said anything when she missed a period. He had been in France at the time and might not have noticed anyway, since that was one aspect of female sexuality he seemed to find embarrassing, perhaps even distasteful, and clearly tried to ignore. But the missed period, together with a slight tenderness of her breasts and an occasional vague queasiness, had decided Andrea that she should make an appointment with Dr. Spann. He had been George's, and indeed Mrs. Evelyn's and Jeremy's, doctor for many years, and when he had called that morning she had known instantly by the delight in his voice that the test had proved positive. She was carrying the child George so greatly wanted.

She hoped that it would be a boy, not only for George's sake but for her own. If it were to be a girl, then there would have to be another child soon. Andrea had decided that she wanted two children. Although she herself had reaped the benefits of being an only child in terms of exclusive attention, she had often wished that she had had a brother. Not a sister, that would have diverted too much attention from her, but it would have been nice to have had a brother, especially an older one. On the other hand, she didn't want to have another child too soon. Thanks to Mrs. Evelyn's motherly presence, she was certain that having children in the house would in no way impede the pleasure she took in being Lady Andrea Harrington, but being pregnant would. She didn't want to spend most of the next two or three years being pregnant; she wanted to have a boy and then wait another three or four years before bearing another child. George would not object to that once there was a male heir to his title. But if it was not a boy he would want to try again as quickly as possible.

"It simply has to be a boy," Andrea said aloud as the Rolls sped toward Oakridge Manor. The drizzle was ending as she passed from Oxfordshire into Gloustershire. The sky

161

was still overcast but the clouds were moving swiftly southward. By the time she saw George, it would be sunny. She was sure of it.

When she arrived at Oakridge Manor, she found George standing in the entrance hall saying good-bye to a dark-haired, handsome young man whom she vaguely recognized but could not place exactly.

"Ah, here you are, my dear. You remember Riccardo Bianchetti, from Venice?"

"From Venice?" Her mind was too full of her own news to make the connection immediately, or even to care very much. But then she did remember. "Oh, yes. The Secret Garden. What a lovely luncheon that was."

"Thank you, madam," Riccardo said, bowing slightly.

Andrea's memories of their honeymoon in Venice had all run together into a kind of impressionistic blur, of breakfasts on the terrace of the Hotel Cipriani, gazing across the busy waters of the basin toward St. Mark's, of days of wandering through the narrow passageways along side canals, of small bridges over the dark reflecting waters that led to unexpected sunlit squares. She remembered the early evenings spent sipping Negronis in the Piazza San Marco, the lingering light turning the great bronze horses of the basicila to gold, the pigeons fluttering away from strollers, the two competing cafe orchestras on opposite sides of the great plaza filling the air with the sounds of "Lara's Theme" or a Strauss waltz.

There had been one wonderful meal after another. A classic risotto with peas upstairs at Harry's Bar; exquisitely tender calves' liver at Le Fenice; braised fresh tuna steaks with garlic and capers at Al Graspo de Ua. And luncheon at what George had called "the Secret Garden."

That morning they had gone to see Tintoretto's vast New Testament canvases at the School of St. Rocco, and then strolled slowly away from the Grand Canal into the warren

162

of waterways, bridges, and small squares that separated it from the Giudecca Canal.

"How in the world do you find your way around so easily?" Andrea asked with a laugh. "I'd be lost in five minutes."

"It's easier than you'd think," George said, taking her arm. "Every little canal has something unique about it. Do you see that house there with the bright yellow shutters?"

"Yes."

"Those shutters have been yellow since right after the war. They repaint them occasionally, but always yellow. Venice is like that. There isn't much that changes. And besides, if one does get lost, one simply discovers some wonderful little corner of the city one's never stumbled upon before."

"I'd do a lot of discovering, obviously."

"Are you getting hungry?"

"Ravenous."

"Come along, then, and I'll show you another hidden wonder."

They walked over arched bridges and around corners. An occasional small boat slid by beneath them. Bright patches of drying laundry hung from balconies, and the shouts of children echoed from some hidden source. A gray cat leapt nimbly from one windowsill to another and lay down to sun itself between two pots of herbs.

At one corner, George stopped suddenly and looked both ways. He made a small clicking sound of disapproval.

"What's wrong?"

"I'm being proved a liar. They've changed the color of that house across the way. But I recognize the carved faces on the balcony. We turn left."

They passed over one more bridge and after going a few paces farther, George said, "Here we are."

There was a walled garden with an open wooden gate. Two large trees, unusual in Venice, shaded the garden from the sun, and under the trees were a dozen tables with blue and white checked tablecloths.

"This is one of my favorite places in Venice," George said. "I call it 'the Secret Garden' because you almost never see tourists here, mostly Venetian businessmen or foreigners who've lived in the city a long time. Maybe for that reason the food is wonderful."

George was quite right about the food. They began with a cold seafood salad of shrimp, mussels, and octopus, very fresh and tangy—even the octopus was tender and juicy. Then there was pasticcio with four cheeses, gossamer layers of pasta sauced with a creamy amalgam of Swiss, Gouda, Fontina, and Parmesan cheeses. Andrea had seldom tasted anything that was simultaneously so rich and so light. While they were eating their dessert, fresh peaches in red wine, a young man wearing a long white apron over jeans and a white shirt, came out of the kitchen into the garden. Andrea noticed him, his curly black hair, intense eyes, and very white teeth, before George did. The young man glanced at them and then hurried over to their table with a surprised smile.

It was Riccardo Bianchetti. George had seemed very surprised to see him. "I thought you were in Birmingham," he said after somewhat awkwardly introducing him to Andrea.

"There was a tragedy, a fire. The restaurant will not reopen for two months. I should have let you know but I thought you would be busy with your wedding plans," Riccardo said. He nodded at Andrea and smiled. For some reason she didn't like his smile. There was a kind of knowing quality about it that seemed almost impertinent.

"Yes, of course," George said, almost shortly. "You're in Venice for the summer, then?"

"Yes, that's so. My aunt needed an operation, not serious, but since I was free it was a good moment. I've taken her place in the kitchen. It is like old times, as they say."

George had explained later to Andrea that he had helped Riccardo get his English working papers and a job as a chef at a Birmingham restaurant that was owned by an acquaintance. Even so, Andrea was somewhat surprised to find him visiting at Oakridge Manor. She was even a little annoyed. She'd known that George had an appointment, and that she might have to wait to tell him her news; she might not have minded so much if it had been someone important. Perhaps, though, that was unfair. He was a fine chef, and George had known him since he was a boy waiting tables at his aunt's restaurant.

Perhaps sensing her feelings, George said, "Riccardo is going to be opening a restaurant of his own in Brighton. There are a number of people financing it, and I've agreed to put up a few shares."

"Oh, I see." Andrea turned to Riccardo. "The best of luck to you. I hope you'll be serving that wonderful pasticcio we had in Venice."

"Certainly."

Andrea had a sudden impulse; she might as well get something out of this encounter, she thought. "Would it be possible to pry that recipe out of you? Or is it a family secret?"

"I would be happy to give it to you, ma'am," Riccardo said, although Andrea suspected he probably would rather not have.

"Thank you. That's very nice of you."

"My pleasure." Riccardo shook hands with George. "Thank you for your help. It means very much to me."

"Of course, Riccardo. Let me know how it all progresses."

There was something about Riccardo that bothered Andrea. On the surface his manner toward George, or herself for that matter, was perfectly correct. But it was as though he were holding himself in check somehow, as though there were things that were not being said.

But then he was gone, and she put the thought out of her mind. As she walked back down the hallway with George, she asked, "Do we have any splits of champagne on ice?"

"I'm sure we must."

"Good. I think I'd like a glass of champagne."

George looked at his watch. "At three in the afternoon?"

"At three in the afternoon."

George stopped and looked at her. "Is it what I think?"

"What do you think?" Andrea asked with a laugh.

"I'm not sure I dare say."

"Well, then, I won't keep you in suspense any longer." She put her arms around him and whispered in his ear. "I'm pregnant."

"Oh, my darling. How wonderful! What splendid news." He held her close, kissing her again and again. "A split of champagne! This calls for a magnum. Come along, we must find Jeremy and Mrs. Evelyn. We're going to have a party!"

Andrea swore George and Mrs. Evelyn and Jeremy to secrecy. She was having a luncheon to celebrate Myra's sixtieth birthday the following Wednesday, and she wanted to surprise Myra with the news, and to ask her to be the child's godmother. The luncheon was already a special occasion in another way. A writer and a photographer from *Town & Country*, who were doing an article on London hostesses, were coming that day. The announcement of her news would make it even more of an occasion.

As Myra's favorite color was pink, Andrea had decided to plan a meal that would be a virtual celebration of pinkness. Mrs. Evelyn, who knew the contents of the house even more thoroughly than George, steered Andrea to a cedar chest in the attic in which she found an ornate Victorian tablecloth embroidered with rose buds. There were no napkins, but Andrea was able to find suitable ones at Liberty's. The china was easy—the Meissen dogwood pattern that had been given to George's grandmother by her dear friend Princess Alexandra as a wedding present. It was a service for twelve originally, but over the years several pieces had been broken; fortunately Andrea was having only eight guests, and there were enough complete settings for ten. As a centerpiece, she used a pink cyclamen, surrounded by eight tiny cymbidiums of the pale pink Castle Hill variety, each tied by a ribbon to a place card, to be taken home as favors. When she had told the florist at Harrods that she wanted eight of that variety of the miniature orchids, to be picked up the day before the party, he had told her it might be difficult to find them, but as always, he had come through. Harrods always did if you gave them enough time.

The menu itself presented some problem in that each course had to be photographed for *Town & Country*. Andrea decided that the simplest solution was to begin with a cold course that could be photographed on the dining table itself before the guests were seated, and to make a duplicate of the main course with which the photographer could take as much time in the kitchen as he needed while the guests were being served.

She wanted to serve a pink champagne, but when she consulted George, as she always did about the wine, he made a face.

"You don't approve?"

"Well, I know it's popular in America, but I've always thought it was loathsome stuff."

"Then we won't have it," Andrea said quickly, but she felt a little put down.

A smile softened George's face. "I don't mean to be rude about it, my dear. It's probably pure snobbery on my part. After all, a great deal of champagne is made from Pinot Noir grapes. They remove the skins very early in the process so as to get a white champagne. For a pink they simply leave the skins in a little longer to give color, so in one sense it's perfectly legitimate. But I've always thought it was inferior, even so. Perhaps you could serve a rosé, say a Tavel. But I would stick with a vintage Dom Pérignon. This extravaganza of pinkness is great fun, I realize, and Myra will be delighted, but it can be carried a little far, don't you think?"

"I suppose it can." Andrea was annoyed, not with George but with herself. He was, she realized, quite right. Pink champagne would be a little too cute, probably. Myra would be amused, but she had to think of the *Town & Country* article as well. She wanted the luncheon to be elegant as well as fun.

"You're quite right, George. Let's do have a Dom Pérignon."

"Fine. I'll see to it, then."

"Thank you, darling. I wish you'd change your mind and join us."

"No, this should be strictly a female affair, I think. They'll be giving you all kinds of advice, I'm sure, when they hear the news. I don't want to intrude."

"How could you intrude? It's your child, too."

"For the next few months, my dear, it is mostly your child. That's simply the way of it, isn't it? But perhaps I'll join you for coffee and receive my congratulations."

"Oh, do. I'd like that."

George put his arms around her and held her close. "I will," he said.

The luncheon was as much of a success as Andrea had hoped. They began with Parma ham, sliced tissue-paper thin and arranged so that it looked like a flat-petaled old-fashioned rose, with slices of avocado curving out from beneath it like leaves. The main course was a hot salmon mousse with a nantua sauce rich with tiny shrimp. The writer from *Town & Country*, a stylish woman in her early thirties named Helen Rawson who was making a name for herself as a food writer, marveled at the smoothness and lightness of the mousse. "I haven't had a mousse this light in a private home ever, I don't think. How in the world do you do it?"

"My husband brought me back a machine from Paris that's quite extraordinary. Apparently you can only buy it from restaurant suppliers. It's electrically powered and does amazing things with purees, but it also chops and even slices."

"You mean one of those professional food processors?"

"That's right."

"You are fortunate. I understand they've developed a small version that's just being marketed for home use in America. I have one on order in fact. I think you're in the forefront of a rage, Lady Andrea. But I doubt if many people will have the true restaurant version."

"Well, I find it almost indispensable. It saves a great deal of time, and it can produce a smoothness that you simply can't get in a blender, even if you force the puree through cheesecloth afterwards. Which takes forever of course."

Just before serving the dessert, a bombe made of layers of strawberry, plum, and cassis ices with a fresh raspberry sauce, Andrea gave Myra the pink envelope she had placed on the sideboard and asked her to read it aloud.

"I hope this isn't another present," said Myra, who had opened her gifts before lunch.

"Not exactly. More of a request." Andrea could not help grinning.

Myra tore the envelope open with dispatch. "Dearest Myra," she read, "Since this is *your* birthday, it seemed an appropriate time to ask you if you would be godmother to George's and my first child, whose birth date will be late in the coming month of May. I hope you will accept this very special but hopefully not difficult duty."

Everyone, including Helen Rawson, burst into delighted applause and began talking simultaneously.

"My dear Andrea," said Myra, with tears in her eyes. "You do me great honor. But don't you think I'm a little long in the tooth to be a godmother?"

"Of course not. You'll live to be a hundred, Myra, everyone knows that. And by then he'll have children of his own."

"Him?" Myra raised her eyebrows.

"Well, I hope so. I'm willing it. George would be so happy. But if it's a girl, you would still be the best godmother any child could ask for."

"Then I accept," said Myra, and got up from her chair at the opposite end of the table, and came to Andrea and embraced her. "We will all put our strength toward willing a healthy child, boy or girl. And now if I may have another glass of that marvelous Dom Pérignon, we will all drink to your health and the safe delivery of your child. Raise your glasses, ladies."

Chapter Seven

ANDREA SAT QUIETLY IN ONE CORNER of the room on the second floor at Eaton Square that George had occupied as a boy. The crib in which he had lain almost a half century earlier, and his father before that, had been brought down from the attic and refurbished. Its oaken slats gleamed with a new coat of varnish. The room had been repainted, and there were fresh bright blue curtains at the windows. In the opposite corner stood the small rocking horse with its bright red reins and real leather saddle, a contributory present from Myra. "Boy or girl, the child should learn to ride," she had said. "A rocking horse is a good beginning."

It was a bright Monday afternoon. The previous Wednesday, May 19, 1971, Charles George Augustus Harrington had been born at 9:03 P.M. But the nursery at Eaton Square was still unoccupied. The crib was empty. Andrea's child, the boy George had hoped for, lay instead within the antiseptic confines of an oxygen tent.

He had been born with a hole in his heart. Sometimes, the doctors said, their voices low and sympathetic but without a hint of the real optimism Andrea longed to hear, such a child could survive for weeks or months, long enough to make an operation feasible. They used words like *prognosis* and *feasible*, and Andrea had been glad to get away from them, to come home and wait in silence.

She had seen Charles only once, just before leaving the hospital herself. He was perfectly formed outwardly; you wouldn't have known that anything was wrong except for the flush on his face as he struggled to breathe, and the slight bluish tinge to his hands and feet that was the result of his impeded circulation. His blue eyes looking up at her from under the plastic tent seemed puzzled, but he did not cry. It was as though crying was an effort that was beyond him. She wanted to pick him up, hold him to her, comfort him, but she could not. She wondered if she would ever be able to do that.

Andrea jumped. Down the hall the telephone had begun to ring. It had been ringing all day, as word spread among their friends. Even Princess Margaret, whom Andrea had met only three times, had telephoned with words of encouragement. George, who knew her better, had talked with her. He seemed buoyed by the calls, and she let him take most of them. She found it difficult to know what to say, but George was unfailingly gracious, the embodiment of that peculiarly British tradition of the stiff upper lip. But Andrea was convinced that underneath his surface calm he was taking it harder than she was. She moved back and forth between the hope that Charles would survive, and a certainty that it would be a miracle if he did. She didn't really believe in miracles, and she found her thoughts wandering to the prospect of carrying another child.

She had had an easy pregnancy, the kind other women envy. She had looked radiant instead of blotchy, as a number of women had commented with a certain tinge of jealousy, an undertone of pique. And she had suffered surprisingly little discomfort. Her back had bothered her some in the final weeks, and she had found it uncomfortable to sleep on her back, waking in the night and shifting to her side. But it had not been as physically wearing as she had expected. Nor had her life been altered all that much; until the last six weeks they had entertained and gone out almost as much as ever. Bruce Halliwell, with whom she corresponded regularly, had even teased her about it, beginning his letters, "Dear Expectant Hostess."

To have another child soon was certainly not what she had wanted or planned, but she felt that it was the only course if Charles did not survive. She avoided thinking the words *live* or *die; survive* was the word the doctors used and she clung to it herself, to its neutrality. There would have to be another child for George's sake. There had been a joyousness about him over the past months that she had found deeply touching. If Charles couldn't be saved, she knew that George would never be able to recapture that sense of excited anticipation even if she did become pregnant again. It would be difficult for them both, she suspected, always wondering if the next child would be all right, but if they didn't try she was certain that nothing would ever be quite the same between herself and George. He had married her to bear him children. She had brought other pleasures to his life, yes; he had said so, and she could feel it in him even when he didn't speak of it. But she wasn't sure that those other pleasures could surmount the loss of his son.

Once again the telephone was ringing.

She stopped rocking and listened. The house seemed unnaturally quiet. It had been that way ever since she had come home from the hospital. Mrs. Evelyn had lost her natural bustle, and Jeremy moved from room to room with the silence of a shadow. It was as though Charles were lying gravely ill here in the nursery itself and not in an antiseptic room halfway across London.

But at this moment the silence seemed suddenly deeper than ever, as though the house itself were holding its breath.

She knew, in a flash of intuition, that George was coming to find her, and that she should not be in this room when he did. She glanced once again at the rocking horse in the corner. It was so bright, so shiny new, but all at once it seemed forlorn. On impulse she went over to it and touched its glossy head, setting it into motion. Then she quickly turned and left the room.

He was running along a street that was both familiar and strange. The buildings along the sides of the street kept changing, as though two slides had been put into a projector simultaneously, so that the eye focused first on one vista and then another. It seemed to be afternoon, but the air was so thick with dust that the light was violet. He turned a corner and the buildings began to fall around him, without sound, the brick walls expanding like balloons and then bursting outward as though they had been pricked.

He heard the sound of a child crying, a baby. He stopped and looked to either side. The sound came again and he turned and climbed over a pile of rubble. A tiny arm extended out from beneath a fallen lintel. He grasped it, and the miniature fingers closed around his own. He pulled, and the arm came away by itself, like the limb of a broken doll. But the fingers were still tight about his own. He tried to throw it away, but could not get it loose.

"Let go," he cried. "For God's sake, let go!"

"George." It was a woman's voice this time. "It's all right, George. It's all right."

"Don't," he said. "Don't touch me. Stop it. Let go!"

"George! Wake up, George. It's all right. It's all right."

"Andrea?"

"Yes, George. It's all right."

"Andrea?"

"Yes. It was just a nightmare."

"Dear God," he said. He was awake now. "I'm sorry," he said. "I'm sorry to wake you."

She was holding him in her arms. He sat up, disentangling himself. "How many nights has it been? Three, four in a row?"

"It doesn't matter. It's all right."

"I think I'd better sleep in the other room," he said, getting out of bed and standing in the darkness.

"You don't have to do that. Stay here with me."

"It doesn't help," he said. "I'm sorry, Andrea. I'm so terribly sorry." He knew he was going to begin to weep, and he made his way as quickly as possible across the darkened room to the door.

174

                              *   *   *

The Gables, an exclusive health club for women, was
situated near Covent Garden. Its pool and saunas and exercise
rooms resounded with laughter and a gossipy hubbub that
would have appalled the husbands and lovers of its members;
male establishments of this sort seldom echoed with anything
more than a splash, a grunt, and a groan. But The Gables,
however much the women who flocked to it might wish to
retain or regain their figures, was first and foremost a gossip
mart, a place to exchange confidences, rumors, and, not un-
usually, lies. With an exquisite understanding of the needs of
their clientele, the owners of the club had designed a central
lounge ringed with high-backed and heavily upholstered booths
where it was possible to talk without being overheard. Only
the occasional high-pitched laugh floating to the ceiling gave
any clue as to the nature of the conversation taking place in
the next booth.

Sitting in one of these booths, Andrea and Myra sipped
glasses of carrot juice decorated with radish flowers, a visual
if not precisely a flavor treat. It was not, Andrea thought, what
she really needed to lift her spirits, but she still had a pound
or two to lose before she would be satisfied that she had
regained her pre-pregnancy figure.

"I know it's a difficult period for you, my dear," Myra was
saying, "But I truly don't see any other remedy than time."

"It's been nearly three months. George simply seems to
withdraw from me more and more. I thought these things
were supposed to be especially devastating for the mother."
Andrea tried to keep the bitterness out of her voice, but she
was not succeeding very well.

"Surely that depends on the circumstances, Andrea. In
this case, it seems obvious that George wanted a child even
more than you did."

"If only it had been a girl."

"Yes, I know. It was rotten luck all around."

"I suppose if we did have another child, it would turn out
to be a girl, just to spite us."

"I don't like to hear you talk that way, Andrea," Myra said sternly.

"Myra, he won't even sleep with me. The day Charles died I told George we should have another child as quickly as possible. All he said was, 'Perhaps.' He's only attempted to make love twice in all this time. And I mean attempted."

"Ahh, I see. I didn't realize."

"I thought it was just the depression. But it's more than that. It's as though any idea of making love were immediately connected for him with the loss of Charles. The thing that's so galling is that I'm quite sure he's having an affair."

"That wouldn't surprise me. It seems quite to be expected in fact. When men are unhappy they usually have affairs."

"With another man?" Andrea said coldly, looking straight at Myra.

Myra was silent for a moment. "Well, my dear, I assumed you knew what you were getting into when you married George." She sighed. "I considered bringing it up, but it seemed a bit sticky, and I didn't think you were exactly naive. There are a few bachelors in their late forties who are womanizers, but they are decidedly the exception. Even among the married men in this country, having a male lover on the side is extremely common, especially among the upper classes. There are all kinds of theories about it, most of them having to do with the atmosphere of all those morbid boys' schools. But since I totally fail to understand the eroticism of rugby football or playing slavey—fagging, they call it, would you believe—to the senior boys, I just accept it as one of those mysterious but very real facts of life. Most wives seem to take it in the same spirit. They'd be far more upset if their husbands were seeing other women. Doing whatever they do with young men is looked upon more as a sort of childish male hobby, like polo. Or as Maggie Courtauld states it, putting up with a husband's taste for buggery is one of the privileges of rank."

Andrea laughed in spite of herself. "Sir William?"

176

"But of course, my dear. He has a mad passion for cockney corner boys. Of course that's hardly unusual. There seems to be some fatal perfume exuded by lower-class toughs that simply overwhelms the English gentleman."

"George's is foreign, I think."

"Even more enticing. Lower class as well?"

"I suppose, although he has very polished manners."

"Dear me, you've actually met him."

"If I'm right, I've met him twice. Once in Venice, on our honeymoon. He was substituting for some relative as chef at a restaurant we went to. A favorite of George's apparently. He called it 'the Secret Garden.'"

"How typical," Myra interposed. "But tell me more."

"George obviously didn't expect to see him there, he was supposedly working as a chef in England. Then I saw him again at Oakridge Manor. George said he was putting some money into a restaurant Riccardo—that's his first name, I can't remember the last—that he was opening in Brighton. I only saw him for a few moments that time, he was just leaving." Andrea hesitated. "You'll like this Myra. I had just driven up from London to tell George I was pregnant."

Myra chortled but at the same time reached out and patted Andrea's hand. "My dear, my dear. Life is full of little dramas we don't even know are happening at the time. More's the pity."

"Well, to tell you the truth, I don't think George was involved with him, at least sexually, then. He may have been before. Looking back, I would say he was, that that was why he was so nervous when Riccardo turned up in Venice. But I don't think there was anything else until—until recently."

"Quite probably not. I'm sure you're right. He probably put all that aside when he married you. The new-leaf fantasy. Why is it that men are so much more successful at fooling themselves into thinking they can turn over new leaves than we women? Now there's a profound question for you, my dear."

"To which I'm sure you have an answer," Andrea said, smiling.

"Of course. Never ask questions you can't answer and you will quickly establish a reputation as a wise old bird. Or a smart fledgling as the case may be. We're realists, my dear. That is the major job of women, to be realistic. That's why I can't abide all this foolishness about trying to achieve equality with men. If we all became as wayward and sentimental as they are, the race would be doomed."

"You make me feel much better, Myra. I knew you would. I still don't know what to do, though."

Myra lowered her chins into her bosom and looked at her. "Do you really want my advice?"

"Yes. Yes, very much."

"Very well, then. First of all, you must start having parties again. You're wonderful at them and it will give you something to do. I'd start with a very large party. Something to show you're out of mourning, as it were. I know that sounds callous, but it's very important to announce in loud tones that life goes on. Even George may be caught up in it all. And secondly, I think you should take a lover."

"Myra!"

"Oh, don't pretend to be so shocked. Realism, my dear. Realism. A lover is just the thing. There are times when it is important to be sacrificial and worry about nurturing one's man. But if he doesn't respond to treatment, then one might just as well take care of oneself. There's no reason for everyone to be miserable, is there? Especially if the one who's making a show of misery already has a lover. That's quite unfair, you know."

Andrea did not reply immediately. She looked down at her carrot juice for a moment and then pushed it aside. "You know, Myra, you're quite right. It is unfair. I think that's what bothers me most. I'm perfectly willing to have another child, or try to. It's George who's wallowing in his misery. It really is unfair."

"Then you must redress the balance, my dear. Let's begin by talking about your party. You agree it should be a large one?"

"I suppose," Andrea said. "Yes, why not?"

"Then you will want to have it at Oakridge Manor."

"Yes." Andrea brightened. "A garden party. In the afternoon."

"A splendid idea. I love garden parties. It gives one an excuse to wear extravagant hats."

Andrea laughed with genuine gaiety.

"I shall buy a new one for the occasion, in fact," Myra said, holding her hands, palms upward, a full foot on either side of her head. "With feathers," she added.

Kevin Willoughby was somewhat surprised when he received an invitation to an end-of-summer garden party at Oakridge Manor. He had not seen Andrea in nearly a year. For a good part of that time he had been in Spain making a lavish costume epic about the Crusades, but Andrea seemed to have dropped him even before he left London. In the first few months after she had married Sir George, Kevin had been to dinner at Eaton Square twice, but he had had the feeling that Andrea's purpose in inviting him had been to prove to him how wrong he had been about Sir George, to show off her happiness at being Lady Andrea Harrington. He had asked her to lunch with him twice after that, but she had put him off both times, saying she would give a call when she wasn't quite so busy. But the call had never come. When he had returned to London from Spain, he heard about the death of her child the previous month, and had sent a letter of condolence, without really expecting to hear from her.

He considered not going to Oakridge Manor, just to show that he was not to be so easily manipulated, but in the end he decided that it would be interesting to see how her marriage was faring after the loss of the child that everyone knew Sir George had wanted so much. Besides, he thought, it never did an actor any harm to hobnob with titled socialites. No doubt there would be a write-up about the party in the papers, or a color spread in some magazine; Andrea had a definite knack for publicity, and he might just get mentioned himself. That was the sort of thing that impressed movie producers, since so many of them were social climbers themselves.

When Kevin telephoned Andrea to accept, she sounded genuinely delighted. "I'm so glad you can come, Kevin. It's been far too long."

The tone of this statement somehow managed to suggest that it was all Kevin's fault. To his annoyance, he found himself acquiescing in this revision of social history, saying, "Well, I was in Spain filming for what seemed like a lifetme." There was somethng about Andrea that always left him slightly nonplussed.

"Oh, yes. There was some disaster with the sets, wasn't there?"

"A fire, yes. But then there were disasters of almost every possible kind. God preserve me from any further epics. Tell me, Andrea, what sort of thing should I wear to the party?" Kevin hated to have to ask that, but he'd rather appear gauche before the fact than after. The first time he'd gone to dinner at Eaton Square he'd worn a dark suit, a very expensive suit he'd had made for himself in Rome, only to find everyone in evening clothes. No one had raised so much as an eyebrow, but he'd felt like a fool even so. He doubted that black tie was exactly the thing for a Sunday-afternoon garden party, even at Buckingham Palace, but he didn't want to take any chances.

"Oh, it's quite informal. Blazers and slacks, that sort of thing. George has this idea that everyone's going to play croquet."

"Oh, God," said Kevin, who was far from adept at that upper-class diversion. "Not with hedeghogs and flamingos, I hope."

Andrea laughed. "No, I always feel like Alice in Wonder-

180

land myself when I play croquet. I swear the wickets move around on their own. But don't worry. There's also going to be dancing."

"It sounds very festive."

"I hope so. I decided it was time to take some pleasure in life again. It's been a difficult few months."

"I can imagine," said Kevin. "One of my sister's children was a victim of crib death. It was a terrible experience."

"I think that would probably be even worse," said Andrea. "To lose what seems a healthy baby. In this case there was no chance to begin to love the child. But that's past. I'll look forward to seeing you, Kevin."

For his part, despite his initial misgivings, Kevin decided that he was very much looking forward to seeing Andrea as well. Driving up to Oakridge Manor the first Sunday in September, he felt a curious sense of adventure. Perhaps because she had rebuffed him, Andrea continued to play a role in Kevin's sexual fantasies from time to time. He was the kind of man for whom the thought of potential conquests or of missed opportunities had a more arousing effect than memories of the women with whom he had actually had affairs. In the case of someone like Andrea, whom he had badly wanted and failed to get, there was always the thought in the back of his mind that someday there might be another chance. Sometimes he would plot out variations on such imaginary future encounters. They never failed to give him an erection, even when he was driving.

There were nearly two dozen cars already parked in front of Oakridge Manor when he arrived shortly after one in the afternoon, a shining array of Rolls-Royces and Bentleys, interspersed with Ferraris and Jaguars. His own brand-new bright red Jag would be right at home, he thought with a grin. From the number of cars, he suspected it was going to be quite a bash.

Kevin was ushered through the house to the broad terrace where Andrea, in an exquisite white lace dress, and Sir George greeted him. Andrea embraced him warmly but Sir George seemed rather distant. At first Kevin thought that his coolness was directed toward him personally, but as the afternoon passed he changed his mind. Sir George was simply behaving in a rather withdrawn manner in general, almost as though he were a stranger at his own party.

From the bar set up at the far end of the terrace, where three red-jacketed bartenders were dispensing champagne, or whiskey if you preferred, Kevin collected a glass of Moët and drifted out onto the lawn. The guests, chatting gaily in small groups, were a classic British mix of politicians, businessmen, artists, and the merely titled. Kevin spotted several well-known M.P.'s, including the Shadow Foreign Secretary; Sir Charles Brockton and the unmistakable Lady Myra in a large pink picture hat; Tony Armstrong-Jones, apparently minus the Princess; and a gaggle of stars of the Royal Ballet, standing in modified fifth position under the trees out of the sun. He found himself involved in a long conversation about Spain with a board member of British Petroleum who had fought in the Spanish Civil War, and subsequently with the wife of an Oxford Don who had seen all Kevin's movies, something that was always an embarrassment considering some of the clinkers he'd been in.

The champagne flowed, Sir George's man Jeremy and two assistants circulated with silver trays laden with caviar, hot miniature puff pastries filled with crab, and tiny cucumber boats stuffed with cold salmon mousse, while a ten-piece orchestra serenaded them from a discreet distance with show tunes.

Kevin was both appalled and fascinated by the lavishness of it all. There were ten tables for eight set up along the perimeter of the rose garden, which filled the air with a last, late-summer effulgence of sweetness. The luncheon buffet was laid out beneath a striped canvas pavilion. The buffet was organized after the fashion of a smorgasbord, with a wide selection of cold dishes and a smaller number of more substantial hot ones. But it was hardly the ordinary smorgasbord sampling. Instead of pickled herring there was truffled lobster salad; Swedish meatballs were replaced by pike *quenelles* as delicate as air. There were great platters of ham, not English boiled ham, but Parma ham from Italy, Black Forest ham from Germany, and Smithfield from America. Pistachios and quail eggs formed an intricate mosaic at the center of boned galantines of duck. Mussels were stuffed with wild rice; rollatines of veal with fresh morels.

It all seemed to Kevin a flagrant example of what his Aunt Emily liked to call "conspicuous consumption," and the contrast with the stews and porridges and fried fish of his childhood made him feel almost resentful. At the same time, it was all so very lovely, each platter an individual work of art. This was not just food, it was a statement about life, basic necessity raised to a level that made one gasp at the sheer beauty of it. Kevin had always felt a certain anger toward those who could afford the extravagance of trying to live beautifully instead of merely attempting to survive. But he was here, a part of this world now, invited in because he had had the good luck to be born with a handsome face and a talent for mimicry. And he was enjoying himself. He was glad to be where he was. Have another bite of truffle, he thought, and enjoy it while you can.

After luncheon, the party divided itself into three groups. The energetic, sporty types, or perhaps those who felt they must atone for eating so much, joined in a round robin of croquet, led by Sir George, who finally seemed to have developed a degree of enthusiasm for the proceedings. Mallets met balls with a steady crack, crack. Groans went up as balls came to a sudden, inexplicable halt inches short of wickets, counterpointed by applause for those with unerring aim. Cries of despair issued forth as players knocked one another's balls out of bounds with sadistic decorum. A second group, overcome by lassitude and looking as though they would have preferred a nap, sat on the sidelines and chatted, joining in

183

occasionally with the groans or applause of the participants.

A third and generally younger group danced on the terrace as the orchestra attempted to bridge the generation gap by alternating Strauss waltzes with Beatles' tunes. Kevin finally managed to snare Andrea for a few minutes, and they danced together to "Michelle."

"You certainly do know how to give a party," Kevin said, as they turned and turned again.

Andrea smiled at him. She smelled of Parma violets, sweet and thrilling. "Thank you, Kevin. It has gone well."

"You're very happy, aren't you, being Lady Andrea? I think this afternoon finally made me understand how much that can mean."

She did not answer at once, looking off toward the croquet field. "I'm very happy today," she said, looking up at his face. "It's been a gloomy time, Kevin. I hoped the party would break the spell. Perhaps it has."

"For you or for Sir George?"

"For both of us, I suppose. But in different ways."

Andrea danced wonderfully, Kevin thought. More than that, she danced wonderfully with him. He hardly had to lead. She seemed to anticipate his movements.

"Things have changed, Kevin," she said. "Tell me," she added, as though it were an afterthought, "are you free a week from Thursday? I have tickets to the Old Vic, and George will be in France."

"Thursday week?" Kevin was taken by surprise. He couldn't really remember whether he was free or not. But he decided that he would be. "Yes," he said, "I believe I am."

"You'll join me then?"

"Of course."

The orchestra swirled into a final flourish, the strings holding the last long note. "Thank you for the dance, Kevin. I think I'd better go watch the flamingos and hedgehogs for a while." She smiled at him, and squeezed his hand. Then she was gone from his side.

Kevin stood at the edge of the terrace and watched her walking away across the vivid green of the lawn in the afternoon sun, her white dress fluttering slightly in the breeze. She looked as cool and inaccessible as ever. But he could not help wondering what she had meant when she had said that things had changed.

Andrea did not really make a decision to have an affair with Kevin Willoughby. She simply let it happen. Although she had always found him attractive, she did not choose him for a lover so much because she wanted him as because he wanted her. The fact of George's turning away from her physically had left her, in some irrational way, with a sense of being undesirable. She knew that that feeling was not uncommon among women in the months following a pregnancy under any circumstances, but George's withdrawal had heightened it. Objectively, she knew that it was nonsense; she was back to her normal weight and had a minimum of stretch marks. In some ways, she thought, she was physically more attractive than ever; there was a new subtle maturity to her that enhanced rather than detracted from her youthfulness. But still she needed proof of her desirability, emotionally more than physically, and Kevin provided that.

Sexually, he was almost too ardent. She had never been involved with a man who was so easily aroused or so inexhaustible. Often he would have two orgasms in a single half hour of lovemaking, with absolutely no diminishment of hardness. Perhaps it was because they saw each other only two afternoons a week; she did not know if he was involved with any other women and did not ask. There was an element of narcissism in him that she hadn't encountered in a man before, either. He was proud of his taut, sleekly muscled body, behaving sometimes with all the uninhibited delight of an adolescent exploring his newfound virility. At first she was almost shocked by the sheer intensity of pleasure he took in sex, but gradually she began to lose some of her own inhibitions in response to his naked physicality, to feel unashamed to touch him or even herself with an openness she had never quite dared before.

At her insistence, they were discreet about their affair; only occasionally did they go out together in the evening during one of George's absences, and then always to the most public of places, the theater or the ballet, often in a party that included other friends. They did not have to pretend that they were not in love, to avoid the secret glances and the covert caresses of those who can think of none but the other, for they were not in fact in love. It was easy to behave as though they were just good friends, since in one sense that was what they were, good friends who happened to enjoy sleeping together. Kevin did not want any deep emotional rapport, Andrea was sure, any more than she did. He was not made that way, she believed; there were too many women in the world. There would be many others after her, and his first love was, after all, himself.

But sometimes they did have lunch together, driving out of London in his Jaguar to Surrey or Kent, occasionally with a particular destination in mind, an old inn like The Talbot at Ripley, or The Crown, built in Chiddingford in the thirteenth century, and sometimes just driving at random, stopping along the way at whatever place took their fancy. One Tuesday in late March, on the first fine day after a week of rain, Kevin suggested that they drive to Brighton and have lunch at an Italian restaurant he had heard was exceptionally good. Kevin often made such suggestions, and Andrea seldom countered them, but on this occasion she wanted to know more.

"What's the restaurant called?" she asked.

"Bianchetti's, I think. Why?"

Andrea gave a small laugh, shaking her head. "I don't think that's a very good idea, Kevin."

"I don't understand."

"Riccardo Bianchetti is George's lover."

Kevin looked startled for a moment and then burst out

laughing. "To use an American expression, you've got to be kidding."

"Nope." Andrea had told Kevin that George had a lover. Kevin, obviously controlling an impulse to say he'd told her so, had simply asked if it was anyone he knew. She had said no, fairly curtly, not wanting to discuss it with him, and he had asked no more questions.

"Have you ever been there?" Kevin inquired now.

"No."

"And you're not curious?"

In fact, Andrea had long been curious. She had even considered asking Myra to drive down with her to have lunch sometime when George was out of the country. But she hadn't quite dared. She and George were getting along quite well, having agreed to lead more separate lives, and she hadn't wanted to take the chance of causing complications. Riccardo was a chef, of course, but he was also the owner, and chefs who were also owners sometimes came out into the dining room. She had thought that could be awkward, and was likely to annoy George.

"Of course I'm curious," she said. "But I think it would be indiscreet."

"Well, of course it would be indiscreet. That's what's so amusing about it. Wife and lover having lunch at husband's lover's restaurant. It sounds like one of those wonderful French farces, with doors opening and closing in the nick of time."

"Precisely," said Andrea.

"Oh, don't be so prissy. George is in France, isn't he?"

"Yes, but I've met Riccardo twice. He'd recognize me if he saw me."

"If he did see you he'd run, don't you think?"

"Probably straight to George."

"So?"

"It would be, well, uncomfortable for him."

"Frankly, Andrea, it seems to me he could use a little discomfort. It seems to me you've been letting the man off very easily. I know how much you enjoy being Lady Andrea Harrington, but everyone in London knows the marriage isn't what it once was. Your famous dinner parties are down from two a week to one every two weeks. It takes the bloom off things a bit, doesn't it?"

"I think people understand."

"I'm sure they do. But are you having as much fun as you used to? The role isn't as juicy as it once was, is it?"

"That's a rude way to put it."

"But I'm right."

Andrea sighed. "Yes, you are right."

"So why not tweak George's nose? He probably won't find out anyway, but even if he did, it just puts you in a stronger position. After all, the man can't possibly divorce you. From what you've told me, you were perfectly willing to try to have another child. It's George who left your bed to begin with, not the other way around. And a male lover to boot. You have all the cards, love."

"I know he's not going to divorce me, Kevin. I just don't want to make things any more difficult."

"I think you're being quite stupid, Andrea. Isn't it time you suggested to George, Sir George, excuse me, that you would like him to pay a little more attention to what you want, that it's perfectly all right with you if he goes off and buggers his Italian boyfriend, or gets buggered, whatever, provided he is willing to put in a little more time playing host and allowing you to live the kind of life you married him for in the first place?"

"You know, Kevin, you have a very cunning mind. A bit nasty, but cunning."

"I didn't grow up in the streets of Lambeth for nothing, love. I take it you do see my point."

Andrea did. There were times when she resented George's withdrawal, times when it made her angry. She had tried very hard not to let it show, partially because she felt sorry for

George and understood his pain, at least intuitively, and partially because she still hoped, however vaguely, that it might be possible to restore their relationship eventually, that George would get over his fear that another child would also be in some way blighted. He seemed to have given up, though, to have come to the conclusion that he was fated to be the last of his line. It was not just the baby, it was the death of that girl he had intended to marry so long ago; each loss in itself might have been bearable, but taken together they seemed to have robbed him of hope, of a sense of the future. But Andrea herself found it difficult to live without some sense of a future. Perhaps it was simply that she was too young still to resign herself to a life that consisted only in the pleasures of the moment. Those pleasures could be considerable, of course. She had a Rolls-Royce to drive, and a beautiful house to live in, or at least inhabit. There was Oakridge Manor. There were parties to be given and to attend. She was Lady Andrea Harrington, and she had made a place for herself in London society. Yet there was a hollowness to it all that disturbed her, and times when it seemed merely a pantomime, a dumb show.

Only the week before she had been shopping at Harrods, buying fresh trout and a half dozen individual racks of lamb, globes of fennel and perfect pearl-white leeks, *cépes* flown in from France and raspberries from God knew where, but far away, you could tell by the price—and the great food halls she loved so much had suddenly seemed oppressive, the party she was preparing for a duty rather than a pleasure. What am I doing here? she had thought. What am I doing here?

Afterwards, she was never quite sure why she had agreed to go with Kevin to Riccardo's restaurant, whether it was out of anger or boredom, or simply mischievousness, or because of some hope that it might change things for the better, somehow alter the pattern of her life, like giving a sudden twist to a kaleidoscope. All she knew for certain was that after agreeing to go she had suddenly felt more alive—slightly wicked and a little giddy, but more alive.

189

*   *   *

Brighton was a good location for a restaurant. After a postwar period of decline as a resort, it had bcome fashionable again as a place to actually live, within easy commuting distance of London and with a bracing seaside climate away from the smog of the central city. Property values had not gone quite as crazy as they had in London, and a considerable number of young solicitors and bankers had decided it was a good place to raise a family, buying up many of the eighteenth and nineteenth century houses that had gone to seed, restoring them gradually to a semblance of their former elegance. It was popular too with writers and actors; Laurence Olivier had a house there. And there were always tourists, come to see the ornate Royal Pavilion with its mosque-like onion domes and lavishly eccentric public rooms.

After a slow start, during which Sir George had lent Riccardo additional money, Bianchetti's had become very successful. The northern Italian cuisine was more refined than that of many of the Italian restaurants in London itself, and it had become a fashionable place to motor down to from London for lunch or dinner. Andrea, almost in spite of herself, was immediately taken with its physical layout, a series of small, intimate rooms on the main floor of what had once been a private house. The walls of each room had been painted a different pastel color, with window draperies of a slightly darker shade. The tablecloths were white throughout, but the napkins in each room matched the color of the walls. It was a charming and even elegant conception, she thought.

The menu listed a number of Venetian specialities, including several risottos, the fish soup called *"Broeto,"* the *Pasticcio ai Quattro Formaggi* she had had at "the Secret Garden" when she first met Riccardo, and the expected *Fegato alla Veneziana*, at which Kevin made a face.

"You can cut the liver into thin slivers and call it by a fancy name, but to me it's still liver and onions and I had far too much of it as a boy," he said.

190

Andrea persuaded him to start with the pasticcio. Recalling how delicious it had been, she was tempted to order it herself, but that seemed a trifle too symbolic of her curious situation. She was, she realized, feeling rather nervous and began to wish she had not come.

Her attitude changed with her first course, which consisted of slices of fresh mozzarella, coated with egg and cornmeal and deep fried and served with a very light fresh tomato sauce. It was a marvelously piquant contrast of flavors and textures. For a main course she had one of the house specialties, slices of a rolled veal roast that had been stuffed with prosciutto and rounds of truffle, and accompanied by sauteed celery root, still slightly crunchy and given an additional perkiness by a sprinkle of Parmesan. It was well worth the 30-shilling surcharge. Kevin seemed equally delighted with his roast pork with rosemary, and cauliflower with anchovy sauce. Andrea was dubious about that combination, but the taste Kevin gave her was surprisingly good, the vegetable itself perfectly cooked, without a hint of mushiness, the sauce sufficiently mellowed by butter so as not to overpower the flavor of the cauliflower itself.

Andrea was impressed. Whatever else he might be, Riccardo Bianchetti was clearly an adept in the kitchen, a fine and sophisticated chef. In an odd way, Andrea was glad of that. At least George hadn't been taken in by a nobody with a pretty face, someone who traded his sexual favors for the kind of advancement he couldn't possibly achieve on his own. Riccardo might be a whore, he might be out for all he could get from George, but there was no doubting his talent or the fact that his restaurant was a solid investment. Andrea had never regarded Riccardo as a sexual or even an emotional rival in the usual sense. She thought that if he had been a woman her feelings would be quite different, but she didn't see how a woman could really fight a man's attraction to another man. And it couldn't really be said that Riccardo had taken George away from her—she suspected that George had been involved with him long before she herself had entered his life. The problem was not Riccardo, but George himself.

She and Kevin were finishing their espresso and had already asked for the bill when Riccardo walked into the room in his white apron and tall chef's hat. He did not see them immediately, stopping to talk with the diners at a table across the room. For a moment, Andrea considered trying to ignore his presence, keeping her head turned away, so that even if he did recognize her he would have an opportunity to pretend he had not. But she instinctively felt that that was the wrong way to handle the situation. She had known this might happen and had come anyway. It was no time to be cowardly about it.

As Riccardo turned toward their side of the room, she looked full at him and smiled her most brilliant smile. Riccardo's face decomposed for an instant into an expression of anger or fear, Andrea was not sure which. But he receovered quickly, and walked to the table.

"Mr. Bianchetti," Andrea said, extending her hand. "You may not remember me. I'm Lady Andrea Harrington."

Riccardo took her hand and bowed slightly. "Of course I remember, Madam. It is a privilege to have you here."

"I'm glad you came through. I wanted to tell you what a splendid meal Mr. Willoughby and I had."

Riccardo barely glanced at Kevin, giving a quick nod. "Thank you. Thank you very much. I'm happy you enjoyed it."

"But I do have one little quarrel with you, Mr. Bianchetti."

Riccardo's eyes widened momentarily. "Yes, what is that?"

"You never did send me that recipe for the pasticcio as you promised. At Oakridge Manor, if you recall."

"The pasticcio? Ah, yes, I do remember. I apologize. If you could perhaps wait a few minutes, I will write it out for you now."

"That would be wonderful. Thank you so much."

"If you will excuse me, then, I'll see to it."

"Of course," Andrea said, and smiled again.

As soon as Riccardo had left the room, Kevin said, "You

192

know, Andrea, you really should go back into films. That performance was worthy of an Oscar."

Andrea grinned wickedly. "It wasn't bad, was it? But I must say he was damn good himself."

"Not really. His eyes gave him away. He was furious, you know. Especially when you asked for the recipe. Are you planning to prepare it for George?"

"Really, Kevin." Andrea tried to muster a tone of indignity, but couldn't help laughing.

Riccardo sent the recipe out with their waiter. Andrea scanned the list of ingredients, written in a small careful hand. "He's left some ingredients out," she said. She'd tasted a bite of Kevin's portion, and was quite sure she had detected a hint of allspice in the béchamel sauce with which each layer of the pasta was lightly coated. She also suspected that he used veal stock rather than the chicken stock he'd listed.

"How can you tell?" Kevin asked.

Andrea explained.

"Well, that's spiteful of him, isn't it?"

"Not really," said Andrea. "I do the same thing myself quite often when I'm asked for a recipe. A first-rate cook can always figure out what's missing if he's tasted the dish. That's part of the fun. And with an ordinary cook, it won't make any difference. The dish won't come out quite right anyway."

Kevin laughed. "You know, I rather think you have more in common with Mr. Bianchetti than George does."

Andrea looked at him. For some reason, she was not amused.

"Quite possibly," she said coolly.

In the basement kitchen of his restaurant, Riccardo Bianchetti picked up an eight-inch stainless steel chef's knife made by Victorinox of Switzerland and flung it across the room. It embedded itself in a butcher-block counter and stood there quivering slightly. "I will kill her," he shouted. "I will cut the whore to pieces."

Two sous-chefs, the chief dishwasher, three waiters, and

Riccardo's first assistant, Alain Becaud, stopped what they were doing momentarily and turned to look at Riccardo. Seeing that he had no further knives in hand, they went back to work. Alain raised his eyes to heaven and walked over to Riccardo. "What is the problem, Mr. Bianchetti?"

"The famous Lady Andrea Harrington was here for lunch."

"Sir George's wife?"

"Si, si. The American hunter of fortunes. Spying on me. She would like to ruin me, I know. She would like to drive me out of the country."

Alain shook his head. "What did she say to you?"

"Niente. Rien. Nothing. She complimented the food. But that means nothing. She should not come here. If she comes here it means that she wishes to make trouble for me."

"Then she would have made trouble while she was here, no?"

"She has influence. She will tell her friends to stay away, that the food is bad."

"But she liked the food. . . ."

"It does not matter. She will lie."

"She came alone or with others?"

"With some young man. He is a movie actor, I believe. Very handsome."

"I think her visit has to do with Sir George, then, not with you."

Riccardo's eyes flashed angrily. "If it has to do with him, it has to do with me."

Alain sighed. "Then you will have to talk about it with him."

"Yes. I will. I will call him in Paris."

Riccardo spent the rest of the afternoon thinking about what he would say. It was important to be careful. Never, not once, had he let George see how much he hated the fact of George's marriage. It had been a betrayal, but Riccardo had understood that it was for having children, nothing more. He had known George would come back in time. George had had other affairs. In fact, he had slept with a great many men. Riccardo knew that, but it did not matter. He was the only one who counted, the only one George loved. Because he himself had been the son George wished for, his son and his lover both.

When Riccardo was fifteen George had found him, working as a waiter at his aunt's restaurant in Venice. His aunt had been good to him, but she had had her own children, and she could not make up for the father Riccardo did not have, or for his crazy mother who did not like to look at him because he reminded her too much of the sailor from Genoa who had married her and then disappeared soon after Riccardo was born. There had been no one to love him until George. George had told him he was beautiful, had made love to him as though he were the rarest treasure, had taught him English and bought him clothes and sent him to chef's school in Milan. And brought him to England.

And then he had married this cunt from America and would not sleep with Riccardo, only help him with money for his restaurant, and talk to him sometimes on the telephone as though he were afraid to be close to him. But that was why Riccardo knew he would come back. George was afraid to be in the same room with him because he still wanted him so much. So he would come back, Riccardo knew. And he had pretended the marriage did not bother him, to make it easier for George to come back someday. So even now he had to be careful what he said to George. He could not allow him to see the whole truth. But he would tell him his wife had come to the restaurant and that he was afraid she would make trouble for him. He would be upset, but he would not call Lady Andrea any names. He would just say he was afraid of her. And he would tell George about the movie actor. That would make George angry at his wife and he would tell her not to interfere, and Riccardo would pretend she was dead, pretend she did not exist.

*   *   *

195

George burst into Andrea's bedroom without knocking. It was clear that he had been drinking. Andrea had never seen him sloppily drunk, it was as though he had too much reserve to allow that to happen, no matter how much he had consumed. But he had had a good deal, she could tell.

She was sitting at her writing desk drawing up the menu for the supper party they were giving after the opera the following week. George stopped a few paces into the room and stared at her. "Hello, George," she said, not getting up. "How was Paris?"

"It ended rather badly," he said. "I had a telephone call from Brighton. Riccardo was extremely upset."

Andrea put down her pen. "Really? Not about me, I hope."

"Well, most certainly about you, my dear. What in the world possessed you to do a thing like that?"

"Don't be silly, George. I had lunch at a restaurant. It was an extremely fine lunch, I might add, and I told Riccardo so. I can't imagine what he has to be upset about." Andrea turned back to her desk with a show of calm. At the back of her mind she was aware that this little scene, which she had half expected, perhaps even hoped for, had started off on too high a note. She'd thought that George would be a little more roundabout.

"My dear Andrea. I thought we had agreed to live and let live. To drive all the way down to Brighton and march yourself into Riccardo's restaurant for lunch strikes me as deliberately provocative. Not to mention the fact that you dragged Kevin Willoughby along."

"George, this is absurd. It was a fine day and we went for a drive." Andrea was about to add that George well knew how little time it took to get to Brighton, but thought better of it. "We didn't go to the restaurant because it was Riccardo's. We went because there's been so much talk about how good it is. I was curious about the food, that's all."

"Nonsense. You were trying to embarrass me, and upset

196

Riccardo, and you succeeded on both counts. Perhaps I deserve your scorn, Andrea, but I won't have you playing games like this in public. I may be a pathetic old fool, but I won't have you flaunting the fact."

Andrea spun toward him, her voice rising angrily. "Has it ever occurred to you, George, that it is embarrassing to me to have to be constantly explaining your absences to people? It's one thing to say you're in France when you actually are, but when I go to a party and someone has seen you at the Oxford and Cambridge Club that very day it becomes just a little awkward. We hardly ever entertain anymore, and I'm never quite certain you'll be here when we do. I wanted to be a wife to you and a mother to your children, George. That's what I married you for. That is truly what I married you for. But if you won't let me be your wife in anything more than name, and refuse to even try to have another child, the least you can do, the very least, is to put up a good front. You aren't even doing that anymore. You can do what you like the rest of the time, but I hardly think it's asking too much to request your presence as host at a little dinner party once or twice a week."

George took two lurching steps forward, his voice rising to a level Andrea had never heard before. "Your little dinner parties," he shouted at her, "are not so little, you know. They cost a fortune. Every one of them costs a bloody fortune."

Andrea was speechless for a moment. Never before had she heard George mention money. Never. "I don't understand," she said at last.

"I can't hide it from you anymore, Andrea. I'm sorry," he said, his voice dropping very low. "I'm sorry. This has all been so wrong. It's not your fault. I know, I know. I never said anything about money. But I've been living vastly beyond my means for years. Even before I knew you. But that's made it worse, much, much worse. I wanted you to be happy. I wanted us both to be happy. I wanted, I wanted—"

George broke off abruptly, suddenly ashen.

Andrea stood up. "George, what is it?"

"I don't know," he said, faltering again. "I don't feel well. I feel— Excuse me. Excuse me." He turned and left the room, almost staggering as he walked.

"George!" For a moment she could not move, a kind of paralysis seemed to come over her. Then, suddenly, tears started to her eyes, and she began to run toward the door.

From the hallway she heard a cry of pain. She heard him fall.

"George," she said. "Oh, George."

Chapter Eight

ANDREA HAD TRIED TO PREPARE herself, but even so she blanched inwardly when she was at last allowed to enter George's hospital room after twenty-four hours of waiting. It was not merely all the monitoring devices attached to his body, and the sense of life hanging in the balance that they conveyed; it was that he looked so old. His gray hair had whitened perceptibly, for one thing. She'd always thought that that was a myth, that it was impossible for a person's hair to change color overnight, but there was no denying that it had. Or perhaps, after all, it was just illusion, and that his hair appeared lighter because of the almost total lack of color in his face. His pallor emphasized the wrinkles in his skin, too, and the flesh seemed to hang with a strange looseness around his neck. He looked not just much older, but immeasurably weary.

"George," she said quietly, taking his hand between hers. The fingers were cold but his palm was sweating.

He moistened his lips, and his Adam's apple moved. "My father died of heart failure, too," he said, in a thin, whispery voice. "He was only forty-three. And my grandfather was young. It's not your fault. Our hearts were never right."

She was not sure what he was trying to absolve her of, their argument perhaps, or even the defective heart of little Charles.

"You're going to get better," she said, although she was less convinced of that now than she had been a few minutes earlier when the doctor, an eminent specialist whom she had met socially on two or three occasions, had said that the first twenty-four hours were critical, that they had got him through that and therefore had reason to hope.

199

George shook his head very slightly. "It's going to be a dreadful mess, Andrea. I'm leaving you with a terrible situation. I'm so sorry."

"Don't think about such things. We'll straighten everything out later." She assumed he was referring to money, as he had just before collapsing the day before. She'd tried to put that out of her mind, and it was disturbing to have it come up again. In the past night and day she had found herself moving back and forth between opposite emotions, feeling guilty one moment and trying to persuade herself that she had nothing more to answer for than George did himself, and finding that when she did not feel guilty it was almost worse. She had been so shocked by George's bringing up the subject of money, and so confused by it, that she had found it easiest to put that question aside, to look on it for the time being as simply a mystery. But now he had brought it up again, and she could not help wondering how badly in debt he really was. The rich, as she had discovered when still a girl, were often the first to plead poverty, but it began to occur to her that there was more involved here than merely being overextended.

"No one really knows," George said. "Not even Stanley." Stanley Poole, George's solicitor, was one of the few people in George's circle Andrea had never much taken to, a man whose reserve seemed to border on contempt for the world in which he moved. He had never been less than polite to Andrea, but he had seldom been anything more. She had thought from the beginning that he was one of the few who truly disapproved of George's marriage, and of Andrea herself, but she had never let it bother her much, since he was the kind of man who seemed to disapprove of almost everyone and everything in one sense or another.

"You must ask for Stanley's help," George said. "He'll do what he can."

"Don't worry," Andrea said, feeling that she was repeating herself but not knowing what else to say.

"You did have a—a good time, at the beginning. Didn't you?"

"You know I did, George. We'll have more of them."

George seemed almost to smile, and his fingers closed slightly on hers. "You're strong," he said. "You'll be all right."

"*You* have to be strong, George. You have to fight to get better."

"I was never much at that."

"At what?"

"Battles. Never any good at it. Only over Germany. But that was revenge. No matter."

The door opened and the doctor put his head in. "I think that best be all for now, Lady Andrea."

She leaned over and kissed George's cheek. The skin itself was warm, but she had the most curious sense that the flesh beneath it was cold. Her mind started to make a connection with something else, some memory, but then it was gone. It was not until she had gone down in the elevator and was leaving the hospital that, as she placed her palm against the revolving door, she remembered.

"History," she said under her breath, and suddenly shivered.

Lady Myra Brockton drew in her breath in a startled gasp. "Extraordinary," she exclaimed. "Absolutely incredible. The nerve of the little rat." She waved the note in the air. "I should keep this, my dear, if I were you. Someday you may wish to use it against him."

"I can't imagine how," Andrea said.

"One never knows." Myra looked down at the tea tray Mrs. Evelyn had brought in. "To hell with tea," she said. "I think we both need a drink. A bit of brandy."

"Yes, of course," said Andrea, getting up and going to the mahogany cabinet where George had always kept brandy, port, and cigars.

The note had arrived only that morning, but Andrea

201

already knew it by heart. It was a very short note, with no salutation, handwritten in the same small hand she had first seen exactly a week earlier at Brighton.

"You killed him," it read. "You never loved him. I loved him and he loved me. You gave him nothing. And you killed him."

It was signed Riccardo Bianchetti.

"Do you want a splash of soda?" Andrea asked.

Andrea brought the glasses back and set them down. "Actually," she said, "it's occurred to me that it could have been worse. He might have shown up at the funeral and started screaming at me in person. From the tone of that note, I wouldn't put it past him."

"Certainly not, my dear. I'm sure he's far too much of a coward to undertake a face-to-face confrontation. Besides, it would have been a scandal, and that wouldn't be good for his business. Even this note is extremely unwise. I shall personally spread the word that no one should ever go near his establishment again."

"I wish you wouldn't do that, Myra. I don't plan to show this note to anyone but you. And he'd assume that I was the one campaigning against him. It would just make things worse."

Myra grunted. "Well, perhaps you're right. I hadn't thought of it that way. But he certainly deserves some sort of retribution."

"What does it matter? He probably did love George. Quite possibly more deeply than I did. It's strange, you know. I thought of asking him to come to the funeral. But it didn't seem . . ."

"Proper," Myra put in. "I should say not."

"The ironic thing is that he's probably going to come out of everything in a much better position than I will. Stanley Poole told me that George signed over the deed to a building he owned in Knightsbridge to Riccardo two months ago. Apparently it was about the only property he had left that was free and clear."

"Aside from this house and the manor, of course."

"No, Myra. They're both up as collateral on loans. They'll probably both have to go. Certainly the manor."

Andrea had never before seen Myra speechless. She smiled wanly. "That's why I wanted to talk with you, Myra. The note is really incidental. It upset me, but in the long run it's not very important."

"I know inheritance taxes are perfectly dreadful. They've created havoc with all the old families. But surely this house can be salvaged?"

"Stanley isn't certain yet, it's all such a mess. George told me so, the last time I saw him in the hospital. But I didn't have any idea things were so complicated or so far gone. Even if the house can be saved, there wouldn't be the kind of income needed to run it."

"Come, now. Stanley Poole is a very clever man. Cold as a dead herring, but brilliant in his way. I'm sure it will turn out much better than you think. It's just the intial shock."

"I don't think Stanley is going to go out of his way to rescue me, Myra."

"Whatever do you mean by that?"

"I don't think he ever approved of me. Too young, too extravagant, and most of all, American. I suspect he even derives a certain pleasure in telling me all the bad news."

"Well, then, you must find someone else."

"He's the legal executor, Myra. You can't get executors changed easily, as I understand it, and when they're as eminent as Stanley Poole, you don't get them changed at all. And don't misunderstand me, I'm sure he will do what he can, not for me, as a person, but simply out of professional honor. But his best isn't going to amount to much. Even the Rolls isn't paid for."

"Dear God in heaven. I had no idea."

"Apparently no one did. Not even Stanley, from what George said. Apparently some of George's creditors were beginning to catch on. It was all beginning to fall apart. I think maybe that's what really killed George, the strain of trying to keep it together. And as he told me very clearly, it was partially my fault. I was spending a fortune he didn't have. But he never even hinted that he didn't have it, not until the very end."

"Well, then, you are not in any way to blame, my dear girl. You mustn't speak of it as even partially your fault."

"No, I didn't know. And I tell myself there's no reason to feel guilty. But it keeps coming back to me that our garden party at the manor last September cost more than two thousand pounds just by itself."

"And a well-spent sum it was, by God," Myra said emphatically.

Andrea smiled. "Yes, it was lovely. I guess I'll have to remember it as Lady Andrea Harrington's monument."

"Don't be ridiculous. You must never forget that you are *still* Lady Andrea Harrington."

"In name, yes. But in fact I am a young American woman with no money who happened to have latched on to a title. With George gone that's the way a lot of people are going to think about it, Myra. If there were money, if I could keep up the same style of living, it might be different. But I have the feeling that without the money, a great many people are going to remember that the title is mine only by marriage."

Gazing across at Andrea reflectively, Myra took a sip of brandy. "Well, you do have a point there. I went through a bit of that when my second husband fell into that crevasse on the north slope of Everest. Or was it the south slope? At any rate, he's there yet, a hero to himself if no one much else. But my mind is wandering. The point is that I do understand what you're talking about. And of course you must have already recognized the obvious answer to your problem."

"I suppose you're going to say find another husband."

"Naturally. That's what we women do, isn't it? But it must be a rich husband. We'll have to check him out thoroughly this time. He needn't have a title, so long as he has the power and wealth to let you live as though you were Lady Andrea.

And don't look at me that way. I know George was buried only two days ago, and I happen to have been very fond of the man. I even wept a bit at the funeral, which isn't usual with me. But you're very much alive and you must think of yourself."

"I am thinking of myself. And one of the things I think is that rich husbands don't fall out of the sky at your feet. George practically did, I know, but that was a fluke. I've wondered sometimes if he would have married me at all if I hadn't reminded him of that poor girl who died in the blitz. And there are also a lot of rich men I wouldn't marry if my life depended on it."

"Of course, my dear. There must be at least a degree of compatability. What I think you fail to understand is that as the lovely young widow of Sir George Harrington you have a far better opportunity to find the kind of man you want than you would have had when you were just a screen actress. You are young and lovely still, you've established yourself in society, you are a highly regarded hostess. You are now a catch, as they say, which you were not to the same degree when you met George."

"Myra, you're impossible." Andrea was torn between amusement and irritation. She had known the kind of tack Myra was likely to take, and in one sense it made her feel better. The only trouble with Myra's advice was that she had conveniently excised from her memory all the pain and difficulty that she must have experienced in between the more triumphant moments of her admittedly remarkable life. And what she couldn't forget, she turned into a joke, like her comment about her third husband's irresistible attraction to lady harpists. Andrea admired Myra's ability to do that, to make a joke of pain, but that was something that she suspected even Myra had more success in doing considerably after the fact.

As Andrea had wandered through the house in the past few days, she had found herself staring at certain objects, or paintings, at the rows of china in the pantry cabinets, at the roll-top desk in George's study, and thinking that it was likely it would all have to be sold at auction, dispersed, a whole history of a family scattered to the winds. Tears had come to her eyes several times thinking of that, not just because she was losing them, but because they belonged together and she had come to love them as a whole, not just as valuable things, but as a kind of entity with a meaning that was greater than the individual parts. She kept thinking that if Charles had been born healthy, then—and would come to a stop. The ifs were too many, and contradicted one another at every turn.

"My dear, I'm so sorry," Myra said, reaching out and patting her hand. "I meant to cheer you up and I've made you cry instead. I'm afraid I do get carried away on occasion. You must forgive me."

"There's nothing to forgive, Myra. You do cheer me up. It's strange. I'm not sure I'm really crying for George or even myself in an ordinary sense. I married George because I wanted a certain kind of life, a material life, yes, but there was always something more than that to it. Especially when I was carrying Charles, I felt it. George was so happy then, and I had a kind of, well, vision of what our life would be. You know, Myra, I don't think I cried enough for Charles at the time. He was part of a kind of dream, you see, and I couldn't let myself think that the dream was gone, too. So I wouldn't let myself really mourn him. But I should have, because that's when the dream died, along with Charles. That was the end of it."

Myra was perfectly still, and silent. Andrea took a deep breath. "So, you see, I'm not sure I want any dreams right now that depend on anyone but me. I'm not sure what to do, but I think it has to be something self-contained for a while. I think I have to depend on myself alone. I've never done that as well as I would have liked to. Oh, I suppose a lot of people would think I was a very self-sufficient person, but in crucial moments I've allowed myself to be shaped by other

206

people's dreams, tried to become part of them. I did that years ago when I let Terry talk me into doing *Past History*— I've told you what a disaster that was—and in another way I let it happen again with George. I want to get away from that kind of situation."

"I'm not sure any of us can really help becoming part of other people's dreams, Andrea," Myra said, with a seriousness that was unusual for her. "But I do understand your feelings. I've had them myself at one time or another. Are you thinking of going back on the screen? That's an awfully collaborative medium, isn't it?"

"Yes. Yes it is. And it's difficult to revive a career in films when you've been out of it for a while. People forget you. And there's always somebody younger and prettier."

"You're still very young, my dear. I hope at least that you will stay here in London. I would miss you greatly. You've been the best audience I've had in years." Myra suddenly chortled. "But you see, there I go myself, trying to make you part of my pleasure."

"Oh, Myra." Andrea stopped for a moment, caught between laughter and tears. "I love you," she said. "I don't think there's ever been anyone who's a better friend to me. I would miss you terribly, too. But I think I will probably go back to New York. I suppose it's a terrible thing to say, but I'm not at all sure I want to be Sir George Harrington's widow. And that's what I'd be here. There are people who would be very kind, I know. But there are others who would feel that I should have been buried with him, if you know what I mean."

"Like the wives of the pharaohs? Yes, I do know what you mean."

"In New York I think it might be different. There I wouldn't be George's widow, I'd be the American actress who went away to make a film and came back Lady Andrea Harrington. There would be a difference. At least that's what Bruce Halliwell tells me, and I think he's right."

207

"Halliwell?"

"Yes, we've been friends since childhood. You met him once at dinner here when he was over on vacation."

"Ah, yes, a very witty young man. A little too witty. Competition, you know."

Andrea laughed. "Yes, I'd love to see you two in a contest. At any rate, he thinks I could make use of what he calls the Lady Andrea bit in New York. He's even suggested I become his partner."

"A partner? What does the man do? I've forgotten."

"He's a caterer. A very expensive, very chic caterer."

"A caterer!" Myra's eyebrows and her voice rose together. "You can't be serious."

"Well, I haven't said yes. I want to think about it for a while. But it could be fun. I have to earn a living, Myra. There may be something coming to me from George's estate eventually, but I doubt if it's going to be much, and it could take years to settle. You know how I love to entertain, and the kind of business Bruce does is with the very rich, where you sit down and work out the entire presentation of a meal— not just the food, but the whole ambience. I think I might be good at that."

"I have no doubt that you would be, Andrea, but it's like going into service. Not like being a housekeeper, I understand that. But even so."

"Yes, that bothers me a little. I'm as much of a snob as you are, Myra. But it seems to me I might as well use some of what I've learned the past three years. That would be one way to do it. And I wouldn't exactly be washing dishes. I'd be a kind of social planner, even a social arbiter from what Bruce tells me."

"I think you're trying to talk yourself into this, Andrea."

"Perhaps I am."

"Well, I don't approve. I think you should stay right here. You know I'll do everything I can to help. You can come live with us and be *my* personal social arbiter, if it comes to that."

"I don't think you need any help, Myra."

"Well, perhaps not. But if you need a job, I'm sure we can find you something very suitable. Charles and I don't sit on all these boards of governors for nothing, you know. I shall talk to him about it tonight."

Andrea was silent for a moment, pondering. "If you like, Myra. That's very sweet of you." But she didn't really think she wanted to do something "suitable." She wanted to do something she enjoyed.

"That's settled then," said Myra. "I don't want to hear any more talk about your going back to New York." She paused, and then, with a hint of mischievousness, added, "I'm sure that handsome Mr. Willoughby would agree with me entirely."

"I'm not so sure about that, Myra. I suspect Kevin liked the situation just as it was, with me safely married to someone else."

"Well, that is quite often a characteristic of lovers, I admit, but when the situation changes, they sometimes change as well. Have you seen him yet?"

"No, he's called, of course, but to tell you the truth, I wasn't quite ready to deal with Kevin. I finally agreed to have dinner with him next week."

"At a restaurant?" Myra looked concerned.

"Of course not. At his flat. And I told him just dinner. I plan to wear black to emphasize the point."

"Isn't that carrying decorum a little far, my dear? Life does go on, after all. And it seems just slightly perverse to start being faithful at this point."

There were times when Myra managed to shock Andrea, and this was one of them. She gave a startled laugh and said, "You know, Myra, you really are rather wicked sometimes."

"Nonsense," said Myra, drawing herself up. "You still have some things to learn, young lady. One of them is that pleasure is difficult to come by and fleeting at best. One must grasp it whenever possible, and if you excuse such lewdness in an old woman, Mr. Willoughby appears to me to be eminently graspable."

To this sally, Andrea had no answer at all.

As it turned out, Andrea need not have worried. When she arrived for dinner at Kevin's the following week, his embrace was the chaste and comforting hug of an old friend and not at all the fervent reminder of their intimacy that she had expected. She was grateful for that; it immediately made her feel more relaxed. It was not, as Myra had suggested, that she felt any after-the-fact sense of fidelity to George. Nor was it a matter of guilt. But she felt intuitively that it was imporant to any future relationship with Kevin to establish things on a new footing, to indicate that for them to see each other did not inevitably involve sex. Beyond that, the events of the past two weeks had left her physically numbed. Sex was simply the furthest thing from her mind.

Kevin had prepared a paella for dinner, a very beautiful paella. He had made it only with seafood, leaving out the chorizo sausages and chicken found in some versions. There were reputed to be as many kinds of paella as regions of Spain. Andrea herself had always preferred the seafood variety of the Mediterranean coast, especially when it was as resplendent as Kevin's, which contained not only the usual complement of shrimp, whitefish, mussels, and clams, but also lobster and even amazingly tender morsels of octopus. It was decorated with bright red pimiento and fresh peas, which stood out elegantly against the brilliant yellow rice. With one taste she could tell that Kevin had used nothing but saffron to color and flavor the rice; most restaurants put in only a few slivers of saffron, since it was worth its weight in gold, and tried to fool their customers by adding yellow food coloring.

"I thought you said you weren't much of a cook, Kevin. This is absolutely marvelous."

"Well, I'm nothing like the kind of cook you are. I was a bit intimidated at the idea of preparing anything for you, in fact."

"People are always saying that to me. But you obviously didn't need to be."

"Oh yes, I did. But I thought I could pull this off. I learned how to do a paella when we were filming at a little seaside village south of Valencia. We had a lot of Spanish extras, and a group of them used to make a paella for themselves for lunch sometimes, in a great big iron pan over an open fire. It was fascinating. Sometimes I bought them some shrimp and clams and they'd invite me to join them."

"I guess there's nothing like learning at the source."

"Especially for me. I hate recipes. Most of the other things I cook are very lower-class English, which I learned by watching my mother, helping usually. Steak and kidney pie, Scotch eggs, that kind of thing. But I thought the paella would be more to your taste."

"It's wonderful, but sometime you must make a steak and kidney pie for me, too."

"All right. But I'd rather eat your cooking. I've been thinking, Andrea, why don't we get married? After a decent interval, of course."

Andrea's fork skidded, sending a mussel shell halfway across her plate.

She looked across at Kevin, who was trying to look nonchalant, but suddenly gave up and grinned. "Surprised you, didn't I?" he asked.

"I think the word is *stunned*."

"You don't like the idea?"

"I don't know what I think. My mind just stopped functioning."

"Well, it seems like a good idea to me. We get along very easily together, we have many of the same interests, and the sex is terrific. That puts us far out in front of most married couples, wouldn't you say?"

"I suppose it does."

"Of course I realize there are drawbacks. You wouldn't be Lady Andrea anymore and I know that means a good deal to you. And most of your ritzy friends would probably disapprove. But I am going to be rich. I'm signing a contract next week with De Laurentiis. Four hundred thousand dollars, plus percentage. And that's only the beginning, if everything goes right. You could go on living fairly much the way you have. I wouldn't want to live at Eaton Square, too many ghosts, but I have my eye on a house in Chelsea I think you'd like."

"Kevin, you're going much too fast for me."

"Well, don't think about it now. Your paella's getting cold. Just keep it in mind."

Andrea shook her head. "Kevin, you don't want to get married. I'm very flattered, but I think you're just being impulsive. Feeling sorry for me or something."

"No, I'm not. Impulsive is what I usually am. This time I'm being sensible. Most women I just want. It's different with you, Andrea. I respect you. I care for you. Besides," he added with a grin, "we'd make a very handsome couple."

Andrea laughed. "Yes, I'll grant you that. And I'm sure being married to you would be fun, Kevin. I even think you'd be faithful for a year or two."

"I was afraid you'd say something like that. People change, Andrea. I've never had any reason to be faithful. If we were married, I would have."

"For a while."

For the first time Kevin looked sulky. "You really don't trust me, do you? But I can't prove it to you unless you give me the chance."

"No, Kevin, I don't trust you. But that's not the main problem. I don't want to *have* to trust you or anyone else. Not right now. Not for some time to come. I don't want to have to trust anyone but me for the time being."

"I thought you might feel like that. But I had to try."

There appeared to be a genuine sadness in Kevin's dark eyes. Yet Andrea could not help wondering if he really would have asked if he hadn't been fairly sure she would say no. Perhaps she was being unfair, but she suspected that Kevin had simply been following through on one of his more elaborate fantasies. Knowing Kevin, the idea of asking her to marry him had probably given him an instant hard-on.

He was sitting silently with downcast eyes. Poor thing, she thought, and, in a reversal of her original intentions, reached out and took his hand.

Kevin was a perfect diversion, she had to give him credit. But for her, at least, she knew he could not be anything more.

And what she needed in the immediate future was not diversion, but a clear direction of her own making. She did not believe that Kevin or anything else in London could offer that.

It was time to go home.

Andrea stood for the last time in the drawing room at Eaton Square. Her bags were in the foyer. At any time now the taxi would arrive to take her to the airport for her flight to New York. And then in the days that followed, the suave young men from Christie's would take over the house, labeling the contents for auction. They were at Oakridge Manor already. She had wanted to leave before they actually began to dismantle the two centuries of Harrington family history that surrounded her, the objects among which she had once expected to spend the rest of her life.

There were gaps here and there. Some things had already been crated and shipped by sea to New York, the relatively few treasures she had wanted to keep for herself. Mostly it was china and silver, things that were beautiful but also useful, things that would through continued use become simply a part of her present life rather than reminders of the past. She had been tempted to take the small Renoir from her bedroom, but it was too valuable; it might in itself bring enough at

213

auction to eventually leave her with a sizable sum after all the creditors, and the inheritance taxes, had been paid.

Andrea heard Mrs. Evelyn rustling across the hall, and called out to her.

"Yes, Lady Andrea."

Mrs. Evelyn's eyes were red-rimmed. Andrea felt terribly sorry for her. Eaton Square had been her home for almost thirty years now, and Andrea suspected that its loss affected her far more profoundly than it did herself. She had feared that Mrs. Evelyn and Jeremy, who had already taken another position, would somehow blame her for George's death, but they had been extremely supportive. Jeremy had apparently known about Riccardo, and even had a good idea of George's precarious financial state. They had both been very good to her, and she would miss them very much, she knew. Myra was going to take on Mrs. Evelyn, a final favor Andrea had asked of her; she had thought it might be difficult for a woman of Mrs. Evelyn's age to find a new place for herself. Despite her strong disapproval of Andrea's decision to return to New York, Myra had agreed.

"I just wanted to say thank you, Mrs. Evelyn. For your kindness, and your help in so many ways. And I promise to keep in touch."

"Oh, Ma'am." Mrs. Evelyn buried her face in her hands, and Andrea went to her and put her arms around her.

"Forgive me, Ma'am. Forgive me."

"Don't be silly. But you'd better stop or I'll be crying, too."

"Yes, Ma'am." But the old woman's body continued to shake with sobs.

The door chimes rang, and Andrea stepped back. "I'll get it," she said.

"No, no. I'll go."

Andrea followed her into the hall, expecting a cabbie. But it was Myra's chauffeur who stood in the doorway.

"Jacob!"

"Lady Andrea," he said, bowing slightly.

"I'm sorry, Lady Andrea," Mrs. Evelyn said, half smiling through her tears. "I didn't even call a cab. Lady Myra said she would come, but she wanted to surprise you."

Andrea gave Mrs. Evelyn a final hug and went down the steps to the waiting car, while Jacob collected her bags.

The rear door to the black Rolls was open and Andrea got in beside Myra. "What a wonderful surprise," she said. "I thought you were angry with me."

"My dear Andrea," Myra said, "I'm perfectly furious with you, as you well know. But if we let a little anger get in the way of things we wouldn't have any friends at all, would we? If you must go, I want to be there to wave farewell. Besides, I wouldn't hear of your taking a mere *taxi*."

"Oh, Myra, I am going to miss you dreadfully."

"I certainly hope so, my dear. I would be most put out if you didn't." And she reached out and took Andrea's hand in hers.

Part Four

Chapter Nine

IN NEW YORK CITY, more cocktail parties, dinner parties, weddings, bar mitzvas, fund-raisers, openings, and even closings are catered affairs than in any other city in the world. Catering there is a multimillion-dollar business, serving almost every segment of society, and every kind of occasion, from Christmas parties at warehouses on the Brooklyn docks to sit-down dinners for twelve at East Side townhouses where the guest list includes the Henry Kissingers and the Oscar de la Rentas. A car dealer in Elmhurst, Queens, may call on a caterer once in his life, for his daughter's wedding, and regret the bill for a year or more, while a Park Avenue widow may have a catered dinner twice a week. It is axiomatic, however, that the Queens father and the Park Avenue dowager will not be dealing with the same firm. A successful caterer never attempts to be all things to all people, even if that were technically possible. A successful caterer makes a fundamental decision about the kind of clientele he wants to attract, and everything from the food he serves and the prices he charges to the manner he affects reflect that decision.

At one level of the catering business are corner delicatessens that prepare, on twenty-four hours' notice, platters of cold cuts and a variety of salads—potato, macaroni, chicken, and shrimp. Sometimes they deliver and sometimes the party giver must pick up the platters, usually made of what Bruce Halliwell called plastic crystal. Upper-echelon caterers would sniff that *that* is not catering at all, but the differences between the lowest and highest levels of the business are in truth a matter of style and cost, and not of purpose, which is simply to provide food that the hosts do not have the time or expertise to prepare themselves. Quality is a different matter. A delicatessen salad—especially from one of the "gourmet" delicatessens that began to spring up in the mid-1970's—may be superb, and a serving of chicken Kiev from a formal caterer can be dry and tasteless despite its cost.

On the second level of the business are caterers that specialize in very large parties, offering a straightforward and basically unchanging selection of menus that cleave to such staples as chicken, roast beef, and lobster Newburg. Some of these establishments, especially those in Brooklyn and Queens, have large dining rooms on the premises that may be hired along with the food and waiters. Often these firms are run by successive generations of the same family, and because their success is built on both reliability and predictability, they are very slow to respond to the latest trend, or as they might see it, the current fads of the more rarefied world of gourmet cooking.

There are hundreds of self-proclaimed gourmet caterers in New York, almost all of them based in Manhattan. Many of them are quite small, highly personalized operations, in which one or two individuals, with a few assistants, plan, cook, and even serve for small dinner parties in the cooperative apartments and brownstone duplexes of the affluent but not really rich, the known but not yet famous. The owner-chefs of these smaller caterers usually specialize in a few dishes that they do particularly well, sometimes becoming known for their expertise with certain techniques, such as puff pastry, or for a particular, slightly exotic cuisine, whether it be Mexican, Japanese, or Moroccan.

At the apex of the catering establishment are a dozen or more firms that fight for—and are fought over by—the elite clientele whose parties are chronicled by *Women's Wear Daily* and the gossip columns of the *Times* and the *Post*. Their menus offer the variety, the quality of preparation, and the glamour of presentation one would expect from the finest restaurants. The variety is necessary because the rich and famous people to whom they cater, in all senses of the word, are constantly going to one another's parties, and no hostess in that milieu would be caught dead serving her guests the same menu she had consumed at another party the week before. Quality of preparation must be maintained because both hosts and guests go out to dinner several times a week, and their taste buds are highly attuned to excellence. And the glamour of presentation must be on a level that makes it worthwhile for one to have worn one's new Halston gown.

Every few years the popularity of one of the top catering firms begins to fade. "They've really become terribly old hat," one hostess will say to another. Or, "Their standards are slipping, my dear. The caviar the other night at Mabel's was entirely second rate." Most often such a fading firm is pushed out by some aggressive and imaginative newcomer, a firm capable of creating fads rather than merely following them, able to outdo the competition in at least one of the three crucial areas of variety, quality, and glamour. Usually such an assault on the bastions of power requires taking a lower profit at the beginning, using even more superb raw ingredients than the competition while at the same time slightly underpricing it. Prices can always be raised later, when the fix is in, and the demand is sufficient. If, of course, the assault is successful.

Bruce Halliwell's firm had reached just such a point of breaking through into the topmost level of the catering establishment when Andrea joined it in May 1974. Bruce's rise had been very rapid. He had left Richard Corliss's firm only three years before to start his own company, which he called Ambrosia, Inc. In those days most catering firms carried the name of the owner, and Richard had warned Bruce that Ambrosia, Inc., was undignified and far too cute a moniker. "People will think you're selling toilet water," he sniffed. But in fact Bruce's move set a new trend; many of the younger caterers began to use equally catchy names. Besides, there was an advantage to having a generalized company name, in that it made it easier for Bruce to foist off his assistants onto some of the hostesses. He had taken full note of the many times that two equally important clients had wanted to give a party on the same night, with both *demanding* that Richard himself personally oversee their particular extravaganza. Everyone knew, of course, that a great many of the parties Richard Corliss catered were left entirely in the hands of assistants, but no really important hostess would put up with that. If she was going to hire Richard Corliss, she wanted to be able to say, "Richard is handling it himself, of course." With a name like Ambrosia, Inc., that kind of problem became a little easier to handle.

Nevertheless, schedule conflicts remained a problem, especially now that he was beginning to crack the A-level party circuit. That was one reason why he had decided that it would be greatly to his advantage to take on Andrea as a partner, quite aside from the fact that he wanted to help her. He could have elevated one of his assistants to a partnership. Paul Boucheron was about ready for that kind of responsibility, and he had lately become the lover of an aging oil tycoon who would do anything for the boy and might be expected to cough up a tidy sum for Paul to buy into the firm. But Bruce was not particularly in need of capital; what he needed was additional clout, and a partner whom hostesses would not feel was merely a stand-in. Few would know who Andrea was, although a piece on her had appeared in *Vogue*, and there had been the *Town & Country* article before that. Some might recall her from her year and a half on Broadway, as well, or her television movies, but that wouldn't carry much weight. What mattered was her title. Not only would that make her acceptable as a star with equal billing within the firm, he was certain it would also bring to Ambrosia, Inc., that extra cachet, the slight *différence*, that could carry it once and for all into the top category.

Andrea needed a job and Bruce needed someone with precisely Andrea's social talents and standing. What she didn't know about food—and from the clippings and letters she had sent him, it was obvious that she had learned a very great deal—he would teach her. He doubted that much teaching would be necessary, except perhaps about the technical aspects of catering. Anyone who could give a garden party for eighty, such as the one described in Vogue, *without* the help of a caterer, belonged in the business.

Ambrosia, Inc., was located in premises formerly occupied by a Chinese restaurant that had always been second-rate and had been finally extinguished by the new rage for the hot, spicy foods of the Szechuan and Hunan provinces; like many Cantonese restaurants, it had been ironically killed off by a new wave of interest in the *real* China. Occupying two floors between Sixty-seventh and Sixty-eighth streets on First Avenue, the space offered several advantages. There was, to begin with, a professional kitchen already in place, which needed only to be updated and expanded. The entire first floor was given over to food preparation, while the smaller second floor served as office space. The location was ideal for a catering firm, being within minutes of the East Side brownstones and Fifth and Park Avenue apartments where the firm's targeted clientele lived, and if it was necessary to get across town to The Dakota or some other Central Park West haven of exclusivity, there were two quick and equidistant routes across the park.

Andrea had arrived from London late on Monday afternoon, May 20, and Bruce had suggested she might like to wait until Wednesday to see the premises, to give her time to recover from jet lag. But she couldn't wait. And so at 11:00 A.M. Tuesday morning, Bruce escorted Andrea around the kitchens for the first time, introducing her to the staff already on duty and then taking her upstairs to his office at the rear of the second floor. Her own office, next door to his, was still being remodeled.

"I'm afraid there isn't much daylight here at the back," Bruce said apologetically. "But when I was planning the layout,

I stood at the front and listened to the racket coming up from First Avenue, and I asked myself if I wanted to spend the next few years yelling at my clients over the telephone or trying to hear them over the din. I decided I didn't want that, and I'm quite sure they wouldn't. They like to think their food is coming from some place with marble floors and gold faucets where a monklike silence is observed."

Andrea laughed, but she decided that once she had settled in she would have to do something to make her office a little more glamorous than it was obviously going to be. She might be talking to clients only over the phone or at their homes, but that didn't mean she couldn't surround herself with a few touches to grace the eye.

Bruce's own office was very neat, spare, and functional. She was a little surprised at that since it was such a contrast to the exotic, sensual ambience of his apartment, where she was staying for the time being. Karen Bolling, with whom Andrea had kept in touch—and who had in fact dined twice at Eaton Square when in London scouting new plays for possible New York productions—had two possible apartments in mind for Andrea, but neither would be available until the end of the month.

"This is a very good time for you to begin to learn the ropes," Bruce was saying. "We have a heavy schedule over the next five weeks, and you'll be able to observe almost every kind of operation we engage in. There are a number of large wedding buffets coming up in June. They're always difficult, not from the logistical point of view, but because the mamas are usually on the verge of a nervous breakdown and can't resist making trouble for themselves and for us. There's a run of end-of-the-season cocktail parties, and the usual smaller sit-down dinners. I'm not going to ask you to actually **do** much at the beginning. I think you'll learn most quickly if you just observe. You might want to keep a notebook of questions you want to ask, and, of course, ideas you have about food or presentation that occur to you. I know how creative you are, and that's going to be very important to us."

Andrea had seldom seen this very businesslike side of Bruce. It didn't surprise her, but she thought it might take some getting used to.

"When you feel ready, I'll have you start dealing with clients directly. July is a slow month in terms of actual engagements, but we'll already be in the thick of planning for the fall season, and you'll be very much involved in that. I don't want to overload you, but your being here is going to make it possible for us to expand some. I want our clients to realize from the beginning that you will be precisely my equal in terms of handling a party. I've already started talking you up, and I can tell from the response that there's not going to be any problem. Now, the first thing to deal with is the datebook. Here, take a look at this."

Bruce handed her a leather-bound notebook with a page for each day of the year. "Turn to June 10."

Andrea turned to the page.

1:00 P.M.   Wedding buffet. 60 persons. Mrs. C. P. Bienstock. The Dakota. 721-8693 (Unlisted) (BH, PB)

5:30 P.M.   Cocktails. 150 persons. Mrs. Stanley Becton. Townhouse, 123 E. 67th. 592-4743 (BH, SG)

7:00 P.M.   Sit-down dinner. 12 persons. Mrs. William Carr. Apartment (service elevator), 761 Park Avenue. 592-2160 (PB)

7:30 P.M.   Sit-down dinner. 20 persons. Louise Richards. Apartment, 320 E. 57th Street. 753-6062 (BH)

"That's a small wedding party for an address like The Dakota, isn't it?" Andrea asked.

Bruce laughed. "You are sharp. Yes, it is. You'd expect them to take over one of the hotel ballrooms. But the groom is Gentile and Papa's very unhappy about it, so it's a low-profile affair."

"I assume the initials refer to who's handling the party."

"That's right. I'm putting in three appearances, God help me. But I'll be leaving both the wedding and the cocktail party almost as soon as they begin, with Paul Boucheron taking over at the Bienstocks', and Steven Grant at the cocktail party. Then Paul does one dinner and I'll go to Louise Richards'. It's her birthday and she especially wanted me to be there, though Paul often does her parties. I'll be doing most of the actual cooking at that one. The dishes will be prepared here up to the point of final assembly and the actual finishing of the dish. I'm not talking about reheating, of course. For a sit-down dinner we try not to do that except with soups, or something like a cassoulet, which we'd make the day before anyway, to let the flavors marry overnight."

"I can see I have a lot to learn. Tell me, why isn't there a Mrs. or a Miss before Louise Richards' name?"

"If you picked that up, Andrea, you're not going to have any trouble learning, I assure you. That's because she insisted long ago that I call her by her first name. Even my secretary calls her Louise, or there would be a Miss there for her benefit. We do a party almost every week for her, so there's a lot of calling back and forth."

"You never put anything in here, though, about what's going to be served?"

"No, we use separate loose-leaf notebooks for that. A whole series of them. And once a party is behind us, the menu goes into the files. In fact, I even keep an alphabetical card file in a safe-deposit box. If we ever lost track of what had been served to whom *we'd* be lost. I should tell you also that in the loose-leaf notebooks we keep a copy of the guest lists. Occasionally, some secretive type will put up a fuss about providing that, but if we can possibly get it, we do. That's because we have clients who go to one another's parties, and we don't want to duplicate menus, unless we're specifically asked to serve a particular dish one client had at another's house, even if the parties are a month apart. That's one of

226

the things that makes us special. A lot of caterers don't worry about that kind of cross indexing, chiefly because they do only a fairly limited number of dishes anyway."

Andrea nodded. "I'm used to that. In London, I always kept a file on what guests had been served what, where they were seated, the colors of the linen, even the china and flowers I used."

"My God," said Bruce. "Maybe you should be instructing me. I guess I don't even need to talk about the endless variations one can ring on basic ingredients. Sole, for instance."

Andrea smiled. "I suppose Madame Prunier gives about two hundred, just for starters. I suspect I could double that if I put my mind to it."

"Wonderful. That's what we need, creativity. Of course you don't have to worry much about people who hire you a couple of times of year, but with someone like Louise Richards, inventiveness is very important. Besides, it keeps the staff on their toes. If you do the same things all the time, the chefs themselves get bored."

Despite a lingering tiredness, Andrea was feeling elated. It was the kind of high she often felt when she was running on nervous energy. She hadn't been sleeping well since before George's death, but now none of the turmoil she'd been through seemed to matter. "You know, Bruce, I think I'm going to love this. It's as complicated as I suspected it would be, but I'm glad. I want to be challenged. And I think it's going to be great fun as well."

Bruce smiled at her. "I wouldn't have asked you if I hadn't known you'd feel that way. It can be great fun, and I love it myself. But it can also be exhausting, and it can be extremely frustrating. There are clients you'll want to strangle with your bare hands, and days that you'll think are never going to end. You have to be prepared for that. Of course, that's why the date book is so important. Sometimes I'm tempted to overload. I think, well, there's a three-hour gap there. We could just fit in that little cocktail party. But I've learned not to do it. It just gets too madly crazy. And our performance suffers. You can't get away with botching anything in this profession. It's too competitive. The waters are full of sharks, my dear."

"Speaking of competition, I had the feeling that Paul Boucheron isn't altogether thrilled to have me joining the firm. Or am I being paranoid?"

"No," said Bruce, laughing. "Just very perceptive, as always. I think he rather hoped he'd be made a partner himself. He's very good, in fact, and I suspect eventually he'll try to make it on his own. But don't worry about it. You'll have the whole staff lapping milk from your hand in no time."

"I noticed that you introduced me to everyone as Lady Andrea. Wouldn't it be a good idea to ask them to call me just Andrea?"

"Certainly not," Bruce said, almost sharply. But then his voice took on a teasing tone. "I'm shocked at you, my dear. To want to throw away an asset like that!"

Andrea felt herself blushing.

"In the privacy of this office, I'm Bruce and you're Andrea. But otherwise, while we're working, I'm Mr. Halliwell and you are Lady Andrea, even when we're talking to the others about each other. And that's not just a matter of being hoity-toity. It's a way of keeping people under control. Things get fairly hysterical at times, and people lose their tempers. You and are in charge here, and everyone has got to know it down the line. It's much easier for a sous-chef to start screaming at you if he calls you Bruce, believe me. If he's been thoroughly indoctrinated in the fact that you are *Mr.* Halliwell, it saves a lot of time spent wrangling. Besides, if you let things get all cozy and informal, you'll have a waiter rushing up to you at a party and calling you Bruce in front of the hostess. Except to Louise Richards and one or two others, I am always Mr. Halliwell to my clients, too. It also helps keep them in line. In fact, even Louise always calls me that in front of guests, and I call her Miss Richards. She's a very down-to-earth lady, but she knows why a certain formality is necessary, from my point of view if not from hers."

"God, Bruce, I feel as though I'd never left England."

Bruce smiled a wicked smile. "What you have to realize, my dear Andrea," he said, leaning forward and lowering his voice dramatically, "is that you are entering what is one of the very few snooty professions left in America."

"Well, if it comes to that, I suppose I can snoot it with the best of them."

"That's my girl," Bruce said, and they began to laugh simultaneously.

June and July of that year passed with a speed that made Andrea feel she had been caught up in a whirlwind. Every evening she would return dead tired to her new apartment on East Sixty-seventh Street, only three blocks from Ambrosia, Inc., and look at the still only partially furnished rooms, the packing cases from England still unopened, and wonder when in the world she would find time to put it all in order. She had very little social life, although she managed to see a few of her old theater friends on various Mondays, that being the one day off for her just as it now was for most Broadway shows. But she didn't really care about a social life. She had wanted to be challenged and there was no question she had gotten her wish. It was exhausting but also exhilarating.

There were some surprises and disappointments. She discovered that aspics, at which she was particularly adept, were far from popular as a catered item. Shimmeringly beautiful they might be, with their intricately decorated layers of ham or crab, but they simply could not be served except at large buffets where there was a wide choice of other dishes. At a sit-down dinner party, there was bound to be at least one guest who wouldn't touch anything in aspic. Besides, they took too much time to assemble, because of the necessity of returning the mold to the refrigerator after the addition of each layer. Time, time, there was never enough of it.

And then there was the matter of innards, or offal, as the

229

English called them. Too many people seemed to think that offal was spelled awful, and it was forbidden even to mention sweetbreads or brains or even calves' liver to clients unless they brought them up themselves. That was something Bruce had forgotten to tell her, and she had to learn the hard way when an elegantly dressed woman looked across at Andrea in her Park Avenue apartment, clutched her pearls in horror, and said, "Ugh."

That had been a bad morning, since the woman seemed to regard with suspicion every subsequent suggestion Andrea made. As Andrea told Bruce later, "I might just as well have suggested serving worms." But on the whole she had no difficulty dealing with clients. As Bruce had predicted, they seemed to be sufficiently cowed by her title, or to take such secret pleasure in the fact that their whims were being indulged by someone with a title, that they caused fewer problems than she had expected. She had been afraid that they might challenge her professional credentials, but between her title and the fact that she was associated with Ambrosia, Inc., clients simply seemed to assume that she knew what she was doing.

By the end of July, in fact, she felt that on the whole she did know what she was doing. The firm would be closed for the month of August, which would give her a chance to put her apartment in order and gather her strength for the September onslaught, when for the first time she would have to carry through on parties she had planned in their entirety. Bruce went to Europe for two-legged game, and she began to wrestle with her packing boxes and shop for additional furniture.

As she unpacked the crates, odd items she hardly remembered having decided to keep cropped up. There were the silver asparagus tongs from Eaton Square, and one of the Chinese vases from the library at Oakridge Manor, each carrying with it memories that she was surprised to realize she did want to maintain. Obviously, she had been in a daze when she selected them in England, but she was glad they were there. Life was a continuity, however much one might try to compartmentalize certain events, however much one tried to seal them off. There were memories that she would cherish, and in her daze she seemed to have selected well those representations of the moments and days she wanted to keep fresh.

There were other things she expected to find. The Venetian mirror from the front hallway at Eaton Square reminded her instantly of Mrs. Evelyn's tearful farewell and of Myra waiting in the car outside, but the remembrance of their loyalty and love outweighed any sadness in the end. An eighteenth-century footstool, a Whistler drawing, a crystal lamp with an apricot silk shade—she was clearly going to have to do some juggling to pull it all together into a coherent decorating scheme. But as the days passed, each treasure found its place and gave her ideas for the new furnishings it was necessary to purchase. The fabric of her new sofa repeated the apricot of the silk lampshade; an ornate little table she found in a Third Avenue antique shop had scrollwork very similar to the Venetian mirror and fitted perfectly into the vestibule. It was an eclectic mix, but then that was all the rage in decorating; people would think that happenstance was deliberate style.

She had not been planning to go anywhere during the month, but then Karen Bolling called to invite her out for a long weekend at her house in East Hampton. Barry Lawrence, who would be opening in the fall in a new comedy Karen was producing, was going to be there with his wife, and she looked forward to seeing them again. But she almost turned down the invitation when Karen added that there was a man she wanted Andrea to meet.

"Oh, God," Andrea said. Like Myra, Karen seemed to feel that what Andrea really needed was another husband. Karen had been very helpful, and very nice, although she had absolutely refused to change caterers and come over to Ambrosia, Inc. "I'll be glad to recommend you to friends, dear girl, but when you come to my house it will be as a guest and not as a servant." Andrea understood that point of view, but she was also somewhat annoyed; it seemed to be a way of saying that Andrea was somehow better than what she was doing, and she'd heard enough along that line from Myra.

"What do you mean, oh God," Karen inquired over the phone.

"I really don't need a matchmaker, Karen. That's what I mean."

"I'm sure you don't, Andrea. But I think you'd like him. He's one of my favorite relatives. I guess you'd call him a relative. His name is Hayes Caldwell, and he's the younger brother of my second husband. What does that make him, my former brother-in-law? These things have always confused me."

"Why don't you try brother-in-law once removed?" Andrea suggested somewhat mischievously.

"I think you're making fun of me. But never mind. You'll like Hayes, I promise you. He's very handsome, and rich as Croesus."

"That just makes it worse, Karen. What is he, divorced?"

"No, his wife died of cancer a little over a year ago. It was very hard on him watching her slip away almost in stages. I think he's just beginning to get over it."

The last thing Andrea wanted to do was sit around and compare tragedies with anyone. But she knew Karen wouldn't let her get away with refusing to come at this point, since she'd already said how nice it would be to see Barry and Maddy. There was no way out of it. She would have to go.

Andrea had been to what Karen called her "beach house" twice before, the last time just before leaving for England and the month of filming at Oakridge Manor. It seemed a lifetime ago, Andrea reflected, but the house appeared just the same, the big white canvas-covered sofas, the huge living room with an acre of glass overlooking the sea, the enormous fireplace with its slightly incongruous built-in electric grill

232

for rainy days, the theater posters on the wall along the stairs, one of them for *Playing by Ear*. Actually there were two *Playing by Ear* posters now, one of them in the upstairs hall. The second poster dated from after Barry had left the show and had Andrea's name alone above the title. It looked as though it had been freshly hung. Karen really was a sweetheart, Andrea thought. On the other hand it could also be considered another message urging her to get out of the catering business.

"Stop being paranoid," she told herself under her breath.

She had arrived in time for lunch on Friday. It was a simple meal, avocados stuffed with crabmeat and a big bowl of scarlet strawberries with the hulls still on, to be dipped in sugar if you chose, but they didn't need it. Barry and Maddy were there, delighted to see her. And there was a youngish Spaniard named Manuel. They ate in bathing suits on the broad deck and Andrea noticed that Manuel's body was quite badly scarred in several places. He seemed oblivious of the fact, lounging around in the scantiest of bikinis. Later she found out he was a retired bullfighter.

There was no sign of Karen's fabled brother-in-law once removed, and he wasn't mentioned, giving Andrea some hope that perhaps one of his oil wells had blown its top and unavoidably detained him. But he arrived later in the afternoon, showing up on the beach where they all lay taking in the sun.

"Hayes!" Karen cried out with obvious delight. She got up from her beach chair and ran toward him as he came down the steps from the house.

"Hello, hello there, sweetie-pie girl," Hayes said, picking Karen up in his arms and whirling her around.

Sweetie-pie girl. Andrea was instantly sure that she was going to loathe him, and wished that he were more than once removed. Or that she was.

But as he walked toward the rest of them across the bright white sand, hand in hand with Karen, Andrea was slightly taken aback. Karen had been right about one thing. He was

233

one of the handsomest men she had ever seen. He was tall, very tall, at least six-five, with broad shoulders and a trim, strong torso. His hair was thick and curly and almost white against his dark tan. But more than anything else it was the energy he radiated that struck her. He seemed to almost vibrate with strength. It seemed to come off him in waves, like the afternoon light bouncing off the sand.

Andrea got to her feet along with the others and stood waiting to be introduced. And Karen did a strange and rather annoying thing. She introduced him to Maddy and Barry, and then to Manuel, and then finally to her.

"Last but not least, lovely lady," Hayes Caldwell said to her in his soft, deep drawl.

God, Andrea thought, what a shame it is you have to talk.

Chapter Ten

IT TOOK ANDREA THE BETTER PART of a year to get used to the cornball and unabashedly chauvinistic endearments Hayes Caldwell dropped into his conversation whenever he was talking to a woman, especially one he knew well. If it wasn't "sweetie pie," it was "honey bunch," or "baby doll," or worst of all, "my little bunny rabbit." She tried to break him of the habit. The first time he addressed her as "my little bunny rabbit," he was telephoning from Teheran; the connection was bad and she was so surprised by the call that she had to let it go. Besides, she had known him less than a month and hadn't made up her mind, quite, whether she was going to become sufficiently involved with him to make the effort of retraining worthwhile. But when he did it again a month later, calling from downtown at the Waldorf where he had just arrived from Alaska, she replied, "Hayes, are you trying to tell me that my nose twitches and I have red eyes? If so, I am not at all complimented."

She was in her office at the time, and Bruce, who had been conferring with her about the menu for a two-hundred-person buffet, had laughed out loud and scored a point for her in the air with his forefinger as he left the room.

At the other end of the line there was a brief pause, and then Hayes said, somewhat plaintively, "Oh, come on, Andrea, you know what I mean. I was just thinking how nice it would be if you were all curled up in my lap right this minute."

There was no answer to that, she would have liked to be there herself.

She tried other tactics. Once he called from Australia and

started off by asking, "How's my sweet kangaroo?" and she countered by saying, "Just fine, you oversized Atlas."

But that didn't work at all. "Are you talking about maps or Greek heroes?" he had asked. "Either way, I thank you."

Finally she gave up and decided to be amused, at least when he was speaking to her in private, but it still made her wince sometimes when he did it in front of other people. Eventually she simply accepted it. Hayes had few if any other failings, and he truly did not understand why any woman wouldn't be delighted to be showered with cute endearments. He had a loving nature and couldn't hide it.

As she had quickly discovered that first weekend at Karen's house in East Hampton, Hayes Caldwell was in every other way a very intelligent and a very nice man, quite aside from being gorgeous. He had been everywhere and, unlike many rich men who flew constantly around the world on business, he actually knew where he had been in ways that went far beyond airports and hotels and fancy restaurants. He could talk about anything from the social structure of elephant tribes to the psychological underpinnings of the Americanization of Japan. He had a degree in geology from Tulane—but although the hard information on such matters as shale deposits was useful and important to him in his business, he had an almost cosmic and thoroughly romantic view of the information of mountains and rivers, continents and seas. It was the fact that the earth *moved*, was still moving, shifting and erupting and reconstituting itself like any living thing that fascinated him, not just that those movements created the likelihood of finding oil or natural gas. He was as interested in anthropology as he was in geology. If a new well came in in some dubious section of the Oklahoma plains, he was pleased and proud because he had been right, but if in the course of drilling, a new Creek burial mound came to light, then he was truly excited and would fly to the spot from across the world, bringing drilling to a halt until the mound could be thoroughly excavated. A new oil well would only add to a fortune already beyond spending; a burial mound was a rare and mysterious message from the past, and Hayes would react with the enthusiasm of a kid who finds an arrowhead on a Boy Scout outing.

Hayes Caldwell was forty-six when Andrea met him, but his boyish enthusiasm for life made him seem considerably younger despite his thick thatch of prematurely white hair. No matter how tired Andrea was, Hayes's arrival in New York, often unannounced, always refreshed her and gave her a new feeling of zest. When he swept her into his arms, giving her one of his oversize bear hugs in greeting, she could almost feel herself drawing energy from him. That was even true in bed. There was an absolute maleness about him that went beyond anything she had experienced with any other man. When he entered her, with slow, sure strength, she always felt as though she were being lifted, carried forward, as though his vitality had become part of her. At the same time he was an astonishingly gentle and tender lover. It never ceased to amaze her that his huge hands, each finger of which was twice the width of one of her own, could caress so softly; she could feel the power in those hands, but it was a power held in reserve, and for that reason all the more exciting. But he could not restrain himself at orgasm; when he came it was always with great uninhibited cries of pleasure, a sound that began as a low rumble and gradually built almost to a shout. It was the kind of sound that Andrea was sure penetrated walls and ceilings into other apartments, and at first she was embarrassed. She had never been very vocal herself in bed, but she found herself beginning to join Hayes in his cries. Partially, she thought, it was because that way his own shouts seemed less loud and less obtrusive, but gradually she discovered a real pleasure, a strange, exciting new sense of liberation in letting herself go, mingling her voice with his in a kind of elemental song.

In the beginning, he was very patient and understanding about her late working hours and heavy schedule. He would fly into town and take his usual room at the Waldorf, and call to let her know he was there. She would tell him when she would be home, and he would let himself in with the key she had given him and be waiting for her. He always spent the night. The room at the hotel was mostly a matter of daytime convenience for him, and she would wake in the morning to find herself nestled in against his enormous warm body. She always slept more soundly when he was there.

Hayes's seeming acceptance of her professional independence apparently stemmed from the fact that his mother had herself been a remarkably strong-willed and determined woman. She had been raised on a vast Oklahoma ranch that turned out to be sitting on a virtual lake of oil. Hayes's father came from an old New Orleans family, although Hayes's grandfather had been an interloper from St. Louis. The marriage between Hayes's parents had been an odd one since his father had been as attached to his New Orleans home as his mother was to the ranch, and they had spent a considerable amount of time apart. Hayes's older brother, to whom Karen Bolling had been married, had spent most of his time at the ranch, while Hayes himself was more or less brought up by his father in New Orleans.

"Yes," Hayes agreed, "it was a strange marriage in a way. But it worked somehow. My parents were very loyal and loving, they just wanted to be in different places. My mother was very stubborn about it, and my father and I did a lot more traveling back and forth than she and my brother did."

"Did you like the ranch?" Andrea asked.

"Oh, sure, it was exciting in a way. But I liked New Orleans much more. If I can ever get you away from here long enough, sweetie pie, I'll show you New Orleans. It's my favorite city in the world and there aren't too many cities I haven't seen."

"Maybe next summer," Andrea said. "During my vacation."

"Promise?"

"That's a long way off, Hayes."

"I wish it were tomorrow, muffin," he said, and caressed her hair with his huge, gentle hand. "You work too hard."

"No, I don't," Andrea said firmly. "Work is a tonic for me, just as it is for you."

There were times, though, when even Andrea felt she was working too hard. Or, if not too hard, then with results that were unappreciated. As Bruce had warned her, there were days when nothing seemed to go right, and she came home in a fury of frustration, not with herself, but with the idiocy of some of the clients of Ambrosia, Inc. One of those days, in mid-February, unfortunately coincided with one of Hayes's visits.

A certain Mrs. Carlson, who had come to the firm for the first time to have them cater a buffet dinner for a hundred people, had called that morning, the day of the party, to announce that somehow or other the guest list had expanded by thirty in the last two days. So far as Andrea was concerned, they would never deal with Mrs. Carlson again; you simply did not spring that kind of surprise on a caterer. She told the woman that, because of the last-minute extra work involved, she would have to charge her double for the additional thirty people.

On the other end of the line there was a gasp. "My husband will murder me," Mrs. Carlson said. "He'll just kill me," she wailed.

"Well, I am extremely sorry, but we have a contract with you for serving a hundred people. I will have to placate the staff with a bonus, and it is in no way our fault that this has happened. If you want enough food for a hundred and thirty at this late date, you will have to compensate us for the problems involved. This is a business, Mrs. Carlson."

"Oh, my God. Oh, my God. I can't believe you're doing this to me." The woman's voice was climbing toward hysteria.

"Mrs. Carlson," said Andrea, in her firmest tones, "we are perfectly prepared to honor the original contract, and have your guests simply make do. But I should warn you that we will not accept any criticism behind our backs. The problem is of your own making. You came to us on the recommenda-

239

tion of Mrs. Billingham, I know, and I cannot have a valued client thinking that we have let you down. I will certainly inform her of the circumstances."

"Oh, no, no, no, you mustn't do that. That would be worse. She's going to be here tonight."

"I am aware of that, Mrs. Carlson."

"Ohhh, all right. All right. This is blackmail, you know."

"It is nothing of the kind, Mrs. Carlson. I must advise you that the contract you signed makes it very clear that extra guests must be made known to us at least forty-eight hours in advance, or that double payment for the additional servings must be made. That contract is a legal document, you realize. I'm afraid that since you are taking this tone about it, I will have to ask your husband to sign a rider to the contract upon our arrival, stating his willingness to pay the additional amount."

Mrs. Carlson sobbed for a minute or more and then knuckled under. The moment she hung up, Andrea dialed Mrs. Billingham. This was the kind of mess that had to be dealt with beforehand, not afterwards. Mrs. Billingham, who was one of the firm's best clients, listened to Andrea's rather toned-down recital of the problem—toned down, except that she did drop in Mrs. Carlson's use of the word *blackmail* with a little laugh.

"Don't worry, my dear," Celia Billingham said. "The woman is clearly as much of a social climber as I thought, with absolutely no idea of how things are done. I will be certain to spread the word quietly tonight that you have done your usual superb job under the most difficult of circumstances."

But even that was not the end of it. Mr. Carlson, in a rage at his wife, signed the rider to the contract but spent the entire hour before the party shouting in the bedroom. On top of that, Mrs. Carlson had failed to warn Andrea about a defective electrical outlet in the dining room, with the result that half the house was plunged into darkness ten minutes before the guests were due to arrive.

240

By the time Andrea got home she was in a thoroughly rotten mood. Fortunately, Hayes was on the telephone to Tokyo, and she gave him a quick kiss and disappeared to take a hot bath, which somewhat restored her equanimity. When she reappeared, in a blue silk sari Hayes had brought her from Manila, he handed her a brandy and said, "You looked like you wanted to kill someone when you walked in, sweetie. I hope it's not me."

"Of course not. It's a miserable dithering wretch named Mrs. Carlson who was obviously raised in the storeroom of a Woolworth's in Jersey City."

Hayes whistled. "Honey, you're really upset."

Andrea laughed. "No, actually, I feel much better for saying that. And the brandy helps. And you help most of all."

"Then come sit in my lap."

"Gladly."

She settled in, feeling the powerful support of his thighs beneath her. "That's nice," she sighed.

"I don't like how tired you look," Hayes said.

"Thanks so much. I do love a compliment."

"You always look beautiful to me, you know that. But I don't think you should be wearing yourself out for these snotty old dames who aren't worth your little finger."

"It was just a bad day, Hayes. And don't worry, I'll never be dealing with Mrs. Carlson again."

"Maybe not. But I think you need a break. I'm flying to Mexico City tomorrow. I think you should come with me, for a couple of days at least."

"Hayes, you know I can't do that. It's a very busy time, with Valentine's Day and the Lincoln and Washington birthdays. We're swamped."

"People get sick, Andrea," he said, very seriously. Just calling her Andrea instead of honey or baby girl showed how serious he really was. "I think you should pretend to be sick before it really happens."

"I'm not going to get sick, Hayes. Most of the time I love it. Today was just one of those ghastly exceptions that prove the rule. I'm doing an absolutely fabulous party on Friday for Lisa Dabney, which I'm really looking forward to. You might even know her. Her husband was in oil."

"Yes, I know Lisa slightly. She took poor Richard for about twelve million I hear."

"Why not? He's the one who couldn't keep his hands off showgirls. In fact this party is a kind of celebration of the final settlement. For sixty of her *closest* friends." Andrea giggled. ":Do you know anybody who has sixty close friends?"

"I think ten is doing pretty well," Hayes said, smiling.

"But, anyway, she asked what I could do for two hundred dollars a person and I said practically anything, and she said wonderful. It's going to be absolutely spectacular. Among other things I'm doing a mosaic made up of four different kinds of caviar, with a design laid out in quails' eggs in aspic that's going to absolutely take people's breath away."

Hayes laughed. "Well, I suppose a few days with me in Mexico City is no match for that. But I wish it were."

"Hayes," said Andrea, looking up into his eyes. "Let me tell you something. I've never seen caviar get a hard-on."

For a moment he looked flabbergasted, and then began to roar with laughter. When he began to regain control of himself, she said, "I wish I could come with you, Hayes. But I can't. Please go on understanding that."

"I'll do my best," he said, and leaned down to kiss her. She could feel his erection rising against the underside of her thigh. She slipped off his lap and knelt before him, opening his robe. It never ceased to fascinate her to watch him grow from a softness that could be encompassed in one hand to a hardness that was bigger than two hands. She held him now in one hand and stroked him gently. "It's beautiful," she said softly.

In the large basement kitchen of David Barber's townhouse, Andrea was overseeing the final decoration of the eighth tray of lobster tartlets being consumed by the ravenous hordes upstairs. David Barber was the latest, and surely would not be the last, in the long line of boy-wonder magazine publishers who, backed by their fathers' meat-packing or plumbing fortunes, descend upon New York from the provinces every decade or so, to found new magazines or take over old ones, firing seasoned editors and hiring nascent geniuses right and left. Sometimes they even took over old-line hardcover publishing companies, which was what David Barber had just done. This party was in celebration of that fact, which meant that a large number of the guests were writers.

Catering a party for writers, whether hack journalists or Pulitzer Prize winners, resembled nothing so much as amassing sandbags to keep back a flood, Andrea had decided. You had to be prepared for the buffet table to be ransacked within half an hour, and it was no good hoping that they would all go home once the food ran out; it was certain that they would remain until the last drop of drink was gone, too, complaining all the while about there being nothing to eat.

David Barber had changed caterers three times in five months, with a resultant bad word-of-mouth for the firms concerned, and Andrea had struck a bargain with the host— she would provide considerably more food than he considered necessary, and anything uneaten would not be charged to him. As she had known perfectly well, there would be nothing left uneaten. In fact, this tray, which she persevered in making look beautiful for people who were by now certainly too drunk to notice, was the final reserve sandbag available, and she was looking forward to going home and leaving her staff to cope with the ruins.

But suddenly through the kitchen door appeared a wandering guest, possibly looking for a bathroom, or, as was to be hoped, the front door. But to Andrea's dismay, the woman said, "Oh, good, I've found you."

It might be that the woman wanted a recipe. That happened sometimes, and it was always difficult to deal with. Or it might be that she wanted to hire Andrea for some future party, in which case she could simply be told to call the office in the morning.

The woman marched right across to Andrea and, extending her hand, said, "I'm Louise Norman."

Dear God, Andrea thought, but managed to say, with at least the appearance of composure. "Oh, yes, indeed, Miss Norman. I'm delighted to meet you."

Louise Norman was a considerable legend in the food world; indeed, she was often referred to by a nickname out of the Greek myths: the Gorgon. She wrote cookbooks and learned and witty articles on food, and reviewed restaurants. Her articles were often as scathing as they were amusing, and through her syndicated column she had the power to make or break the career of chefs, caterers, and other cookbook authors, and even to influence the destiny of commercial food products. Bruce had once said that she overate to compensate for an acute case of virginity, adding, "You never know where the bitch is going to strike next."

She was indeed somewhat overweight, and a homely woman as well, although Andrea thought she could have improved her appearance considerably by the simple expedient of washing her stringy brown hair. There was no one Andrea was less in the mood to contend with.

But to her surprise, Louise Norman was all smiles. "I've been hearing a great many good things about you, Lady Andrea. And your cocktail buffet tonight bears them out. So beautifully presented and also absolutely delicious. That's not very common these days. I've become very suspicious of elaborate presentations. They so often mask inferior preparation of the food itself. But everything tonight was as good as it looked. What's more you didn't run out of food, which is most surprising considering the crew that was assembled up there."

"Thank you so much, Miss Norman. I'm very flattered. I know how high your standards are."

Louise Norman gave a quick smile at this recognition of her own importance. "I was especially taken by the Oriental chicken wings. So very tender and moist. And a very clever idea for a party like this. It slows down the wolves just a bit since they can't simply pop them in the mouth and swallow."

Andrea laughed. "Yes, that's exactly what I had hoped."

"I'll tell you, my dear, the reason I came to find you is that I would so much like to interview you for an article I'm doing on catering. For the Sunday *Times* magazine. Quite an extended piece."

"I'd be delighted," said Andrea. "I'm sure Mr. Halliwell will be very pleased, too."

"Oh, I'm not all that interested in Bruce Halliwell," Louise Norman said with a wave of her hand. "Naturally, I'll mention that you're partners, but it's you who arouses my curiosity. You're rather an oddity in the catering business, you know."

Andrea wasn't quite sure what to say to that, but Louise Norman had fixed her with an inquiring eye and was obviously going to wait until she got a response. "I suppose you mean having a title?"

"Well, yes, that is unusual, and my readers will be fascinated. But it's also a profession in which one finds almost no women at the top. The Gay Mafia won't have it, of course."

"I beg your pardon?"

"Oh, come now, Lady Andrea, don't play at being naive with me. The catering business in all the major cities is run by a Gay Mafia, as you perfectly well know. There was a woman just last year in San Francisco named Maribel Greenwood who was doing very well for herself until she was overheard saying something about how sick and tired she was of all the faggots in the business. So the word went out, and all those cute waiters and barboys suddenly just stopped showing up to serve. They'd say they'd be there, and just wouldn't show. She was ruined in six months."

Andrea had already heard the story, in fact, and she did know perfectly well what Louise Norman was talking about, but all she said was, "Well, I haven't had any problems at all."

"Very diplomatic, my dear. Well, I'm sure you're tired

and I won't keep you any longer, but I'll give a call and we'll set up a time when I can talk to you at more length."

"I'll look forward to it, Miss Norman. Thank you so much for your interest." Andrea extended her hand.

"My pleasure," said Louise Norman, shaking hands. "I like to help those who seem deserving."

The next day, Andrea reported this encounter to Bruce in detail. She was worried that he might be offended that Louise Norman wanted to interview her and not him, and explained that she had been afraid that not to agree would be a serious mistake.

"Of course, my dear Andrea, you did exactly the right thing. To say no to the Gorgon is like slitting one's own throat. And I'll make it absolutely clear to everyone that I'm delighted with the whole thing. Just to keep all my fellow faggots from muttering darkly that you're attempting a coup against me. The Gorgon is quite right about that, of course, but I'm surprised she'd come out with it so directly." Bruce laughed. "The Gay Mafia! The boys will love it."

"Well, I hope she doesn't bring that subject up again."

"She may, you know. I doubt if she'd dare discuss it openly in her article, but she's a whiz at being nastily suggestive. If she does bring it up, just repeat your sentence about not having any problems and smile sweetly. She can't put words in your mouth, and in fact wouldn't. For all her snideness, she's very careful about quotes. It makes it difficult for anyone to fight back if she gets her quotes right."

"How in the world did she get to be so powerful?"

"Brains, ambition, and a talent for assassination." Bruce smiled. "Actually, I'm very glad this is happening. It could do you a lot of good."

"You mean us."

"No, I mean you. There's a possibility, just a possibility, mind you, that I may decide to get out of this rat race."

Andrea looked at him closely, startled. "I hope to God you're joking, Bruce."

"Well, I've been approached about the idea of running the food end of a big new complex that's being built in Key West. They're talking about a lot of money, and it would be much less of a hassle than this business. And I keep thinking of the sun and all the beautiful young men who troop down there to lie in it."

"Well, I can understand the temptation, but what in the world would I do without you?"

"Take over the firm and run it yourself, of course. You've learned more in one year than I managed in three."

She could do it, of course. She had no doubt in her mind about that. "But you couldn't just give it to me, Bruce. I'd have to find some way to buy you out. After all, it was you who made the initial investment and built it up. I may be called your partner, but I haven't any real financial equity."

Bruce waved his hand airily. "Oh, we could work something out." He gave one of his sudden mischievous grins. "You could always put the touch on Hayes Caldwell."

"No, I wouldn't want to be in that position with Hayes. But I've heard from London that George's estate is almost settled at long last. There may be something left for me, after all."

"Well, don't let's worry about it now, anyway. It wouldn't happen for six months or so, and I may lose interest in Key West. Maybe I'm just tired. I can't wait for August first so we can get our buns out of here."

"Only six weeks. Where are you going in Europe this year?"

"Absolutely everywhere, my dear. I'm taking Rusty on the grand tour."

Rusty, a would-be actor whom they'd been hiring as a waiter the last few months, was Bruce's latest conquest. "Well, that should be fun, if not exactly restful," Andrea said, teasing.

"Who said anything about rest? Rusty is not the type to stick around long, and I figure I might as well get as much as I can while I can get it."

"He is gorgeous."

247

"My dear Andrea, you don't know the half of it. The boy is to die."

"Well, I'm just going to collapse for a week on the beach at East Hampton. But then I have to gear myself up for New Orleans."

"Fabulous city. You'll love it."

"I certainly hope so, Hayes will never forgive me if I don't."

"Is Hayes still muttering about you working too much?"

"Not as much. I glare at him when he starts and he lets it go. It isn't really the work, of course. It's just that he'd like to have me drop everything and fly off with him to Rome or Rio or wherever at a moment's notice."

"For his sake or yours?"

"That's a good question."

"Getting possessive?"

"I'm afraid so," said Andrea, sighing. "I'm afraid so."

They flew to New Orleans in Hayes's company jet. Since he flew all over the world with it, Andrea expected a good-size plane, but when she actually saw it for the first time, looming on the concrete outside the private terminal at La Guardia, she was astonished. "It's huge, Hayes," she said.

"The *Magnolia?*" Hayes laughed. "Just a little three holer."

"A three-holer?"

"That's what pilots call them. It's a Boeing 727." He pointed up to the plane. "Three engines, you see, one on each side and one on top. It's just about the most reliable jet there is."

"It must cost a fortune to run, though."

"Sure. But it saves money in the long run. You can get where you want when you want to. There are about twenty-five of them in corporate use in this country."

"I suppose you fly it yourself," Andrea said, smiling up at him.

"No. I go up and sit in the co-pilot's seat sometimes. I

248

have a license for the little Lear jets, but it would take a month of training to get one for this baby, and I can never find the time."

Andrea took his arm. "Well, I'm awfully glad we both found the time for this trip. I'm really looking forward to it, Hayes."

He leaned over and kissed the top of her head. "You and me both, baby girl."

The interior of the plane was outfitted lavishly. The main cabin was more like the library of a home than the interior of a plane, with beige wall-to-wall carpeting, maroon leather chairs, bookcases, stereo equipment, and a fully equipped bar. There was a galley equipped with both a microwave oven and electric burners so that one could heat up catered food or start from scratch. At the rear of the plane were two small sleeping cabins and a bathroom with a circular shower trimmed in brass.

"It's just beautiful, Hayes. No wonder you like flying around the world so much."

"I'm glad you like it. It was custom designed by Air Research of Los Angeles, the same company that outfitted *Air Force One.* I would say only the best, but in fact that's the only company in the country that does this kind of thing, so there wasn't much choice."

Andrea ran her hand down the door to the shower. "Does this produce enough water for two?" she asked.

Hayes looked at her and gave a sly grin.

Andrea laughed gaily. "Well, I've never had a shower in a mid-air before."

"Let me go up front, then, and find out how soon we can get this crate off the ground."

Since Hayes could refer to his 727 as a "crate," Andrea was not in the least surprised to discover that his "house" in New Orleans was in fact a mansion, not quite as large as Oakridge Manor but a good deal bigger than the house in

249

Eaton Square. It was surrounded by a wrought-iron fence whose uprights were capped with intricately molded representations of corn husks, a formal, pillared white house dating from the 1840's with a three-story central section and two-story wings at each side. The house was run by a black couple in their early sixties, Henry, who was as correct as any English butler but who at the same time conveyed a warmth and kindliness that was profoundly Southern, and his wife, Emily, who from the start treated Andrea like a queen, unpacking her suitcases for her and constantly asking if there was any little thing she could do to make her more comfortable.

Andrea didn't say anything about it, but in a way the attentions of Henry and Emily made her slightly uneasy, bringing back memories of her life in London, memories she had tried very hard to put out of her mind. Perhaps it was her imagination, but she detected in this couple, so devoted to Hayes, the kind of longing for a mistress of the house that Jeremy and Mrs. Evelyn had once displayed. Their welcome and the house itself cast a kind of seductive spell, as she suspected Hayes had known they would.

But then New Orleans itself was seductive. It did not take her long to realize how truly a son of that unique city Hayes was. Unlike native New Yorkers, who take the city almost for granted, or Chicagoans, who are aggressively proud, as though trying to make up for some secret lack, or citizens of Los Angeles, who are constantly discussing the contrast between Los Angeles and New York in a defensive tone, Hayes Caldwell loved New Orleans with a tender and complete passion. He was proud not only of his own house, but of the entire Garden District, proud not only because it was exclusive, but because it was beautiful.

"I don't believe there is a residential district in any city on this earth that has as much grace or loveliness as these streets," he said, and Andrea would have believed him even if he had *not* been everywhere. There were parts of London and Paris that were grander, certainly, but she doubted that such charm could be found anywhere else. Perhaps it was the trees, the magnolias and willows and great copper beeches. Perhaps it was the huge gnarled wisteria vines, the brilliant magenta bougainvilleas, the contrast of bright light and deep shadows. But whatever element it was that seemed to predominate, the overall effect was one of a calm and slightly mysterious beauty that was not just a visual pleasure but in some curious way deeply moving. It made her think, and then say aloud to Hayes, "It's strange, but this is somehow the way human beings really ought to live, all of us."

"Yes," he said, smiling. "That's just it."

But it was not merely the Garden District that Hayes loved. It was the great river that had been tamed and channeled. It was the streets of the French Quarter, the quiet side streets and the noisy tourist-packed jazz bars and strip joints of Bourbon Street. "There are people who hate the fact that parts of the Quarter are so sleazy," he said. "But there's always been a certain licentiousness to New Orleans, and if you took it away you'd be killing part of what the city is."

Andrea understood Hayes's proprietary feelings about his city, but even so she was a little startled at how insistent he was that she experience it *his* way. Their second evening there, they were to have dinner at Antoine's, and as they were sipping a Ramos Gin Fizz on the shadowed coolness of his terrace beforehand, he said, "I hope you won't object if I order for you this evening."

Andrea thought that she did rather object. Hayes had already pressed the gin fizz on her, having made the drinks himself. She didn't ordinarily like gin, or sweet drinks in general. Luckily, it so happened that she found the concoction of gin, egg whites, and orange-flower water, sweetened with confectioners sugar and vanilla extract, and amalgamated with lemon juice and light cream, far tastier and more refreshing than she'd expected. But a drink was one thing; putting herself in someone else's hands for an entire meal was another. Antoine's might be one of the most famous restaurants in the world, but there were many who said that it was not up to the level of its former glories, and she wanted to test it out for herself. Besides, in terms of her own eating pleasure, she liked to go with the mood of the moment. That was in one way contradictory, she was willing to admit, since as a caterer she provided people with meals that had been planned weeks or even months in advance. But that was also just the point. She was on vacation, and she didn't want to have her eating programmed for her.

Responding to her hesitation, Hayes added, "I realize you know a great deal more about food than I do, sweets, but you have to understand that Antoine's is really two restaurants. There's a public restaurant that tourists line up for an hour to get into, and there's a private restaurant that's almost a club. They're on the same premises, of course, and they have the same kitchen. But I want you to experience the true Antoine's, the one that's really a family restaurant that New Orleans people go to week in and week out all their lives."

"It sounds like '21' in New York," Andrea said, beginning to fear the worst. In her opinion, restaurants that people went to as though they were clubs were almost always boring.

"Not really. You'll be surprised, I think. But I do want you to have the dishes that Antoine's does best, better than any place else."

"Well, I was certainly planning to have the Oysters Rockefeller, if that's what you mean."

"Yes, we'll start with those."

"Is the recipe truly a secret or is that just hype?"

"It is one of the few true secrets I know of. Jules Alciatore invented Oysters Rockefeller around the turn of the century. As the story goes, he was having trouble importing snails from Europe and he wanted to find a substitute that made use of a local product. They say almost nobody ever cooked oysters in those days, so the whole idea was new, not just the sauce. Of course, almost every restaurant in New Orleans of any pretensions makes Oysters Rockefeller these days, and there are hostesses around the city who swear they've discovered the secret, but I don't believe it. They're not the same. When you see a recipe it almost always includes spinach as one of the greens pureed for the sauce, but the proprietors of Antoine's swear they never use spinach at all."

Andrea had never heard Hayes talk about food in such detail. "You are an expert," she said, teasing him a little.

"Well, honey, the first time I was taken to Antoine's by my father I was seven years old. We would eat there at least once a week. I figured it up not long ago. I've eaten at Antoine's close to fifteen hundred times."

Andrea was stunned, and must have shown it, because Hayes grinned and said, "Oh, I'm kind of laggard. I travel so much you know. But I've had the same waiter since I was fifteen. He's in his sixties now. His name is Ellis."

"You always have the same waiter?"

"Of course. When I make a reservation I call and ask for Ellis and he takes care of it all. Every old New Orleans family has its own waiter. It's the way things are done."

Andrea decided it was pointless to argue. "All right, then, what am I going to eat?"

"Well, there are two main courses I want you to sample. I know how you like to trade back and forth between plates, so you can have either one and I'll have the other and give you a taste. One of the dishes is chicken with *sauce Rochambeau*. It combines boned chicken and sliced ham with two sauces, one of them a brown sauce and the other a béarnaise. There isn't a better chicken dish in the world, I promise you."

Andrea laughed. "And I believe you. What's my other choice?"

"A simple tournedos with *marchand de vins* sauce. Except that the beef is like butter and the sauce is out of this world. You can have it with about half a dozen different sauces, but you can't beat the *marchand de vins*."

"Hayes," Andrea said, "why don't we just hurry on over? You're making me very hungry."

Forty-five minutes later, they arrived at Antoine's. Hayes guided her firmly past the long line of tourists to an unmarked and nondescript door farther up the street. He rang a small bell, there was a discreet buzz, and he opened the door on a long, unadorned corridor. At the far end another door opened and an elderly black man in a tuxedo poked his head out and perused them. "Oh," he said. "Good evening, Mr. Caldwell," and he then stepped fully into the corridor to hold the door for them.

They entered a very large, rectangular room with a very high ceiling. A rose-gold light that seemed to envelop the white-clothed tables and bentwood chairs with a beneficent glow like something out of an early Impressionist painting filled the room. They passed among tables of animated diners to a smaller, quieter room at the front of the restaurant. A large portal allowed a glimpse into still another large dining room—the room, Hayes explained, in which those who were waiting in line at the main entrance would be seated.

Almost as soon as they were seated, a short, portly man with white hair approached them beaming. "Good evening, Mr. Caldwell," he said warmly. "It's a pleasure to see you."

"Good evening, Ellis. You're looking well."

"Thank you, Mr. Caldwell. I seem to keep on with it."

"Ellis, this is Lady Andrea Harrington. She's one of New York's most important caterers, and she's never been to New Orleans before, so we'll want to make it a very special evening."

"Of course, we'll be honored to serve you, Ma'am. May I bring you a drink, or would you prefer to see the wine list?"

"I think we'll have a bottle of Taittinger '73 to begin with," Hayes said. "Lady Andrea is very fond of champagne, and her first visit to Antoine's gives us reason to celebrate."

As Ellis left them, Andrea smiled at Hayes and said, "You know, Hayes, I do feel like celebrating. I'm very happy."

"I can't think of anything I'd rather hear you say. Shall we stay with the champagne all evening, then? Or would you rather go on to a wine?"

"Champagne."

Ellis returned with two glasses and the bottle of Taittinger. The softness of the pop as he removed the cork indicated that it was perfectly chilled. He poured a small amount into Hayes's glass to be tasted. When Hayes nodded his approval, Andrea's glass was filled and then Hayes's. He lifted his glass and said, "To us."

"Do you wish to see a menu now, Mr. Caldwell?"

"I think Lady Andrea would like to have one to look at, but we already know what we'll be having."

"The Oysters Rockefeller, I assume?"

"Yes, indeed, Ellis. Lady Andrea will take the *Poulet Sauce Rochambeau*, and I'll have the tournedos. Beyond that, the souffléed potatoes, and a *salade Antoine* for me and the *avocat éventail* for Lady Andrea."

"Very good, Sir."

After Ellis had left them, presenting Andrea with a menu before he did so, Andrea said, "You didn't tell him what sauce you were having with the tournedos. Or does he know?"

Hayes smiled. "He knows. He also knows I like it very rare, just the other side of blue."

"It's almost like having a family retainer, isn't it?"

"It is like that, honey. For many of us Antoine's is a second home."

Andrea looked over the menu, which was entirely in French. On its cover was a brown and white reproduction of a nineteenth century painting of the interior, which was surrounded by a representation of a lacy placemat. She was surprised at how reasonable the prices were. A tournedos for $7.75 was remarkable, even if the *marchand de vins* sauce was extra—a mere $1.25 extra. One of the most expensive dishes, at $8.50, was *Pompano Pontchartrain,* and she asked Hayes what it consisted of.

"A fillet of pompano with soft-shell crabs on top. Some people feel that fish is somewhat overcooked here, but Ellis always sees to it that the fish chef gets it right for me. When we come back sometime, that's a dish you might want to try."

Ellis brought their oysters, the half-shells arranged on a pan of rock salt, the oysters topped by the very dark green sauce. It was pungent, aromatic, and very rich, the underlying oysters plump and juicy. "No spinach?" she said, tasting carefully. "Well, there must be parsley, maybe watercress. Celery. Green onions?" She was guessing, really. The sauce was such a complex of flavors, that all somehow married into one, that it was impossible to be certain. "There must be a little Pernod, though," she said, suddenly sure of that.

Hayes was grinning. "I can just see you going back to New York and experimenting, sweetheart."

"Well, of course. But I can see how it could be kept a secret. It's very complex. And wonderful."

As she ate the oysters, she paused for a bite of the wonderful hot French bread that had been brought along with the oysters. Good as it was, though, it had a dismaying tendency to crumble in every direction, and Andrea began trying to clean up the mess.

"Don't do that," Hayes said, almost as a command.

Andrea looked at him, startled.

"It's a New Orleans peculiarity," he explained. "Our best bread always crumbles like that, and it's considered bad form *not* to scatter it all over the table."

Andrea was amused. "That's a clever way of getting around a problem, isn't it?"

Superb as the oysters had been, Andrea was even more delighted with her chicken; it was incredibly rich and she had wondered beforehand if the use of the two different sauces might not be heavy as well, but the result was that kind of celestial richness that manages to practically sing. She also had a bite of Hayes's tournedos, which was as tender and flavorful a piece of beef as she had ever tasted, and the sauce another marvel of piquant complexity. The souffléed potatoes, presented in an openwork basket woven of potato strips and deep fried, were another wonder, so good she thought she could go on eating them for hours. The avocado salad was an intriguing combination, beautifully presented, with thin slices of avocado in a fan shape, topped with two anchovy fillets in the form of an X, centered with a dollop of caviar, and served with a fine vinaigrette.

"Hayes," she said. "I am in heaven." She blew him a kiss. "I'm so glad I let you choose. It really is wonderful."

"Well, honey, we could come here all the time, you know. All you'd have to do is marry me."

Andrea had known that was coming, but she wished that he'd waited a few days, until the end of her stay in New Orleans. Then it would have been less awkward. "Why do men always propose to me over dinner?" she asked, trying to make light of it.

"I suppose that's because you're so luscious, sweetheart. I didn't know anyone else had proposed to you lately, though."

"Not lately. It was just after my husband's death, before I decided to come back to America."

"Well, I'm awfully glad you turned down whoever it was, or I might never have met you. But I hope you'll see things differently this time."

"Oh, Hayes, let's not spoil this lovely evening."

"I'm not going to pressure you, honey. But you just think about it some."

"Must I?" Andrea asked, and gave a little laugh.

"Well, you're getting to be very important to me, little lady."

"You're important to me, too, Hayes. You know that. But I like things the way they are. Besides, I have plans of my own."

Hayes's face darkened. "What kind of plans?"

"Business plans." Andrea found herself absentmindedly neatening the bread crumbs once again. Hayes glanced at her hand and she stopped. "Bruce is considering becoming involved with a new resort complex in Key West. If he does, I would probably take over Ambrosia, Inc., all by myself."

257

Hayes was silent for a long moment, staring at her almost without expression. Then he said, "You know, sweetheart, I wish you could have known my mother. You're just as independent and ornery as she was."

"I think I'll take that as a compliment," Andrea said. "In spite of the *ornery*."

"It was meant that way. I'd rather it was a compliment I didn't have to make, though." Hayes sighed. "Well, then, I guess we'd better have some coffee and *crêpes suzette*."

"Dear God, Hayes, *crêpes suzette*? How can I possibly eat any more?"

"You'll find a way," Hayes said, "once you get a whiff of them. Antoine's has the best there are in this world. Besides, Ellis would be disappointed if he didn't get to show off with the chafing dish." Hayes paused. "Especially since he knows you're a professional yourself," he added. And then he smiled.

Chapter Eleven

THE ITEM IN *WOMEN'S WEAR DAILY* for May 6, 1975, began,

A catered affair of a special sort took place last night at Broadway producer Karen Bolling's East Side townhouse. The party was in honor of that choicest of purveyors to New York's social nabobs, Lady Andrea Harrington, celebrating her assumption of sole ownership of Ambrosia, Inc. to be known henceforth as Harrington's. Former partner Bruce Halliwell, who kept everyone amused with his famous one-liners, is departing for warmer and more relaxed climes to assume leadership of the posh new Key West resort SunSea. What made the occasion unusual was that the party was catered by arch-rival Richard Corliss—"friendly rival," both he and Lady Andrea insist. But the lavishness of the buffet was such as to indicate that Mr. Corliss did not want to lose the opportunity to show off in front of the competition.

Among those present were several of Lady Andrea's most important clients, including art collector Mrs. Celia Billingham, wearing a silk dress inspired by one of her favorite Mondrians. Perennial Broadway charmer Barry Lawrence, with whom Lady Andrea once co-starred in one of her previous incarnations (as the actress Andrea Nilsson), attended with his wife, Maddy who, on being asked the secret of their long marriage, replied, "He never makes movies." Food critic Louise Norman caused a considerable stir with her new permanent, and uncharacteristically refused to offer any comparison between the culinary prowess of Mr. Corliss and Lady Andrea. "They're both wonderful in their different ways," was all she would say.

On the sidelines, it would be noted that both Mr. Corliss and Lady Andrea are about to have some new competition.

Restaurateur Riccardo Bianchetti, originally from Venice but now a British subject, whose purely Italian catering service has taken London by storm, has plans to conquer still another country, and will be opening a branch in New York in the fall. What makes this truly interesting is the word from one of my London sources that Lady Andrea's late husband, Sir George Harrington, was one of the investors in Mr. Bianchetti's original restaurant in Brighton. Now don't tell me the world isn't an absolutely *tiny* place!

"Did you see this?" Andrea asked, slapping the copy of WWD down on Bruce's desk.

Bruce, who was busy cleaning out his drawers, nodded. "I thought I'd let you discover it for yourself, my dear."

"Not that it comes as any surprise," Andrea said. "Myra Brockton has been keeping tabs on Riccardo right along, and she wrote me more than a month ago about this. 'The little rat is about to swim the Atlantic,' is how she put it, as I recall. But it was a shock to see the news come out in this context. Where in hell does that rag gets its information?"

"Probably straight from Riccardo. It's part of the naughty genius of WWD to find these things out and then sit on them until they find the most titillating moment to drop them."

"Well, it pisses me off."

"Really, my dear, such language. Perhaps we should pass the word among the boys that Mr. Bianchetti deserves a rather frosty reception in New York."

"I doubt if it would do any good. Riccardo is extremely good looking and they'll all be rushing around trying to see who can get him into bed first."

"Well, we'll just have to let it be known that the dear boy has a chronic case of the clap. Some irradicable strain he picked up from a gondolier."

Andrea laughed. "Now that's a thought."

"Does Riccardo really worry you?"

"In a way. Perhaps it's silly. But our little world is indeed the very tiniest, and I won't have that bastard going around whispering to people that I was responsible for George's death. I must say it even bothers me to have word get out that he was George's lover. I'm surprised WWD didn't suggest that a little more openly. Or is that something else they're saving for future titillation?"

"Could be. There's not much you can do about it, Andrea, except to get your own version into circulation first."

"Bruce, I don't even know what my version is, except that life is complicated."

"That's far too blandly truthful, my love. If you're going to counter a lie, you have to do it with a better one. Why don't you suggest that Riccardo was blackmailing George, bleeding him dry, and that that's not only one reason for his heart attack but also the reason that there was so little left of his estate. People already know that it took almost a year for you to get hold of the money you bought me out with, and it'll sound extremely plausible."

"You know, Bruce, you really are terribly clever."

Bruce grinned. "You noticed," he said. "I'll tell you what. I'll pass the word among the boys, and you get on to Louise Norman. It's just the kind of thing she loves. We'll have everybody feeling sympathy for you, and if Riccardo Bianchetti starts maligning you no one will believe a word of it."

"I think I ought to casually mention this little matter to a few select clients, as well."

"Absolutely. You're extremely well liked, Andrea, and respected. I think Riccardo Bianchetti is going to find it difficult to make much headway in New York. Oh, he'll get clients, but not the ones who really count." Bruce picked up the paper. "You know, this little item in WWD may prove to be a blessing in disguise. If the link between you and Riccardo hadn't got out, it would be more awkward for you to broach it. Your clients are going to be curious, and some of them will bring up the WWD piece themselves. Then you can go into your act without appearing too overt about it."

Andrea reached over and took the paper out of Bruce's hand. "I think I'll go read this through again," she said, and then gave a good imitation of a Myra Brockton chortle.

Under its new name, Harrington's became more successful than ever. Toward the end of her partnership with Bruce, there had been some feeling among the clients of Ambrosia, Inc., that Andrea was if not more proficient at least a bit more imaginative than Bruce. He had not been unaware of the fact, and although he and Andrea had never really discussed it, Andrea suspected it had been a factor in his decision to make the change to SunSea. As sole owner, she was able to put her own special stamp on the entire organization, so that even when one of her assistants was in charge of a party she knew— and more important, her clients knew—that it would reflect her own style in every detail. One aspect of that style was to provide every guest at smaller sit-down dinners with a menu written in calligraphy, the colors of the paper and ink echoing that of the flowers or linen or china. For large parties, printed menus, set in a type face that particularly suited the ambience of the occasion, were distributed.

On the organizational end she made one innovative change that she had once suggested to Bruce, but which he felt was more trouble than it was worth. Whenever possible, she now took Polaroid photographs at each party, snapping the buffet table just before the guests arrived, or photographing some special dish before it left the kitchen. The photographs were added to each client's file as an additional aid in avoiding duplication. It also gave her proof to the contrary if, as sometimes happened, a client claimed that a given party was "exactly like" the one Andrea had done for someone else last month. When that problem arose, Andrea could now produce pictorial evidence that in fact the two parties were considerably different.

With Bruce gone, she gave additional authority to Paul Boucheron, naming him *chef de cuisine,* and cutting him in

262

on a small share of the profits, but even so she was busier than ever. And that was causing problems with Hayes. He had become increasingly unhappy with the catch-as-catch-can nature of their relationship even before she had taken over the firm. He had tried very hard to talk her out of doing that in the first place, attempting once again to persuade her to marry him. Her refusal still rankled, she knew, and he was stopping over in New York to see her less often than he had.

When he did come to New York, she did her best to rearrange her schedule so that she could spend more time with him, but often he gave her so little notice that it wasn't possible. It was almost as though by popping up unannounced he was giving himself an excuse to complain about her lack of attention to him, as though he were trying to wean himself away from her. She had gone to Europe with him for two weeks in August, and they had had as beautiful a time as she could remember, spending a week in Rome and a week touring the Greek Islands. But that only seemed to make matters worse. He wanted her with him all the time, and simply couldn't understand why, if she loved him, she didn't want that, too.

One Monday night in late October it came to a head. For once he had let her know a week in advance that he would be in New York, and she had decided to surprise him by cooking dinner for him at her apartment, even though they were supposed to go to Katja's, the shining Art Deco restaurant on East Fifty-eighth Street that had become all the rage.

But when she announced that they were going to eat at home, instead of being pleased, he was annoyed.

"Now why in hell are you doing that?" he said. "Christ, Andrea, you spend night and day nine months a year cooking. Give it a break and come out on the town."

Andrea was irritated herself, but tried not to show it. "But that's just the point, Hayes. If I can cook for the world, why shouldn't I cook for the man I love once in a while?"

Hayes looked slightly abashed. "I'm sorry, baby girl, I'm

being rude, aren't I? You were just trying to do something nice. I know. But the idea of having you cook for me just makes me think about what it could be like if you'd marry me. It makes me sad. And frustrated as hell."

"Hayes, we can't keep going through this." She sat down beside him on the sofa, which she'd just had recovered in a nubbly fabric, as blue as the Aegean, that Hayes had bought for her when they were in Greece.

"I know we can't. Or at least I can't. That's the trouble, sweety pie. I hate this business of seeing you on the fly every couple of weeks. I think about you all the time in between, and I just get more and more upset."

She put a hand on his arm and looked up at him. "I think about you, too, Hayes."

"Then why in God's name won't you marry me? What's the point in all this long-distance thinking about each other when we could be making love and traveling around the world together? Why does someone like you, someone who got used to servants and mansions, want to hold down a job when you don't have to? It's crazy."

"It's not a job, Hayes. If it were just a job, I'd give it up in a minute. It used to be that, that was all women ususally did have. Jobs. But now they have careers. That's what I have, a career. And it's one thing to give up a job to get married, but it's something very different to give up a career."

"Spare me the women's lib, Andrea, for God's sake."

"It's not a philosophy, Hayes. It's something I feel."

"You know what I think? I think you're afraid that if you married me, you'd be bored."

"I'd never be bored so long as I was with you, Hayes," she said, rubbing his arm. "But you know you're as much of a worker as I am. You fly all over the world constantly, and I couldn't go with you a lot of the time. I'd be in the way. You probably won't admit that to yourself. But it's true. And I wouldn't want to go with you all the time. I can't imagine anything drearier than sitting in some hotel suite in the middle of a Middle Eastern desert waiting for you to come back from the oil fields. And beautiful as New Orleans is, much as I love your house there, I think I'd be bored waiting at home for you, too. I'm just not that kind of person.

"You have to understand, Hayes. I love what I'm doing now. For the first time in my life I've got something that's truly mine, that really belongs to me. I'm not acting in a play or a movie that somebody else wrote, or with somebody else telling me how to play a scene. I'm not spending somebody else's money, trying to live up to what I think they want of me, the way I did with George. I'm not anybody's appendage, and I tell other people what to do instead of the other way around. For the first time, I own my own life. And that's a wonderful feeling. Maybe I'll get tired of the catering business eventually, want to do something else, or even nothing. But right now I want what I've got. I love you, Hayes, truly, I do. But if I married you I know I'd regret giving up what I have. And that wouldn't be fair to either of us. It would just make a different kind of problem between us."

Hayes shook his head. "I know. I know everything you're saying means something to you. But, dammit, Andrea, I'm not the kind of person who can deal with this kind of situation we're in. I want a wife, someone to come home to. That's important to me, I need it. The house in New Orleans seems so empty. My life seems empty sometimes. This way we're living just isn't for me, sweetie pie. I'm not saying good-bye, or anything. I don't know if I could. But there are times when I think maybe I should look for a woman who'll at least meet me halfway. I don't know whether I could feel about any other woman the way I do for you. But maybe I should be looking for her, it seems to me."

Andrea felt a great sadness, the possibility of tears, and she closed her eyes momentarily. She was going to lose him. Maybe not right away, but eventually. Part of her wanted to give in to him. Part of her being ached to satisfy him and would weep to lose him. She could simply throw up her hands and say, "I love you too much to lose you." She could say those words with conviction. But the moment she had said them she would begin to regret that she had. The other half of her would be miserable instead of joyous at having abandoned what she had achieved. And she was certain the regret would eventually poison the love she did feel for Hayes.

It simply couldn't be.

"I understand, Hayes," she said. "I wouldn't blame you for looking for someone else. How could I? It's not the fault of either of us that we're the people we are. It's sad, it makes me very unhappy sometimes that I can't bring myself to just say yes, yes, yes, to you. But I can't."

Hayes had tears in his eyes. He kept them wide open and the drops did not fall. "I'll always care for you, baby girl," he said. "But I think we're beginning to make each other unhappy. I think maybe we shouldn't try so hard to keep it going. Maybe if we back off a little, we'll get a different perspective. Maybe one of us will change."

"You mean maybe I'll change," Andrea said very quietly, and without any hint of accusation.

"No. Maybe if we don't see each other very much for a while, I'll realize that even as it is, it's better than anything else. Or maybe you will. I don't know. But I think this is getting to be a strain for both of us."

Andrea wanted to weep but would not let herself. She called on every reserve she had and said, simply, "I wish that weren't true, Hayes. But I think it is. I think you're right."

Hayes stood up suddenly. "I think I'd better go," he said. "I think it's better if we aren't together tonight."

Andrea nodded and got up herself. Hayes embraced her briefly, and she felt the strength of his arms. But then he let her go, as though he had no more energy to give.

"Let's promise to keep in touch, though," he said. "Let's call once in a while."

"Yes," she said, and they looked at each other, and then he turned and was gone.

On a hectic day in early March a telephone call came through to Harrington's from Los Angeles. Paul Boucheron was on another line, and Andrea took the call only because it was long-distance. The day was over-scheduled and she really didn't have time to talk.

"Am I speaking with Lady Andrea Harrington?" The man's voice was quite deep, and strangely sexy. It also sounded as though it belonged to someone who was used to giving orders. The accent was definitely New York.

"Yes, this is she."

"Good. This is Sid Fogel. I want you to do a party for me when I'm in New York next month."

The name was vaguely familiar to Andrea but she wasn't sure why.

"What kind of party did you have in mind, Mr. Fogel?"

"Dinner. I guess it would have to be a buffet. It'll be about sixty people."

"I see. On what date?"

"Whatever date you're free between the nineteenth and the twenty-third. I don't want one of your assistants."

Andrea began to feel somewhat annoyed. Mr. Sid Fogel seemed a little too aggressively self-important. "My assistants are superb professionals, Mr. Fogel."

"Sure. So are mine. They're still assistants. I want the best, and I'm told that's you."

"That's always nice to hear, Mr. Fogel, but I do have a very busy schedule. Did you hear about me from a client of mine?"

"That's right. Marc James over at NBC."

Marc James was a senior vice-president for programming who had much better manners than Sid Fogel. Andrea guessed Fogel must be a producer. He had that don't-tell-me,-I'll-tell-you tone. Marc James was a good client and she didn't want to offend him, but she wasn't at all sure she wanted to deal with Sid Fogel.

"Maybe I should tell you the party's for Liza Minnelli. There'll be lots of press."

Andrea wasn't sure she believed him. He'd said Andrea could choose the date that suited her, and it seemed unlikely that Liza Minnelli's own calendar was so empty that just any old night would do. Still, lots of press was always helpful. "I'm looking at my date book, Mr. Fogel. It's rather difficult. The only night I could offer you would be the twenty-first."

"Fine. I'll be in New York for a couple of days next week. I understand you like to see the premises."

"Yes, it makes planning much easier if we know exactly what kind of floor plan and kitchen facilities we'll be dealing with."

"Okay. I'll be there on Tuesday and Wednesday. When would you like to come round?"

"Wednesday afternoon at two o'clock would be good."

"That suits me. The address is 115 Central Park West. I'll see you then."

"Yes, Mr. Fogel," said Andrea with a slight tartness, "you will."

When she arrived at his eighth-floor apartment overlooking Central Park the following Wednesday, Andrea fully expected Sid Fogel's domicile to be decorated in the worst of glitzy bad taste. She had done a little research on Mr. Fogel, and discovered that he was indeed a producer, had in fact made a fortune out of the most demeaning and idiotic game shows on television. Anyone who came up with an idea like "Honeymoon Roulette," in Andrea's opinion, had to be a lout, and she was seriously considering various excuses for getting out of the commitment altogether. After all, no contract had yet been signed.

But she was surprised, both by the apartment and by Sid Fogel himself. He was tall, over six feet, handsome in a slightly offbeat way, his lean frame attired in a gray cashmere turtleneck and dark gray wool trousers of continental cut, with no pockets in front. The apartment was modern, with leather sofas, Wasilly chairs, and chrome and glass tables, the rooms brightened by a number of contemporary paintings, including a Stella geometric and a fine example from Trova's "falling man" series. There was nothing crass about it; it was restrained, even elegant.

Sid Fogel showed her the kitchen, which though not large was well equipped, with both a conventional gas stove and a microwave oven, as well as an oversize combination refrigerator-freezer. There was also a narrow butler's pantry with an extra sink and considerable counter space. It was, all in all, a better space that she often had to work with. The layout of the apartment in general was also well suited to a large buffet, with a bar in the large living room. Andrea always liked to have drinks and food served in separate rooms. It avoided traffic jams.

"I don't see any problem at all, Mr. Fogel. Why don't we discuss the menu?"

"Fine. Would you like some coffee? I've just made some espresso."

"That would be very nice."

He looked over several sample menus Andrea had brought while they sipped coffee from handsome brown and white Dansk cups. "These are just to give you an idea of the general composition of the buffets we serve in the various price ranges," Andrea said. "We can also accommodate you in any requests you have for particular kinds of food or special dishes."

"Well, I happen to be very fond of oysters."

"On the half-shell?"

"What about fried?"

"I don't really recommend that, Mr. Fogel. We try to avoid doing last-minute frying of any kind, not only because it's time consuming but because it tends to create a rather strong odor in the host's apartment. And if we do something such as fried oysters before hand, to be heated up, I find they tend to get mushy."

269

"That makes sense. What about Oysters Rockefeller? Could you do them?"

Andrea could not help a wry smile. "Yes, in fact, I could. They also should be cooked at the last minute, but since you have a microwave, there should be no problem."

"Good. I want this to be a very special party. How about the galantine of duck you have listed here? That's not exactly your everyday fare, is it?"

"No, and it always seems to be very popular. That is, of course, one of our more expensive offerings, because of the time involved in preparation."

"I don't care about price, Lady Andrea. Just charge me what's necessary."

Andrea's misgivings had by now evaporated. Sid Fogel wasn't going to be at all difficult to deal with. They discussed the menu for another half hour, and then, as she was putting the samples away in her suede attaché case, preparing to leave, Sid Fogel asked, "Where do I know you from, Lady Andrea? Have you ever done television?"

"Yes, I did some television movies, and a couple of feature films, but it was some time ago."

"That must be it. It's strange, though, I feel as though I've met you. What name did you act under?"

"Andrea Nilsson."

"Oh. Of course. That's it. I saw you on Broadway, in, umm, *Playing by Ear*. Twice, in fact, the second time from the first row. That's why it seemed as though I actually knew you. You were wonderful in that. I wanted to meet you, in fact, but in those days I didn't have the connections."

Andrea smiled. "It seems a very long time ago."

"Yeah, it must be ten years," Sid Fogel said, with a certain lack of gallantry.

"I'm afraid so."

"Oh, don't get me wrong, Lady Andrea. You're the kind of woman who grows into her real beauty."

"Thank you, Mr. Fogel."

"Have you ever thought about doing television again? Not as an actress, but with a cooking show, something like that?"

The idea had in fact crossed Andrea's mind, but Harrington's absorbed too much of her time for her to have given it any real thought. "I think Julia Child has that market cornered."

"Not necessarily. She and Graham Kerr had shows on at the same time for a while. Different kinds of show, different time slots. There's always room for a new approach."

"Well, Mr. Fogel, if you come up with one let me know." She said it flippantly, and never expected to hear anything more about it.

Sid Fogel's party was a great success; even Liza Minnelli showed up, however briefly, with Halston in tow. A month later, Sid called Andrea again, but this time it wasn't about a party. "I've been thinking about that television show," he said.

"What television show?"

"The cooking show. You said to let you know if I came up with a new approach."

"I wasn't really serious, Mr. Fogel."

"Call me Sid. Look, couldn't we talk about it? You must have a day off occasionally. Let me take you to dinner."

"Well—"

"Where would you like to go?"

Andrea pondered for a moment, unsure that she wanted to get into this at all. But, why not, she decided. As a kind of test of his seriousness, she considered suggesting that they go to The Palace, but decided that the prospect of shelling out a hundred dollars a person or more wouldn't faze him for a moment. Besides, she was curious where he would take her if left to his own devices. "Why don't you surprise me," she said.

The following Monday he picked her up in a limousine and they drove crosstown to the Café des Artistes, which

271

George Lang had just rescued from years of decline, not only restoring culinary excellence but also refurbishing the charming murals of very naked but utterly innocent wood nymphs that adorned the walls. As she had suspected, Sid Fogel did not really have a new approach to a television cooking show, beyond flattering her that she had a personal quality that would carry the day.

"I don't really see that I'm all that special," she demured.

"But you are, Lady Andrea. Say, do you mind if I just call you Andrea?"

"No." Andrea was amused; she could tell from the beginning that Sid Fogel was one of those people who found her title obnoxious.

"The thing is, Andrea, that it's always a matter of personality that makes a show of that sort go. It's not that Julia Child is a good teacher, though she is. It's that she's so endearingly down home about it. That makes people like her, especially since she's dealing with all that complicated French food. It takes the intimidation out of it. Now you, you're different. You're elegant, but you also have a way of making food sort of sexy."

"Sort of sexy." Andrea was beginning to get the feeling that Sid had other things on his mind than a television show. "Tell me, Sid," she said. "How many women over the years have you managed to lure out to dinner by telling them you thought they'd be terrific on television?" And she took a bite of quail.

Sid smiled. "Dozens," he said coolly. "Usually I invite them to my apartment, though."

"Well, at least you're honest. Does it work?"

Sid nodded. "Often enough."

Andrea laughed. That didn't really surprise her. She decided that she was beginning to like Sid Fogel.

"Look, Andrea, I'd like to sleep with you. I'd be crazy if I didn't. I wanted to do that ten years ago when I saw you on Broadway. But I'm serious about this show. You may not

272

know it, but my reputation in the television business is pretty gross. Sure, other producers, the network executives, they'd all like to have had my success, but they make themselves feel better by telling themselves I did it with real trash. They say I have no taste. They're wrong. I do have taste. But I know that most of those millions of schmucks out there who turn on their sets over their TV dinners don't. Trash makes them happy and it makes me rich. Even so, I'd like to put a little polish on my image, show the bastards that I can do a class show as well as anybody else."

Andrea was a little taken aback by this confession, both by the tone of it and the implications of it. It had been a very long time since a man had come on to her so directly, or someone she didn't know well had talked so frankly. People she'd only met once or twice usually watched their language around Lady Andrea Harrington. In a way, Sid was refreshing. Sometimes she got tired of people's false fronts, their attempts at talking and behaving the way they thought someone with a title would expect.

"You're nothing if not frank, I'll say that."

"I'm me, Andy, I'm me. That's one of the best things about me."

"Andy? That's a new one."

"You don't like it? Sorry."

Andrea laughed again. "I don't mind. I've been called a lot worse things in the last couple of years."

"Like what?"

"Sweetie pie. My little bunny. You name it."

"Must be a Southerner, right?"

"Right."

"Oil, cattle, or peanuts?"

"Everything but peanuts. Does that man from Georgia really have a chance, do you think?"

"Carter? Why not? People want somebody they never heard of. There's something wrong with everyone they already know."

"I quite like him, but Hayes said it's too soon for a deep-South President."

"Hayes? Is that the sweetie-pie oil man?"

"Yes."

"Terrific name. Last names as first names are very classy. I take it he's still in the picture?"

Andrea considered for a moment. "Not really. He's a marvelous man. But he wanted me to marry him, and I wouldn't, so he's off courting a widow with soybean futures, to make me jealous. It isn't working. She's a reformed alcoholic, she broke a leg riding to hounds, and she hasn't a brain in her head. As I told Hayes myself, it's difficult to be jealous of a woman who can't drink, can't walk, and can't talk."

Sid Fogel suddenly erupted with laughter, causing several other diners to turn and stare. Ignoring them, he said, "Now that's my kind of sentence."

Andrea had almost immediately regretted saying it, but was now glad he was amused.

"Why wouldn't you marry him?" Sid asked, and then began answering his own question. "I remember from years ago. It just came back to me, you'll see why, a scene in a movie called *The Long Hot Summer*. They made it from a Faulkner novel although you'd hardly know it. A fun movie though. There was a scene where Joanne Woodward said to Paul Newman, 'I'm nobody's little rabbit.' Loved that line. God, she was good. You see why I thought of it."

Andrea had never seen the film, but *saw* exactly. "Yes, that's part of it," she said.

"So if you want a career more than you want to get married, you should think television, Andy."

"I'm doing very well, Sid. Very well."

"Yeah, I know. But you could do better. You could be really famous, right across the country."

"Maybe I could. But I know how risky television is. Why should I give up what I have to take a chance like that?"

"You mean your catering business? You wouldn't have to give that up."

"I don't think you realize how time consuming a business it is, Sid."

"You tell me you have great assistants. Superb professionals, I think you said. So you delegate a little more authority."

Andrea smiled tolerantly. "Except that a lot of my very best clients demand my personal services. Just like you."

"Okay, point taken. But you take a month off every summer, right?"

"Yes. August. To recuperate."

"Sometimes just doing something different is a way of recuperating. A show would be very different. So you take two months off instead. How much catering is there in July?"

"It's a slow month."

"So, if you took July and August off, we could tape most of the shows in that period, maybe even all of them. A season these days is only thirteen shows. And if Dinah Shore can do five hour-long shows a week, you ought to be able to do two or three half-hour ones, if everything was fully worked out ahead of time."

"You make it all sound a little too easy, I suspect."

Sid shrugged. "You let me worry about that. That's what a good producer's for."

"And you're one of the best?" Andrea teased.

"You said it, kid."

Andrea laughed. "And nothing if not persistent."

"That's right. You can say no now, but I'll keep on bringing it up until you say yes. You're a natural. Pretty, sexy, experienced in performing, an expert in your field. And there's another angle, you know. If you're up there on that box, people are going to be knocking down your door to have you cater their parties. It won't even matter if they can't get you personally. Just to be able to say it's your firm will be enough. People like to get close to media stars any way they can. Hell, you could open a West Coast branch, spend some of your time there, some here, double your profits. Think about that side of it."

Andrea was not ready to admit it to Sid Fogel yet, but she was intrigued. There could be a great many side benefits involved. She'd been thinking for some time about doing a book on party giving. It was common knowledge that Julia Child had made a small fortune from her cookbooks not just because they were damn good but because of the exposure she got from television. It was the difference betwen good sales and phenomenal sales. And a successful television show would put Andrea on an entirely new footing in her profession. She would not just be one of half a dozen top caterers, but one of the few superstars of the food world. It could happen. If she really put her mind to it, in fact, she had no doubt she could make it happen.

"Am I beginning to get through to you?" Sid asked.

"Well, it does seem like something worth thinking about."

"Good. That's progress. After dinner why don't we go back to my place, have a nightcap, and talk about it some more?"

Andrea smiled at him. "I said think about, Sid. And let's take one thing at a time."

"Sure. In that case, why don't we have dinner again next week?"

Andrea considered briefly. "Yes," she said. "Why don't we?"

"This is the beginning of something very big, Andy. I promise you."

"Well, we'll see."

"You and I will make a terrific team, I'm sure of it."

"Will we?" said Andrea, and gave a little laugh.

Part Five

Chapter Twelve

SID FOGEL STOOD IN THE SHADOWS near a doorway at the rear of the grand ballroom of the Beverly Hilton. He had been there about ten minutes, waiting for Andrea's award to be presented. Knowing that it would come almost at the end, he had timed his arrival perfectly. He hadn't intended to come at all, but his curiosity had got the better of him; he wanted to hear Andrea's acceptance speech, wanted to know firsthand how she handled herself, and whether she would even mention him. But he did not want her to know he had been there and was prepared to duck even further out of sight if anyone he knew should pass by on the way to the restroom or making an early exit. Let her stew, he thought.

On the oversize screen at the rear of the stage, Andrea's face suddenly flashed into gigantic presence. He knew what was coming. He had seen the series of edited clips from "Gourmet Adventures" beforehand. Andrea would like the presentation, he thought. It had been the idea of the award program's director, Dick Simpson, to show Andrea proceeding from soup to nuts as she interviewed some of her more famous guests, but he had put his own staff to work culling out the appropriate clips. It had been a gesture of affection, but he hoped its actual effect on her now might be to bring her to her senses, to make her realize how much she would be losing if she stuck to her exaggerated money demands. The anger he had felt at lunch that day began to return, and he clenched his teeth together hard.

The short recapitulation of the show ended, and the president of the Independent Broadcasters Association appeared to say, "It gives me great pleasure to present this special

279

award to a very lovely and talented woman, Lady Andrea Harrington."

A spotlight picked Andrea out as she rose from her table. Far back as he was, Sid could see that she looked smashing. The bitch always looked smashing.

Andrea accepted the inscribed silver tray and moved to the microphone. For a moment she simply stood there smiling as the applause quieted down, stood there with that cool and yet somehow sexy elegance that had attracted Sid to her from the beginning. If she was under any strain, she certainly wasn't showing it. But then Andrea wouldn't, Sid thought.

"My thanks to the members of the board for voting me this special award, and to all of you for a very lovely welcome," Andrea began, her slightly husky voice perfectly calm. "It is my belief that the success of 'Gourmet Adventures' has shown two things. First, it proves that there is a very large television audience for programs that differ from the standard fare without being limited in their appeal to some special elite. And secondly, it demonstrates that independent television is not merely a supplement to the major networks, but a strong, imaginative alternative."

In spite of himself, Sid chuckled. That's it, baby, he thought, feed their egos.

"Television, as we all know, is a profoundly collaborative medium. I therefore want to thank all those who have worked with me over the past two seasons, the guests who so graciously agreed to appear on the show, my superb creative and technical staff, my director, Bill Hornsby, and most of all, my producer, Sid Fogel, who sadly could not be here tonight. It was Sid who persuaded me to do the show in the first place, and it could not have been such a success without his continued faith. Ladies and gentlemen, thank you once again."

Sid shook his head. You had to give her credit. Not only had she brought it off as though nothing were wrong, she had, Sid realized, just set him up to play the villain. He should have known. It was just like the story she'd told him about how she'd handled that former lover of her husband's,

Riccardo Bianchetti, when he'd come to New York. She'd gotten her story across first. Stupid of me, Sid thought. He'd considered getting the rumor out that afternoon that he was going to drop the show, but he'd held back, hoping she'd come around. Damn it, he should have beaten her to the punch. With Andrea, you couldn't afford to waste any time making feints, you had to go after her before she decked you herself.

Sid Fogel grimaced. He turned sharply and went out the door behind him. He'd been had and he knew it. But he'd only lost one round. He'd back her into the corner yet.

Andrea and Rick arrived home from the awards ceremony about midnight and opened a bottle of the superb Chardonnay from the case Robert Mondavi had given her for Christmas. She'd done a show at the Mondavi winery near Oakville the previous fall, and had become a devotee of Robert's wines. She was particularly fond of the Chardonnay, and, God only knew, she deserved a reward for the way she'd handled herself at the awards dinner. Considering the disaster of her lunch with Sid, and the tension she'd been under as a result, she thought she'd played it all just beautifully. Rick, of course, didn't really understand what she'd accomplished. As she lay stretched out on the white love seat in her bedroom with her feet in Rick's lap, he suddenly said, "You know, Andrea, you really surprised me when you said all those nice things about Sid in your speech. I didn't even expect you to mention him."

Andrea cradled her glass of Chardonnay in her hands. "It's called politics, Rick. The word will get back to Sid, and it will put him on the spot. He can't really denounce me as a greedy bitch after I've praised him to the skies, can he? Or at least not so easily."

Rick's brow clouded for a moment, as he thought that through. Then he smiled and said, "Oh, okay, I get it." He stroked her leg gently. "You're so damned smart, Andrea, it's hard to keep up with you."

Andrea smiled back at him. "Thank you," she said. Rick,

she'd come to realize more and more, was simply not too bright about some things. If his career did take off, he was going to need an awfully good manager, or he'd find himself getting screwed at every turn. But in a way, that was one of the things she liked about Rick. After Hayes and Sid it was something of a relief to have a lover who never told her what to do, or argued, or tried to organize her life—though there were also times when it seemed a little boring.

"I wish I didn't have to go back on location tomorrow," Rick said, his hand encircling her ankle.

"I know. But tomorrow's going to be very busy, and I have to fly to New York the day after, so we couldn't be together for a while anyway."

"Yeah." Rick sighed. "That makes it worse. What time is your flight? So I can call before you leave."

Andrea hesitated. "It's still a little vague, Rick. I'm not taking a commercial flight. Hayes Caldwell is flying in from Singapore, and refueling in Los Angeles before going on to New York. So he offered me a ride."

"Oh, I didn't know." Rick frowned.

Rick knew Andrea and Hayes had been lovers, just as he knew that she had been involved with Sid. Andrea had always thought it was strange that even though Rick disliked Sid personally, it was Hayes he seemed to be jealous of. And that was despite the fact that she saw Sid constantly and Hayes only very occasionally. Perhaps he sensed that Andrea had cared for Hayes much more deeply than she ever had for Sid, although she tried not to let it show.

Andrea reached out for Rick's hand. "Don't look so worried," she said. "Hayes and I are just old friends, you know that."

"From your point of view, I guess so. But I get the feeling Mr. Hayes Caldwell wishes it were otherwise."

"Oh, don't be silly, Rick. As I recall, the one time you met Hayes, he was being extremely attentive to that copper heiress from Brazil."

"That was just for your sake," Rick said.

Andrea took a sip of wine. Rick was probably quite right about that—about some things he wasn't so dumb. "Look, Rick, if it really bothers you, I'll take a commercial flight. But it seems a waste of money. And it's so much more comfortable on Hayes's plane."

"No, it's okay. I'm sorry."

Andrea had fully expected that answer. In fact, she wouldn't have offered to take a commercial flight if she hadn't known Rick would back down. "Good. Because I don't think it's wise to get into this kind of nonsense. If you aren't careful I might decide to be jealous of that lovely young thing you're co-starring with."

To Andrea's surprise, Rick blushed. "Barbara Benton? You've got to be kidding. She's barely speaking to me."

"Perhaps that's because you don't pay enough attention to her," Andrea teased.

Rick shrugged. "That's her problem," he said.

"Good." Andrea set her glass down and reached out to Rick. "As you pointed out, we won't be seeing each other for a while. I think we should make love, don't you?"

Rick beamed at her. "Oh, yes," he said.

Andrea opened her eyes for what seemed the hundredth time. Through the drapes she could see the slight translucent glow of the dawn. She knew she was going to feel like hell all day, but in a way she was glad to see the light. It would be better to get up than to just lie there and suffer.

After the wine they had drunk, and Rick's energetic lovemaking, she had expected to fall asleep very quickly and easily. She had been very tired, but her mind would simply not let go. Just as she had been on the verge of falling asleep, she had snapped back to wakefulness with a jolt. Her body craved sleep, but her mind wanted to go over the lunch with Sid again. And again. She tried thinking of other things but that only proved to be worse. It was as though her memory had

283

gone on a rampage, throwing up incidents and voices at her with a surreal disjointedness. It seemed to her as though she had slept almost not at all, one of those strange nights when the line between consciousness and unconsciousness was so thin that there were times when you didn't know whether you were asleep or awake. In either state, her head had buzzed with images, words, bodies, voices. . . .

Hayes was making love to her. She could feel his strong body, hear him suddenly shout with pleasure, except that abruptly it was not Hayes but Kevin, straddling her, looking down at her, smiling with that self-satisfied, boyish grin of his.

George. He was terribly old, saying money, money, money in a dying voice, she didn't want to think about George. Terry, then. What had Terry been like as a lover? She could hardly remember. It was strange. She couldn't see his body, but his voice came to her out of the darkness like a blow, "You've got to be more commanding, Andrea."

Commanding. She'd learned that. Somebody had told her so. Sid had told her so. Commanding bitch.

Wake up, wake up, it's all right, George. Sweetie pie, it's all right.

Hayes. She came back to Hayes. He had never called her bitch. Sweetie pie bitch.

You want too much. You spend too much. You want too much.

This isn't for me, sweetie pie.

I'm not saying good-bye, good-bye, Hayes.

You want too much.

Andrea threw back the sheet with a convulsive jerk and got out of bed, standing too quickly, so that she half-staggered for a moment. Rick stirred slightly on the other side of the king-size bed, but did not wake. He was dreaming, she could see the outline of his erection against the silk sheet. Despite all her thrashing around, Rick had wakened only once, for a few seconds. He always slept soundly. It was one of the blessing of naiveté, Andrea supposed.

She pulled on a negligee and made her way through the house as quietly as possible, turning on only the occasional light. The early-morning sky was still white as she passed under the glass roof of the foyer. She hoped to God it would be a day when you could see the sun; the smog kept getting worse and worse all the time. In the kitchen she made herself a cup of hot milk and sat down at the table next to the French doors onto the terrace. She took a few sips of milk and then, elbows resting on the table, sank her head betwen her hands. Her eyelids felt heavy and scratchy and she let them close for a moment.

You want too much.

Andrea sat up with a start. "You've got to snap out of this," she said aloud. And after a moment, added, "Sweetie pie."

There were things to do. Things that had no connection with Sid Fogel or "Gourmet Adventures," thank God. She was glad she had planned to go to New York; a change of scene would help. The New York Arts Society was holding its annual gala at the Metropolitan Museum on Friday, and she had decided to oversee the evening personally. Although she had absolute trust in her staffs on both coasts, she always liked to be present for major occasions, especially organizational galas and charity fund-raisers. They always attracted a considerable amount of publicity, and her active participation reinforced the impression that despite her status as a television personality she was still very much in charge of Harrington's. That public perception could be more important than ever now; having reached the impasse with Sid, she suspected that the catering firm was once again going to become the central focus of her life, at least for a while. She always had that to fall back on.

Andrea sighed. Fall back. That was the trouble. She didn't want to go back a step. She wanted to keep going forward. What was the use of it all if she couldn't keep going forward, if she couldn't become more powerful, more famous, and, yes, damn it, if there weren't more money? If she had to fall back, would it still seem worth it?

She'd turned down Kevin because she wanted to owe nothing to anyone but herself. She'd sacrificed Hayes to her ambition. And she'd used Sid—though that was only fair, since he'd used her, too—to gain a new kind of respectability. She felt her anger rising again. She'd come too far, and worked too hard, and given up too much to be slapped down again now. She couldn't let that happen.

The morning light was streaming through the kitchen windows, and she could see the tops of the cypresses along the walk to the pool swaying slightly in the wind. A strong breeze was always a good sign in southern California; it carried away the smog. It was going to be a bright, clear day. That was something, at least.

Andrea's Rolls, with her assistant, Gabriella Crowley, at the wheel, swept down Sepulvada toward West Imperial and the terminal for private planes at Los Angeles Airport. Between them on the caramel leather seat lay the morning edition of the *Los Angeles Times*. Andrea tapped her long fingers against it, fuming. In Baxter Robinson's column there was a brief item that read, "There's word around town that a certain glamorous lady is asking for so much money that her hit television show may be dropped by the producer. It's said he's in such a snit he walked out on the lady at lunch the other day." That was all, but it had put Andrea into a rage when she had read it only moments before.

"So much for the loyalty of Rabbits named Robinson," Andrea was saying furiously. "I'll never speak to him again."

"Of course you will," said Gabriella calmly. "It could have been much more specific, Andrea. That kind of blind item could refer to half a dozen people. I wouldn't worry about it. After all, you expected Sid to drop the word, and at least it didn't happen until after the awards dinner. Considering all the tributes you gave him there, most people won't even think of you. Especially since Baxter printed them yesterday."

"The miserable snake in the grass," Andrea snapped. "Albino snake."

Gabriella laughed. "I think snakes eat rabbits, Andrea."

"Well, you may think it's funny. But I don't."

Gabriella frowned. "What's the matter with you, Andrea? It's not like you to take things so hard."

"I'm sorry, Gabriella," Andrea said. "You're the last person I should take things out on. But the last two nights have been awful. My whole life keeps running through my head, all jumbled up. And I've been having so many dreams about Hayes. To tell you the truth, I wish I weren't flying with him. I've even had fleeting moments of thinking I should have married him, God help me."

"What are you talking about, Andrea? You've told me many times that you were so glad you didn't succumb to the temptation to marry Hayes Caldwell. That you would have just been his lovely wife and never had the chance to become what you have. I truly don't understand."

"I don't understand either. It's strange. When Hayes called last week and we discovered we were heading for New York the same day, I jumped at the chance to travel with him. I told myself it was just because it was so easy and luxurious. But, you know, I think that maybe in the back of my mind I was looking forward to showing him all over again that I didn't need him, telling him I was signing a new contract for a lot more money. I was so damn sure I could twist Sid around my little finger."

"Look, Andrea," Gabriella said as she pulled the Rolls over to the curb. "We're here. If you don't want to fly with Hayes, I'll go aboard and tell him you couldn't make it. I can say that because his plane was going to be on the ground for such a short time, you were afraid a message wouldn't get through. Do you want me to do that?"

"No." Andrea shook her head, and then smiled. "I'll pull myself together and put on a good act. I've always been good at that."

"Now that's the kind of talk I like to hear. But promise

me when you get to New York you'll get some sleep. Forget about Sid. He'll come around in time. He's just trying to pressure you, through Baxter or anybody else he can. It'll work out. I know it will."

Andrea hugged her. "Thank you, dear lady. You're a treasure."

"You're a treasure, Andrea. Don't forget it. Sid's not going to forget it, either. I promise you."

"All right."

"And get some sleep."

"I'll try."

Andrea got out of the Rolls with her one small bag—she had a complete wardrobe in New York—and walked into the terminal.

As the *Magnolia* became fully airborne and made a wide circle to the east, Hayes Caldwell unbuckled his seat belt and went to the bar to break out a bottle of Dom Pérignon.

"Heavens, Hayes, it's not even noon yet," Andrea said, unstrapping herself as well.

Hayes looked over at her. He could sense her tenseness just from the way she sat forward on the edge of the maroon leather chair. It was the kind of chair that made you want to sink into it, but she held herself upright. And now that they were in the air she was sitting forward on the edge of the cushions as though she were afraid to relax. When she'd come aboard she'd seemed very lively and gay, but there had been something willed about her laughter, as though she were giving a performance. And she had looked more tired than he had ever seen her. Lovely, of course, and as stylish as ever in an apricot wool suit and pale green silk blouse. Andrea always looked lovely to Hayes. But her eyes were slightly bloodshot and there were half-moons of weariness below them that makeup could not disguise.

"This is a special occasion, honey," Hayes said, removing the foil and untwisting the wires around the cork. "I don't get to see you very often, you know. When old friends get together as seldom as we do, it deserves a celebration."

Andrea smiled, but it was not the kind of full, dazzling smile Hayes would have liked to see. "I suppose it does," she said. "It really is good to see you, Hayes."

Hayes held the cork in his right hand and turned the bottle against it, to prevent the cork from flying into the air. The champagne was chilled to just the right point, so that as the cork came free there was no sudden overflow. He poured out a glass for each of them.

"You know, Hayes, you open a champagne bottle with the finesse of a true sommelier. I think you missed your calling."

"Well, I always did think it was kind of crass to send the cork shooting across the room and spill half the bottle. That's locker-room stuff, if you ask me." He came out from behind the bar with a glass in each hand, and gave one to Andrea.

"To old times," Hayes said, almost without thinking, and was suddenly afraid that Andrea might take offense.

But she smiled. "To old times."

They each took a sip of champagne and then there was a silence, filled only by the drone of the engine.

"I guess it's none of my business," Hayes said finally, "but you seem a little down."

Andrea looked away from him and took another sip from her glass. Then, as though having made a decision, she looked him directly in the eye. "Things are rather a mess, Hayes. I don't like to admit that, especially not to you, but it's the truth. You'll find out anyway, so I may as well be the one to tell you."

"What's wrong, honey?"

"I've had a serious argument with Sid Fogel. About money. If I don't back down, he's threatening to cancel 'Gourmet Adventures.' "

"I'm sorry, Andrea. I know how much that show means to you. But can't you work out a compromise?"

"I think the only compromise Sid would accept is for me to come crawling back to him on my hands and knees. I won't do that. I deserve what I asked for, and I know for a fact that in terms of the potential profits for next season it wouldn't be any hardship for him to give it to me. But it's more than money. It's a matter of pride. For both of us, I suppose. Stubborn pride, I guess some people would call it. But it makes it difficult to find a way out."

Hayes didn't know what to say. He wasn't used to Andrea's showing her vulnerability. God only knew, he'd tried to reach through to it before, with damn little success. The thing that surprised him most was her saying that she especially didn't like admitting to him that she had problems. He understood that, all right. The real difficulty between them had always been her insistence on making it clear that, love him or not, the most important thing in her life was the fact that she could damn well take care of herself. Sometimes it had seemed to him that in trying so hard to prove that to him she was really attempting to convince herself.

For her to let down her guard now, even a little, made him want very much to take her in his arms and comfort her. But he suspected that would be exactly the wrong thing to do. He'd never managed to get Andrea out of his system. The other women he'd been involved with in the past three years never seemed to quite measure up. The strange part of it was that the quality they most seemed to lack was precisely the strength of spirit, the independent fire, that made Andrea put her career first. He had often wondered whether Andrea ever regretted not marrying him. Maybe, for the first time, he was seeing a hint that she did. But he was sure it would be fatal to press the point.

"The man's in business, Andrea," he said, deciding to stick to surface facts. "He's not going to throw away a profit-making venture just out of stubbornness. It would be stupid."

Andrea smiled wanly. "You don't know Sid. He'll go to any lengths to prove that he can't be pushed around. Besides, he has so many other shows on the air, or in the planning stages. My show is just one corner of his empire, Hayes."

"Well, isn't it also just one corner of your empire? You've got Harrington's. And I see copies of your party-giving guide stacked to the ceiling in all the bookstores. You can do other books, can't you?"

Andrea nodded. "Yes, of course. Of course I can." But she still looked bleak. "I guess I'm just very tired."

"Well, I've always told you . . ." Hayes let the sentence drift off.

"Go ahead, Hayes. Say it."

"There's no point in picking up the threads of old arguments, honey."

"Then I'll say it for you. I work too hard."

"Are you just saying that for me, or admitting it to yourself?"

"I don't know. I've been doing a lot of thinking the past two or three days. Not very straight thinking, really. But I . . ." Andrea shrugged.

"We seem to have a lot of unfinished sentences around here," Hayes said as lightly as he could.

"Yes. But I think I'll leave that one unfinished."

Hayes hesitated for a moment and then asked, "It wouldn't have anything to do with wondering what you're working so hard *for*, would it?"

Andrea suddenly sat back in her chair. "Is that what you'd like to hear me say?"

"Not really."

Andrea looked surprised. "No? I would have thought it might give you a lot of satisfaction."

"No, baby, you're wrong about that. I think it would make me sad."

Andrea stared at him. And then to Hayes's astonishment, her eyes filled with tears. He had never once seen her cry before.

"Hey now, baby girl," he said and went to kneel beside her chair, enveloping her in his arms. "It's all right. It's all right." For a long moment she remained in his arms, but then he felt her take a deep breath and she pulled back from him.

"I'm sorry, Hayes," she said. "Forgive me. I'm behaving like a child."

291

Still kneeling beside her, Hayes said, very quietly, "I love you, Andrea. I still love you."

Andrea shut her eyes. "Don't, Hayes," she said, almost whispering. "Please don't."

Hayes stood up. "I think you still feel something, too."

Andrea opened her eyes and gazed up at him.

"I don't know what I feel, Hayes. I'm sorry. I shouldn't have come with you. I knew it was a mistake."

"No, it wasn't, sweetie pie. We belong together."

"Oh, Hayes, please stop."

"I have to say this, Andrea. I have to. Maybe we could go back to where we were. To hell with marriage. Just back to what we had."

"I don't want to talk about this, Hayes. Not now."

"But sometime?" he asked, and could not keep the hope out of his voice.

Andrea would not look at him. "I don't know, Hayes. I truly don't know. Perhaps. I have to sort things out."

Hayes reached down and squeezed her shoulder lightly. "All right," he said. "That's something. I won't press." He paused a moment. "I haven't told you about the Chinese banquet I went to in Singapore," he said. "Have you ever eaten fried fish eyes?"

Andrea gave a quick, grateful laugh. "As a side dish or a main course?" she asked.

Cruising at thirty thousand feet, the *Magnolia* flew eastward above the Arizona desert.

Chapter Thirteen

SHORTLY ARTER 11:00 the following morning, Andrea arrived at her office at Harrington's. Despite jet lag, or perhaps because of it, Andrea had slept soundly the night before. On the flight across the country Hayes had shown *The Philadelphia Story* from his stock of old movies. Cary Grant's efforts to win back Katharine Hepburn reminded her a little too forcefully at moments of Hayes's plea that he and Andrea try to revive what they had had together, but she suspected that he had selected the film unconsciously rather than deliberately, and she had made no objection when he suggested it, thinking only that it would be a way to pass the time without getting into any more deep emotional waters. By the time Hayes dropped her off at her apartment on East Sixty-seventh Street, she was so tired that she'd gone immediately to bed. The flight from Los Angeles had apparently had the effect of finally sapping her of the strength even to worry, and she had fallen asleep almost at once.

When she arrived at Harrington's, Paul Boucheron presented her with an enormous bouquet of yellow roses in honor of her award from the Independent Broadcasters Association, bringing them into her office and offering them with a deep bow.

"Oh, Paul, they're gorgeous. How sweet of you."

"I am not the only one passing out bouquets. I have something here for you to read."

"What is it?"

Paul handed her a copy of *New York* magazine. "It came out yesterday with Louise Norman's latest piece on New York caterers."

"Good, I take it?"

"For us, wonderful."

"Well, God knows I've paid my dues to Louise."

Andrea's relationship with Louise, which had begun so well Andrea's first year in New York, had almost foundered when "Gourmet Adventures" had first gone on the air. Louise had panned her flat, writing that she had expected something far more *adventuresome* from Lady Andrea Harrington than just another cooking show, particularly one that focused primarily on what she had called "froufrou and frills—all very pretty, of course, and ladies who have nothing better to do than play bridge and spend money will no doubt think it's all very soigné, but I find it merely frivolous."

Andrea had been furious at first, even though she told herself that Louise was just jealous. The entire food world knew that Louise had always wanted her own television show. In the fall of 1976 she had managed to get a slot for herself on "The Today Show," but she had proved so unpleasant, and so unglamorous at the same time, that she'd quickly been dropped. Still, her attack on "Gourmet Adventures" had come as a shock to Andrea. Previously, she had always been extremely complimentary, and Andrea had even come to regard her as a friend.

After her initial rage, though, Andrea had begun to realize that Louise was quite right, and her column had acted as a stimulus toward Andrea's rethinking of the show, leading to her proposal to Sid that they take the show out of the claustrophobic studio setting to interview chefs and celebrities in their own restaurants and homes. It had been those changes that had eventually brought "Gourmet Adventures" its great success, and Andrea, at Bruce Halliwell's suggestion, had written to Louise to thank her for the part that her criticism had played in revamping the show's format. Louise was not used to having her brickbats repaid in gratitude and had been utterly disarmed. She had told Andrea privately that she continued to find the show "a trifle elitist," but in print she had been

294

very flattering, writing that in its new format "Gourmet Adventures" provided "the kind of vicarious pleasure one gets from reading *Architectural Digest.*" That still got across the elitist point, of course, but in a way that attracted viewers rather than scared them away.

Andrea had subsequently cemented her friendship with Louise by having her on the show. She was not a very good guest, but Andrea had coupled her with André Soltner of Lutèce, one of Louise's most cherished restaurants, and it had all gone off very well. Still, with Louise, you never quite knew what might happen, when she might turn savage.

Andrea took the copy of the magazine from Paul and quickly scanned the paragraphs concerning Harrington's, which Louise proclaimed one of the city's top three caterers, along with Richard Corliss and Glorious Foods. The comment that pleased her most read, "I had expected the quality of Harrington's food to decline as Lady Andrea turned more of her attention to the production of her deservedly popular television program, 'Gourmet Adventures,' but her New York staff, from *chef de cuisine* Paul Boucheron on down, have been so thoroughly trained in Lady Andrea's methods and approach to the serving of sumptuous and imaginative feasts, and are, like herself, such complete professionals, that there has not been the slightest falling off."

She would have to get a copy of the article off to Sid by express mail, Andrea thought, with the words *deservedly popular television program* underlined in red. Doubly underlined, in fact.

"I'm so happy to see her recognize your importance," she said to Paul Boucheron. "It's about time."

Paul's long Gallic face seldom betrayed his emotions, but for once he positively beamed. "There is even more."

"More?"

"Oui, oui. On the last page. When she talks about Riccardo Bianchetti."

Andrea looked up sharply. "Riccardo?"

295

"You will be amused, I think."

Mention of Riccardo always made Andrea slightly nervous, and she turned to the final page of the article with some misgivings.

Bianchetti's has unhappily failed to live up to its original promise. In operation for three years, this firm seems to be mired in the past. Any catering firm that devotes itself to a single cuisine in this period of increasingly eclectic tastes in food is perhaps asking for trouble, of course. This is not to suggest that Italian cooking at its best is not without variety or that it cannot attain the heights of culinary delight. It is without question one of the world's most interesting and, at times, exalted cuisines. But there are difficulties in terms of the demands of the catering business. Aside from such all too commonly encountered dishes as lasagna and cannelloni, the great Italian pasta dishes must be prepared at the last minute. While this is perfectly possible in a restaurant kitchen, it is hard to carry off successfully in the circumstances of a catered affair for more than a few people. The repertoire of Bianchetti's is thus somewhat limited, and when the firm does attempt a dish like *Linguini ala Primavera*, the vegetables, whether mushrooms, snow peas, or broccoli flowerets have often been cooked beyond that point of bright crispness that gives the dish its charm. On occasion, even the pasta itself is gummy.

In terms of variety, one wonders why Bianchetti's has not ventured into the cold pasta salads that Word of Mouth has had such success with. I suspect that the problem lies with the fact that Mr. Bianchetti is a classicist in a world of experimentation. Cold pasta salads are in fact more an American than an Italian dish, just as pizza as we have come to know it, with a great number of possible toppings, is really an American adaptation and extension of the original Neapolitan tomato and cheese torte. Bianchetti's has been noted in the past for some of its more elaborate dishes, including a veal roast stuffed with truffles, but even those dishes are not what they once were. Just as Lady Andrea Harrington divides her time between Los Angeles and New York, so Mr. Bianchetti commutes between his London and New York establishments, but unlike

296

Lady Andrea, he does not appear to have been successful in training his staff to the point where they are able to carry on as though he were present even when he is not. It's rather a shame.

Andrea was in one sense delighted to see Louise take a slam at Riccardo, but at the same time it gave her a slight chill. From what she had heard, he had intially been quite successful in New York, but had never managed to attract the kind of clientele she herself enjoyed.

She had only run into him a few times over the past three years, once at a meat wholesalers, Imperial Veal & Lamb on Fourteenth Street, another time at Bridge Kitchenware, and twice at Bloomingdale's. The first time she had made a point of shaking his hand and wishing him well, as though she had never received the note he had sent after George's death. He had been very stiff, though superficially polite; only his dark eyes gave any hint of his dislike of her. Otherwise, they had merely said hello in passing. On the most recent occasion, in fact, six months ago, he had barely nodded to her.

"Riccardo is going to be furious," she said to Paul. "I really wish Louise hadn't made a direct comparison between us. After all, she knows something of the story." Andrea was not sure how much of the story Paul actually knew, but she was certain Bruce Halliwell had told him a good deal of it.

"Louise Norman is a malicious woman, Andrea. She likes to make trouble."

"Well, I hope that in this case she doesn't succeed. Do you have any idea how Riccardo's firm is doing financially?"

Paul shrugged. "Not well. He was never able to attract the elite clients. And Louise is quite right about his failings. I think he is not in very good shape."

"And this won't help."

"No."

Andrea sighed. Too much of her past was being thrown up at her these days. The last subject she wanted to dwell on was

297

George and Riccardo. That was past history and she wanted it to stay that way.

Andrea sat up suddenly, startled by the curious ways of the mind. *Past History.* That wasn't anything she wanted to think about either. But there had been a line in her final speech —it came back as though it were yesterday: "History does not really become the past until every person who lived a particular moment of it is dead. Only then does it stop interfering with the present. Sometimes even then it won't relent."

She shook her head.

"Is there something wrong?" Paul asked.

"Just silly memories. Let's get down to work, Paul. Have you got all the menus and charts for the gala at the Metropolitan?"

"Everything."

"All right. Let's make sure we haven't any problems."

The Fountain Restaurant of the Metropolitan Museum of Art had both advantages and drawbacks as a location for a catered dinner. Aesthetically, it was a dramatic setting, but one that was marred by a certain shabbiness of detail. The long, high-ceilinged room with its large rectangular pool at the center, the white fluted pillars rising at the pool's edge to support the vast skylight masked by a white pleated canopy, gave the impression of a dining room aboard an ocean liner of the 1930's. Unfortunately, the cloth of the canopy was badly stained in several places, although that fact was less noticeable at night, when no light penetrated the expanse of glass above it. The surface of the tables around the pool was Formica, which was not a problem; for the gala Andrea was covering them with white tablecloths, complemented by black and white checked napkins which echoed the mosaic tiled floor. But there was nothing that could be done to disguise the tackiness of the white vinyl chairs. The tables were also small, ruling out any possibility of individual flower arrangements.

The pool and its statuary almost made such niceties re-
dundant, however. The sculptures, the work of the Swedish-
American Carl Milles, were based upon the Greek myth of
the nymph Aganippe, from whose fountain on Mount Helicon
the waters of artistic inspiration had been believed to flow.
The nymph herself was represented by a nude figure reclining
on a pedestal at the far end of the pool, playing with a bronze
fish in the water below her. On either side of her, at the corners
of the pool, there were statues of a faun and a centaur, while
across the shallow waters of the pool itself, five slender bronze
statues representing the arts raced joyously homeward from
Aganippe's spring, holding aloft the symbols of their artistic
inspiration, whether the column of the architect or the lyre
of the musician. It was, Andrea thought, a charming and
exuberant sculptural group, a centerpiece worthy of gala
circumstances.

But the room did present some practical problems. The
kitchen, which produced light meals and sandwiches during
museum hours for the hordes of visitors, was large and well
equipped, but its situation at the far end of the pool, beyond
the statue of Aganippe, meant that waiters had to travel a
long and circuitous route around the perimeter of the pool to
reach the tables near the entrance to the dining room. Since
the museum served cafeteria style, the placement of the
kitchen was no problem during ordinary usage. But for a sit-
down dinner for three hundred guests, and of the kind planned
for the Arts Society gala, if everyone were to be served a hot
meal within a reasonably short time, Harrington's was going
to have to employ more waiters than usual.

Andrea and Paul Boucheron had planned the menu to
minimize the difficulties involved. The first course, a colorful
layered terrine of fresh vegetables, was most flavorful as it
approached room temperature, and thus could be put in place
while the guests were being served drinks in the Greek gal-
leries just beyond the dining room entrance. The second course
was a hot scallop bisque. Because of the smallness of the tables,

299

Andrea did not want to use covered soup dishes, since there was virtually no place to set the covers aside while eating. Instead, each serving was topped by a puff pastry crust, which not only kept the soup hot but added a touch of elegance as well.

The main course was to be a *navarin* of spring lamb, a dish at which Paul Boucheron was an absolute master. Because it was essentially a stew, it would retain its heat on the long trek from the kitchen to the far reaches of the dining room, but thanks to Paul's artistry, no one would consider himself to be consuming a mere stew. Paul used morels rather than ordinary white mushrooms, rounds of celery root rather than the usual green celery, and tiny Belgian carrots no longer than one's little finger, braised together in a veal stock flavored with fennel, basil, garlic, and fresh juniper berries. It was the kind of dish that kept revealing deeper complexities of flavor as it was eaten, combining the richness of meltingly tender lamb with the sprightly freshness of the individual vegetables.

It was always a great success. Paul had often been asked for the exact recipe, but resolutely refused to part with it. Andrea was one of the very few people who knew that he used juniper berries, tied in a white cheesecloth sack so that they could be removed before the dish was served.

At 8:15 that evening the gala was in full swing. The first-course plates had been removed, and Andrea and Paul were supervising the transfer of the heavy white porcelain soup bowls with their golden pastry caps from the huge wall ovens to the waiters' trays. When dealing with anything as delicate as puff pastry, a few extra portions were always prepared, in case insufficient puffing or overbrowning of any of the crusts occurred; Andrea wanted to make certain that only perfect specimens were carried away to the dining room. Suddenly, out of the corner of her eye, she caught sight of an unexpected movement at the big industrial ranges off to her right where the *navarin* was gently heating in eight-quart stock pots. She turned to get a better look and saw a man in a waiter's jacket hovering in front of the ranges.

Andrea strode quickly toward him. They needed every hand they could get; she hadn't hired extra waiters so they could wander around the kitchen peering at the food. As she approached the range, she saw that the man was actually stirring one of the pots.

"What the hell do you think you're doing?" she said angrily.

The man turned to face her, and Andrea stopped dead a few paces away from him. It was not a waiter.

"Riccardo," she gasped.

He stared at her, his handsome face distorted by a strange, almost maniacal smile.

"What are you doing here?" she asked, her heart leaping in sudden anxiety.

"Perhaps I just wish to see what makes you so successful. That Norman woman, that cunt, says you are so good and I am so bad. But I see nothing so wonderful here. It is just because she is your friend. You have always wanted to see me ruined. I know that is true. So you asked her to give me a terrible review. You have wanted to destroy me always because George loved me instead of you. You have wanted to drive me out of business. But soon you will not be in business, either, Lady Andrea. That is such a comedy, you calling yourself Lady. You were never a lady, only a selfish bitch. A woman who would kill for what you want, the way you killed George." Riccardo's voice was low, but it was filled with a cold hatred that frightened Andrea.

"I think you had better leave right away, Riccardo," Andrea said, trying to keep her voice from trembling.

"Very well," he said, and smiled that strange twisted smile again. "I have done what I came for."

"What do you mean?" Andrea looked beyond him to the ranges where the *navarin* simmered. She had seen Riccardo stirring one of the pots—he could easily have tampered with the food.

Past horror stories flashed through her mind. The fired waiter who had put broken glass into the minestrone at Rug-

301

gero's, the chef at La Boule who had urinated into the *coq au vin*. Those restaurants had survived the incidents, but there were others that had been bankrupted because something had gone wrong in the kitchen. Only two months earlier, La Constanza, one of San Francisco's most successful restaurants, had gone out of business because a few customers had come down with hepatitis, spread by a sous-chef who hadn't even known he was ill. The year before a large restaurant in New York's Chinatown had closed because word got out that a couple of improperly cleaned chickens had given a half dozen diners salmonella poisoning. It was the worst fear of every caterer and every restaurateur that something like that would happen. It was a very human business, and unwashed hands, or an angry fit, or simple carelessness could have disastrous results. There were so many things that could go wrong, and so many easy ways to ensure that something would go wrong if one wanted revenge.

"Have you done something to the food, Riccardo?" Andrea could hardly get the words out. She turned and called out, "Paul, Paul, come here."

Riccardo laughed. "Taste it," he said. "Taste your pitiful *navarin*. You will not know. Perhaps I have done something, perhaps I have not. But if I have and you serve it, what might happen? Who knows? There could be many very sick people. But if you do not serve it, the party will be ruined. Yes? Then we will see what people say about the great Harrington's. The image will be ruined then, too. Is that not right, Mr. Boucheron?"

Paul had come rushing to Andrea's side as Riccardo was speaking, and now raised his hands as though he were going to attack him. "Tu es fou," he yelled. "A crazy man. *Bâtard*."

"I'm going to call the police," Andrea said. But she did not move. All at once she felt a great rage welling up from the pit of her stomach. It was as strong as the fury she had called out of herself so many years ago on the stage of the Colonial Theatre in Boston, and she heard her voice issuing

302

forth with the same icy rage. "You say I have always wanted to destroy you, Riccardo, but you're wrong. You have everything backwards. I never hated you, not until now. It was you who hated me, because I took George away from you. And you would never have had him back if our child had lived. He came back to you out of despair, not love. He came back to you to wallow in his unhappiness, not to find joy. George thought he was unworthy and his relationship with you made it easier for him to loathe himself exactly because you were so unworthy of him. That is the truth, Riccardo. You were utterly unworthy of him."

Riccardo looked wildly around him and then dashed to a side counter where the set of Sabatier knives Paul always carried with him on the job were waiting to be repacked. "I will kill you," Riccardo screamed, his voice echoing off the tiled walls. "I will kill you." He picked up one knife and flung it toward Andrea. As she darted to one side, it flew past her and clattered against the range behind her.

"You cunt," Riccardo screamed, picking up another knife and coming toward her, the ten-inch blade glinting in the fluorescent lights.

Moments earlier the kitchen had been a hubbub of activity, but suddenly everything was absolutely still, her staff and the milling waiters frozen into immobility. Then, all at once, several men started rushing toward Riccardo. But he had too much of a head start on them and was already within ten feet of Andrea. She turned and ran through the door to her left leading into a side pantry where another door opened directly onto the dining room. She glanced back and saw Riccardo coming through the door behind her. She kept running, straight on through the pantry and out into the dining room itself. Startled diners looked up from their soup, and conversation came to a straggling halt beside the pool. She crossed the breadth of the room and turned the corner, half falling against a table as she did so. There were shouts and the screams of women and the sound of chairs overturning. "I've got him," a voice called out, and Andrea stopped and looked back.

Half a dozen men were struggling with Riccardo, tuxedos and waiter's jackets bobbing together as they tried to hold him. The diners at the end of the pool had scattered in several directions. Throughout the dining room people were standing. Riccardo still had the knife in his hand, his arm raised high above his head. He had been pushed back against the statue of Aganippe and as he flailed there he suddenly slipped and fell heavily into the reflecting pool itself.

Andrea put her hands to her face as he fell. He came down on the bronze fish below the statue, impaling the left side of his neck on one of the sharp upturned fins. For a moment he thrashed violently in the shallow water and then was still. There was a single instant of terrible silence in the dining room, then it was broken with screams. The water surrounding the bronze fish was slowly turning red with Riccardo's blood.

For the first time in her life, Andrea fainted.

Andrea arrived home at her apartment shortly after ten o'clock, numb with shock and exhaustion. The gala had come to an immediate end following Riccardo's impalement, which was just as well, since she still did not know whether he had tampered with the *navarin* or not. The police were running laboratory tests on it at Andrea's request, although from their point of view it didn't much matter—you couldn't very well bring charges against a corpse. Two doctors had helped pull Riccardo out of the pool, but he was already dead. The razor-sharp fin had severed his jugular vein and entered the base of his brain. It made Andrea shudder to even think of it. She had tried not to look at the pool while the police were interviewing her; the sight of the bloodied water made her ill.

Most of the guests had left as quickly as possible, except for those who had actually struggled with Riccardo, who stayed to be questioned by the police. A few other guests, including Karen Bolling, who had been on the organizing committee, and Louise Norman herself, had remained to bolster

Andrea's morale. Louise actually seemed to be enjoying herself, commenting to Andrea, "My dear, I never imagined a column of mine could have such impact." Andrea thought that the time might come when she would be able to laugh at the memory of that remark, but at the moment all she could do was to shake her head. One of the things that worried her was the prospect of people making a joke of the incident. She was quite sure that within the food world it would be regarded as an absolutely delicious scandal. God only knew what effect it would have on business. The strange thing was that she was not sure she even cared.

In the past week it seemed as though one element of her life after another had slipped beyond her control. She had been so confident that she could talk Sid into giving her anything she wanted and she had been utterly wrong. Her feelings about Hayes, which she had believed she had firmly in perspective, had suddenly dissolved into confusion. And now there was Riccardo. She stood at the window in her living room and looked down on the darkness of East Sixty-seventh Street below her. Tired as she was, she also felt a strange restlessness. She knew she couldn't sleep. It was hard even to sit still in one place. All at once she began to tremble. Riccardo's death had distracted her from fully realizing that she herself could have been killed. "Oh, my God," she said. "It could have been me."

Karen had invited her to spend the night at her townhouse, but Andrea had said that wasn't necessary, that she would be all right. Now she wished she had accepted. Because she wasn't all right. She felt terribly alone, and worse still, afraid. She hadn't been truly afraid in a very long time. Even when George had been lying in the hospital, his heart choosing between life and death, she had not felt this kind of fear. Then she had felt a specific fear, a justified one. But what she felt now was not like that. It was a sense of the ground giving way beneath her, of a chasm opening just in front of her, the kind of fear that came in dreams, all the more terrifying for being unfocused and irrational.

She thought of calling Bruce in Florida, or even Myra in London. Either one of them could be expected to come up with a witty epitaph for Riccardo, and words of kindness and wisdom for her. But she needed something more than that. Perhaps she could reach Rick in Nevada, but he would not know what to say, would not really be able to emphathize. Rick, she suspected, had never been truly afraid. He was lucky in that; he simply didn't know enough to be afraid.

But even the most empathic words would not be enough. She wanted to be held, the way her father had held her as a child when he wakened her from a nightmare. She wanted to be held close and physically comforted, to feel the warmth of strong arms about her, to put her face against someone's chest and feel the beating of another heart.

Hayes. She wanted Hayes.

Andrea stood for a long moment by the window with her face in her hands. There were a hundred reasons not to contact Hayes. It could be a dreadful mistake. But she wanted him with her, wanted him dreadfully. Just for once, she told herself, go with your feelings and not your head. Just for once.

She turned from the window and went to the telephone to call the Waldorf. The hotel operator rang his room.

She prayed that he was in. He had said he would be in town for four days, but he might be at the theater or a dinner party. It wasn't even eleven yet. There was one ring, and a second, and a third.

"Hello."

"Hello, Hayes."

"Andrea! How's my girl?"

"Your girl is just terrible. I need you, Hayes. Could you come over here right now? I'm at home."

"Of course, I can come. Are you all right?"

"No, Hayes. But I will be when you get here."

There was a momentary pause. "I've always wanted to hear you say that, baby girl," Hayes said. "I'll be right there."

306

Hayes held her.

He stroked her hair as she sat in his lap and told him what had happened that evening. She told him quickly, in a rush of words, but it was only at the end that she was able to let her fear out. "It scares me so much that someone could hate me like that," she said, and began to sob, her face pressed against his chest.

"It's all right, sweetheart. It's all right. He was crazy. It didn't have anything to do with you. With crazy people it never has anything to do with the people they hate. It's just anyone they imagine is against them. It's all in their minds."

"I know that. But it still frightens me." Andrea pulled her head up. "I'm getting your shirt all wet."

"Doesn't matter, baby girl. Go ahead and cry. I've got more shirts than Gatsby did."

But she didn't need to cry anymore. She began to undo the buttons of his shirt—he hadn't stopped long enough to put on a tie—and rubbed her face against the soft curly hairs of his chest.

"I think we better move our base of operations, baby."

"Ummm. I think so, too."

He picked her up and carried her into the bedroom. He set her down on the edge of the bed and knelt in front of her and reached behind her to unzip her dress. Gradually he undressed her completely, kissing each newly exposed part of her body. His huge hands cupped her breasts and he took each of her erect nipples gently between his teeth, teasing it with his tongue. He put his face against her abdomen, holding her to him. "God, I've missed you," he said very softly. "You smell so wonderful, you feel so good."

She ran her hands through the thick curliness of his hair and down the side of his face, and then she sank back onto the bed and pulled him to her. "I've missed you, too, Hayes. I don't think I let myself know how much I've missed you."

When he entered her, Andrea put her hands over the taut muscles of his buttocks, holding him hard against her. She did not want him even to move, not yet; she wanted simply to lie there and feel him deep within her, as though there were no possibility of their bodies ever being separated again. Hayes moved his knees up under her, lifting her with his arms around her torso, pulling her up against him until she was completely free of the bed itself, sitting astride him, her breasts pressed against his chest, and he held her there, not moving, and their mouths opened to one another's.

I'm home, Andrea thought. I'm home.

They made love for almost an hour, and then Andrea fell into a profound sleep in Hayes's arms. At dawn, they woke, it seemed almost as one, and in the thin pearlescent light moved against one another again, with brief, wild abandon.

When she awoke again it was past noon. Hayes was not beside her and for a moment she felt bereft, but then she heard sounds from the kitchen and knew he was still there.

She got up and washed her face and combed out her hair, put on a slinky blue satin robe, and went to find Hayes in the kitchen.

"You're up," he said, with a huge smile, and held her to him and kissed her.

"What are you up to out here?" she asked, her arm around his waist.

"A little brunch."

"Moving in on my territory, I see."

"Not exactly. I found a can of artichoke bottoms in the cupboard, and I thought we'd have some poached eggs on them, with hollandaise sauce. But I'm afraid the hollandaise is separating."

"Oh, we can fix that. Just add a teaspoon or so of cold water and beat it like hell. It usually comes back."

"Do you want to do it?"

"Of course not," Andrea said, smiling. "It's your brunch."

Hayes added the cold water and began to beat furiously. "It's working," he said. "What do you know."

308

"Well, then, let's eat. I'm starving."

"Me, too. But after all, we did have a rather energetic night."

"A wonderful night," Andrea said.

They carried the plates into the living room and ate from the coffee table, sitting side by side on the sofa.

It had been a long time since Andrea had slept so late. In her world during the past few years, time for herself, time to do nothing, time to waste, had been a luxury she could seldom afford. She had always been fully aware of the life Hayes could give her in a material way, but as she sat beside him eating the brunch he had prepared, she reflected that she had never given much thought to the more intangible pleasures that could be hers if she married him. His presence beside her at this moment made her feel protected, cared for. That was not something she had believed was important to her, but perhaps she had cheated herself. Perhaps that mattered more than she had been willing to admit.

"This is lovely, Hayes. Thank you for letting me sleep so late."

"Whoops," Hayes said. "That reminds me. I took the phone off the hook so you could go on sleeping. I figured you deserved to sleep as long as you wanted."

"Oh, thank you, Hayes. I'm glad you did."

"Shall I put it back?"

"I suppose you'd better. The number's unlisted, so I won't be getting any calls from the newspapers about last night, but they may be worried at the office."

Hayes got up and returned the receiver to the cradle. Just as he turned away again, it rang.

"Shall I get it?" he asked.

Andrea nodded. "Please."

"Hello. Yes she is," Hayes was saying. "One moment."

He turned to her frowning slightly. "It's Sid Fogel," he said, with his hand over the receiver.

"Oh, God."

"Shall I say you're in the shower?"

"No. I'd better take it."

Andrea went to the telephone, patting Hayes's cheek as she took the receiver from him.

"Hello, Sid."

"Are you okay, Andrea?"

"Yes, I am. I'm just fine," she said, smiling over at Hayes.

"I was worried. I called your office and Paul Boucheron told me what happened last night. I understand you made the front page of the *Post*."

"Terrific," Andrea said sarcastically.

"Well, actually, it can't hurt. Television star attacked by mad caterer. It's good stuff."

"Television star?"

"Yeah, I've got good news for you, Andrea. I'm still mad as hell at you, you understand. But three little letters have changed things some. ABC."

"What do you mean, ABC?"

"We've got an offer for the show. Prime time. We're going network, kid."

"Prime time?"

"What's going on?" Hayes asked from across the room.

Andrea shook her head and put her finger to her lips.

"That's right," Sid said. "I wish I could take credit for it, but I can't. Apparently your vice-president friend over there, Marc James, has been pushing to get your show for some time. And your remark the other night at the awards dinner about independent television being not just a supplement to network fare but a real alternative had some effect. Not to mention that you've been killing the networks during your time slot in the big cities. They look at numbers, like I've always said, and they figure if you can't compete, steal."

"So what happens?"

"So we're going to sign with ABC. What do you think happens?"

"You'll still be producing?"

310

"Bet your sweet ass."

"What about money?"

"The budget goes up, kid. You can have your extra seven thou a show."

"Well, now, Sid," she said, in her best Lady Andrea Harrington tones, "I think we'll have to talk about that a little further. After all, with a network budget . . ."

"Andrea," said Hayes.

"With a network budget," Andrea went on, "it seems to me ten thousand a show would hardly be asking too much."

Sid laughed. "I figured that was coming. You never give up, do you, you greedy bitch?"

"No, you manipulative bastard," Andrea said sweetly. "I don't. Not when something is really worth having."

Andrea could feel Hayes's presence across the room behind her. She knew she ought to be able to turn toward him, to look at him and smile. But she couldn't bring herself to do it.

"Ten thousand," she repeated to Sid. "That really ought to be possible."